IN HIS STEAD

A Novel by Judith Sanders

In His Stead

A Father's War

A NOVEL BY

JUDITH SANDERS

IronWord Press

"TRUTH IS MY ANVIL."
----- Mahatma Gandhi

Leland, North Carolina

Published by:
IronWord Press
Suite 200, 1115 Willow Pond Lane
Leland, NC 28451
www.ironwordpress.com

Other books by this author: *Crescent Veil*, biocriminology at its best.

Cover design by George Foster, fostercovers.com
Interior design by Dorie McClelland, springbookdesign.com

Library of Congress Control Number: 2012949099
ISBN: 978-1-938573-82-8 (hardcover)
ISBN: 978-1-938573-83-5 (softcover)
ISBN: 978-1-938573-86-6 (ebook)

Author's Note

Three years ago on Thanksgiving James Williams approached me with his thoughts for a story. He was trying to write this novel himself but gave up. He gave me his outline and I attempted to put his feelings and passion to words. I hope this novel has done that for him.

In the writing of this novel, I found myself totally absorbed by the main character, Thomas Lane, and his dilemma. His passion and need to protect his children is not unique to a specific gender but is shared by all parents regardless of the language we speak, the design of our clothes, or the geographical location in which we raise our children.

I believe there is some Thomas Lane in each of us. And my wish is that his path toward peace for the sake of his children can someday be a reality for all the world's children.

—Judith Sanders

Foreword

It was late in the evening of March 5, 2007, when a loud banging pulled me off the couch. I thought my seventeen-year-old daughter was knocking because she had again forgotten her house keys. But I was terribly wrong. When I opened the door a combination of panic and fear struck me. My daughter's best friend and her mother were standing there crying.

My little girl, my Paige, was in trouble. She had been in a terrible car accident. I was told that my wife and I needed to get to the hospital now! Before I could move I had to have the answer to one question. I asked the unthinkable: "Is my little girl alive?"

My only answer was the uncertainty that filled their teary eyes.

When my wife and I arrived at the hospital we were told her injuries were extensive and we would be told the specifics after testing.

My wife's expression warned those around us. *Get out of my way. I will see my daughter right now!* And within a few seconds we were running down the hall of the emergency room to our Paige. As we arrived she was being transported for a CAT scan. We managed a brief glimpse as she was rolled by. All the gut-twisting words in the dictionary could not describe the torment going on inside my mind and body when I saw my baby. Bleeding and broken, her beautiful face tarnished with blood, bruises, and tubes will be forever etched in my mind.

My wife's best friend, an OR nurse, joined us as we waited outside the scan room. As they talked I took the opportunity to step away. I wandered down the hallway, uncertain where I was going until I found an empty room.

I consider myself a pretty tough guy and I have never begged for anything in my life . . . that is until that night. All alone in the basement of the hospital I dropped to my knees and pleaded, "God, my life for hers. Please, if a life is needed, take mine not my daughter's." As the tears soaked my cheeks and collected in my hands I repeated that same prayer over and over. I begged Him not to take my little girl because I had failed as a parent to protect her.

Nothing can prepare a parent for something like this. The next time I saw my little girl, she was unconscious and on a ventilator to help her breathe. I found myself taking breaths in tune with the ventilator to ensure it was working. I felt so helpless, so weak, that I could barely find the strength to stand on my own two feet.

Because of the extent of Paige's injuries, especially the trauma to her head, the physicians thought it best to put Paige in a medically induced coma. Waiting for the doctors to tell us that it was time to decrease the medication and bring her out of the coma was agonizing. Finally, the meds were stopped and the days ticked by as we stood vigil, cried, and waited for her to open her eyes and come back to us.

Deep in my heart I wondered which day God would make the trade. I was ready to make good on our deal. Of course, I continued my prayer negotiation, to let me look into my daughter's beautiful brown eyes and see her smile one last time.

Then it happened. I was standing along the side of her bed rubbing her forehead, whispering a song to her. All of a sudden her eyes opened. It was a brief connection. The doctors had previously said that *if* she awakened she would go in and out. But for my wife and I, that one look put our world back on its axis. The room quickly filled with medical personnel to celebrate. Once again, I quietly slipped away to another empty room, sat down, took a deep breath, and reaffirmed my offering, "My life for hers, Lord." As I waited, I wondered how he would take me. Would it come as a heart attack? I sat there running my hand over my chest waiting for something to happen as I speculated on what a heart attack felt like.

Today, four years later, I am still waiting. The years have passed, my daughter has recovered, and we are both still here. I am so very, very grateful for having my daughter back.

Yet, I do not sleep that well for the safety of my eighteen-year-old son concerns me. He informed me he is thinking about going into military service. My thoughts immediately turned to how I could change his mind. The idea of him so far away from me in a distant place was bringing back my sense of helplessness. In 2007, I almost lost one of my children due to circumstances beyond my control and now I was being asked to give one up without a fight. Not a chance. I'm their Dad and go-to guy. Don't I have an obligation to speak out?

As my son and I talked about military service, I realized he needed my support. But I also knew there was no way I could let him march into harm's way. I said to myself he can join, but before I would let them take him to Afghanistan or some other war zone, I would go and fight in his place. He changed his mind and never went.

As I thought of what I would want to do if my eighteen-year-old or, eventually, my thirteen-year-old decided to enlist, the plot for this story emerged.

In My Son's Stead is dedicated to all of the children on both sides fighting in conflicts started by grown men and women. I did not serve in the military. I am patriotic yet, I find myself thinking, what right do we have as parents to send our children off to face the horrors of war? They are children after all, our children. No matter how old they are, they are still our little boys or little girls. Period! And while there is a breath in my lungs and a beating in my chest I will protect them at all costs, even if it means giving my own life for theirs.

My hope is that this story causes a conscious awareness of the price of war, and more importantly, the high value of our children's lives. They are, after all, all we really have that we can call our own.

This statement represents everything that I am. I have three fantastic children; Paige, Connor, and Robert, and a beautiful wife, Sharon. I would gladly forfeit my life for any of them. Their happiness and safety are the sole concern of my life. Each day that I share with them gives me the strength to forge ahead no matter how hard times can get. My days on this earth would mean nothing without my family.

—*James Williams*

".. . in September 1780 he entered into the service of the United States in Granville County North Carolina as a substitute for his father James Aiken Sen., in the 1st Regiment of North Carolina militia Commanded by Col. Moore . . ."

Excerpt from
The Southern Campaign American Revolution Pension Statements & Rosters

Chapter 1

THE NEWS ARRIVED ON MEATLOAF NIGHT. That would be Thursday. It had always been Thursday. When they heard it, Christine, Tom's wife, had sliced her finger cutting tomatoes. He wrapped the wound with a glittery pink Band-Aid usually reserved for his young daughter. *And the weather had been . . .* Thomas Lane Sr. paused. His gaze rolled up as if checking a list suspended in the air. He couldn't remember if it had been raining or the sun was shining. Had it snowed? He marveled at how he recalled most of the tiny details of that tragic day with perfect clarity. Why had the weather escaped him? A man should remember if it had been balmy or slushy, damp or dry, on the day his oldest son died.

Sweat beaded at Tom's temples now, just as it had that Thursday three years ago when the nondescript US military vehicle stopped at their house—3 Black Hill Street, Hardscrabble, Pennsylvania. From his chair at the head of the dining room table, Tom had had an unobstructed view of his porch and the street beyond.

When the chaplain and the casualty officer stepped out onto the cracked sidewalk, they stopped to straighten their class-A uniforms. Then they paused on Tom's creaky front porch and both gave the faded American flag tacked to the railing a somber look. Next came the tap-tap-tap on the front door.

They were late. While the family had been eating their meatloaf and watching the evening news, they had already seen Thomas Lane Jr. die on national television.

But the US Army has its rituals, and so the family gathered in the tiny living room as the chaplain said his prayers and called Tom's son a hero. Patting Tom and his wife's cold hands, the Chaplain struggled to find words to reach an emotionally deadened family. He told them they should be proud.

When the chaplain had completed his platitudes, the casualty officer continued with practicalities. He gave them the details of their dead son's travel itinerary. Did they want him buried at Arlington or somewhere close by?

Tom still didn't recall much of that conversation. But the last thing the casualty officer said pierced Tom to the core. His oldest son would be coming home "in a box."

His boy in a box?

They never got to see him.

Tonight, as the fragrances of Thanksgiving dinner lingered in the air, Tom wondered for the millionth time if they had buried all that had been his son. Was anything missing? Somehow his child had become like a puzzle, a puzzle that Tom could never solve because he didn't have all of the pieces. He tried again to make sense of it.

Why had Tommy sacrificed himself? Why had he joined the army? Had he felt compelled to be a Ranger like his dad? Why hadn't he, Tommy's father, done more to protect his child?

And lest he ever forget, Tom could watch his son's death on YouTube anytime he wanted. He needed to see it again tonight.

Tom sat in front of his blank computer. His home office was set up in one corner of the dining room. His sweaty hand felt slick against the mouse. He made sure he was alone—Christine and his daughter were asleep upstairs, worn out from the holiday; Donnie was away at college —if you counted across town as away. Tom's search engine took him straight to the video and he clicked play.

As the three-minute clip began, Tom watched the glowing monitor. He braced himself before the videographer staggered, then took a deep breath as the narration began: "Allah—" The rest of the suicide bomber's words were blotted out by the screams of Afghani adults and children scrambling for safety. The assembled military personnel ran for the protection of nearby houses and stores.

A lone American soldier fought against the fleeing tide. As he sprinted forward he did something most unexpected. He stripped off his Kevlar vest and shouted out, "Bomb! Bomb! Hit the deck."

The terrorist had no time to react. The American soldier catapulted onto the bomber's back, locking him and the pack slung over his shoulder in a tight embrace. In an instant the soldier rolled into a narrow gully at the side of the dirt road, embracing the bomber.

A violent explosion sent earth and fire rocketing into the sky. The sulfurous yellow ball, an animated inferno like the devil's breath, expanded and overflowed the ditch. The camera, although knocked out of our correspondent's hands, continued to record as roasted flesh, blood, and dirt rained down over its lens.

Tom cringed, but he did not turn away.

The video had reached the Internet in record time. Thousands of people saw the Kevlar shield and Thomas Lane Jr. bear-hugging the bomber as he protected everyone in the Kabul marketplace. Everyone except for himself.

Tommy's death had been national news. His was a *heroic death*. So many people had said those very words to Tom. Even now, after one thousand and ninety-five days, it meant nothing. Hero or not, Tommy was still dead.

Tom stared at the static on the computer screen, his mind mesmerized by the compelling, horrifying images he had just seen. He placed his palm flat against the screen, a black, grim shadow against the snowy background, as if the warmth was pulsing from the son he loved and not from a heartless machine.

Somehow, as he watched, he shared his son's last breaths.

Tom clicked the mouse and the screen returned to his young daughter's screensaver—a blue sky and bouncing spring flowers. The sudden transformation from the previous dismal images to the playful blossoms left Tom gawking for a few seconds.

He swiped his face with his calloused hands, the motor grease visible under his nails. His gesture to erase his sorrow did nothing. His eyes turned liquid and red.

It's as if someone flipped the off switch on Tommy's life.

Guided through the darkness by the small lights of the microwave and the DVD player, Tom moved through the rooms, repeating his nightly ritual. He checked the windows, making sure they were tightly closed and latched. The bolt on the back door was in place. As he walked through the kitchen, he passed Tommy's high school graduation picture on the refrigerator door. Next to it was another photo, taken at Arlington, of his wife holding this same high school picture and kneeling next to their son's tombstone.

"My boy," whispered Tom to the sleeping house.

He moved to the living room, locked the front door, and headed for the stairs to go to bed. The heat came on. The old pipes in the duplex shuddered as the boiler forced steam through the radiators.

With the birth of each of his three children, Tom had pledged to God that he would be a good father and protect them. But the best he had been able to do for his family was to put locks on the doors and windows.

Chapter 2

"Tom. Tom, wake up!" Christine shook her husband's shoulder.

The ringing in his ears grew louder. He came fully awake. Tom jerked upright to sit on the edge of the bed. Both feet hit the floor with a thud.

"What the hell?"

He rubbed his half-open eyes with one hand and grabbed the phone with the other as he glanced at the clock. It was two in the morning.

"Who? What! Donnie, where are you?" He felt his wife's body press against his back. A little tremble passed from her to Tom.

"Donnie, let me talk to the police." *Not this shit again,* thought Tom as he turned to his wife. "He's OK. Minor accident." He held up one hand to silence her as the police officer came on the line.

"Yeah. Yeah. I understand. I'll be right there to get him." He slammed down the phone.

Chapter 3

"DROP ME AT MY DORM," slurred nineteen-year-old Donald Lane. "I have work tomorrow. Or is it today?" His saliva bubbled as he giggled. His faded black jeans, creased leather jacket, and rumpled black T-shirt smelled of smoke, beer, and vomit. Dried blood marked the spot on his left ear where his stud had been ripped out.

"Wipe that shit-eating grin off your face. It's Thanksgiving, for Christ's sake. Your mother worked all day on that meal. Now it's splattered on your sneakers. Do you know how a call in the middle of the night upsets her?" Tom glanced at the passenger seat. His son's head lolled on the headrest. "Donnie. I'm talking to you."

"Yeah, yeah. Tell Mom I'm OK."

"Wise up, kid. If you had been the one driving drunk, I would have left you behind bars. Then you'd know your actions have consequences."

"Right. Are you going to give your 'Be a man' speech? No f-f-father-son shit. Let me sleep."

"When are you going to grow *up*?"

"Never, if I have to end up like you."

Tom jerked the steering wheel over sharply and veered onto the shoulder of the road. He turned off the truck and swiveled to face his son.

"What's going on here? You've been giving me nothing but attitude for months now."

"Gee, you noticed."

"This can't still be about me missing your punk band thing?"

"It was a competition, a war of bands. And we won that *thing*! Just forget it." He waved a limp hand at his dad. "I guess I have to be a star athlete like . . ." Even drunk, Donnie knew when to stop.

"Like your brother? Is that what you were going to say?" Shocked more by his thoughts than Donnie voicing them, Tom did what he always did—he changed the subject.

He had never had a problem connecting with Tommy. His second son was different in personality as well as looks. Tommy had looked like Christine, blond and blue-eyed. Donnie was his dad all over—tall, lanky, with olive skin and the dark brooding eyes of an Italian godfather. Maybe that was why he was hard on Donnie. Tom saw too much of himself in the boy.

"Donnie, you are underage. Do you remember Judge Brice's warning?"

"I'm a soldier. Soldiers drink, right? You did. Tommy did."

"The National Guard is weekend soldiering." Then he mumbled, "You know nothing of war."

The boy looked away, folded his arms on his chest.

Tom had said more than he intended. "Listen, son, when I was—"

"I'm ignoring you. Get the hint?"

Disgusted with his son and in a flash of anger, Tom released Donnie's seat belt, grabbed his son's shoulders, and pinned him against the window. "What is it with you?" He stared into Donnie's blurry eyes. "Nothing but crap comes out of your mouth. I'm not taking your shit like your mother does. And that's not what I am sending you to college to learn!"

"You didn't send me to college. I'm paying my own way. I'm doing it the hard way."

Tom relaxed his grip. "Why can't I get through to you, boy? The guy you were riding with is going to jail on this DUI. That could be you. You think giving me lip is the right answer? You visit your friend after he's been in jail for a month, then see how hard your life could get. Christ, you don't even know what I'm talkin' about."

Donnie slid from his grasp. "So are you going to tell me, like . . . if I had any balls like my big badass Army Ranger brother and dad, I'd be able to do it all! Like classes and two part-time jobs." He smoothed his long hair off his face. "Why are you hassling me? I'm doing what you and the judge wanted. I'm staying in college and doing the march-ing thing."

Tom watched his son attempting to count jobs and classes on his fingers.

Donnie ended up staring at his waggling digits. "Tonight was a break, that's all. And I don't even know the guy who was driving."

Tom huffed. "You get in a car with some drunk you don't know? Geez, Donnie. You could've been killed." He paused for a second to calm himself, then snapped the seat belt back around his son and started the truck. They drove home in silence.

When they pulled up to the curb in front of the Lane's faded green duplex, half of a clapboard house that the army built after World War II, Donnie said, "Hey, this isn't my dorm."

"I'm not driving all the way across town tonight. You'll sleep at home. I need to get some rest." He spoke more loudly as he said, "I work for a living! People like your mom, this family, and my employees depend on me." After he got out of the truck, Tom slammed the door and walked around to the other side.

He watched his son struggle to find the door handle. Donnie care-lessly let the truck's door bang against the telephone pole. "Right. Work." His fingers attempted to snap out an imaginary tune as he sang, "Work, work a work a . . ." Donnie staggered. "I need my guitar." He mimicked playing it as he attempted to dance.

Tom went to help his son, but the boy pushed him away.

"I don't need your help!" Donnie staggered. "Dump me on Mom. Right! You go run away, go disappear at the shop. Do your twelve, four-teen hours of bullshit."

Tom watched his son lean heavily against the low chain-link fence that enclosed what was generously called a front yard. It was a grassless eight-by-eight-foot patch of earth; each of the six houses attached to his in a long row had the same setup. Tom had the end unit, so he had a short driveway and a freestanding one-car garage, although it sat at an odd angle.

"Donnie, let me help . . ." He reached out.

"Nope." The boy yanked his arm away from his dad. "You go . . . When I get back from doing my 'pretend soldiering' in Afghanistan . . . I'll give you a call, Dad."

Tom froze in his tracks. "What did you say?"

"My Guard unit is setting sail." Donnie's arms pinwheeled in the air. He almost fell. "No, that's not right. Army lingo . . . deploying." Donnie snickered and brightened. "Hey, I got a great idea. Maybe I'll go to Canada. Isn't that what they did in your day? Of course my supersoldier dad would never have done such a thing." He wiped the slobber off his chin with the back of his hand.

Tom couldn't speak. He had no spit. He was dry as the Iraqi desert where he'd fought. He glanced at the curtains moving in the front window. Christine peeked out, then disappeared. She opened the front door.

Donnie saw his mother and attempted to straighten up. His fingers combed back the long bleached pieces of hair hanging in his face with the rest of his spiked, dyed black hair. "Hey, Mom." He staggered up the steps, across the small half porch and inside. That was as far as the boy could manage.

Inside, Tom took over and deposited his drunken, fully dressed son on the couch.

Christine hovered. She covered her son with a quilt. She smoothed his hair. "Tom, did you argue?"

He lied, "No."

"Let him sleep it off. He's just a boy." She tugged on Tom's sleeve. "Come to bed."

"In a while. I'm wide awake now. I'll watch some TV. When I get sleepy I'll be up."

An hour later Donnie rolled over and belched.

"Here's a garbage can if you get sick." Tom pulled his chair up next to Donnie. "We are going to have a talk in the morning." Tom shook him. "Did you hear me?"

Donnie didn't answer.

Tom watched his son sleep for a long time. "Just a boy," Christine had said. She was right. "No scars on your knuckles," Tom said softly.

When Tom had joined the army, the streets had already prepared him. He had defended himself with his fists and against the threat of a knife. Sure, he had been the same age as Donnie and Tommy when they joined the military, but he was a hard eighteen, motherless, with an alcoholic father.

In the army Tom had seen, heard, and done things that would have shocked his wife and children. Things he would never disclose to anyone but God. His sons, especially Donnie, were virgins when it came to the irrational hate, violence, and physical brutality one man could hail down on another.

Tommy had been in a few scuffles, and football had toughened him up. As the oldest he had always been his brother and sister's champion. He had defended many of the kids in the neighborhood from Ralph, the local bully.

Donnie had never been in so much as a shoving match at school. How would he cope in combat? *Another son?* That thought pinged around inside Tom's mind. And Canada? What was going on in his son's head?

Tom pushed back in his beat-up old green recliner and settled in for the night. The footrest extended only halfway. He reached down and yanked it up. In his annoyance he broke one side, and now the footrest tilted to the left.

He closed his eyes and took several calming breaths. Thinking maybe he needed some help, he mumbled a prayer. *God help me. Parenting. That's what they call it. I tried. Did I get it all wrong, Lord?* Then in his own defense he said, *Donnie's had a lot more than my father ever gave me.*

Tom was ashamed of the response that popped into his mind. *So, is that justification for giving your second son less of yourself?*

Chapter 4

AFTER A SLEEPLESS NIGHT TOM STILL MANAGED to shower and be waiting when Donnie came out of the house at six thirty the next morning.

He was determined to head Donnie off. He knew the boy would try to flee rather than risk another quarrel. So in spite of the cold November temperature, not a surprise for eastern Pennsylvania, Tom stationed himself along his son's most likely escape route at the back of the house.

Tom watched his son sneaking out the side door, book bag slung over one shoulder, still in the clothes he had slept in. The warped storm door was tricky to close. Donnie worked the ill-fitting bent aluminum door like a practiced thief.

When his son thought he had made a clean getaway, Tom spoke up. "How are you getting back to campus?"

At first Donnie was startled. Then he turned and saw his dad leaning against their dilapidated shingled garage. He came around quickly. "I'm catching the bus."

"I'll take you."

"No. You go on to work." He walked a few paces away.

Tom followed. "We need to talk. Get in the truck."

Tom walked closer, hands buried deep in his jacket pockets to keep them warm. Distracted this morning as he made his own version of an escape before his wife woke up, he had forgotten to pick up his gloves.

"No."

"Get in the truck or I'll put you in it!" The thick white puffs shooting out of Tom's mouth and nose added more weight to his heated words than he had intended.

Donnie stopped. His head hung low for just a heartbeat before he managed to marshal some of the previous night's defiance. He hooked both thumbs in his belt loops, his backbone straightened, and he stared back at his dad wordlessly.

Feeling the fire sparking between them, Tom's tone softened, "Okay. I'll make it a request. Please get in the truck."

Father and son slid in next to each other. They rode for ten minutes without speaking. The heater was on full blast, but it still felt cold inside the truck to Tom. Finally he asked, "You want me to stop at Dunkin' Donuts for coffee?"

Donnie only shrugged and continued to look straight ahead.

"What happened? Did you get a rod shoved so far up your ass now you can't turn your head and even look at me?"

"I see you," Donnie said turning.

During that brief face-to-face Tom saw a heap of sadness in his young son's bloodshot eyes.

The kids and their touchy-feely stuff were as foreign to Tom as the unexplored regions of outer space. He usually left that soft territory to his wife. Of course, he and Christine's relationship was another matter. She was the only person he had ever allowed to glimpse what was inside him. But even with her he had been cautious. He had some untouchable black zones. He didn't know when this had happened. Perhaps it was a result of his father's abuse, a gradual numbing due to pain, regret, and grief. He had read articles that talked about children growing increasingly anesthetized to block out painful memories. Was he one of those? Had he been a good soldier because he lacked emotion? Perhaps that had once been true, but not anymore. His son's dying had awakened in him a sleeping giant of intense feelings.

He suddenly realized he was ignoring Donnie. "How's the ear?" Tom tugged on his own ear, then pointed at the Band-Aid on Donnie's. Tom wished the other two earrings, one in his son's eyebrow and the other hanging from his right ear, had also been lost during last night's intoxication.

His son mumbled, "OK."

Tom pulled into the Dunkin' Donuts and up to the drive-through window. "How do you take it?"

His son didn't answer. He gave him a look that said *you should know.*

He realized he was being tested and wasn't putting any points on the board.

With two steaming coffees in the cup holder between them, he drove to Donnie's dorm.

When they arrived and his son started to jump out, Tom put a hand on his arm. "Don't. Have some coffee."

Relenting, Donnie remained in the truck. He picked up his coffee but didn't drink.

"Son, you need to talk to me."

Donnie remained mute.

"OK, I'll start. What's this about you going to Afghanistan? Or the running away to Canada bullshit? You scared or something?" Bad choice. Big mistake.

"If you're going to yell at me and rough me up again, I'm leaving." Donnie opened the door, and a blast of cold air rushed in.

Tom's defenses went up. "I've never hit you in your life!" Tom gulped down a breath.

Donnie shifted, ready to step out. His hand paused on the door handle.

"No. Don't leave." Tom's voice lost some of its edge. "You talk. I'll listen. Promise."

Donnie started slow. "I saw through your plan from the beginning. You thought if I put on the uniform I'd give up music. Give up being me." His words gained momentum. "The first thing out of your mouth when I said I don't want to go is you think I'm a coward. I'm not stupid. You want me to be like Tommy. Well, I'm not him!" His eyes filled with emotion.

Tom felt his face blanch as if his son had hit him with a baseball bat. But was Donnie's assumption accurate? Maybe he did want his son to be levelheaded, strong, decisive, and brave like Tommy. In that moment he hated himself. *"Dead" was like Tommy.* Tom was stunned.

"I can see your mind going. You're afraid to admit what you're thinking."

Ashamed of his thoughts, Tom recoiled and kept silent.

"Go on and ask me! Am I a coward?"

When he finally found his voice, Tom said, "Being scared and being a coward are two different things. Besides, I thought you wanted to join the Guard. You said you liked it. Christ, Donnie, you could be top dog in your unit. I know you've got it in you."

"I never said I liked it. You said that . . ." Donnie's voice deepened as he mimicked his father. "'The Guard is better than community service and taking out garbage at the shelter. And you'll get a signing bonus so you can go to college.'"

Returning to his own voice, Donnie continued. "My choices were jail or join the Guard and have the money to go to college? You and Judge Brice decided my life. Not me."

Tom had been reaching for his coffee and stopped.

"Can't you get it through your head—I can't be Tommy!" Donnie held his head in his hands as tears gathered. "You lost your favorite son, but I lost my only brother."

To cover his shock, Tom picked up his mug. His hand began to shake, so he put it back in the cup holder.

A few heartbeats later Donnie added, "And I'm serious about Canada."

"Son . . . if you run away to Canada, you'll become a fugitive." Tom's next words were slow and distinct. He couldn't make a mistake. He had to convince his son to stay the course. "This is serious business in the military. After thirty days you are not AWOL but deemed a deserter during a time of war. The army can and will issue a federal warrant. It will remain valid and shadow you for the next forty years. Desertion," he couldn't believe he was saying the word in connection with his son, "will destroy your life. If you're caught you'll do time. And army time behind bars can break you. Nothing will ever be the same for you."

"Always ready with a lecture." Donnie wiped his nose on his sleeve. "You know all the rules. But none say what you're really thinking."

"I'm trying to understand what's going on inside your head. You need to know the real world is hard."

Donnie's lips curled up with discuss. "You think I don't see what's going on in the world! I see it every night. It sits in Tommy's empty chair at our dinner table. The world is ready to explode, and no one is trying to remove the fuse. Christ, this war is the longest in our history. The economy is in the toilet. Even if the army hadn't called me up and I graduated from college, do you think I'd find a job? What am I supposed to do with my life? What options do I have? Tommy was looking for a career and . . ." He didn't finish.

"Give it time. Things will change. Donnie, there will be another solution. And it will be something better than running away."

Donnie looked up at his father sheepishly. "Ten minutes of talking, and the only thing you heard was that your cowardly son may become a fugitive. I don't need this. I've got to go."

"I can help, Donnie. I know I haven't been around much lately, but tell me what you want me to do and I'll do it." That was a weak response. Fathers were expected to have all the answers. But so much hurt had come out of Donnie that Tom was at a loss to cope with it.

"What can you do, Dad?"

Tom stared at his son. Was he that useless as a father?

"Uncle Sam never loses. Didn't they teach you that in Ranger school? I can handle it. I'll take care of this. Relax, Dad. Maybe I'll get a new song out of this experience." Tom watched an uncertain smile turn up the corners of his son's young face.

Donnie checked his watch. "Hey, I need to get to work."

"Yeah. Sure. Work." He gripped Donnie's shoulder and looked into his eyes. "So we're good?" He slapped him on the back.

"Yeah, sure. Tuesday night, I'll be home for dinner." Halfway out of the truck Donnie turned back. "Dad, there is one thing you could do for me." Tom nodded. "Tell Mom about me leaving. After Tommy, I can't . . ." He swallowed hard. "I don't want to set her off. She is just starting to smile again."

Tom's usual retort, "Do your own dirty work," would have been automatic any other day. But not today. Hadn't he just told his kid he wanted to help? "Yeah, sure. I know how to handle your mom."

Donnie jumped out of the truck.

Tom sent a weak wave after his son. Donnie didn't turn back to catch the gesture.

Are we good? he had asked, and Donnie had implied they were. *That's a pleasant piece of fiction*, thought Tom.

He couldn't remember the last time he had spent time fishing or playing pool with Donnie. This was the most talking they had done since . . . Tom didn't know when. He waited and watched his nineteen-year-old son amble down the sidewalk toward the campus bookstore, where he worked. His kid still had that same hitch in his gate, just like when he was little. His right foot toed in.

Tom stared after his boy, and in his mind's eye Donnie morphed into a shy little five-year-old getting on the school bus for the very first time, his small hand holding his big brother's.

Tom had watched his son walk away from him that day, too. But today neither he nor Donnie were excited or anticipating a great adventure. There was no last flash of a smile as his son stepped onto the yellow bus. This time his son had not turned back to his father to get a final nod. *It's OK, it's safe.*

Have I lost this son, too? Is giving his mother and sister bad news all I can do for my boy? Is this one thing the sum total of my accomplishments as a father? Am I ready for another son going off to war?

Tom didn't really want to face the answers. Then he added, *Now who is the coward?*

Chapter 5

It was eight o'clock Monday morning, and although the workday started at seven, Thomas Lane heard his employees leisurely rolling into the parking lot. Well, Tom decided, he'd let them be. If Donnie hadn't interrupted his post-Thanksgiving glow, he too would have lingered around the house. But Donnie's news had extinguished the warmth of that occasion. Selfishly, he thought, *I never have an opportunity to cut myself some slack.*

The weekend had been long and agonizing. He still had not broken the news to Christine. He saw today as another of those elastic days that stretched on, wearing him thin, and took forever to end.

This morning the gravel crunching under car tires seemed unusually loud and annoying. *Damn ugly, low-hanging clouds! Can't wait to dump your snow and slow down my deliveries.* Tom wasn't sure whom he was talking to when he glanced up. Could be God. Could be his own frustration hanging over him. He felt chills roll over him. Either way, snow wasn't impossible. They often had snow by Thanksgiving.

Christmas is just around the corner. It's been hard enough without Tommy. This year, will it be without Donnie? Tom's throat felt thick. Time was trampling all over him.

In the past, the run up to the holiday had been casual, gleeful. Now winter wanted to race in and deliver its gloom in a mad rush. Somewhere in Tom's mind he wondered what the weather was like in the Middle East right now.

His son's Guard unit had been called up. That message was still mulling around, gathering strength, inside Tom's brain. He usually met his challenges head-on, with the tenacity of a bulldozer, but this time that would definitely not work. There was a gap between father and son, his only son. He felt it as surely as the ache in his joints.

My nineteen-year-old son is going to be shot at and shoot other people. My son's Guard unit has been called up. Over and over, like an evil mantra, those words ricocheted in Tom's thoughts. Finally, the resulting force of his enlightenment almost threw him to his knees. He braced himself against his workbench. *What have I done?*

Tom took a moment to talk to God. He begged, *Please undo this. Give me a chance to make things right.* Tom had been leaving him messages, but so far he hadn't received a response. *Geez, Donnie. I thought the Guard was a good idea. Keep you out of trouble. Now this. How am I going to explain this to Christine? Why me, God?*

The parking lot was almost full. Soon Thomas Lane's little world, his machine shop, would be buzzing behind its dull concrete walls, and he would be expected to do his share. The oblong building could easily double for a World War II army barracks. But the sturdy structure suited its task—sheltering hard work that paid off. Tom's business was a safe island in the center of a high-unemployment storm.

Did I get it wrong, God? Donnie's hurting words returned. *Twelve or fourteen hours . . . Was it . . . is it bullshit? I work six days a week to put meat on the table. A lot of tables. Or was it just an excuse to shun the sorrow and drama that filled the house in Tommy's absence? I used to spend more time at home when the kids were little. Why did I quit them? I should have taken them on a family vacation every year.*

Instead, Tom had escaped to work. The business had always come first, as he struggled to build something out of nothing. Suddenly it all didn't feel so important anymore.

He shuddered. *I should have gone to Donnie's band competition.* His head hung low. Tears threatened.

Tom had seen the horrors of war. Big, strong men terrified, sweating in panic. Now another of his sons was going to be one of them, one like him. Tom had thought he had felt all that fear had to offer. But until today he had never felt its *helplessness.*

He glanced up and out the window. Debris floating on the river was hung up, and the waves splashing over it distracted him. He remembered picking this location because the Susquehanna River ran just fifty yards away from the Dumpster behind the shop, and for a fisherman that's a small picture of heaven. Its grassless shores were holding in muddy waters, running high and deep. Soon chunks of ice would be clinging to the banks in dirty brown slabs.

"No fishing today," he said to the view out the window. Fishing . . . both his boys loved to fish. Just like their dad. He and Donnie hadn't been fishing together since Tommy died.

"Hey, Prez, would you take a look at this?" Joe was one of Tom's twenty-six skilled craftsmen.

Tom was so deep inside his head that at first he didn't understand Joe was talking to him. He took the pad and the piece of steel Joe was holding out. He double-checked the calculations. He didn't permit mistakes. Not from his men or himself. But Tom wasn't infallible. Donnie's deployment was proving that in a big way.

Tom pulled his cracked and stained fingers through his thinning brown hair; the few grays he had were in his sideburns. His receding hairline lent an air of thoughtfulness to his sharp, noble features.

Bowed over his bench, he looked smaller than his actual six feet. He checked the layout Joe had drawn and a sample piece of the steel he'd marked where a sequence of cuts would be made. "Meticulous attention to accuracy" was the slogan on Tom's business card. But today it wasn't happening. His mind was too attached to Donnie.

Get on with it, damn it. You're the boss, for God's sake. Do your job! He was surprised his inner trembling had not set the steel he held dancing.

"Looks right, Joe. If you need me, just give a holler." He forced himself to keep moving. "Time to check in with the office queens."

Massaging his throbbing head, Tom walked the few paces to his office, a box within a box. It contained a couple of dented filing cabinets, three recycled metal desks that were crunched together, and two long fluorescent tubes dangling overhead on long wires. The ceiling was the roof fifteen feet overhead; the bare unpainted drywall ended at seven feet. When you sat at the desk and looked up, years of dust and cobwebs floating on the exposed steel beams waved hello.

Tom had hired the queens, Cecilia and Goldie—both pushing sixty hard, uphill—eight years ago to track supplies and accounts. He hated the paper stuff. The women ruled over the paper and all the men, and that included their boss. Tom was just fine with that.

"Good day, ladies." He tried on a smile for the first time that day, but couldn't hold it in place.

Goldie and Cecilia chatted and shoved invoices in front of him to sign. He did as he was told, and it was over by lunchtime. His thoughts immediately raced back to Donnie.

Maybe he should have gotten that second mortgage on the house? But even that money wouldn't have been enough for tuition. It always comes down to the almighty dollar.

Crap! His fist smacked the desk.

"What?" Goldie jumped. For a second Tom wondered if she knew that her salt-and-pepper hair was in rollers. And why was she wearing that glittery sweater? It looked weird with jeans and her white orthopedic sneakers.

Cecilia whispered, "Goldie has a lunch date." She gave Tom an eyebrow wiggle, as if that explained everything.

"Whatever. I was just thinking about money. Economics? You know, the stuff that runs the world?" Tom rubbed his thumb and fingers together.

The roach coach, fat and steamy, rolling up to the front of the machine shop entrance interrupted his rant and announced the time.

"Lunch," proclaimed Goldie, who had been watching out the window for her date to pull up. The sparks in her eyes had Tom feeling sorry for the man she was about to meet.

Tom watched the two women giggle like scheming schoolgirls. Cecilia sprayed Goldie with perfume until Tom was choking. He waved goodbye and wished Goldie good fishing as she made for the door, pulling out rollers as she walked.

The lunch wagon horn honked twice. All the employees responded as though an exterminator was spraying inside the building. The doors scraped open. The workmen swarmed out toward the tantalizing vapors rising to the heavens from the portable kitchen's gaping side window. The aroma of sausage, onions, and burgers cooking on the griddle made Tom's mouth water. He was tempted to break his diabetic diet.

Cecilia saw him leaning toward the door and warned, "Don't even think about it. I promised your wife I'd keep an eye on you."

"Well, Christine isn't your boss. And if you use both eyes, you'll get a really good look at me walking to that truck." His index finger stabbed the air. Tom threw his half-moon reading glasses on his desk for emphasis and linked his arms across his chest like one of those Secret Service guys guarding the president.

Cecilia hesitated a few seconds, then closed her greasy pink lips. She snatched her coat from the rack and wrapped it snuggly around her doughnutlike waist as if it were a bathrobe.

Tom held the door open for Cecilia with a gentlemanly flare as they joined the crowd outside.

Grabbing something wrapped in greasy wax paper, Tom paid and rushed back into the sanctuary of the warm lunchroom.

The place reeked of stale coffee, cigarettes, and metallic dust. Fluorescent lighting had leeched all the color from the walls years ago. Orange plastic chairs were scattered in disarray around indestructible picnic tables. Two long lines of three tables each sat ready for their occupants.

Within seconds, the room was a beehive of activity. It was like this Monday through Friday. Never changed. Tom had learned to like this sameness. And today it was a safe haven from his present sea of sadness and self-pity.

He watched the normal rhythm of his employees. Every day he saw the same actions and the same people. He fleetingly wished he could hide away in that sameness. But he knew they were counting on him to help them provide for their families. Did they know or could they see that he wasn't doing such a good job with his own?

The sound of chairs scraping on the painted cement floor melded with the voices of the jabbering workmen as they pulled up to the tables. Three minutes was all it took to fill every chair. Routine was a good thing—eating, gabbing, playing a quick game of pinochle, and sitting in the same location, with the same people, day after day. Each person had a place. So why did Tom feel so lost?

He considered himself to be one of them, no better, no different. During lunch, he and his army buddy Frank were the ones to beat at pinochle.

He had spent seventeen years in this very chair, wearing this uniform: a blue shirt, with his name written in red inside a white oval over the pocket, and dark blue work pants. "Clothes make the man," someone had said. Well, Tom's clothes were just trying to do the right thing for his family. For his kids he had wanted better, wanted more—jobs where his sons could wear those Dockers, maybe even a suit, and his daughter, Chrissy, a gorgeous fourteen-year-old with honey-blond hair, could wear high heels. Jobs with IRAs and 401(k)s. He hadn't been able to give that to Tommy, and now he was falling short with Donnie, too.

Ed spoke up from the opposite end of the table. "Hey, Tom, George and I will take you on. Tell Frank to get ready."

"Not today guys. I'm waiting for a call. Hillary Clinton needs my advice." Tom forced a chuckle.

The chair across from Tom rumbled and creaked.

Looking up, he saw just what he expected—his best friend pulling up in his usual spot, wearing the same uniform as Tom. Of course, Frank's clothes were two or three sizes larger and shorter. Frank unwrapped his lunch of sausage, peppers, and onions on a kaiser roll. He was a little bit like one of those obsessive-compulsives. Tom supposed that Frank being a single guy had something to do with it. He watched his friend's repetitive actions.

Frank laid out the sandwich in the exact center of its wrappings. Then he checked to make sure he had his requested two napkins. Now he should say, "These sandwiches can be messy. But it's all tasty grease." And he did.

Frank and Tom usually carpooled, but today Frank had taken the bus to work after his dentist appointment.

"Won't it hurt to chew?" Tom asked.

"Nope. I'm still numb."

Tom watched as Frank lifted the lid off his coffee, added three sugars, and closed his eyes to inhale the ambrosia before he took his first sip. At last, Frank was ready. He always started with his sandwich. He would alternate back and forth: bite of sandwich, sip of coffee, bite of sandwich. He would finish just as the thirty-minute lunch break was ending.

At last Frank looked up, and his bulldog mug froze in mid-chew.

The first clue for Frank that the world was off its axis must have been the sausage-and-egg sandwich sitting untouched in front of Tom. His second clue, the one that made him put down his own food and break his ritual, was Tom pulling on a Marlboro red.

"What the hell . . . it's been fifteen years since I saw that. What did I miss while I was at the dentist?"

Tom took a long drag, tilted his head back, and exhaled to give himself time to pick the right words to fit his sadness. He rocked on the hind two legs of his chair, watching his small bluish donation join the rest of the smoke cloud that was hovering above them.

"I guess you're off the 'secondhand smoke will kill ya' kick," said Frank. "What's with the face? You forget to put a blade in?" Frank scratched at his left cheek.

As a rule it would have bothered Tom to be less than orderly. But not today. The hollow circles hanging under his shit browns, the ones his wife called "bedroom eyes," were a new addition, too, but he didn't care.

"It's the boy," Tom said, finding his voice. "I made a big mistake."

Frank slid the cigarette out from between his friend's fingers. He smashed it in an ancient turquoise plastic ashtray. "Go on."

"Yeah, you're right." Tom picked up the hard pack as if reading the fine print. "These sticks don't taste as good as they used to." Gulping at his cold coffee, he said, "Geez, just a few days ago we were gorging ourselves on turkey and apple pie, and having a few beers on my front porch. Now I can't even remember the taste of Christine's cooking."

Frank cocked his good ear toward Tom as he did a poor job of wrapping his sandwich in foil. "So . . . ?" He wiped some drippings off his hand and pants with a napkin and lifted his coffee to his mouth. He leaned forward against the table. His friend would get to the point when he was ready.

Tom delivered the bad news full frontal. "Well, Donnie's unit has been called up. They're sending him to Afghanistan. And I heard fear and anger talking for him last night. He's even thinking about going AWOL to Canada."

Tom noticed the hand holding Frank's coffee quiver. Then with a practiced hook shot, Frank tossed his lunch in the garbage. Slumping forward, he glued his elbows to the table and rubbed between his furry black eyebrows with his clasped thumbs.

"I don't know what to think or do for him. Now that I think back, weeks ago Donnie mentioned a few things . . . civilians, even children, were being killed over there. I didn't pay much attention. I should have listened better. Stuff like that bothers him." Visions from Tom's own military service, ugly things he had never shared with his kids but dreamed of all too often, snaked back to join him in the lunchroom. He drew back. "Tommy and now Donnie . . . Christ, Frank, none of this shit was in my plan." Tom paled.

Frank maneuvered in closer when his friend's face paled. "What is it? You going to get sick?"

"No. It's nothing. Nothing." Tom slapped at his own face. "A headache." He sighed and without water gulped down three Tylenol tablets he pulled from his pocket.

"Is it the dreams again?" asked Frank. "The one where you are drowning in the sand, smothering?"

"Yeah. They started up again. Don't get all Catholic mystical and start crossing yourself like it's some kind of celestial warning," Tom sighed.

"I'm worried about the kid. He got the word during his weekend training. Thanksgiving night he got drunk as a skunk. I had to get him out of jail. He's on a first-name basis with half the police force. Not good. On the way home we got into it. He blasted me pretty good. He had a lot stored up inside him. I guess it sort of flew out during his drunken rambling. And I didn't come off looking too good. I haven't seen him since I dropped him back at school Friday morning." Tom wiped cold sweat from his forehead onto the sleeve of his work shirt. "He wants me to tell his mom and sister."

"Did you?"

He blurted out, "No!" Then lowered his voice. "I don't know how." Tom sucked in more air. *Duty* and *honor*, the army way, were words Tom believed in, concepts he had experience with. He had passed on his thoughts to his sons. Tommy believed in them, too. "When I suggested the 'hero on call' plan for Donnie, I thought it would put the kid on the straight and narrow, and, besides, the war was supposed to be over. I never thought his unit would see action beyond the firing range at Fort Dix. Especially not combat. Never this." Tom's hands balled up into white-knuckled fists. "I'm such a dummy. I should have let Judge Brice give him community service. But, oh no. Instead I butt in and push him into the Guard."

"Hey, don't beat yourself up," offered Frank. "It wasn't just about the money, although he wouldn't be in college without it. Finding pride in yourself and your country in the corps was worth a shot. The boy was in a really bad place back then."

"Yeah. You're right. But you know what bothers me?"

Frank shook his head no.

"I'm afraid his second thoughts, too much thinking, will get him killed. You've seen it happen." Tom held his head as if it had suddenly gained weight. "He shouldn't be going, Frank. I just couldn't admit he wasn't the warrior type. Christ, he writes poetry and sings it on his guitar. He was always the peacemaker. Turning the other cheek. Quoted

Gandhi and Martin Luther King. You'd think it was the sixties all over again. Never uses his brawn. I couldn't relate to that, but I was proud of him. When Rocky, you remember him," Frank nodded, "tormented him, Tommy took over."

They both sat in silence, thinking.

Tom caught his second wind. "When we quit the army, I wasn't expecting my kids to be taking over where we left off. Wasn't one son and thirteen years of my life and yours enough, Frank?"

Grabbing the packet of cigarettes, Frank pulled one out, stared at it for a minute, then broke it in two and discarded it in the ashtray next to Tom's. "It's like a time warp. Donnie is the same age as when you joined. It's you . . . us all over again."

"In my worst nightmares, I never thought Donnie would ever have to go. He only agreed to the plan because I made the big concession that he could study music. That was the plan. My plan. My fault.

"Shit!" Tom jolted out of his chair and walked to the other side of the room, next to the vending machines lining the wall. "Shit!" His elbow thumped the wall.

A few of the guys glanced at Frank and Tom. They waved them off.

"Tom, there was nothing wrong with either of us serving our country. Kept me out of the gangs."

"Yeah, but that doesn't mean I want both my sons to go through what we did."

The bell signaled lunch was ending.

"Tom, let's face it. There's always a war. I want Donnie to stay safe, too, but . . ." Snorting back his own gathering tears, Frank took out a big red bandanna. Self-conscious, he swiped at his crooked flat nose. It had been broken several times during his youth when Frank thought he could become a professional boxer. He stuffed the bandanna into his back pocket before anyone saw him.

A lifelong bachelor, Frank always said that Tom's family was his family. Anything that hurt one of them, hurt the other.

Clearing his throat, Tom smacked his friend on the back. "Thanks.

But I got Donnie into this. Now I have to find a way to get my son out of it. My job is to fix things. And right now I'm doing a piss-poor job."

QUITTING TIME WAS CLOSE WHEN TOM CALLED FRANK over to his workbench and they bowed their heads close in secret conversation. "Cecilia just told me something." He whispered, "Do you remember the Ricca's kid, Freddie? His parents, Sophie and Angelo, live in our row, but down two blocks?"

"Went to grammar school with Donnie, right? Same age. They played in Little League together. His father is the editor of the newspaper."

"Yeah. Freddie enlisted in the army right after graduation. He's dead. Killed by a roadside bomb."

Tom took an oil-stained rag and wiped a splattering of the tears slipping from his eyes. He imagined the path that had brought him to this day as though it was diagrammed on a set of blueprints.

"The Ricca's kid joined the army for the money, too. Angelo had laughed and agreed when I said, 'It's sort of a college fund, since I don't make enough to help my son but make too much for Donnie to get a free ride.'"

And that was how Tom had justified suggesting his second son's enlistment to his wife. Now this! Would Christine remember all Tom's cajoling and blame him?

Tom's next words came out all quivery. It took him a moment before he could spit the rest out. "Frank . . . nineteen. The Ricca's kid was nineteen. Same as my boy."

God, what am I going to do to fix this? I'm a dad, his dad. My job is to protect him, keep him safe. That's what dads do. Isn't it?

Chapter 6

TOM HATED BEING RIGHT ABOUT WHAT THE DAY would be like. The ten-hour grind had felt more like twenty. He was surprised his extreme exhaustion wasn't seeping out of his pores.

On the ride home, Frank and Tom didn't talk much, both held silent by deep thoughts.

Pulling in at his house, Tom could see Christine had beaten him to the single space in the driveway. Their old garage would accommodate only one vehicle, Tom's prize 1969 Chevelle Malibu SS 396 hardtop coupe in metallic fathom green. It was the one thing his alcoholic father had cared about. When Tom inherited it and had sons, he vowed the car would be a conduit, not a division, between father and sons. Tom was glad that so far that common love between him and his sons was intact. The Malibu held the privileged inside-garage slot, and Tom had to park his pickup on the street.

Dragging his body out of the truck, Tom glanced over at Frank. His friend moved like a robot that needed oiling. Tom smirked. He decided they both were walking like some used-up old men had replaced their almost fifty-year-old bones.

Frank shuffled to the center of the street that separated their houses. Then, turning back, he said, "I'll think of something. Promise." He gave a halfhearted salute.

Tom watched him walk away, Thermos in one hand, house key in the other, his head bent and his eyes locked onto his shoes.

Ready to also do a bit of shuffling, Tom took a deep breath and started up the cement walk in front of his house. He took the three steps onto his half of the front porch, then stopped to check the soles of his shoes. Paint chips and a few pieces of dead leaves were sticking to the soles. He wiped his feet on the mat. He didn't want to irritate Christine, especially not tonight.

He followed his natural impulse and inhaled. His nose was searching for the savory aromas of his wife's cooking before he even opened the door. Taking another whiff of what most often made his stomach sing, he experienced a personal first. The scents traveling in the air didn't excite his appetite.

Tonight was the night. His son had given him the duty. Donnie was staying at his dorm and Chrissy would be home late, so the timing was as right as it would ever be. Tom knew his family. His son couldn't stand to see his mom unhappy, and Christine would need some crying time to brave up before she could face her son and daughter.

It all added up to another sleepless night in the making.

The moment Tom crossed the threshold, the old clapboard duplex moaned and groaned. The radiators gave him their standard greeting—clangs and whistles. He swore he could see the heat going right out the single-pane windows along with half his annual income. He reprimanded himself: *I should have installed a new system, replaced those singles with doubles, and gotten new storms.* But then he remembered that Chrissy had broken her ankle playing soccer and he'd had to cover the gap between what the orthopedist charged and what the insurance paid. Next summer, definitely next summer, house improvements would be at the top of the list.

The heating system clunked as loudly as it could, as if in reply.

Tom felt its objection ripple the soles of his feet. "Shut up. I'll give you an overhaul this summer." Tom figured the boiler knew not to talk back.

"Are you yelling at my house again?" Christine was acquainted with her husband's quirks. Like talking to inanimate objects: the house, the car, and . . . and sometimes even God.

Tom ignored her comment, "Do I smell chicken?"

"And mashed potatoes, green beans, and biscuits. I also made a green salad. It's all on your menu."

"Did you fry the chicken so it gets those crispy brown flakes?"

"Absolutely not! We are watching our cholesterol. Remember?"

"There's a whole lot of eyes on me lately," Tom said, under his breath.

"So, Cecilia caught you cheating on your diet. Did you hit the lard wagon at lunch?"

"Geez, she's got the hearing of a bat," murmured Tom. Then, as he took off his shoes and left them by the door, he called out, "You're like the CIA, but smarter and prettier." There wasn't any reason he couldn't give her a little sugar before he was forced to rub in the salt.

Hanging his jacket on the stand in the hallway, Tom started up the steps for his customary after-work shower. The heat came on and the house complained again, with a clang and a hiss.

"Shut up or I won't fix you," Tom grumbled.

"Tom . . ."

"Yeah."

"Take your time. This is Chrissy's late night."

Tom called back, "Cheerleading, right?"

"That's why I love you. You know the schedule."

He almost said that he was counting on that schedule.

Bracing one hand on the wall, Tom dragged himself up. He'd managed to mount three steps, then stopped. His skin made contact with the cold leaching through the plaster of the outside wall. Gripping the wood railing with the other hand, he turned and saw movement out of the corner of his eye in the living room at the bottom of the stairs.

He stepped back down and caught the heavy green insulated curtains doing a jig at the front windows. Maybe they wanted to register their objections to his neglect, along with the rest of the house. "Even the damn house is ganging up on me," murmured Tom.

Crawling under the mass of olive green, he checked each window. Two were unlatched, and the air was pushing through the one-inch gap. Locking them was like plugging just one hole in a crumbling dam. It was all he could do. His failures were showing up in bunches.

He glanced at the front lawn, trying to remember just when it had turned brown. He should have thrown some lime on that postage stamp, but when did he have the time?

He headed to the shower. All the way up the stairs he wondered what the right words were? He needed soft ones for Christine.

He threw his soiled work clothes in the hamper and braced himself on the sink. The knots in his shoulders and neck muscles didn't realize the porcelain was supporting his weight, so they stayed tight.

Tom froze. He stared at the guy in the mirror, the guy who knew all his secrets. A slight gap between his front teeth, a chipped eyetooth that was a gift from his father, and deep lines that Christine called smile lines but that reminded him of a map of the Grand Canyon all added up to one ugly, dumb mug. And now that man was about to be exposed. After tonight, the charade would end.

The image in the mirror jeered at him, whispering, *You're powerless, weak, and pathetic. You can't take care of them, shield, and protect them. You never could. It was all just an illusion.*

The punches kept coming. *If you had been a better provider, your sons wouldn't have gotten into this mess. Hell, you were doing what you wanted, starting your own business. You turned your back on jobs in companies that had college assistance, savings plans, and regular hours. And why? So you could be the big man, owning your own business. Making all the decisions without a thought for anyone else. Running to conventions, giving your family less and less of your waking hours, letting the job eat you up. And don't deny some of those hours were spent with a fishing pole or a pool cue in your hand.*

Sticking up for himself, Tom shot back, *That's the nature of a man. I was making something from nothing.*

Where Tom came from, gender roles were well defined. Men worked with their hands, drank beer, and went bowling, or, as in Tom's case, played pool after work and on Friday nights. Women bore children, had meals on the table when their husbands walked in the door, and took care of the house. That was what Tom's family life had been—that is, until his mother had died.

Faint memories of his mother slipped back into place—the fresh scent of clothes dried on the line outside; bedsheets tucked tightly around him, making him feel warm and safe; doing his homework at the kitchen table under his mother's watchful eyes, to the smell of garlic.

The devil in the mirror whipped out at him, *Liar. You never worked on that dream. You left everything that had to do with the children to Christine. She ran the carpool circuit, checked out their friends, and kept them safe. Sure, occasionally you played with them, when it was convenient. You're just like your father. Didn't he let your mother work herself into the grave? What did you teach your kids? How to play pool? I bet you even dreamed of one of your sons turning into a hustler.*

"Hey," said Tom to the wise guy in the mirror, "I made some money with that stick."

Yeah, right! Then lost it all. That fast money never lasts. You pushed Donnie onto the hard path when he needed money for college. And why? Because it was easy for you. Your son is right where you put him!

Tom thought the creep in the mirror was right. The veil hiding his incompetence had some holes. And, he wondered, would his family ever admire and respect him again?

Christine called from the bottom of the stairs. "Tom."

He balled up a clean hand towel and dabbed at the perspiration that had popped out on his brow. Lint dotted his scruffy dark whiskers.

"I can't come down. I'm in my underwear." He hung over the railing and looked down at her. "What?"

"I think we should go over to the Riccas after dinner. Pay our respects. I made a pound cake."

At those words, the piano Tom had been carrying on his back all day turned into a baby grand.

Chapter 7

THAT SAME EVENING, RIGHT ACROSS THE STREET, Frank was pacing around the living room of his two-bedroom white Cape Cod as though he was marching into battle. His meaty, white-knuckled fists hammered out a beat, a determined beat, with each of his steps.

Frank glanced at the phone. "Don't you dare ring!" A call at this hour most often meant a dinner invitation.

"Not tonight . . . I couldn't plaster on a fake smile," said Frank to the phone.

"Nope. I wouldn't do it. Even though Christine's cooking is the food of the gods."

He salivated. He gulped down temptation. "A diversion. That's what I need."

He clicked on the TV and the news blasted. Frank recoiled when he heard CNN's Wolf Blitzer tallying up the day's casualties of war.

"Why do I turn that damn thing on the minute I walk into the house?" Frank screamed. "Bad habit!"

He glared at the TV. "The more blood, the better for your ratings, right? You sons of bitches! Since when is war a spectator sport, you dummies? You've set up your own little coliseum network so everyone can see our boys being thrown to the lions. You're no different than those damn depraved Romans! Let our boys do their jobs and come home. Stop putting their every move, good or bad, under a magnifying glass! Isn't combat enough pressure for them?"

He clicked it off and threw the remote into the chair sitting in front of the vile electronic instrument. Frank's eyes shifted to the pictures in silver frames on top of the TV, of him and Tom in Iraq, smiling, Tommy in his class-A's, giving a big thumbs-up.

"Kids. God, all so young." Frank cleared his throat. "So many years," he murmured to the photo. "I had a lot more hair then, too." His stubby fingers rubbed over the shiny circle on the top of his head.

Frank and Tom had a history. They'd served side by side during Operation Eagle Claw in 1980, kicked around the Persian Gulf in 1983 during the Chad incident, and were involved with the support team for the assault on the hijackers of the *Achille Lauro*. They had taken part in the expelling of Iraqi forces after the invasion of Kuwait and stuck together through February 1991, during Operation Desert Storm.

After thirteen years of service, when Tom was thirty-one, he and Frank had exchanged the army way of life for the life of neighbors. He had been there when all of Tom's children had been born, and had cried with his best friend when they buried Tommy.

At least three nights a week Frank was still at Tom's elbow, but now it was at the dinner table. Tom would call over and complain; it would go something like, "Christine made stew. Could you do me a favor and come over? Or I'll be eating stew sandwiches for the next month." Or, "She cooks like the Steelers are coming for dinner. Help me out here, buddy."

Frank chuckled at the thought as his stomach growled. He looked down and jiggled the rounded heap of flesh hanging over his belt. "Shut the hell up."

Frank glanced at Donnie's high school graduation photo. "You're a carbon copy of your old man, kid. None of Christine's Irish DNA in you. You sucked up all your old man's fiery Italian genes, dark hair, and olive skin. A lot of lean meat. The way your dad was when he joined up."

Frank's stomach complained again. He stomped into the kitchen and threw a frozen something in the microwave.

He put two napkins on his TV table, popped the cap on a bottle of Heineken, grabbed the remote, and turned the TV back on. He flipped to the History channel, vowing not to check CNN for the rest of the night.

Tom was certain Christine had the scent. He had always known she was gifted, but tonight she was proving it yet again. He got the "vibes."

Snuggling close on their chilly walk back from the Riccas, she started sending out little probes. "Did you have a good day? Is everything OK at work? Are you having any more problems with the delivery truck?"

She hadn't asked him anything like that since the business had turned the corner, leaving the red zone and floating into the black. Tom tried to keep to short answers, "Yes. OK. The truck's running like a champ." He wasn't ready for more just yet.

"Check out the moon, honey."

"Tom, how can you think about sex when we just left that house full of sorrow?"

"Just because I point out there's a beautiful full moon doesn't mean I'm romancing you. Unless you want me to?"

"We know all too well what Angelo and Sophie are going through. Their pain. It's etched on their faces, and you can hear it in their voices. Telling them things will get better just isn't enough. Their grief is still too raw."

"I almost didn't recognize Angelo. The man has completely given up."

"Well, I can understand. We expect our children to outlive us. Losing Tommy was my worst nightmare. When we were in the kitchen, Sophie said she wants to join her son. Oh, Tom, what should I do? I told Angelo. But . . . the depth of the woman's depression. They have lost their only child. If I hadn't had two other children to care for, I think I might have thought like Sophie." Christine sighed. "The pain never leaves, but in time the days do get more tolerable."

"Christine, you can't do anything but be a friend. And you are doing that."

"You're right. But I will never forget the way death permeated every corner of their house. Like it was something tangible hanging in the air." She shivered.

They continued on in silence.

It WAS A LITTLE AFTER NINE when the couple walked in their front door. Fearing his wife would resume the inquisition, Tom rushed upstairs.

"Stomach's acting up. You might not want to come to bed until the toxic cloud dissipates." It was a half-assed delay, like a kid not wanting to face up to a bad report card. But Tom gave it a try.

Christine followed Tom. "I'm not afraid. After all these years I've built up immunity to your toxins."

She went into the bathroom to do her nightly beauty stuff.

"You know you don't need all that stuff," Tom said while sitting on the toilet.

He had never understood why his wife used all those lotions and creams. Tom believed she was the person the word "beautiful" was invented to describe. And in this he wasn't lying. Christine would be forever gorgeous, inside and out. He watched her brush her shoulder-length hair. Little wisps of spun gold curled around the brush. Her fingers pushed a few strands off her ivory forehead.

Tom was tempted to let his fingers play in those silken threads.

For a long time now, he had realized she was too amazing, too good for him. And that was stating the obvious and underlining it. He often imagined her smiling as she waved her wand over him, distributing a few sparkles of her magic, which smoothed out his rough edges and showed him the merit of gentle words. Real beauty could do that. And she took him knowing he would be forever a work in progress.

Tonight Christine lingered in front of the mirror.

Now Tom felt a little ridiculous for thinking there was even a slim chance his wife would fall for the old stinky gas ruse. For God's sake, with a woman who'd been washing his dirty underwear, he had nothing left to hide. He flushed, washed his hands, and made for the bedroom.

Sitting on the side of their four-poster alone in the dark, Tom took a moment to take in the scents of their marriage: his talcum powder, Christine's lilac soap, and the perfume their two bodies made. Their togetherness swam around him. He had used every neuron and still had nothing in the way of hope to offer her. And he knew it was time—time for his confession. A profound sadness came over him.

Tom heard the soft patter of his wife's bare feet coming down the hall. He braced himself. And then there she was. Her slim body made a cotton T-shirt look as sexy as a satin gown. Her arms were folded over her chest, and her head was tilted against the doorjamb. Her blue eyes caught the moonlight and swallowed him whole.

When she reached to turn on the lights, Tom's voice tiptoed through the darkness, "No, Christine. No lights."

The filmy curtains at their single window were pulled open. Tom watched her walk toward him on the path the full moon had laid down.

"You look like a goddess come down to earth especially for me. Come here, honey," said Tom, patting the mattress.

For a while they sat in silence, shoulder to shoulder on their bed—the bed where all their children had begun. The place where everything Tom had tried to build was born.

Pressing up against each other, they held hands like shy teens on a first date. Tom marveled at their shadowy silhouette on the wood floor. He liked the way they looked.

"Tom?" Her voice was gentle, always full of love, even when she was yelling at him. "Last night . . . you didn't fall asleep watching television, did you? You spent the night in the recliner because . . . ?"

She waited.

Tom stuttered, "It's D-D-Donnie. His guard unit, the Fifty-Sixth Stryker Brigade, has been . . ." He didn't need to say more.

Christine's slim hands jumped to cover her face.

But Tom needed to see that face. It was the source of all his strength.

"I'm sorry, honey. . . ."

He bent down on one knee at his wife's feet.

"Forgive me, Christine?"

Slowly and with what he hoped was tenderness, he pulled her hands away. Putting one finger under her chin, Tom brought her eyes up to meet his. The light coming in the window was just enough for him to see the heartache filling her pools of blue.

Holding on to her hands, he sat back down on the bed and started wiping at her tears. He put an arm around her as she sagged. He felt clumsy, the back of his big abrasive fingers mopping across her small velvet cheeks. Tom wasn't as cautious when he wiped at his own.

Then they fell back onto their bed and just held each other. They rubbed each other's bodies as if massaging away this crisis. Their hands became hungry as their bodies became needy. Eventually the energies generated by their fear and sorrow overwhelmed them. Relief could only be found in fierce, wild lovemaking.

IT WAS WELL PAST MIDNIGHT before the waters of passion receded. Tom's own well of sorrow was now bone dry. But he knew the drought was only temporary. There would be more floods.

Looking into Christine's beautiful face, his gut twisted. Before he knew it he whispered, "Baby, I'm sorry. I'm so very sorry."

Listening to her sobs during her restless sleep only increased Tom's torture.

He faced up to his complicity. His error in judgment when he had agreed and encouraged Donnie to sign up for the National Guard wasn't just a mistake, it was a disaster, one compounded by his parental complacency. With a single blow he had done irrevocable damage to the family. Tom had experienced this kind of intense pain after Tommy's death. And now that hurt resurfaced, hot and fresh, to besiege him.

The soldier had failed. He was no better than his own father, who had chosen to desert him and live inside a bottle.

Tom had promised Christine he would take care of them. He had broken his word. He had neglected his fatherly responsibilities. Tommy and now Donnie would suffer from his failure. The sins of the father . . .

Suddenly Tom wanted to shout out and curse God. But for the sake of the woman in his arms and her need for rest, he kept silent.

He swore an oath to God that he would do whatever it took to make this right. In his head he pledged he'd be there for Christine, for Donnie, and for Chrissy. His wife's abundant courage had its limits. Christine had forgiven him tonight. She wouldn't let him keep the blame or carry that burden. And that made his pain all the more intense.

"Baby, I won't let you down. I promise."

Losing another son could not be left to chance. Tom knew too much of the mortality of men. He had seen it visited on the young and the old, the weak and the strong. There had been many opportunities for him to die in combat. But he had escaped. Why? Sometimes, after a nightmare, he felt as if that question had been burned into him, a tattoo on his conscience. But the thick scrapbook in his mind, so full of ghosts from his past, was getting heavier. He would not—no, could not—fathom Donnie's face on a page next to Tommy's in his book of death. Nor would he allow Donnie to start his own gruesome album.

Tom fought to steady his breathing.

He was so tired of sorrow and, its accomplice, regret. He had lived with them and delivered them. Dark memories are the worst kind of torture.

"God," Tom whispered, "give me something. Anything to hang some hope on. Help me find another path. One that keeps my son from stepping up to death's door. I am the one who should be invited in. Heaven knows I have knocked at that address too many times. It is time for this man, he pounded on his chest, this man who thinks himself a father, to take action."

Then Tom wept—for his mother, for the son he had lost, for his wife, and for the father he desperately wanted to be to his son and daughter.

The full-size bed Tom and Christine had been sleeping in all their married life suddenly seemed too small for all the misery it held.

FRANK AWAKENED AT THREE A.M. with drool dripping from the corners of his mouth. His meal had congealed into a lump, still uneaten, on the TV table. Two bottles of beer and the start of a third had been supper.

He wiped the fog from his eyes with the heels of his hands.

As his vision cleared and his senses returned, he noticed the History channel was still playing—at this point, a two-hour special about the Civil War.

He stared blankly at the screen and reached for the remote. He'd tortured himself enough for one night. It was time for bed. Tomorrow wasn't going to be any better than today.

Then, for some reason, his thumb paused over the power button. He looked around the room as if someone had just tapped him on the shoulder.

"Tom, is that you?" He turned. Nobody was there. He figured sleep still had a hold on parts of him. But something was nagging at Frank. His eyes focused on the flat screen.

The show was almost over when a graphic scrolled across the bottom of the screen. It said, "You are watching *In My Son's Stead,*, a reenactment of a common law widely used during the Civil War."

"Whoa!" Frank's thumb jumped to hit the reverse button. When he was at the beginning of the show, he TiVo'd it.

Frank leaned forward in his chair and watched as a small troop of five Confederate soldiers rode up to a small farmhouse. It wasn't a typical rich Southern plantation. The farm belonged to a poor family.

A mother, a father, and a boy of maybe sixteen walked tentatively out onto the porch. They huddled close together as if a storm was coming.

The officer in charge slid down off his horse. When he was at the foot of the porch and in front of the family, he said, "We're looking for conscripts that have failed to report. I'm here for your son."

Frank let out a sigh.

The mother's arms locked around her boy. "We have already lost one son to the war. Don't take our boy, please, please! He's all we have," she screamed.

The father pulled his family aside to calm them. The soldiers would take his son no matter what he said, and it could get rough. The army had the law on their side.

The officer stepped up onto the porch and closed in on the family.

The farmer pushed his family farther behind him to safeguard them.

But instead of yanking the boy out of the mother's arms, the officer walked to the opposite end of the porch. He signaled for the father to follow him.

Frank inched closer to the set. He turned up the volume.

"Look," the captain said, in a low voice, "I have a son of my own." He winced, and the father could see that this soldier was a compassionate man.

"Listen closely, and think before you answer, farmer." The officer's eyes moved from side to side. It was obvious he didn't want his men to hear. "There is a law, it's common law—some of the rich plantation owners do this using their slaves—that allows for someone else to stand in your son's stead. Speak up if you want to invoke this law. This is your only chance."

The captain quickly retreated off the porch and back to his men.

The father glanced once at his wife and sixteen-year-old boy. Then his voice rang out strong and certain. "I will go in my son's stead."

Frank fell back into his chair with a belly-grunting huff. "Well, I'll be damned!"

Chapter 8

ON TUESDAY MORNING, watching Frank cross the street with a spring in his step annoyed Tom. It was seven in the morning, and his rotten mood was sliding downhill and gathering momentum. By the time Frank opened the door and jumped into the truck, Tom was close to decking his friend for his inappropriate smile.

Poor Frank must have read Tom's mind, because as soon as his butt was in the seat he said, "Hold on, Tom . . . I know this looks bad." His hands were up with his palms out, ready to defend himself.

After a friendship spanning decades, Frank should have remembered that no sleep had always equaled a short fuse for Tom. And two sleepless nights in a row had set his buddy's nerves jumping, as though 220 amps were running through his veins.

Tom snapped back, "You've got that right. And where's my coffee?"

"Oh, the coffee." Frank hit himself in the head. "Geez, sorry. I'll explain. But first, how's Christine?"

"How do you think? Smiling on the outside, sopping up tears with the corner of her apron when she thinks nobody is watching. She's dropping the bad news on Chrissy after school today. Which reminds me, come over for dinner."

"No. No, I couldn't. Your family will . . ."

"Cut the crap. You're their favorite uncle. And with Donnie there, you can help me hold my mouth in check. I don't know what to say or even how to act around my own son. I want to keep it light, normal, and I need your help. We'll play a game of pool after, like we used to."

"Okay. What's Christine cooking?"

"Beef and noodles."

Frank licked his lips. He was already savoring the meal. Maybe it was because he hadn't eaten much yesterday.

Tom turned the key and, inching away from the curb, barked, "So, are you going to tell me why you're wearing that shit-eating grin? I don't often start my day by punching out someone, but this is the kind of morning I can make exceptions."

"I got something. I mean, I saw something last night that might help."

"What are you talking about?"

For the next fifteen minutes, Frank gave Tom a blow-by-blow account of what he had seen on the History channel.

Tom tried to wrap his brain around Frank's theory, but this morning's ride to work was something out of Dante's *Inferno.* As they hit pothole after pothole, it seemed to Tom the street had given birth to more cavities overnight; it made concentrating challenging.

Tom lowered his window and let loose on the cop at the corner. "Why don't you put some unemployed people to work fixing these craters?"

The cop yelled back, "Move it!"

"Easy, Tom." Frank put a hand on his friend's arm.

"Yeah, yeah," said Tom, cranking the window up.

"You're telling me this Disney film," which, in actuality, it had been, "could be an accurate portrayal, the real deal. Have I got this right?" Tom's wired mind fired off words like *outrageous* and *impossible* inside his head.

Frank nodded, then added, "It's history."

"Huh." A law that could help Donnie? The only laws Tom was familiar with pertained to his business, like the federal excise tax law on trucking. But a law that could actually help? Was it possible? He had to think. "I can't get my head in the game. I need coffee."

Dunkin' Donuts was Tom's usual choice, but he needed to drive away the fog in his mind sooner rather than later. When he spied a Starbucks sign coming up at an easy on-and-off exit off Route 87, he jumped for it. Today they would join the suit-and-tie types.

Tom walked up to the cute little girl at the counter and ordered. "Coffee. Two."

"Have you tried our Frappuccinos? They're excellent."

"No, just coffee." Over his shoulder Tom asked Frank, "What the hell is a frappa . . . ?"

"Okay, and . . . ?" she asked.

"Coffee. The brown brewed water you sell." Tom's hands started dancing in the air, and he hoped she understood blue-collar Italian sign language.

She still stared at him, as if he had just asked for a drink from the Fountain of Youth.

Frank tapped Tom on the shoulder and pointed at the sign overhead.

"Good God," marveled Tom. "When did coffee need its own menu?"

Taking charge, Frank ordered. "Two grandes, Sumatra blend."

When the girl behind the counter realized she was talking to some-one who spoke her lingo, she began to chant, "Caf or decaf, foam or no foam . . . ? Skinny Carmel Macchiato is our special. And we have some organic blends . . ."

"Keep it simple. One sweet, the other black," countered Frank.

"Nice going, Frank. I never knew you spoke a second language."

Tom and Frank managed to get two coffees and get back on the road, but because of all the time they had spent in negotiations for their brew, they hit peak traffic. Tom cursed. He was going to be late meeting with a potential client. "This week sucks."

"So, what do you think?" asked Frank as he inhaled and sipped his Sumatra.

"Think?" They were four deep at a light, standing still. Tasting his coffee, Tom scorched his tongue. "Damn it."

"It's coffee, and it usually comes hot," quipped Frank. "Take the lid off."

"Now, why didn't I think of that, Einstein?" Sarcasm was Tom's release valve. He put the lid in the center cup holder, and cursed when just two cars in front of him made it through the light because of all the jerks crossing in front of them who had run the red.

With road rage flaring inside him, Tom toasted Frank and tried his coffee again. "By the way, this Sumatra isn't half bad. If it wasn't like being under the gun to get a cup, I'd go there again."

While Tom blew on his coffee and took minuscule sips, it came to him that Donnie might soon be under the gun, literally. He turned to Frank. "This common-law thing seems a long shot. But I have to do something. And more words won't do it. He shuts me out. I need to take some kind of action. Show rather than tell. Right now this 'in his stead' scheme is all I've got."

"But if it is authentic, still in the law books, then maybe . . ." Frank's energetic chatter slowed to a trickle.

"Yeah, I get it. But who could we get to take his place if we legally could?"

Frank rubbed his chin as he thought. "Maybe some homeless guy. Or someone on death row."

"Right—they're going to let a murderer out of jail to join the army," scoffed Tom. "Where will I get the money to pay him?"

"You could take out a second mortgage," said Frank. "That would be enough incentive, especially in these economic times, for some unemployed bum to do it."

"The bank refused to approve a loan unless I made improvements. I couldn't afford the repairs on the house before, so what makes you think I could come up with that kind of cash now." He paused. "I should have sold the Chevelle."

"No, not Mona. That's your kid's inheritance. Donnie loves her. I'll keep thinking," said Frank as he drank his coffee.

A jumbled memory, one he tried to suppress, started to play in high definition on the screen in Tom's mind. He was bathed in an eerie green light and could hear the rattle of hundreds of rounds, preparing the helicopter's landing zone. He was clinging to a canvas seat, stomach and nerves churning, body sweating under the weight of his pack. He heard the sloshing of water inside it as he snapped on his night-vision goggles. He was back in the Middle East. It was just like before. He was blindly riding into an arid darkness.

"Tom? Tom, what are you ruminating on?"

"Nothing." He swallowed. "Maybe we should make sure this old law is legit before we go any further. No sense pointing the gun if we don't have any ammunition."

"You could check it out on the Internet," suggested Frank. "I don't know much about computers, but everyone says that if it exists you can find it in cyberspace."

"This is Tuesday, so Goldie and Cecilia go out to the cafeteria for lunch." Tom knew everyone's schedule. "Come to the office after they're gone. Then we can be sure no one will be poking their noses into our business. We'll Google it and take it from there."

HANGING OVER HIS BOSS'S SHOULDER at 12:04, Frank was mumbling in Tom's ear, "Let it be there . . . let that law be valid."

Tom's thick, oil-stained index fingers tapped timidly over the keyboard. Searching, he didn't know who was more nervous—Frank, who seemed to be praying that the movie had all been true, or himself, wondering what he would do next if it was.

Tom put in "Civil War" and "in my son's stead" and punched Enter. The first eight references they read through were about the Civil War. It wasn't looking good. And it was taking a long time. The queens would be back to the office soon.

Tom clicked on every search result. A.J. Stead & Son Agricultural Buildings, W.T. Stead on the death of his son, and Christina Stead, author, all were of no use. But when Tom began to read the third listing on the second page of results, his hopes burned a little brighter.

When George Washington was forming the Continental Army to fight against Great Britain, James Harris was the first man to substitute a slave to fight in his place. That was in 1780, toward the end of the Revolutionary War. After that, and during the entire Civil War, many men would go off to war in the place of a son or, if they were rich, would pay someone or even send a slave to stand in their stead.

"Listen to this Frank. When President Lincoln instituted the draft in 1863 you could purchase a substitute to take your place for as little as three hundred dollars. Andrew Carnegie paid an Irish immigrant to fight in his place during the Civil War. J.P. Morgan and Grover Cleveland did the same thing. Southern plantation owners sent their slaves to fight and die for them. Here is a son who went for his father, James Aiken. But there was no money involved." Tom added, "It says here it became 'common law.'" He rocked back in his squeaky metal chair and took a calming breath. "Woo."

Frank plopped down at Goldie's desk opposite him. The seconds dragged on as they stared at one another, letting the knowledge that they had found the damn law sink in.

"Hey, what's 'common law'?" asked Frank, jerking upright.

"Good point. I guess we better know."

Tom returned to pecking on the computer. "It's laws based on precedent instead of statutory law."

"So . . ."

"It means it's real. Holy shit. Here, here it is." Thumping the desk with his fist, he sent the neat stacks of invoices in all directions. "Damn, it's still on the Pennsylvania law books."

Some people say that at moments like this a silent, numb feeling sets in. But there was nothing calm going on inside of Tom.

He listened to his heart pumping as hard and fast as it could. Thoughts like, *What do I do next?* and *How will I pull this off?* were crashing over him like waves. When the tide went out, exposing the tough reality of the situation, Tom took a minute to catch his breath before he said, "This could work."

His next thought was of Jim Small, an old army buddy.

"Is Small still practicing law?"

"Yeah. He's some bigwig district attorney down south." Frank caught up to Tom's thinking, "Yeah! He'd loved this kind of shit, a real challenge. Have you heard from him since Tommy's funeral?"

"No. But at Arlington he said to call if I needed him. I'll send him an e-mail with this information we found and tell him about Donnie. Then follow up with a call tonight. If I can get him on board . . ." Tom hit enter and added, "Here goes all the information we found. I think I did it right."

"Now all we need is . . ." Frank didn't finish his thought.

Tom looked over at Frank, ready to thank him for coming through, but his co-conspirator's somber face stopped him. Frank's hands were shaking. He had to interlock his fingers to force them under his control. His broad, clean-shaven face was damp. Frank's normal cocky smile was a straight, taut line, something akin to a line in the sand. Tom could see fresh sweat staining Frank's work shirt.

Then his brown hound-dog eyes bore into Tom. Frank said, "I've been thinking."

"Sounds dangerous," kidded Tom.

"There's only one way to make this work." He sucked in more oxygen. "I'm going instead of Donnie." The words crawled out of Frank's mouth as if a stealth approach would make them more palatable. Wrong.

"No! No way!" Tom blurted.

"That's how I am seeing this," said Frank. He jutted his jaw out, giving Tom his bulldog face, but Tom wasn't buying it, not this time.

Tom's hand sliced through the air. "I won't allow it."

"Who, then?" Frank asked as though they didn't already know the answer.

"Well, even if I could find enough money to bribe someone, I can't do that. Paying someone to fight for you is just wrong. I would be sentencing someone else's son or daughter to . . ."

Frank's right knee jerked up and down at a discordant beat.

"What if the person got killed because of me? Another body to add to my count." Tom took a moment and felt the Chinook he had been on earlier in his mind become tangible.

Frank tried again. "See, that's why it has to be me. Let me do this. I'm the logical choice for this job. I wouldn't be leaving behind any wife or kids." Frank's body wasn't moving an inch; his stiff mouth moved as though cartoon lips from some creature had been plastered onto his mug. "I can do this."

"Right. Like I would let my best friend go for my son and me," said Tom. "That's not happening."

The red deepened on Frank's face as he stood up and let his sizable bulk loom over Tom. He sucked in his gut, pulled up his pants, squared his shoulders, and said, "That best friend shit flows both ways." Then his voice softened. "Look, Donnie is as close as I'm ever going to get to having a son. I wouldn't be leaving anyone behind, and my DD214 discharge form says I'm combat eligible for reenlistment, too."

"Yeah, right. You mean until you have to run a mile with that belly hanging over your belt and your emphysema kicks in. Even if that fireplug you call a body were in shape . . . no, I couldn't let you do it."

"Yeah, well what about your diabetes? You aren't ready for the Olympics, either."

"I'll deal with my diabetes. I'll lose weight, take my pills, and watch my diet. I have three weeks to prepare, and I have been jogging regularly, so I'm ahead of the game." Tom's voice slowed. "I appreciate your offer, Frank, it means a lot to me, but this is a one-man mission, my kid, my assignment." After all, reasoned Tom, my mistake got Donnie into this. I am personally culpable for the spot my son is in. Besides, I kind of like this James Aiken."

Frank cracked a half smile and got up to pace. "So you're going to pull an Aiken. Only reverse it. Instead of son for father, you're going to do a father for son."

"Yeah, an Aiken. I'll do an Aiken."

Frank and God had come through for Tom. They had delivered the answer to his prayers. But God was tricky. He'd made it a package deal. Come to think of it, He only made package deals. Like when you're a kid wishing for a pony for your birthday and then you get it. But on the pretty bow around the four-legged creature's neck, there's always a tag that asks whether you are willing to take on the shit that comes with this gift.

Was Tom ready? The answer was hard for him to digest. He looked over at Frank. On this assignment he would be going it alone. But until the time came for him to line up and step onto that plane for Afghanistan, he would need Frank. "I could use your help putting this operation together."

"Okay, I'll back you up, like always. Sure," Frank whispered. "So what's our next move?"

Tom heard Goldie and Cecilia talking outside the office door. They'd be bursting through any minute.

Tom hurried to say, "We'll let Jim handle the legal issues. When he gives me the green light, we'll find a way to convince Donnie to let me take his place."

"I remember," Frank recited, "phase one is initiating. Have a clear idea of the campaign's military, political, economic, social goals. In this case Jim, our legal eagle, will be flying cover. Our goal: taking Donnie out of the action."

"The planning and executing phases won't mean a ~~damn~~ thing if we don't get my kid on board."

"Well, I remember what it was like digging holes in the sands of Iraq," said Frank dubiously. "And Donnie's not going to be a slam dunk, either."

"Yeah, but look at it this way. It can't be harder than the peace process." Tom took a breath. "The world has been wishing for peace in the Middle East for a very long time. We keep sending in troops, but the sands of war keep falling right back in and plugging up any progress."

"And the United States military can't hold back a whole ~~damn~~ desert."

"Exactly."

Frank and Tom were always on the same page.

"To overcome something like a threat of terror," Tom said, "you'd have to be able to see inside the hearts of men."

"And that's not happening, so . . ."

"So, Frank, we are going to save a few hearts of our own. I am digging my heels in. I'm refusing to let the reckless greed and hate of some men destroy another of my sons. This war can't have Donnie."

A small envelope in the corner of the computer flashed. He opened his e-mail to read Jim Small's response. There were only two words; "I'm in."

Chapter 9

ON THE RIDE HOME AFTER WORK, Tom reviewed his life. His mistakes were numerous and of the PhD variety: piled high and deep. And what was worse, they far outweighed his accomplishments.

The most important decisions he had made for his sons had been wrong. He had let his stubborn pride cloud his judgment. And that horrific blunder negated any good he might have done for his family in the past. Now Donnie's life was in jeopardy.

His decision to follow his heart and marry Christine was left out of Tom's dark equation, but he needed to, had to change this trend he saw and rectify his mistakes. And after a lengthy discussion with Jim Small he might just get his chance. Jim had told him to be patient, give him some time, and let the plan ripen. So that was what Tom was trying to do as he stepped in his front door.

As he prepared to take a shower, he mapped out his evening. He'd keep it light. Listen to his kids without barking at them. Glue a smile on his face and enjoy something akin to a normal night at home. He had just one foot in the shower when the house said, "No way."

The water pipes choked, then coughed up a rusty little stream in spits and spurts.

"I'm going to replace all of you with your copper cousins if you give me any more grief, you temperamental, corroded pieces of shit!"

Tom lathered up and hurried to rinse under the meager flow. The pipes protested in gagging bursts, and suddenly the water turned glacial. He jumped out of the shower, still arguing with the plumbing, and came face-to-face with Christine, who handed him a towel.

"I wouldn't pick a fight with the plumbing if I were you, or icicles will be hanging from some of my favorite parts."

"Yeah. That shower always gets the last word."

Through the years, Tom had often wished for a second bathroom, something grand. But it would have never worked for his family. They needed to share the sink, compromise on who got the first and hottest shower, and keep in mind whose towel was whose. Sharing is part of life. Christine had taught him that living as a family, close together, teaches you that stuff.

When he accepted the towel, a dark blue one that Christine had color-coded as his, she gave him one of those looks, the kind that makes you drop your cloaking shield so you can see her antennae fully extended, scoping out your vibrations.

"It's nice that you are home early." Christine checked her watch. "Four thirty is a new record."

"I needed to be here, inside these drafty walls."

As Tom dried off, he watched his wife displaying her greatest gift: caring. She took care of her family as though each of them were precious works of art, canvases to which she added a considered stroke every day. Her slim, nimble hands had helped form each of them.

Tom wondered why he hadn't noticed that before.

"Did I do this"—his hand made circles in the air—"get the marriage and family thing all wrong?"

"What?" Her eyes widened. Her probe retracted. "Oh, you're worried about your relationship with Donnie?"

He nodded and wondered, *How did she know that?*

"He'll come back to you. You planted some good seeds when he was younger. Teens are like wild stallions. We have to give them their freedom, but they'll come back home when they miss the herd. Donnie loves his family and you."

"And how about you? Did you need some of that same freedom?"

"Are you asking me if you held me back from having a career?"

"Yeah." Tom rested his elbows on his knees. The past few days of roller coaster emotional stuff had been draining.

"Well, there was a time when I wanted to be a nurse. In high school I volunteered at the hospital."

"Did you wear one of those pink-and-white dresses?" Tom eyebrows danced seductively.

"Yes. I was a candy striper."

"I never knew that. I bet you looked cute." He thought about that for a second. "You would have been a great nurse. You like people. And you care about them."

"But I use those skills right here. Don't you see? And what better job could there be than taking a drafty old pile of wood like this house and warming it up with love, food, and laugher. We transformed this into a home."

"You did it, not me." Before she could object he asked, "Was it enough?"

She worked her way around the bathroom, picking up her husband's dirty underwear and putting it in the hamper, then lingering so they could connect. Connect was what they did best. When they were in sync, their world hummed; when they were out of sync, Tom couldn't function worth a damn. It amazed him how such a fragile creature could wield so much influence over every part of him—mind, body, and soul. With a single look or just one word, her slender, five-foot-four-nothing body cast an all-encompassing shadow.

At last she said, "This is me . . . my dream job. I loved staying home to raise the kids. I didn't want to miss a moment of their lives." She laughed and held out her arms as if she were hugging the house and everything in it.

Then Tom watched her eyelids narrow and zero in on him.

Her voice turned serious. "Are you ready to talk now, Tom?"

There was no reason to beat around the bush; the woman already knew he had something to say. "Frank found something that might help Donnie. Jim Small is checking it out."

Tom went on to explain the movie, their Internet research, and what he was going to do.

The color in his wife's delicate skin fluctuated, her lips quivered, and tears rushed into and out of her deep sea-blue eyes. As he watched her heart get tossed about, he felt little pieces of his own breaking away.

He braced for an all-systems breakdown, like the one from the previous night, but then Christine surprised him. When he thought about it, she had been surprising him every day of their married life, so why should today be different?

"Don't think for a moment, Tom Lane, that you are making this decision alone. You are talking about one of my babies and my husband here."

She was wagging her pointer finger at him like a stern schoolteacher, but he didn't care. He wanted to go to her, kiss that finger, and put his arms around her, but she held him off.

"Do I have this right? These are my choices: a husband or another son? And don't give me any of that bull about honor and duty."

Echoes of Tommy, thought Tom. But before he could dwell on the past, the fierce look on Christine's face stopped him.

"The danger is real. Put Donnie in the line of fire . . . or you." Her small pink fists were trembling as she rested them on her slender hips.

Tom thought she was close to swearing, which was a once-in-a-millennium occurrence for her. She hadn't practiced it enough to be proficient, so when she did swear, most often the whole family laughed.

She was usually good at checking her temper. But right now her cup was almost full, and Tom could see George Carlin approaching the rim. Tonight he wouldn't laugh.

Christine ranted for a cool fifteen minutes, and there were a few times when Tom wondered if she had written the sailors' dictionary of swear words, because she used some combinations that not even he had heard before.

When she stopped to take a breath, Tom grabbed his chance. "As usual, you get right down to it, honey. But look, I have the most military experience, and because of my age, they'll stick me at a desk; at the worst, I'll be a grease monkey. They'll be ready to kick my old flabby butt back across the Atlantic after one tour. Donnie, on the other hand . . . the young and eager ones, well . . . And I've got the business going good. You can depend on Frank to run it, so you won't be living just on army pay. And I am . . ."

"Expendable?"

"Only temporarily."

"Listen and never forget. You are not expendable, Thomas Lane. Never!"

The blue in Christine's eyes grew as dark as combustible charcoal. Tom wisely decided to keep his mouth shut.

"You promised after we lost Tommy that the family would stick together. ~~Damn it~~, Tom, don't you remember?"

Of course, he did. That was the reason he needed to do this. He needed to step up and stand in for Donnie and for Tommy. And once again he had selfish reasons. He needed this for himself. He couldn't face that guy in the mirror too many more times without owning up that his time had come to step up. Death was too much a part of his replaying dreams. He would not allow his remaining son to take a seat in that realm where loss of life, limb, and insanity reigned.

Tom turned back to his wife.

"Now you want me to make nice, like some brave little army wife on a TV show, wave the flag and smile as you disappear into the night! ~~Like hell~~ I'm putting on that face. It's not happening."

Christine paced. Since the bathroom was tight, Tom sat down on the toilet with a towel wrapped around him to give her flailing hands room. He raised his arm like a kid in school asking a question, but when her eyes bore down on him like twin photon torpedoes, he lowered it.

"So you are going to play the lighthouse, stand on a hill and show Donnie the way to safety?" she asked.

"I never thought of it that way, but I like it." That was definitely the wrong answer.

"Are you insane?"

Her fingernails dug into the soft flesh of her upper arms. She was holding on as tightly as she could to herself or, Tom thought, maybe to her own sanity.

"I've put you in a terrible position. I know that. But listen for a minute, honey." Tom gently touched her hip. She stopped, unfolding her arms and motioning with her hands as though *she* was the Italian —*Go on.*

"We live in a damaged, wounded society. A gray society. We're like a school of fish that clumps together and changes direction in a flash. We don't know which way we should swim. This leader will give us revenge for 9/11, that general will win the war and stop the terrorists. We don't know what we want: power, glory, oil, democracy, or victory. But it sure as hell doesn't look like we want peace. And we aren't going to rid the world of the hate some men have for us by going to war with them. But I can give changing our piece of the world a shot. To do that I have to participate in the change. I have to make ripples. No one will notice my ripples in the sea of war. But Donnie will feel their effect. He will be safe at home with you. The family will continue. This is important to me."

"You are important to this family. Don't ever forget." She acknowledged her husband's soulful confession with a half smile. She wasn't easy.

"OK, I'm a little agitated right now, so give me a chance to think, Tom."

One heartbeat passed before she whirled on him. "How long have you and Frank been working on this?"

"Frank just told me about it today. Honest. Like I said, after what he saw on the History channel. You've heard Donnie talk. He's scared. That worries me. Sure he knows the military manuals front to back. But it's not about the book, it's the action. At a dangerous moment, you can't think, you have to react."

"Great! You're talking about being shot or blown up . . . like Tommy." A heavy sob and her next words got caught in her throat. "Damn it to hell, Tom Lane, I don't like the choices you give me. And I don't know what I'd do if something happened to Donnie *or* you." She started pacing again. Two steps each way. "Now I know how Solomon felt."

"You always needed to know it all. Remember how you always told the kids to think of the best and worst that could happen? And then they'd be prepared. You said, 'It can't hurt as much if you know everything.' Christine, this is just the worst-case scenario."

"You make it sound like you're going to the dentist, not into combat."

She glanced at the mirror, took a towel, and cleaned the steamy smears. Tom guessed she wasn't aware of the tears dotting her cheeks.

Her eyebrows came together. "Do you think this scheme of yours could work? It is pretty farfetched. I mean, it is possible you will show up and the army will throw you off the bus. You might be home for dinner."

"But there's no doubt Donnie will be gone if I don't try. I have to give this a shot, Christine. I couldn't live with myself if I didn't."

"Have you heard Donnie talking this up to his friends?"

Tom whispered, "He looked up to Tommy. He's emulating him."

She straightened another towel. Her hands trembled.

"The boy's naïve. Covering up his fear with false bravado." He almost let slip something about his and Donnie's previous argument but caught himself.

"Tom, what would you say to convince him?"

"I'm working on that," said Tom.

Christine threw her hands up. "Why does God make life so difficult?"

Now Tom found himself sticking up for God. This was a reversal in their roles. "Wars, like global warming and oil spills, are all man-made. So don't be blaming God, honey." He pointed up to the cracked bathroom ceiling. "We are going to need him on our side." It was time for Tom to calm things down. "We can do this. We have been through worse. Remember how worried we were when Chrissy was born premature?"

"And when you were getting the business going," said Christine, laughing and crying at the same time, "and we didn't have enough money to buy Christmas presents, so I repainted some junk I bought at garage sales? Those toys were the most hideous colors."

"Or when I almost lost you, when that drunken driver broadsided you." Tom's voice quivered and started to break up. "I guess it's my turn to put us to the test." His throat felt thick. "Christine, I'm sorry, but this is the way it has to be. I'm going to try and go for Donnie."

Tom was doing it for Tommy, too, but he didn't need to say that.

When married as long as Christine and Tom, you could hear each other's unspoken words as clearly as those that were vocalized.

"You don't have to take a test, Tom. You're above the rest as far as I am concerned. If you weren't the kind of man, the kind of father, who was willing to risk your life for our children, I wouldn't love you so much." Christine continued. "You grew up unloved, and yet you still know what loving is all about."

Tom stared at his wife with wonder. How did she know he was comparing himself to his own worthless father?

"Don't doubt yourself, Thomas Lane. You are nothing like that sperm-donating drunk. He was never a dad. When you changed your name from Lanci to Lane, you severed that connection. You may not have been as active in your kids' lives as they wanted you to be, but you are a good father and a good provider."

Her praise weighed him down with more guilt. Tom wanted to be punished—another irrational leftover from his father. Before each beating, the bastard would say, "You've been bad, Tom. Admit it." And the child that had been Tom would frantically search his mind for the smallest infractions to confess. Was that why Tom didn't tolerate mistakes? Anything lower than a B on the kids' report cards and he had preached to Christine to get after them. Yes, there was still a bit of Lanci in him. He felt shamed by Christine's words of praise. They were rocks around his neck, pulling him down to the darkness lingering inside him.

"Don't. I don't deserve your praise. I should have taken better care of Tommy, my family. This plan . . . I don't know."

"I understand what you are planning to do, Tom. I don't like it. I can't see any of this scheme of yours happening. That doesn't mean I'm not counting on a miracle, just a little one with an all-around happy ending."

"That's what I love about you. You're a miracle maker." The quaking in his voice was hard to control.

"All day I thought about Tommy, the Riccas, now Donnie." She paused. A quivering sigh made her shoulders slump. "How many more families will be destroyed before this is over?"

"I don't know, honey. A better question might be how many wars do we fight before we understand a lasting peace isn't a by-product of war?" Tom picked up her hands and kissed both palms.

She stroked his face, giving him the tenderness he needed but didn't deserve. Then she asked, "Remember that Roberta Flack song from the seventies, 'Killing Me Softly with His Song'?" Tears ran down her cheeks like a raging river, melting Tom's resolve.

He nodded. His heart swelled with her tears. She bore the pain he was pouring on her petite shoulders like a queen.

"This family is me. I am part of each of you. My body feels the pain from a small splinter just as acutely as it does the anguish of one of Chrissy's emotional meltdowns. You are telling my whole life with every word, Thomas Lane."

He grabbed her, desperate now to feel his arms around her, to have her close. He pulled her onto his lap and crushed her body to him. He couldn't get enough of her.

They smothered each other with their love, a thirst that had never been quenched. Tom stroked her back, cried, and kissed each of her tears.

Christine backed away from Tom, and as she started taking off her clothes he let his towel drop to the floor.

Amazed that she had more to give him, Tom followed her into the bedroom like a dog on a leash. How did this incredible woman know his strength came from their union? In his darkest dreams she had often come to pull him back . . . back to her, to his family, and to life. And now the darkness was circling once again. And she was here for him.

They didn't have sex. Instead they gave each other comfort all tangled up inside love. The making of it was long, passionate, and steamy. It was the kind that leaves permanent marks inside you and lives a lifetime in your memory. And Tom was hoping it was the kind that never could be lost, not even after death.

Chapter 10

THE MEAL THAT EVENING STARTED OUT like a wake but picked up a little cheer when Donnie began to tease his sister. He had several probing questions for her new boyfriend and wanted fourteen-year-old Chrissy to arrange a one-on-one meeting for him.

Chrissy did one of those moves girls do so well and threw her hair back with a flick of her head. Tom noticed today her nails were shamrock green, with little flowers stuck to each tip. She had her mother's spun gold for hair, but Tom's rich walnut-brown eyes with long dark lashes. One look from them could bring a stampeding herd of cattle to a full stop.

Tom's eyes strayed frequently to Tommy's empty place at the table. It remained available as if they all were still expecting him to walk in the door and sit down. Tom still felt his oldest son's presence at every meal.

Tom noticed that Chrissy's eyes filled with tears every time they strayed from her plate to Donnie. Her somber face broke its unyielding poise for a second or two as her brother persisted.

"So . . . what's his name? Where does he live? What does his father do?"

Tom watched his son flexing his biceps, making them dance as he talked. They all laughed. Chrissy blushed and was flustered. It was perfect. It was his family.

Chrissy giggled. Donnie had finally managed to break through her sad shell.

"I'm still going to be checking out your boyfriends. Just because I'm not going to be here doesn't mean he gets by without a full inspection from every member of this family." Donnie gave his uncle Frank a wink.

Frank smirked.

Tom jumped in to break the thin layer of ice that still lingered between father and son. "Absolutely," Tom said, backing up his son. Of course, he would be the one doing the boyfriend inspection from a distance, but now wasn't the time for that reveal.

"Frank, more beef and noodles?" offered Christine.

"More? Any more and Donnie will have to help him carry that watermelon he calls a stomach home," Tom declared. "He's eaten three helpings."

At last Donnie made eye contact with his dad. He smirked and fake-punched Frank's belly.

Christine smiled and said, "He always eats at least three. He's complimenting the cook."

"He's going to compliment himself right into the next notch on his belt, the way he's going," Tom said. "Pack up the leftovers for him while we adjourn to the pool room."

Tom turned to Frank and Donnie and rubbed his hands together, like Scrooge counting money. "Gentlemen, warm up your pool cues." He stood.

Donnie vacillated. "I'm meeting the guys. And I have my last final tomorrow—economics."

"Economics? Since when does a guitar player need economics?" Tom sniggered. "If you're switching things around, how about a squirrel chaser like park ranger Jackson? You used to help him fill the bird feeders at Christmas. Now you're throwing in banking. I don't get it." All table talk and smiles ceased.

"Dad, I haven't wanted to be a forest ranger since I was ten years old." Donnie shot back a cool glare at his dad with an unspoken, See what I was saying? You don't know a thing about me.

"In September Donnie switched to a dual major—economics and music." Christine smiled at father and son to warm the space between them.

"I discussed it with Judge Brice. He suggested the dual major. I guess you missed that meeting." Donnie shifted.

"Sorry, son. I guess you outgrew me helping you with your homework and I lost track."

"I better go." Donnie stood.

"No. Please. One game," pleaded Tom. His hand slipped onto his son's shoulder. He gave it a fatherly squeeze.

Donnie tensed, looked at his mom's pleading face, then brightened a little. "Sure. OK, one game."

"I can beat you both using one hand and my belly." Frank's jest had them all chuckling.

"That I'd pay to see," joked Donnie.

As Tom waddled toward the basement door, displaying his own love of Christine's beef and noodles, Donnie perked up and said, "I feel a challenge coming on."

Tom noticed that his son rubbed his hands together just like he did.

In single file, they went down the stairs and into Tom's favorite part of the house, the low-ceilinged, pipe-clanging basement. And there, like an emerald island, sat his jewel, a genuine Brunswick slate-topped pool table.

"Do either of you know who said, 'Billiards is a health-inspiring, scientific game, lending recreation to the otherwise fatigued mind'?"

"Abraham Lincoln," mocked both Frank and Donnie in unison.

"Dad, you have to get some new material."

"I'm just reminding you both that pool is an ancient game, an elegant pastime, played by presidents and other famous people, like Carnegie, J.D. Rockefeller, Vanderbilt, and Henry Ford." Tom finished chalking his cue and tossed the chalk to his son without taking his eyes off Frank.

Donnie casually scooped it up in midair. "Hey, Uncle Frank, for an assignment he once made me do the history of the game of billiards."

"And you got high marks," said Tom, and adding mentally, Now the frost is thawing between Donnie and me.

"You remembered that?" Donnie beamed.

Mentally Tom gave himself a gold star.

"But you forgot someone on your list. General George Custer," said Donnie.

Frank and Donnie laughed.

Tom thought the mention of Custer was a bad omen.

Tom loved this part of the day. Starting from when each of his boys turned five years old, evenings had found father and son, or sons, gathered around the pool table in the basement.

Both boys had started playing from an elevated platform Tom had built around the table so his sons could be at the right height. Of course, the platform was long gone. But the competition and affection—even though fathers only mentally say these things—between father and sons had gained both depth and dimension over the span of years they had played the game together. That is, until his oldest son had gone into the army and his younger son became a teenager, and Tom had mistakenly left his youngest son to his own devices. *I guess they don't outgrow needing their father.* He reprimanded himself and threw away his gold star.

"OK, Dad. Prepare to be scalped," said Donnie.

"You better look out, kid, your father almost turned pro." Frank didn't need to stick up for his friend, but he liked to be part of things.

"Don't get cocky, kid. Remember what happened to Custer." It warmed Tom's heart to be bantering once again with Donnie.

"You taught me all you know. So less chatter and I'll even let you break," countered Donnie. "Now we'll see who comes out on top. Are we on for a friendly wager?"

"You're on," countered Tom.

The first game lasted forty minutes, and the kid cleaned his father's clock. They went to the best of three. Tom claimed victory over the second game, and his boy won the last.

Donnie crowed like a rooster announcing dawn. He strutted and mimicked blowing on his fingers to put out an imaginary fire on his hot, talented hands. He placed his cue in the wall rack like it was the holy grail.

Tom had never enjoyed losing so much. His love for the boy inflated with every antic. He hadn't realized how much he had missed this father-son brand of communication.

"That's my baby." Donnie blew his cue stick a kiss. "OK, Dad. That will be twenty bucks." Donnie rubbed his palms together and offered them, as if the deal was sealed.

"I remember when it cost me a banana split. I think his need for cash might have something to do with a young lady named Nancy." Tom's eyes shifted to his son, who affirmed he had the correct girl. "She goes to college up north," Tom explained to Frank. He added, looking at a surprised Donnie, "Yes, your mother and I talk." They laughed and he asked, "Can I owe ya, kid?"

"Oh, no you don't. Never welsh on a bet," said Donnie. "It's the measure of a man. You taught me that."

Tom winced, as though pulling money out of his pocket was painful. "I guess it's going to cost me," he groaned, fingering the bills in his money clip.

"Tell you what." Donnie's eyes sparked. "I'll take a weekend with Mona and we'll call it even." His son laughed at his own impossible proposal.

Tom had once said his Malibu lady had an enigmatic smile like the Mona Lisa, and the name had stuck. Of course, you had to be a car lover like Donnie and his dad to appreciate that smile.

"Ah, Mona," sighed Tom. "She's at her best when the sun glints off her classic chrome grill lips; and that graceful ridge of the hood gives her that sexy, pouty expression." Tom had drawn that picture a thousand times. "She, like the real Mona Lisa, smiles with attitude. And for any red-blooded man, one look into those big, round twin beams and you're a goner." Tom saw his son get caught up in the fantasy. Of his two sons, Donnie was the one who had always been as much in love with Mona as he was.

Then Tom's dreamy look disappeared, and he said, "You've been trying to wheedle that car out of me since the day you turned seventeen and got your driver's license." Tom found a twenty and threw the money on the pool table. "It's not happening today, kid."

Donnie said, "But you know I have to keep trying. She already told me she needs a younger man."

They all laughed.

"Well, someday, when you have a better understanding of what it takes to make a classy lady like Mona happy, she'll be yours."

This playful jousting was required and had accompanied every Sunday night game of pool as Donnie was growing up.

"Did I hear Christine say she had made a chocolate cake?" Frank interrupted.

And like a punch to the head, the remedy to his dilemma hit Tom. As they walked upstairs, he gave Frank a knowing nod. He could guarantee Donnie would agree to his plan.

Chapter 11

"I'M TELLING YOU, THIS WILL WORK."

Tom hated Frank's mute bobblehead impression. He continued the one-sided debate. "Why not? I'll goad him into a game of pool. You'll egg him on, like he's afraid to play me for higher stakes than gas money. Frank, when you've got him hooked, I'll reel him in. Donnie's coming off a two out of three win, so his confidence is high."

It was only Wednesday morning, and he had already done a week's worth of strategizing. Tom's brain was firing on all cylinders. He and Frank sat in the parking lot at Starbucks sipping Sumatra, and it seemed to him that he was coming up with dozens of ideas and Frank none.

"I could get addicted to this blend," Tom said, changing tactics and rolling his eyes. Even his comic drama didn't prompt Frank's tongue to shoot back some sarcasm. Now his friend's silence was really getting on Tom's nerves.

"Say something, for Christ's sake! Me doing all the thinking is giving me a headache."

"Sorry." Frank slipped his coffee cup into a holder. "But this is a little too real for me. I should have kept my lips buttoned! We are talking about a lot of lives here. My big idea"—Frank's hands jumped wide apart like a fisherman talking about his catch—"is going to mess up your family. Christine must want to hire a hit man. And what if this backfires and my plan gets you . . . Jesus, Tom, what are we doing?"

Tom noticed the dark five-pounders hanging under each of Frank's eyes. They weren't new, but they had gotten heavier since yesterday. He knew his friend was one to carry his burdens deep inside. But that had to stop. He needed Frank to be sharp and committed.

"Number one, this is my plan. You aren't taking the credit or the blame," said Tom, sticking his face closer to Frank's. "Second, nothing, and I mean nothing, can shake Christine and me apart."

Tom saw Frank's eyes leave the floor mat and jerk up from under their thick red lids. Frank's glower reminded Tom that the man across from him knew all his secrets, even the deep ones.

Frank had been in Iraq and witnessed Tom's torment. His friend had taken full responsibility for each man wounded or killed on his watch. Sure, Tom knew it was combat and people would get hurt, but he had adopted the attitude that every outcome was a result of his actions and decisions. After a firefight that killed or wounded more than half his squad, something had snapped, and Tom had dropped into a valley of depression. All alone, he could never have climbed out. It was the first time in Tom's life that he didn't have a strategy to defeat the enemy. When the enemy is you, it's a no-win scenario right from the beginning.

Despair was all Tom saw for his future. His grief channeled his judgment to but one conclusion. Eliminate the problem. That was when Frank had stepped in and taken over.

The two men had kept that secret. It was a mistake Tom was ashamed to share with anyone but his best friend and God. It had been after many sleepless nights in Iraq that Frank had awoken one morning and found Tom sobbing and caressing his sidearm. Frank had seen other men suffering with Post Traumatic Stress Disorder. Frank had saved Tom. He had taken care of him, and made sure he got the help he needed. Frank drove Tom to every appointment with his therapist. Frank's actions, support, and advice had saved more than just Tom. They gave his best friend a marriage, family, and a future.

Now Frank felt crippled, unable to take action because he knew about Tom's haunted past. Was Tom so depressed that he was again ready to fall on his sword? Was his friend planning a suicide mission?

Tom read Frank's thoughts. "Buddy, I'm not there. Believe me. I'm thinking from love, not from desperation or sorrow. I intend to come home. And I need you with me on this to make that happen."

Frank said, "You're sure?"

"Well, I'm not going to kiss you to prove it, if that's what you want. I hope that doesn't crush ya."

They both laughed.

"Can we get on with this now?"

Frank was cautious but nodded.

"Frank, some day when Donnie is a father he will come to you and thank you. He'll understand how a father feels . . . how he loves his children. And if the worst happens, my family is going to need your support. I don't want anyone ever thinking this is the wrong decision. Thinking that way will tear them apart. This is my game, all my decision, and my only alternative. It's time for me to stand up straight and stand in for my son. Speech over," said Tom as he swiped his dripping nose on his sleeve and started up the truck.

As the V8 roared to life, Tom tried to convince himself that he believed the sermon he had just given Frank. If—and he had to be honest with himself, it was a big *if*—he expected to pull this off, he had to stay focused, wipe away all doubt. To inspire others to trust in his plan, he had to exude self-confidence, show no weakness. The slightest hint of vulnerability and he'd be defeated before he could even begin.

The army had taught Tom the importance of a positive mental attitude, and that attitude was coming in handy once again. He may no longer have been the sergeant, pumping up his team, leading the way, and keeping them safe as they followed in his footprints. But he was going to prove to himself that he could be the leader of his family. They followed where he led. The buck stopped with him. And it was up to him to keep them all on the same path. Solidarity was the sole direction that held a guaranteed secure future for Donnie. Little did his family know—and he included Frank when he thought of his family—that it was them standing behind him, especially Christine, that keep him moving forward.

Ever since Frank and he had hatched this scheme, Tom had been giving himself an assortment of these pep talks. Beads of sweat trickled down his back despite the chilly early-December air. Tom felt it but ignored the dampness of doubt. He would not—no, could not—allow it to seep in and erode the foundation on which he was building his case to protect Donnie. Psychologically, Tom was already in the battle.

"You can say what you want, Tom, but I know how you work." Frank took a sip of his coffee and added, "I've heard that speech before, Staff Sergeant Lane."

"I'll be a lonely private, if this works. Remember base manpower, just feet marching to the beat."

"You're kidding! I thought when you re-up, it was at your former rank."

"Yes. But I'm not re-upping. Remember, I want to be Donnie."

"Man, this plan is losing its shine," said Frank.

"So let's plot it out, just like a military maneuver."

Tom and Frank had their plan to coerce Donnie into agreeing to the switch mapped out before they pulled into the parking lot at the shop. They agreed it would be harder for Donnie to turn down his father's challenge if he had an audience, a group of his friends present when Tom challenged him. They also intended to play on the father-son rivalry, heat things up a bit before they brought out their secret weapon.

"Does Christine know about this pool game for all the marbles?" asked Frank.

"Yeah. I gave her a rough idea of what I was planning. She listened, then laughed at me and said it would never work."

"Hey, isn't Thursday night date night?" Frank also knew his adopted family's schedule.

"Right. Great. Donnie and his friends always hang out around the pool table until nine or ten before they make their appearance on the social scene. So Thursday it is."

Tom found himself holding his breath. In two days he'd be playing a game of pool that would decide his son's future. Could things get any crazier?

Chapter 12

THIS TIME THE "BLACK," Tom's PTSD, had added a new twist to his nightmare.

The sand was thick and consuming as usual. But it was green, and chest deep. Tom struggled, desperate to rescue his arms from its sucking grip. His legs fought forward two steps. The sand dragged him back one.

Two contenders, father and son, were stranded in this bottle-green sludge. They calculated each move. Danger waited for the winner, lingering torment to the loser. There would be no clear victory, yet one had to triumph to save the other.

The young boy in front of Tom was ready to shoot through the sixth of the fifteen floating gates. Success.

Now just nine gates remained, trembling on the tide. Tom's hands stretched out for the closest gate. His workman's stiff fingers skimmed the smooth edge of the post just before the sand sucked him under. He fought against the green beast, swearing it would not beat him. Not today, not him.

Tom surfaced, choking. He tried to spit, to expel the taste of the grit. But he had no saliva, no moisture left in him. This "sea" was draining him dry. He missed a gate. Another entry loomed closer. He swam for it. He had it in his grasp and passed through. The last gate remained. Tom's mind quickly plotted the many ways he could approach it. But time was running out. He had to choose the right strategy, the winning moves. One slip and the world would shatter.

Suddenly the rifle he carried became a long pole. Someone, maybe Tommy, whispered, "Dad, use the hook at the end of the pole." If Tom grasped it properly, he could use it to line himself up with that wretched gate to triumph. Beyond the gate was the "black," its jaws open, hungry, waiting for him.

To win meant to be taken. This time he pushed down the urge to run from it. He had made his decision. The "black" can't have Donnie. He would go into the "black." The pole slipped from his hands. It rolled away, fractions of inches from his fingers.

"TOM, TOM, WAKE UP." Christine shook his shoulder. "I didn't expect my meatloaf to send you into a coma."

The green sand in his mind dissolved, replaced by his lumpy recliner. His personal angel, Christine, hovered. Tom was stretched out flat, still in the same position he was in when he collapsed after their Thursday-evening dinner. He usually caught the news, not a few z's, but all these nights of twilight half-sleep were getting heavier. "How long was I out?"

"About an hour. You looked too peaceful to wake."

Peaceful? God, there was a lot Christine didn't know. He wanted to keep it that way.

Christine whispered in Tom's ear.

A spark flared in his body; she was telling him one of those secrets that their children would never believe and didn't need to ever hear, the kind that turned parents into people just as youthful, at least in the parents' minds, as themselves.

Smiling, Tom watched Christine moisten her lips. His wife added a cute little head tilt that suggested more than idle interest.

Damn, if she wasn't flirting with him.

Christine leaned in again. Her right breast skimmed Tom's shoulder. "Perhaps a replay later, my bear. Grrr . . ."

Bear was her pet name for Tom, especially during and after great sex. And Tom admitted the woman did know how to get into his troubled mind and make some bright spots. Even if her proposition was available for only a limited time before reality cut in, he thought about taking her up on the offer.

Tom supposed this was his wife's way of putting aside some of the drama going on inside her. God knows, they both were as taut as Gertie's garters (one of Tom's mother's favorite expressions). But Tom and

Christine decided it was important to let their lives play out with some normalcy for their children's sake.

"There are two logical reasons for marrying a guy like me: for sex or my good looks," said Tom so only Christine could hear him. He tried for a hint of his old charm and gave her *the smile*. "Until now, I had always thought you chose this gorgeous mug."

The couple's banter was like foreplay that hung around to become afterglow. Whereas foreplay warmed things up, afterglow kept the pilot ignited. One of those marriage perks. Great stuff. Christine moved in.

Her lips skimmed the edge of his ear, then she followed up with a slow kiss that brushed by his cheek and sent major waves south of the border.

"I always have been way ahead of you," said Christine. "I knew where your talent was before you did."

Then, turning her back to him, with a seductive swivel of her hips, his wife swayed back into the kitchen.

Tom let out a controlled, soft wolf whistle as he thought, *That woman certainly knows how to wield her powers.* A woman in an apron with a dish towel in her hands—who would have thought that could be sexy? He nodded his approval as she exited.

Tom's down-to-earth philosophy on marriage was as basic as doing laundry. Things occasionally got a little dirty, soiled with sorrow, as in what the two of them had gone through with Tommy and what was going on right now. After all, shit happens, that's why they invented detergent.

But if you care, you put it through the wash and it comes out nice and clean. Then when you look out at the clothesline at those fresh duds, all you see is the good stuff—sexy smiles, the first steps of your kids, all the laughs, the loving and hugging.

Tom rubbed his chin, thinking about how many people underestimate the power of the hug. Making frequent and casual contact was one of his personal favorites. He considered it a way to keep the love showing. Like a minute ago, when Christine had come up to him. She knew he needed one of her special, personal Band-Aids, one she'd drawn a happy face on before kissing his hurts and making the pain disappear.

That was what his wife's playful contact had just done for Tom. She had put a Band-Aid on his troubled soul.

Tom heard some snoring and looked over at Frank. He was drooling on his V-neck T-shirt. He had put on clean blue work pants to come over for dinner. Tom was dressed the same. Weren't they a pair?

"Hey. You ready?" He poked Frank. "Get up."

Rubbing his face awake, Frank sat up on the sofa. The whole family knew Uncle Frank was a notorious after-dinner snoozer.

Part of Tom wanted to delay or at least linger in the afterglow of Christine's flirtation. But he had a mission, a bomb to deliver. He called out, "Christine, where's Donnie?"

"He and some of his friends are playing pool."

"Perfect," said Tom, slapping Frank's knee. And then Tom bowed like Fred Astaire asking Ginger Rogers for a dance and said to Frank, "Shall we?"

From the top of the stairs Tom heard the great sound of young laughter. He had one foot on the second step when the laughter abruptly stopped and the two older men felt the mood turn sour. They waited to do a little more recon.

"So, how are you feeling?" asked Ahsan, a slight young man with a mind twice as big as his body. He was Donnie's keyboard go-to. He and Donnie had been best friends since kindergarten. Tom knew the boy and his parents very well.

"I feel like a winner. How do you think I feel, with all your money in my pocket?" Tom saw his son point with his cue at his friends.

From the steps, Tom and Frank watched Ahsan take his shot. The four ball ricocheted off the edge of the pocket.

Resting on his stick, Ahsan pressed the conversation. "Donnie. You know what I mean. Picking up a gun, Afghanistan, fighting in the war . . . what do you think?"

"Yeah," asked Luke, the muscle-bound athlete in the group. He wasn't in the band, but hung around because he liked the music and Ahsan's sister. "You've got, what, two weeks left? Then it's off to the big party."

"Grow up, Luke," snapped Donnie. He pulled back from the pool table. "It's not going to be a party."

"Don't be a wiseass. You know what I mean, Donnie. The war . . ."

"Yeah. Sorry. I think they're nuts! The government, that is. Did you hear on the news tonight how we are paying the insurgents?"

"Insurgents?" Luke asked. "Like, as in the guys we're fighting?"

Tom knew Luke wasn't the smartest kid. But he was impressed that Luke was interested in the news.

"Pay them to do what?" asked Nate, the most recent addition to Donnie's band and group of friends. Donnie had met Nate at college. The kid played bass guitar.

"To not shoot at the American supply lines," Donnie answered. "What's that about?"

Tom decided to let go of the spy routine. The creaking stairs announced his and Frank's arrival.

"Did you see that on CNN, Dad?"

"No."

Tom's eyes automatically scanned his son's clothing. The hard-core rocker duds made him frown. *Is he deliberately the exact opposite of Tommy?* wondered Tom in light of their recent discussions.

Donnie was wearing baggie black pants for date night. Both the pants and his black Grateful Dead T-shirt had strategically placed holes. His prize black leather jacket hung over the newel post at the bottom of the stairs. The dangling buckles on his scuffed midcalf boots jingled as he moved around the pool table. Tom noticed that his son and his friends all followed the same sinister dress code. The only thing that was different among the band members was the placement of the white streak in their hair. Luke, on the other hand, stood out from the group like Mars in the night sky in his new blue jeans and white oxford button-down. His natural brown hair was cut close and neat.

Huh, thought Tom. *Where are Donnie's earrings? What's that about?*

"Dad, did you hear me? Paying the enemy. What do you think?"

Opportunity blossomed. Tom said, "That's my tax money at work."

"Stupid. We come off like a two-headed dog—one head eats you while the other head catches and offers you dinner."

Tom noticed his son miss an easy shot.

"I don't get it!" Donnie stood back to let Ahsan take aim.

Tom was both proud and stunned that his nineteen-year-old son possessed such insight. "Yours is not to question why . . ." said Tom. He purposely didn't finish the rest of the quote. His tactic was to pry the gates to sedition open a little at a time.

"Yeah," said Nate. "You're the man. Army strong. Goin' to be a hero like your brother . . ." He thought a moment and changed course, "The girls will be falling all over you. They love a man in uniform."

Tom watched the fantasy forming in his son's young mind. As the boy moved around the table, Tom admired the kid's strokes. Tommy had been good at the game, but Donnie was great. The pool cue belonged in his youngest son's hands.

"These guys are pushovers," Donnie said, indicating his friends and looking at his dad.

"Right," Tom said. He noticed Donnie had his own cocky look. "But what did I tell you about crowing before dawn?"

"Never count your money until the deed is done," Donnie recited as though he was being quizzed and expected a good grade from his dad.

"And don't be pinning any medals on your chest just yet," added Tom as hurting time crept closer. "Heroes come by them the hard way."

Everyone in the basement heard the tang of pain that slipped into Tom's voice.

Donnie winced. "Dad, do you think I don't know what I will be facing?" He sunk the eight ball, and Ahsan threw ten bucks on the pool table.

"I think you are a teenager who hasn't had enough failures in your life," snapped Tom.

Donnie walked over to his dad. "You think playing baseball for Coach was easy? I came home bruised and hurting every day."

"That's my point, kid." Tom added a little pepper to his voice and kept pushing the label *kid* at his son. He watched Donnie cringe as if he was being harassed by a pesky mosquito.

"You came *h-o-m-e* every night, kid." Tom stuck his face into Donnie's space, though all he wanted to do was put his arms around his son. Instead, Tom put a Kevlar vest around his heart, just as he had around his body when he served in Iraq. "But, like you said, you can handle it."

"Are we there again? News flash. Your son is not going to become a fugitive. Watch me. I can man up. I'll do the job," stated Donnie for the record.

Well, at least he's putting all thoughts of running to Canada at rest. That was a relief. Tom had a chance to make it work now.

Donnie's friends hooted and hollered their support and patted him on the back like he had just hit a home run. "Yeah, you're the man," someone yelled.

Tom saw the anger and disappointment on his son's face as the boy realized his father didn't share his confidence. Donnie needed his dad's support. But, then, that was Tom's point.

"Any of you going over to the Middle East?" Tom turned on the other boys. Silence answered. But now Tom had drawn a line. A generational line, which would yank Donnie's friends over to the boy's side. And that gap could help Tom.

Tom faced his son. "You aren't going to have any recover time in Afghanistan. No teacher, coach, or parents patting you on the shoulder, saying, 'It's OK.' 'Poor little boy.' 'You'll do better next time.'"

Frank chimed in. "Your dad knows what he's talking about, Donnie. You should listen."

"Why are you talking to me like this, Dad? You're afraid I won't live up to your standards? Are we back there again?"

"Well, I do have the experience. I know I could do the job better."

"Right," snorted Luke. Grumbles bounced off the low ceiling.

Good old Luke, thought Tom. He just wanted to kiss him.

"Maybe when you were younger, Dad, but . . ."

Now was the time for the tricky velvet glove. "Donnie, how about I go in your place?"

Nervous laughter darted between the young people. One look from Frank and Donnie's friends sobered.

"I won't embarrass you. You think I won't measure up to you or Tommy?"

"This is about you and me. Not about Tommy." Tom leaned in closer to Donnie and spoke in a soft but firm voice. "You are my son and I want to help you."

"No way!" Donnie marched to the far side of the pool table. "That's ridiculous! Besides, I'm not wimping out." Donnie's face turned fire-engine red. "We're here to play pool. Let's play."

"Tell you what. I'll play you for it. You think you're so bad with that stick." Tom saw his words hit home.

Donnie's shoulders slumped. "Dad, that's a fool's bet. The army won't take you. What are you playing at?"

"Mr. Lane, you're old," said predictable Luke.

"Then what have you got to worry about? Maybe you don't have enough to beat me. Or maybe your mouth is running ahead of your skills." Tom kept up the pressure.

"Dad, I could beat you . . . again . . . anytime." Donnie had a little of his father's vinegar in him. "And like you could really go in my place. I don't see that happening."

One of those damned ominous clouds that had been following Tom all week appeared in the cellar over the pool table. Of course, he was the only one who could see it, but the people all around him felt its presence.

"Afraid?" countered Tom.

Donnie tried cutting through the cloud cover. "No." He huffed. "Are you for real? Come on, Dad . . ."

Tom nodded, his eyes cold.

He let his kid talk. Donnie was setting himself up, making all of Tom's next moves easier.

"OK. At last, some real competition. I'm up thirty bucks. I'll play you double or nothing. These guys are making me feel guilty for taking their money. But . . ."

Tom had laid the foundation. Now all he had to do was take the bricks Donnie was handing him and build.

Frank gave Tom a slight nod. They were on course.

Donnie finished, "You know what happened the last time we played, Dad. I took two out of three games. But who's counting." Donnie accepted his friend's hoots and high fives, then patted his bulging pocket.

This was getting better and better.

Until Donnie's friend Ahsan spoke up. "Hey, we told the girls we'd pick them up at nine." Ahsan checked his watch. "If you start another game, we'll be late."

Quickly, Frank spoke up. "Go on, kid. I don't think you should press your luck. Your Dad's looking a little too eager. Take what you've won and spend it on Nancy."

Donnie just stood there, staring at his dad as if he had grown another head.

Tom's face remained stony.

Donnie's friends started up the stairs. Ahsan pulled on Donnie's shirt-sleeve. "Come on. Let's go."

Donnie had one foot on the bottom step.

"A man doesn't back down. But then, you're just a kid. Run, don't walk." That was all Tom had to say.

Donnie stopped in midstride and turned back. "You're on. Eight ball. One game. If you win," he turned to his friends, "then you can see if the army will take you. I'm thinking they'll laugh until they pee their pants."

"Yeah, old man," chimed in reliable Luke.

Ahsan was ready to join in the spirit of the game. "Hey, what does Donnie get when he wins?"

Donnie followed his friend's lead. "Yeah. What's in it for me? Are you going to double what's in my pocket?"

"Chicken feed." Tom dug into his pocket, pulled out the keys to Mona, and threw them on the table. "I feel real lucky tonight."

Donnie's mouth dropped. He rubbed at the sparse whiskers on his chin. His rich coffee eyes lit up like twin beacons.

Frank stepped closer to the table, between Donnie and his father. "Are you crazy, Tom? You're talking about your Malibu here."

"Is this your way of saying I'm ready for Mona?" Donnie's eyes connected with his dad's.

"Yeah. But you have to earn her. It's a give-and-take world kid. Are you ready for it?"

Again Frank interfered, just as they had planned. "This isn't fair, Tom. You're teasing the boy." Frank started to pick up the keys.

The way Frank added the word *boy* was a nice touch. Tom could see the dig hit pay dirt, as Frank had intended.

Donnie's face lost its warm smile. He reached out and placed his hand over Frank's. "Stop." He turned. "So I get Mona when I win. That's the bet you want, Dad?"

Tom had him.

Nate said, "This whole idea is crazy. Don't do it."

Tom cautioned himself to remember next time that Nate was smarter than he'd thought.

"The invitation expires in thirty seconds. You get Mona and I get to go to Afghanistan in your place. This is your chance. Can you man up?" Tom picked up another brick.

"Come on, Donnie." His chorus of friends was getting into the act. "Do it. It's Mona."

"This is a one-time offer," Tom said, getting deeper into this dark drama. He let his son mull it over for a few seconds.

"Do it, Donnie," said Luke. "Mona's sweet."

Ahsan added, "You can take him."

Frank did his part. "I don't know, Donnie. Your dad is pretty good. I wouldn't if I were you."

Tom saw the answer in the gleam in Donnie's eyes before he spoke.

Donnie was a fisherman, and his dad was surprised he hadn't recognized bait when he'd heard it.

"You're on," said Donnie.

Tom walked over to him and stuck his hand out.

"Are we clear? I win, I go. You win, you get Mona."

Gotcha! Tom's son had swallowed the worm—Mona's keys—hook, line, and sinker.

Donnie said, "Crystal. I agree."

"We'll shake on it," insisted Tom.

As Tom grasped his son's hand, he squeezed it harder than necessary. Not to hurt the kid, but to let him know this was serious. "Then it's a deal," Tom said. "And . . ."

"You never welsh on a bet," Donnie finished. Then he gave his dad a cocky smile and said, without turning away, "Uncle Frank, rack 'em."

Frank gathered up the fifteen hard-resin balls lying around the table, eight solid-colored and seven with stripes. Like a shepherd bringing in his sheep, he corralled them inside a wooden triangle. When all but the ivory cue ball was captured, he reorganized the solids and stripes so they were evenly distributed. With flare, Frank showed Donnie and his father the eight ball and then dropped it dead center inside the triangle. With his fingers inside the back of the rack to make sure all the balls were packed tight, Frank slid the rack over a white dot in the center at one end of the table. Satisfied, he carefully removed the wood frame and backed into the shadows.

Side by side, father and son stepped up to their green battleground.

Donnie's friends scurried to be out of the way to give them a clear field. Ahsan sat on the cellar steps, while Nate and Luke leaned against the washer and dryer. Tom noticed they seemed as excited as hungry pigeons on a crowded boardwalk.

"We'll lag to see who goes first," suggested Donnie.

His father nodded agreement. "You first."

Donnie powdered his hands and chalked his cue, the stick Tom had given him for Christmas last year. The kid didn't glance at his dad but instead hoisted his cue and lined up with the cushion at the opposite end of the table.

The objective was not to hit the rack of balls but to run the cue ball down the table, make contact with the cushion at the far end, then come back to nudge the opposite cushion. That was a lag.

Tom watched his son take his stroke. The cue ball hit the first cushion and then the second and came to a rest about four inches from the rail.

All Donnie's friends clapped and yelled, "Nice."

Don't get too confident, Tom reminded himself. With a lag, the ball that is closest to the second cushion wins, and that player goes first.

"Not bad." Tom couldn't help letting some pride sneak out.

"See if you can do better. After all, you taught me all I know, Dad."

"Yeah, you're right. But . . ."

At that point, Frank stepped up behind Tom with a three-foot-long white leather case. He flipped the top open. Inside were two butts and four shafts.

Gently, Frank drew out two pieces of a nondescript-looking pool cue and screwed them together. Tom watched Donnie's eyes widen. The boy had never seen this cue before tonight.

"Is that a Sneaky Pete?" Donnie asked.

From the steps, Ahsan said, "It looks like a regular cue to me."

Donnie whirled on the kid. "That's why they call it a Sneaky Pete. Pool sharks hide their expertise by making it look like they grabbed a house cue. But it's not, it's a . . ."

Tom looked into his son's face and answered, "a Bala."

"Oh, geez," said Donnie as both hands jumped to hold his head. His smile evaporated.

"What's that?" asked Nate from the washing machine.

"It's a Balabushka. It's one of the best pool cues in the world," explained Donnie. "Tom Cruise was supposedly using one in *The Color of Money.* Of course, it was a replica."

"It's just a pool cue. How much better can it be?" asked Ahsan.

"You think. . . . The owner of the Bala named the Dove was offered ten thousand dollars for his cue but didn't take it."

Ahsan's eyes went wide and shifted to the ceiling.

Donnie's eyes locked on his dad's. In them, Tom saw a newfound respect forming.

Donnie asked, "So Uncle Frank's stories are all true. You hustled."

Tom didn't answer; instead, as in his hustling days, he let Frank take care of the details.

Holding out the Bala for Donnie to see, Frank said, "She's legal. Justice is her name. Twenty ounces and fifty-eight-and-a-half-inches long."

Donnie took the stick as if he might burn his fingers on it and hefted it.

"You giving up?" Tom's shit-eating grin would have annoyed anyone. "Now's the time to tell me." He knew when he asked the question that Donnie wouldn't quit. Mona, the glory of a win against his dad, and now the Bala staring the boy down were screaming at Donnie to take the challenge.

Tom analyzed the slow, easy grin growing on his son's face. And he knew exactly what was going on. The boy was picturing himself dancing in the praise that would surely follow such an astounding win. Tom should know. He had been there and done a few victory dances in his time.

Those conquests appeared dingy in Tom's memory right now, especially when he looked into the face of his youngest son. Victories of the heart, reflected Tom, those were everlasting.

Regrouping as fast as he could, Donnie said, "You may have the stick, but we have the same skills. You're not scaring me."

"So, no turning back."

Donnie nodded.

Tom knew his son's throat was too dry to speak.

It was time to bring Donnie down a peg, to add a little more to his load and let some doubt creep into him, which would weigh the results in Tom's favor. He had to win. The game of pool was once his life, and now it was Donnie's. But this wasn't a game.

"I may have taught you all you know, but I didn't teach you all *I* know."

Tom took the small square of blue chalk and placed it where Donnie's cue ball had stopped. Frank handed him a cloth, and he rubbed down his stick. Then he powdered his hands with a fine talc he took out of a side pocket of the case. There was enough friction in the basement. Tom didn't need any between the cue and his bridge hand.

He chalked the tip of his stick. A miscue, the tip sliding off the ball, was not an option Tom would consider. Knees slightly bent, he looked down the length of his cue. He imagined it warming to his touch, like an old friend saying, "Glad to see you, buddy."

The light hanging over the center of the table started to swing. Tom glanced up. Christine must still be working in the kitchen.

Tom picked up the cue ball, placed it on the table, and went to work. His eyes narrowed. The field of green wool became Tom's whole world. His stroke was smooth; his hands were steady. He took the shot. The cue ball bounced off the first rubber and headed back to the second. Barely kissing the rail, it stopped so close to it that no light could get between them. Tom didn't smile. This was business.

Low *oohs* and *ahs* hung in the dusty basement like bats in an attic. The below-ground space around the pool table became a tomb.

When Tom straightened up, took the cue ball, and got ready to set up for the break, all eyes followed him as though he had turned into a newly risen beast.

They were right. There was a snarling Rottweiler in the room, and it was Thomas Lane. He saw Donnie's friends pull back. His son's eyes jerked from side to side. Tom felt mean and cruel. That was the way this had to be done. Clean cuts.

"We're here to play pool, right?" said Tom.

"Yeah," said Donnie, clearing his tight throat.

Tom noticed his son was looking around, maybe for some kind of out or protection. But this time his father wasn't there to give it to him. Not tonight. "Frank, hold the stakes."

Frank scooped up the keys.

Tom turned to his son. "I don't need your promise in writing, do I?"

"Dad."

The disappointment in his son's voice tore at Tom's heart.

"Of course not. You taught me better than that," countered Donnie, his voice stronger now, tinged with anger. "Break. Let the pain begin."

Tom pulled out the second butt from his case, unscrewed the first one and replaced it with a heavier one.

"Hey, Donnie, what's your father doing? Is that legal?" Luke's mouth was at it again.

One stroke at the table and Tom had become unapproachable.

"Yeah, it's legal," Donnie answered. "He's got a breaking cue. Gets more action." With both hands wrapped around his own cue, Donnie rested his chin against them and became a stone statue.

Tom chalked up and set the cue ball down just a fraction to the right of center and just off the rail.

Frank rapped Donnie on the arm and whispered, "Watch and learn." Then Frank thought again and said, "Tom, wait." There was something he had forgotten. It was in his hand. Frank offered it to Tom.

He took the toothpick and planted it at the corner of his mouth. "Like old times," said Tom. "Thanks."

Frank explained to Donnie, "Your dad used to smoke. Had a cigarette hanging out of his mouth every game. Like he couldn't play without it. Didn't even light up half the time. But he gave it up, so . . ."

"The toothpick," finished Donnie.

As Tom roamed, he went through the fundamentals in his head. After all, it had been a while since he had played for such high stakes. Relax your bridge arm and don't bend over as far when you're breaking as you normally would for other shots. The basics whirled around him. Use a closed bridge formation; it will be more accurate. Move back on the stick to allow for more acceleration. The old ways came to life. He felt like an alcoholic who was eager to jump off the wagon. He was ready. In fact, Tom was greedy for it.

He turned the cue ball over a couple times, placed it, then put his whole body into his shot. For Tom, a great pool player in action had always been nothing short of water over silk. The game had it all, elegance and strength.

The cue and Tom moved through the shot, and he was pleased to hear that old familiar echo of balls scattering and thumping into pockets.

Donnie walked over to check them.

But before he could speak, his father said, "I have stripes. The ten and the fourteen balls went in the back left pocket and the nine in the side."

In eight ball, one person has solids and the other stripes, and to win you put all of yours in, then sink the eight ball last.

"Yep," said Donnie. He checked the lineup of the remaining balls. "You're lucky you didn't scratch, Dad. You left the cue ball hanging over the pocket. You haven't got a second shot." Donnie snickered.

Tom knew his son was being his own cheerleader, and he hated to crush him, but he said, "Eleven ball in the side pocket."

While Tom had been talking, Frank had replaced the butt on his stick. He took it and used it as a pointer. Then he powdered his hands and chalked up.

One of Donnie's friends moved up next to him. They exchanged glances. And Ahsan whispered, "He can't make that shot, can he?"

Head down, Donnie looked over an imaginary pair of glasses at his dad and said, "Show me."

Tom liked how his boy was taking this.

He walked around the table, checking the angles. Then he went back to the cue ball. Tom prompted himself: *When you play pool, remember, you don't think of just one shot; as in chess, you need to plan the next couple of moves.*

He found his line and let his cue do its stuff. The red-striped eleven ball rumbled into the pocket.

"That was tricky," whispered Luke.

"Just a little English," Tom said to his audience. Again the Rottweiler circled. He had left himself in perfect position for the thirteen.

With a blur of orange, Tom sunk it. He moved around the table, checking each ball in relationship to the others. After each shot the table changed. It was a dynamic, flowing sea. Tom's dream trickled back into his mind. Here was that green sea. The toothpick was shredded.

"Twelve ball." He tapped the intended pocket. Tom took his stroke and sunk it.

But the rust of Tom's unused skills leaked out. He had left the cue ball in tenuous position for the fifteen ball.

Should he use a bridge? Was that what the stick in his dream had symbolized? Was God sending him a message? He looked up but didn't see him hanging on the plumbing.

He circled the table a few times.

Donnie smiled, "You put too much on that last shot, Dad."

He lined up on the solitary remaining striped ball. Tom stopped and again wiped his hands. When he took the shot, the ball stopped short and was left hanging on the rim of the pocket.

"Huh!" Donnie smiled. He swaggered closer. "Do you mind if I try some of your powder?"

"Sure. If you think it will help ya, kid." Tom's unexpected smirk turned his son's smile to a frown.

Tom had planned and buried the cue ball among the other balls. He was forcing Donnie to make a fantastic shot in order to put anything in the pocket. Tom doubted his son could find a way out of this fix.

"Didn't leave me much," said Donnie. Like father, like son; the tension he must have felt inside didn't show. He circled as he calculated.

"That's the nature of the game." Tom could see the boy's mind working the angles, planning the next shot if he made this one. This is what he had taught him, and Donnie was remembering it all.

"If it was me, I'd play it safe," suggested Tom. "Bury me behind your balls."

"Thanks, Dad, but I have my own style."

Tom could safely say he had never been more proud than he was during the next few minutes. Donnie went flat out. His kid lined up, checked everything, and used a massé that brought down the house.

Tom had to hold himself back from joining the celebration in order to keep the pressure on.

"How did you do that?" asked Ahsan.

Luke jumped up to fist-bump Donnie. "You made that cue ball take a sharp left, go around the fifteen without touching it, and you sank the two ball. Awesome!"

Donnie's eyes leaped back to the table. "It's not over . . . yet." He looked to his father.

God, thank you for this boy was all Tom could think of at that moment. Donnie was much stronger and more mature than he had given him credit for. And his son was going to need all that strength very soon.

Donnie had left himself perfectly lined up for the seven. He glanced up at his father just as he made his move. He shot and the ball fell into the pocket. He sunk the one and the six. His cue was a blur as the three dropped. The five followed on the next shot.

This wasn't looking good were the unspoken words being communicated by Tom and Frank's glances.

Donnie lined up and quickly sank the purple four ball.

Tom decided it was time to bring in the big guns. He silently prayed. *Hey, my kid is running the table. What are you thinking? Give me a break here, God.*

Donnie's friends gathered around him, slapping his back.

"Back off," Donnie warned them. "It's not dawn . . . yet. I have to sink the eight ball, then we crow."

Tom knew the shot was a slam-dunk. The eight ball in the side pocket. He could make that shot in his sleep.

Donnie lined up. His cue floated forward to strike the cue ball dead center.

Tom held his breath, thinking of more things he should have promised God.

Then the best for Tom and the worst for Donnie happened. The boy miscued.

After Tom thanked God, he turned to his son. "It's always the little things that get you. You forgot to chalk up." His son didn't want to hear this final lesson on the game of pool, but his father delivered it anyway.

Perspiring, Donnie collapsed back against the washing machine.

Tom casually powdered his own hands. Never let them see you sweat. Then he chalked up.

Frank edged up closer to Tom and whispered, "Watch your feet."

That little mistake, not keeping at least one foot on the floor when he shot, had cost Tom a hundred thousand dollars during a tournament. He cautioned himself not to get sloppy now. There was no emotion showing on Tom's face; it was all churning inside.

All he had to do was sink the fifteen and the eight ball. The Donnie phase would be complete. Then Tom would gather his troops—Frank and Jim, his lawyer—and take on the US Army. There was no way his son was going to Afghanistan.

But first he had to make a two-bank shot, being careful that the cue ball hit the fifteen before the eight. Tom calculated the correct amount of English he needed. Once again he looked at the overhead pipes, thinking God wasn't making this easy.

He rubbed more powder over his hands. A river of anxiety was seeping out through his skin and rolling down his arms in salty rivulets. He grabbed a towel and wiped down both of his arms and between each finger. He chalked up and softly blew on the cue.

"You didn't leave me much, kid."

Donnie just smiled.

It was a nice smile.

Tom stepped up. Then he stretched out over the table with the full length of his body.

He spied his son's eyes shifting to check his father's feet.

Good boy. Smart boy. Thanks, Frank—all ran through Tom's mind. He took his shot. The ball seemed to be moving more slowly than usual. For once the old drafty house kept still, and everyone in the basement held their breath.

The cue ball rebounded off the far cushion, took a left turn, and kissed the side rail, hitting the fifteen ball a little left of center. As the fifteen was impacting the back of the pocket with a thud, the cue ball careened a fraction to the right, making contact with the eight ball at the side pocket. The cue ball and the eight ball lingered in their gentle caress at the lip of the pocket.

If Tom accidentally sank the cue ball, he would lose.

"Come on, baby, show me your English," Tom sang, encouraging the cue ball to shift off to the right as he had planned.

The basement door opened with a bang, and Chrissy called out, "Is anybody down there?" When no one answered immediately she switched off the light.

"Hey!" It was a united scream.

When the light came back on all heads darted from the stairs back to the table. The eight ball had disappeared. All that remained on the battlefield was the white cue ball.

Tom and his son gave each other a single glance, then walked over to the pocket and looked in.

The eight ball was resting safely cradled in the side pocket.

Chapter 13

WHO KNEW SALT COULD BE CATHARTIC?

Tom awoke to a light snow, just three inches. He had already shoveled his driveway and sidewalk. He was stretching the job out, to give himself more time outside the house for uninterrupted thinking. He had salted just about every surface that needed it and some spots twice. That included the walkway of Nana Swartz, the ninety-year-old widow who lived in the other half of his house. Still Tom lingered in the cold, waiting. But for what?

He rolled the coarse rocks of salt in his hand and watched them spill from between his gloved fingers. The moment they hit the ice, the crystals created heat.

He should be so lucky. Just to touch something and change it instantly was a power he could use about now.

But he had no magic—just two hands and one brain. And even though he was working all he had, his best wasn't cutting it. His heart told him he had created a gap between his son and himself.

Tom stared up at those damn lousy clouds. *God? You could jump in here any time and put my feet on a different path. I'm open to suggestions.*

The street was quiet. It was seven on a Saturday morning. But this silence was different. This was a hushed peace, the bliss only a blanket of new snow can create. It was a temporary calm.

He left the bag of salt on the front porch just in case Mother Nature dumped on him again. Tom's small universe was out of control. His intention was to help his son, not alienate him. But it wasn't happening. Donnie had stormed out of the house after the pool game Thursday night. Father and son hadn't spoken since.

So, God, if I sometimes whine to let you know I'm feeling the bumps in the road, please forgive my grumbling. Tom couldn't stand complainers, not even when he was one of them.

He inched by Mona to stow the snow shovel on the sidewall inside the garage.

The garage, a detached structure with aged asphalt shingles instead of siding, sat in a corner of the backyard and barely held one car. It leaned to the southeast, as if a strong wind had changed the building's original course. It had been frozen in that position forever. Tom had worried for Mona. The son of one of his workers was an architect and had checked out the garage for him. The architect found it was as solid as the leaning tower of Pisa, which was likewise 3.99 degrees off center.

The wind came up, and Tom heard a few shingles flapping. It also delivered the smell of coffee. Christine was warming up the house. He briefly thought that if they had a newer house, he wouldn't be able to catch those aromas. And he would miss that. Though his bank account would be better satisfied with a lower oil bill, the sensible side of Tom chimed in.

Mentally, he pinched himself back to this moment. He tugged on Mona's silky-soft protective cover. It slid away slowly, like a stripper exposing small amounts of creamy, sexy flesh a little at a time.

"Mona. You have been a loyal lady. Sorry I had to prostitute you. But Donnie would only bite if you were the bait."

The thorn in Tom's side was that all his phone calls to Donnie's cell had gone unanswered. The silence was ripping his insides to shreds. The boy had called his mom but refused to talk to his father.

But tonight Donnie would be home. They needed to talk; those words crawled on a banner in front of Tom's eyes like a headline in Times Square. His son needed to understand this wasn't a warped joke. Tom did intend to serve in the army in his son's place. It was crucial they settle their differences. This was an acute time in both their lives. Tom couldn't report for duty with this unresolved wedge of tension keeping them apart.

Leaning one hand on Mona, Tom looked up at the rafters and said, *God, give me some words so Donnie will understand.* He waited, and when nothing came to him, Tom got a little ticked off. *Come on. You can't be shoveling snow, too. Honk three times if you're up there and open for business. A little sign . . . anything.*

"Beep, beep, beep!"

"Holy shit!" Tom almost fell over. Startled, he grabbed Mona's door handle to steady himself. He must have looked like he was having a heart attack or something, because when Donnie rushed over to his dad, the kid was pale, too.

"Geez, Dad! Are you all right?"

Tom nodded. "Sure. Yeah." But he felt his body all over to make sure he wasn't lying.

"Didn't you hear me when I honked?"

"Oh, yeah. I heard that."

His son's cheeks were returning to frosty pink, so Tom supposed his were also.

"Hey, Mona's going to catch a cold." Donnie took the cover out of his dad's hands and began to tuck her in. "Don't worry, baby," he said to Mona, "I'll make sure you're nice and cozy."

Tom watched his son replacing the cover and wondered if there were quirky genes for chatting to non-life-forms, because it seemed as though he had passed his on.

"I came over early to help you with the shoveling, Dad."

His son's smile lacked its youthful confidence. The unspoken *and to make peace* hung in the air. Fathers notice that kind of stuff.

"But, as usual, you beat me to it."

"I couldn't sleep. I didn't want to wake your mom, so I came out here and got started."

"Me neither," said Donnie. "I was thinking about that game of pool we had."

"A bet is a bet." He gave Donnie his best fatherly, putting-my-foot-down face. "I'm going."

"A serious decision like this isn't made into a game. I resent your total lack of even talking to me. We should have discussed it man to man."

"You're right, of course. I guess I didn't know how to approach the subject, and as usual I went about it all wrong. But we're there now, so . . ."

"Are you telling me or asking me?"

"I'm sorry, OK. Don't get mad again. I'm willing to discuss this rationally. But when we are finished talking, I am still going to take your place."

"You are the most hardheaded person I know."

"Your head isn't too soft, either, son."

They played a little who-blinks-first game, going eye to eye, until Tom said, "OK. You first, Donnie."

"It's simple, Dad. What you want is not possible and you know it." His son's eyes were pleading.

Tom could see the boy checking for weak spots in the argument, but he wasn't going to let him find any. Of course, Tom's greatest weakness was Donnie, but he kept that soft spot undercover.

"The truth is, I know it is possible." Tom inched by Mona to the back of the garage near his little workbench. He began to straighten the tools.

Donnie followed. "Dad . . ."

Tom felt his throbbing arthritis attacking his joints. He rubbed at his knees.

"Dad, are you listening?"

"Sure. What did you say?"

"I asked how do you think you can pull this switch-off?"

"I'll take care of it. You don't have to worry."

"There you go again. Treating me like I have no say, but I do!" Donnie took a breath and then lowered his voice. "This is my skin on the line. And you're too old. They won't take you."

"Maybe according to you, but not to the United States Army. I've already checked it out."

"So you've been planning this . . . for how long?"

"Drop it, Donnie!" Tom hadn't planned on hitting Donnie right between the eyes with reality this way, in the garage, but now was as good a time as any. "It's my business. Like I said, I'll take care of it."

Donnie locked his arms in front of him and widened his stance as though he was getting ready for a bout with Mike Tyson.

"A stupid game of pool versus a stint in the army. Do you hear yourself?" Donnie's hands were flying around. "You'll take care of it. Like I can't! Like I'm still a kid who needs his parents to wipe his nose and his ass? I can take care of myself. I've had enough of this sick joke of yours. I'm going!" Donnie's thumb pointed at his own chest.

Tom wanted to send him to his room and tell him not to come out until he could make sense, but to Donnie it was perfectly logical. In this instance, Donnie thought it was his dad who was coming off half-cocked.

Tom struggled not to lash out with hurting words that would plug his son's ears and prevent him from understanding. He was firm but calm as he emphasized, "No, you are not going!"

Father and son came nose to nose. So much for staying calm.

"I have been trained and I'm half your age. It's time for me to make my own life. Have experiences that test me. I need to do this, Dad. I'll show you and all my friends that I'm no pussy. This is something I can do. I'm ready."

"You know your job? Tommy loved being a soldier and he knew his job." Tom's head ballooned with his son's naïve boasting. "You've never had a full-time job in your life. And the army will be a tough boss."

"I'm leaving!' Donnie turned away.

Now was the time to drop the boy who thought he was a man feetfirst into the blood, guts, and sludge of war. Tom didn't want to expunge the glorious images his son had formed of soldiering, because he and Tommy were part of that picture. But Donnie had pushed Tom over the edge of the precipice, and now Tom would take him down to the land of reality.

"Wait. Please." Tom forced his voice and heart to be temperate. "It isn't like in the movies, son." He signaled Donnie to follow him. "Come. Sit down."

They went back over to Mona. Tom pulled off her cover, and they sat side by side in the front seat.

Donnie's breath was coming fast. Misty clouds rose in front of him.

By the time Tom was ready to speak, Donnie's inflamed face had lost some of its heat. But Tom could still see determination ready to ignite in his son's eyes and his locked-down posture.

"Many people ask why men go to war, son. Like there should be one uniting reason. But there isn't one. If you ask a hundred soldiers why, they'll have a hundred different reasons: maybe to overcome fear, for a woman, for the money, to show their courage, to get behind a righteous cause, God, country, or maybe to stand next to their friends. Each one is enough justification. And a soldier has to have that in him. After 9/11, Tommy found his reason." Tom's right fist came across his chest to his heart. "A soldier has to believe with all his strength and heart that his reasons are just." His voice softened. "I don't see that in you, kid. But I feel it pumpin' true in me."

Donnie started his rebuttal, but his father held up one hand.

"Give me a chance. Listen, please." Tom's tongue froze. Revealing your dark side wasn't done easily. It took him a few seconds before he started again. "Frank and I were Rangers with the Seventy-Fifth. Fort Benning was our home turf. We lived ready. We could be deployed to anywhere in the world within twenty-four-hours notice. We had special skills: airborne, air assault, direct-action operations, raids, infiltration and exfiltration, and so on."

Tom could only say this if he looked straight ahead.

"Of course, we'd been watching Bush senior on the tube, so we knew our time was coming, and we wouldn't need the twenty-four hours. We had been locked down on base for weeks, hopping ourselves up, cleaning our weapons, packing and unpacking, and waiting. We were always waiting. The waiting is the worst." His voice lowered. "It's like waiting to hear the doctor come out of the operating room and tell your family if you are going to live or die. . . . Everyone was thinking about that, but not saying it."

He heard Donnie shifting, but Tom still didn't turn to him.

"Your uncle Frank and I were the quiet ones, having been in that waiting room many times. We were preparing; it was written in our eyes. But the new grunts talked and laughed, working themselves up into a frenzy, as if their boasting would give them an edge in keeping death away. They were trying to glorify what they were about to do. Pull out that just cause. Say brave things, in case the press overheard them and their words would be sent home and make their families feel proud. But we old-timers knew we were merely faceless, nameless expendables. Statistics that would show up on *Wikipedia* years later: 'KIAs: 6.' Gee, isn't that great, so few casualties. Not great if it's you or your buddy mangled or dead, and your family is getting the official visit. Will you ever forget that day when the chaplain came to our front door?"

Donnie's chin quivered.

Tom gathered some breath and went right on generating the gloom.

"War or preparing for war was my world. Stay focused. Stay strong. Live another day. That's what you are thinking about at the beginning and end of every day when you are getting ready to be deployed. Cleaning up your trash, leaving nothing undone behind. When the time comes, you think you have hardened yourself, that you are combat ready. But when it happens, you never are.

"One of many times, Frank and I were standing behind a mud wall outside of Fallujah. The Gulf War was having a difficult birth. There were eight of us. We infiltrated before the bombing started. We were recon. Located targets and called in the information. Then all hell broke loose. The British dropped two laser-guided bombs meant to take out a bridge that crossed the Euphrates River. They missed their target; more than a hundred civilians died and even more were injured. Our position was exposed. We were dodging the Republican Guard, angry civilians, and our own bombs. The coalition forces attacked again with four more laser-guided bombs. Two went in the Euphrates, one hit the bridge, and one hit a marketplace. More men, women, and children, dead and dying."

Tom took off his gloves and wiped the perspiration from his face. His steamy breath rose to the roof to join Donnie's dissolving wisps.

"Frank and I, along with the rest of my squad, stayed tight as we were picking our way out of there to our extraction point. Frank was at my elbow. I heard him breathing. We were using our night vision. I didn't hear anything before blood splattered my face and fogged my goggles. I heard him fall. I bent down over him. The bullet, a forty-five millimeter, had entered the back of his head. When it exited, it tore his face off. No doubt he was dead."

"But Dad . . . "

"Let me finish. These eight guys were my squad, my responsibility. They meant more to me than anyone else in this world. I wasn't going to leave Frank behind. So I dragged him by the collar over rocks, sand, dirt, and even some dying civilians until we got to the extraction point."

"We spread out to secure the area while we waited for the helicopter to touch down. And for the first time, I bent down over Frank, my best friend, and you know what the first thing that came to my mind was?"

The shake of Donnie's head was scarcely discernible.

"I'm glad it's not me. Do you believe that? Here was Frank, or so I thought. A guy as close to me as a brother, and all I could think of was . . . how glad I was to be alive. I soon found out it wasn't him. But it still didn't change the way I felt. My squad, my guys, were the reason I was there. I wanted to keep them safe, bring them home. But I had changed. Other things, like your mom . . . were more important, and what I was thinking about? I had lost my cause, and with it my edge."

Donnie asked, "Was that when Tommy was born?"

"Yeah." Tom swallowed and patted his son's knee. "A few months later, when I had a chance to get out, I took it. Oh, Sullivan, that was the guy with no face, wasn't the first guy I had listened to as he died. But I knew for sure I didn't want to see or hear death again. And I sure as hell was needed more at home than somewhere else. Am I still proud of my service? Absolutely. Do I love my country? Yes.

"Now, let me ask you, Donnie: Are you prepared for the civilian casualties? Do you really think we need more revenge for the 9/11 attacks? Do you believe we can bring down al-Qaeda or the Taliban? Do you believe we should stop supporting Israel? Do you think the United States will ever pull out of the Middle East and leave behind all interest in that oil-rich region? Can we stop terrorism?"

Tom had never had a serious political discussion with his son, but perhaps he should have.

"Dad, all of those are justifications to fight."

"Are they yours? Can you own one of them? Make it your just cause?"

At first Donnie didn't answer. Then he switched gears. "Dad, we have to fight terrorism. We can't give them a second chance to hurt us."

"Which one of my questions are you answering yes to? If you have what you consider to be your motivation, lay it on me. What will you be killing for?" Tom wouldn't let his son change course. "And there is a good chance you will be seeing action! It might be a man in a turban, a child in the cross fire, or a fellow soldier who stepped into your sights for a second by mistake. Could be you never see the results of your actions. But your actions are focused toward people and conflict. Think about it."

Donnie shifted his weight, as though he was uncomfortable in Mona's leather seats, which Tom knew was impossible.

"Because if you can't say yes, then you don't believe in this war and you shouldn't go where your heart doesn't lead you. I do believe, with all my heart, that what I want to do is the right thing for this family."

When Donnie started to speak, Tom knew the red, white, and blue was rising to the surface.

"You served. Tommy did. . . . Now it's my turn. I took an oath, made commitments. Isn't that what you wanted me to do with my life . . . commit?"

"This isn't choosing a college course of study, Donnie."

Tom gave his son something with which to remove the hook that was in him.

"Letting somebody you don't even know decide your future because you're afraid to speak out, fearing someone will label you unpatriotic.

Now, that is disloyal to the principles of this country. The founders of this country fought so you would have the right to speak freely, whatever your opinion. And it seems we have liked war. We have been involved in too many conflicts since our nation's birth. And yet the wars continue. I have fought so you won't have to. That's what they told me when I joined up. And yet here we are again. I figure I have the right to say, 'Not another son. Not this time.'" Both of Tom's hands balled up into tight fists. "I am going to take them up on their promise. I am going in your place so you won't have to."

Donnie just stared at his father. He looked about ten years old, his eyes big. The questions written on his youthful face were, "What do you think? What should I do, Dad?"

Weightiness fell over them. It was as if they had reached their destination, and it was both a beginning and an end. This was their last long look at a sunrise before it disappeared forever.

"I have only one more thing to say. Something I hope you believe. You have said a number of times that you think I wanted you to be like Tommy and me. But that is not true. I think we have fought because you have too much of me in you. I don't want you to be me. I want you to be you. You are already better than me. That is all I have ever wanted. I wanted you to be more than me."

Now it was Donnie's turn to stare out the front windshield. "You're right." Donnie's eyes flooded. "You're right about everything. I don't hate anyone. I never wanted to be a soldier. I—"

"I pushed you into it. It's OK to say it." Tom's lips felt like dry paper. "Believe me, son, during war, boys may become men, but men also become wounds. Watching, hearing, and living with suffering all around you changes a person—even now I can close my eyes, see Iraq, and smell the strong odor of blood. It creates pictures in your mind that can never be erased. These are the souvenirs we bring home and the lesions we all carry; some conceal them . . . some cannot. Is it wrong for me not to want your young mind to be stained forever?"

Tom thought about his own ghostly keepsakes. He had often thought if he had a second chance, it would be different. Well, miracle of miracles, here was a rare chance for a do over.

"I don't know what to do, Dad."

Tom pulled his son into a quick bear hug. And for an instant, Donnie felt like a newborn curling into his father's shoulder for the first time. A tear slid out of one of Tom's eyes, and with it Tom had a vision of the helpless baby Donnie had been, with a head of hair like one of those Russian fur hats. God, he'd had so much hair when he was born.

He also remembered the first time their eyes had met. It had just been two hours after Donnie's birth when Tom first held his son, and even though the medical books said babies couldn't focus that early, Tom knew that Donnie had seen him. It had been as though this little wrinkled "thing" was saying, *"Hey, Dad, I'm your son, and I've been waiting to meet you. I knew I could depend on you to hold me tight and keep me safe like this."*

Tom wondered when he had let that feeling slip away. Why had he wallowed in sorrow and chosen work to replace their wonderful connection?

Now Donnie was looking at his dad as if he had never seen him before. It wasn't the same wonder he'd given him at the pool table when Tom had pulled out the Bala. No. This was very different. He was staring at him as though he could see his father's soul seeping out. If he did see that part of Tom, no wonder the boy kept silent, because Donnie would have been looking at himself.

Now Tom's tears flowed.

"Donnie, I love you. I want you to do this for me. Let me go. I'm asking for this one favor. It's for the family: Tommy, your mom, and Chrissy. Your mom is heartbroken. You are my just cause."

"Dad, I never thought about what this would do to Mom, Chrissy, or you. I should have known. And . . . I have been thinking of Tommy a lot lately. I miss him, Dad."

"We are all ripples in a stream, son. And your deployment would cause a storm in the family's small pond"—then he admitted—"and my life." Tom's breath came in ragged, frosty puffs. He had never talked like this before, and he wondered if God was Edgar Bergen and he had become Charlie McCarthy. Another prayer had been answered.

"But, Dad, you can't protect me forever. The army doesn't care about our bets. And what do I say to my friends?"

"You tell them what your uncle Frank told me when Tommy was born. There are three stages of a man's life: He believes in Santa Claus, he doesn't believe in Santa Claus, he is Santa Claus. I'm giving you a chance to be Santa Claus to your kids someday."

"What you are hoping for is pure fantasy. Just like your ho, ho, ho used to be." They both chuckled. "But I liked hearing it."

"I know this might not work, but just let me give it a shot. Hey, and you'll get Mona."

"Dad, I love Mona because you love Mona." Donnie's long face sobered. He looked down at his shoes. "I understand what you are trying to do. But don't be disappointed when it's me flying to Afghanistan. You can't win when you pick a fight with the government."

Tom shrugged. "And by the way, where are your earrings?" He pointed to his own eyebrow and earlobe.

"I thought it was time to take them out before I reported for duty and my sergeant ripped them out. And I also . . ." Donnie took off his ski cap to expose his shaved head.

"Put your hat back on before you catch cold, kid."

"And, Dad, could we keep this crazy idea of yours just between us? I'm not sure how I'm going to handle this with my friends. And if it doesn't happen, I won't have to take the abuse. I know I'm choosing the easy way out. But no lecture, please."

"Our decision to swap places stays just between us . . . for now. I know you'll feel the backlash from your old dad's crazy antics. It's not going to be easy for you. The path of least resistance would be to not make waves. But you can drown even in still waters, son. Remember that."

Chapter 14

LATER THAT SAME AFTERNOON, Donnie and his friends met at the Wings on Fire Café, which also happened to be the only place that had pool tables in Donnie's neighborhood.

Wings was one of their regular hangouts. Even though Donnie and his friends weren't old enough to drink, the owner let them play pool. Donnie was good for business. He had such a great reputation that sometimes the local cops stopped in to watch him play. And because the beat police were friends with Tom, they kept an eye on Donnie.

The place was nothing but a single-story brownstone, a slice of times gone by. The building appeared cramped, shoved in between a shiny new drugstore and a small thrift shop. It was the kind of place that looked from the outside like it was a bar, had always been a bar, and could never be anything but a bar. The long, polished wooden runway with its brass foot-rail was the first thing you saw when you opened the door. It traveled down the left side of the room and disappeared into the dim green lights over the pool tables at the very back. Booths and small, round tables hugged the wall and any free floor space. The ceiling was high and covered with tin. The same pattern of tin was repeated halfway up the walls. The place was reminiscent of a tunnel. And this tunnel was generally filled with local traffic.

But today it was sparsely populated. A couple of the patrons were unwelcome.

"Am I gettin' this right? Your *daddy* is going to try and take his little boy's place . . ." Rocky's acne-pocked face twisted into a tight skull. He took a long drag on his cigarette and let the smoke stream out of his nose, as though he were a gangster in a movie.

Donnie glared at Luke. "You told him?"

"Sorry. I didn't know it was a secret." Luke sank down in his chair.

Donnie missed what should have been an easy shot.

"Poor *baby*, afraid of putting on the uniform. Is that it?" Rocky could have been the poster child for poor nutrition with his slight frame, sallow complexion, and sunken eyes, and cheeks that made his features appear razor sharp. Today he wore a faded black T-shirt imprinted with a leftover slogan from the sixties, "Kill a Commie for your Mommy," printed on the front. His pale, dirty hands raked through his unwashed brown hair.

Rocky's subordinate, Tiny, whose christened name was Claude, was equally difficult to ignore. Tiny picked and chewed at the bloody stumps of what once had been his fingernails. If that annoying habit wasn't enough to make him impossible to overlook, at his last physical the doctor had to send Tiny over to the butcher to use the meat scale to weigh him. Tiny was huge.

Tiny snapped the straps of his bib overalls. His cherry-red rosebud lips curled back to show each Chiclet-like tooth.

Rocky hiked up his low-riding pants and reminded Donnie, "Hey, dummy, I'm talking to you."

Donnie's first encounter with this tag team had been when he was in the sixth grade. Rocky and Tiny were eighth graders. He had been walking eight-year-old Chrissy home from school. Rocky, who had gone by Ralph back then, and Claude had bushwhacked them. Tiny, who even then had been a major package of blubber, had sat on Donnie while Rocky forced Chrissy to watch him set fire to each and every spider in her science project. She had won a blue ribbon; it had also gone up in flames. Donnie's relationship with these two punks had never changed.

"Knock it off, Ralph. Keep your Pinocchio nose out of my business," said Donnie. "We're just playing some pool." He moved to the other side of the table.

Ahsan walked around the table, checking the line for his shot.

"Game off, *boy*?" Rocky's eyes stayed on Donnie. Then he leaned hard into Ahsan, just as he was taking his shot.

Ahsan missed and rubbed his ribs where Rocky's bony elbow had made contact. The cue ball skewed off to the side.

Watching from behind the bar was the manager and owner, Mr. Olesh. As the troubling scene developed, he picked up his phone.

"Oh, sorry," slurred Rocky, stepping back. "Hey, loser," he said, pointing his cue at Donnie. "How's that little sister of yours? She's turning into quite the sexy little fox. Huh? Right." He nodded as he licked his lips.

"Don't you have to be somewhere?" asked Donnie. "Like over at welfare, snatching purses? Hey, I always wondered, do you report to the IRS the money you steal from those old ladies?"

Donnie had been amassing a ton of feelings over the last couple of days, and now his body stiffened. He wouldn't throw the first punch, but beating on Rocky would be something to take the edge off, especially when Rocky was being unusually annoying. But Donnie turned away from his antagonist.

Rocky's face twisted, and he raised his pool cue back over his shoulder.

Luke, a guard on the college football team, stepped between Rocky and Donnie.

Donnie turned. "Leave him to me, Luke." Then his icy dark eyes froze Rocky's sneer. "When their backs are turned . . . that's your style? I'm not taking your crap anymore." He put one hand on Rocky's shoulder and squeezed. "You want something, Ralph?"

"Getting physical isn't your usual style, boy." Rocky snarled.

Donnie's second hand clamped onto the other shoulder. Rocky shrank down under Donnie's viselike hands. "Maybe I'm changing my style. You chickenshit piece of . . ."

Rocky cringed.

Donnie released him and shoved him back.

Rocky rotated his right shoulder, as if to stimulate circulation. His pool cue, which he had twirled so he could grip it with its heavy end up, like a club, slid through his hands to the floor.

Donnie said one word, "Worthless," before returning to his friends. He would no longer be one of Rocky's victims. He had too much going on inside him. Agreeing to his father's proposal seemed supportable when he was looking into his father's pleading face. But out here in the real world, the father-son switch made him uncomfortable in his own skin. He felt guilty, as though he had committed a crime and was waiting for the police to drag him away. Conflicting emotions boiled inside him. He had lost control of his life, even his ability to play pool.

He tracked Rocky until he put the cue in the rack.

Luke sat back down at the round table with Donnie, next to Nate and Ahsan. "Hey, Donnie . . . I'm sorry."

Donnie sipped on his coke, watching Rocky and Tiny regrouping in a side booth in the shadows. "Forget it." Rocky was berating Tiny for not coming to his aid.

Tiny and Rocky took sips from a shared flask that was hidden under the table as they debated. All at once Tiny stood and meandered past Donnie, only to circle back around. He came up next to him and said, "Let me sweeten that for you." He picked up Donnie's glass and poured hot sauce into it.

"Now that brings back fond memories," said Donnie. "What are you, a third grader?"

"Oh, let me make a contribution," said Rocky as he took Donnie's glass from Tiny and hocked up a green loogie, deposited it into the glass of soda, and placed it back on the table.

Donnie pushed the contaminated sludge as far away as possible. His hands balled up, the knuckles drained of blood.

"So your sister? Looking ripe for picking. Yeah, Tiny and I were just saying how we would like to get to know little Chrissy better. I need something to take the edge off. She'd do." Rocky smiled, showing his crooked buckteeth. Then he smacked Donnie on the back. "Wouldn't you like a little nephew that looked like me?"

Donnie bolted out of his chair. The crash of it hitting the floor ricocheted around the bar as though a Smith & Wesson .38 had been discharged. Donnie's face burned. He wanted this—hell, he welcomed it.

Luke held Donnie back.

"I'm going to get to know her a whole lot better." Rocky stuck his thumbs in the belt loops of his pants. The tops of his boxers puffed out above his low-riding jeans. The coarse dark hairs at the center of his white stomach curled out over his underwear. "You have a problem with that, *boy?*"

Tiny nodded and chortled as Rocky hiked his crotch to show Donnie precisely where his interest in Chrissy centered.

"Go for it," said Luke, releasing Donnie.

He was on him before Rocky could react. Donnie picked him up by the front of his shirt and slammed him into the wall. Both of Rocky's feet dangled off the ground. "Stay away from her, Rocky, or I'll mess you up so bad there won't be anything left to put in your coffin," threatened Donnie. He shifted one hand to Rocky's throat and held him against the wall with his other hand and the force of his own body.

Luke and Nate blocked Tiny from participating. The giant man backed away around the table.

Pulling Donnie's arm, Ahsan urged, "Let him go. He can't breathe. He's had enough. Donnie! He's not worth a run-in with the police."

"Shut up, towel head," barked Tiny, sidestepping around Luke and Nate.

At that moment Frank and Tom arrived.

Tiny belly-bumped Ahsan, sending him colliding into an unoccupied table. He rolled onto the floor.

Luke came nose to nose with Tiny. "You want to try that again with someone your own size, blubber boy?"

Mr. Olesh, a sixtyish, gray-skinned man, hurried over. "What's going on here?" He patted his aluminum baseball bat against the palm of his free hand. He said, "I told you two not to come into my place. Rocky, Tiny, get out!"

"Thanks for the heads-up, Olesh," Tom said, sliding up to the group. "We'll take it from here." He spoke softly as he approached Donnie. "Let him go, son." He placed a hand on Donnie's arm. "Let him go."

Donnie released Rocky, but his eyes remained locked on him as if he were the red bull's-eye on the dartboard.

Luke backed away from Tiny a couple of yards. "You too, Luke." Frank inserted himself between them.

Nate helped Ahsan to his feet.

Rocky retreated until he was next to Tiny.

"What's all the yelling about," asked Rocky. "You called your old man for help, *boy*? Does he do everything for you?" He rocked his hips. "There's no problem. Unless it's the great Donnie Lane is off his game." Rocky chanted like a child reciting a nursery rhyme, "Donnie Lane is off his game. Donnie Lane is off his game." He snapped his fingers to accompany the beat in his head and did an off-balance dance.

The manager warned, "Get out, Ralph, or I'll call the police." Pointing at Tiny, he added, "And take that mountain with you." He raised the bat. "Go! Out the back. I don't want anyone to know your sort even comes in here."

Tom whispered something in Olesh's ear.

"Just go. I'll give you a get-out-of jail pass this time." He lowered the bat.

Rocky's bloodshot eyes flashed dark and predatory for a second. He and Tiny back-stepped toward the rear door as if ready to leave. Then Rocky stopped.

Tom kept one eye on Rocky as he and Frank pulled up chairs next to the boys.

"Okay. Sure, we'll go, but first . . ." Rocky staggered over to a withered old man alone in a dark, back-corner booth by the exit.

The man sipped from a fat glass of amber liquid. He appeared lost within himself and oblivious to Rocky.

"I want this gentleman here to tell me what he thinks of our pool shark, Donnie," hissed Rocky, shaking the thin, zombie-like man.

The man flinched, as if waking up, even though his heavy lids had been open the whole time.

"Just leave him be," suggested Tom. "I know you're hurting, Rocky, but . . ."

Rocky ignored Tom. Instead he preached to his audience, pointing

Donnie out to everyone in the place. "He's letting his *dad-dy* go instead of him to Afghanistan. Listen up, Mr. Ricca." He nudged the dazed man twice. "Tell us what you think of this candy-ass wimp."

In the background, Tiny chortled, like a sick walrus.

The old man, white whiskers outlining his watered-down face, slowly pulled away from his isolation. A blank pad and a pen, the tools of his trade, remained on the table. "For God's sake," pleaded Tom. He started to stand, but Donnie pulled him back down.

"Ignore Rocky," said Donnie. "He's all talk and no action."

"Big talk from a kid who always lets someone else do his fighting. First your brother and now your dad." Rocky snorted. He had had so much alcohol that he leaned to the left.

Mr. Ricca's hollow body uncoiled. His hunched spine seemed to resist any action. Finally he was standing, but he swayed on his feet as if he had just exited the Tilt-a-Whirl. He trembled inside his oversized suit. His hawklike face scowled. With one shaky hand, he waved everyone off. Still bent, even when standing, he started to sit back down and melt back into himself.

Rocky put an arm around the withered man, forcing him to stand. He marched Mr. Ricca toward Donnie.

The manager, Mr. Olesh, said, "Rocky, leave him. Don't you know about his boy?"

"Yeah. So . . ." Rocky whimpered. "Ain't we all got troubles?" He made an effort to pull himself together. "I bet Mr. Ricca here has a few choice words for Donnie." He pointed an accusing finger.

Rocky kept Mr. Ricca under tight control. It was as if the old man was Rocky's personal puppet. Once they were in front of Donnie, Rocky asked again, "What do you think of Donnie letting his father take his place? Your brave son gave his life," he stammered and whimpered, "for his country. You have a right to tell Donnie here what you think of his unpatriotic cowardly conduct." The last two words were slurred into one.

Mr. Ricca squinted at Rocky, then shoved him aside. He swayed. Then he took two shaky steps forward until he was leaning over Donnie.

Everyone could see Donnie's eyes misting over.

Tom started to stand, then sat back down. "Hey, Angelo. How are you doing?"

Not everyone knew that Donnie had known Mr. Ricca's son, Freddie. Or that Mr. Ricca had been his Little League coach. Donnie respected the man. He often read Mr. Ricca's column in the local newspaper. Mr. Ricca lurched back into Rocky as if the power of Tom's voice had thrown him off balance.

"Dad," said Donnie, while his expression said he was unprepared for the alteration that had occurred.

"The man's spirit has drained away," said Frank.

Mr. Ricca moved even closer. He looked into each person's face as if to get the right distance to bring them into focus. They stopped on Donnie.

Ahsan whispered to Donnie, "Is he . . . was he our coach?"

Donnie nodded. This was the man who'd made him believe after a 1–10 Little League season that Donnie should never lose hope. And he had come to support Donnie at his band concert.

Tom covered Donnie's hand with his own. He should stop this. But it was a lesson, one his son eventually would come up against. Perhaps he was being cruel, but now his son could see what he had been struggling to describe with just words—death was a ravenous thief.

"Donnie, stand up and give Mr. Ricca your seat," said Tom.

Donnie gulped down the few comforting words he was about to speak, imagining how the man must hate the sight of him. He was alive. Freddie was dead. His brave son had served. Donnie stood there like a weak child who had agreed to let his father take his place.

Donnie stood up and pulled out his chair.

Mr. Ricca's sunken eyes turned up to him. "Boy . . . ?" Both hands felt over Donnie's chest, making sure he was flesh, substantial. Feeble mumbles fell out of his mouth. Then Mr. Ricca grabbed Donnie and hugged him so fearsomely that Tom was afraid the exertion would break the fragile man.

"Angelo . . . are you OK?" Tom put one hand on his arm.

"Donnie . . . Donnie. My boy . . ." He wept, his shoulders shaking. He clung to Donnie as if he was a granite pillar and they were experiencing a tornado.

Everyone in the bar moved closer.

"Sit." Tom helped Mr. Ricca onto a chair. As the frail man sat, Tom turned to Rocky, "Join us, son."

Donnie glared at his father as he pulled up another chair.

Rocky waved off Tom's offer. He and Tiny moved apart from the group.

"When Freddie deployed, he took our lives with him." Mr. Ricca's pale tongue attempted to wet his desiccated lips. "At first, we thanked God for his phone calls and e-mails. And then five months after his arrival in Afghanistan, we began to dread them. But still we needed that contact, a sign that our boy was OK, alive. The war, what he was doing, was devouring my boy. He was proud when he left home, but he soon turned inward and angry. He had always been a tenderhearted child. Freddie loved the boys he fought with. They were his reason for fighting. He even made friends among the Afghan people. The environment, the suffering, and the stress took its toll."

Ahsan offered Mr. Ricca a glass of water.

"Thank you, son." Mr. Ricca patted Ahsan's cheek.

Mr. Ricca rubbed his temple, remembering details. "Freddie couldn't sleep. He was determined to stay with his buddies and finish his tour. He had sixteen days before rotating out. But my son's soul was wearing thin."

Rocky and Tiny watched and listened from the shadows.

Mr. Ricca took out a handkerchief and wiped his watery eyes and nose. "Freddie was a good boy. A happy boy. But the war took all that away from him."

He sipped the water and frowned.

"This war is leaching the humanity out of our children. They are taught to kill, told they need to kill or be killed. How can our young people's values survive inside this storm where death is the norm? These boys and girls are serving, defending us and finding their purpose in the brotherhoods they form. When they return home, separated from those friends, with skills that don't fit into peace, they feel as useless as a car without wheels."

Tom put an arm around the bereaved man's shoulder.

His lips vibrated like the silent beating of a crow's wings. Mr. Ricca started, then stopped twice more, before saying, "I received this letter."

Mr. Ricca pulled a wrinkled letter from his inside jacket pocket. He unfolded it as though it was a fragile lost scroll written by Jesus Christ.

"The way this is written, it is as if Freddie knew he wouldn't be coming home to us."

He broke down. His face disappeared into the cavity of his crossed arms resting on the table.

"Let me help you home, Angelo." Tom started to stand up.

Mr. Ricca looked up. "No." He leaned in to Donnie, holding out the letter, "You read it. Then you will know . . . a father's love . . . a father's loss."

Every fiber in Donnie was telling him not to take the letter. But the desperation in Mr. Ricca's eyes begged him for this morsel of his son. So Donnie read:

> There are many things we have left unsaid, Papa. Things that are not usually said between men, fathers and sons. But although you never vocalized on a daily basis how much you love me and how proud you were of my accomplishments, I thought you should know you have left nothing unsaid. Your actions and your life showed me in a much more meaningful way what your lips could not.
>
> When I was trying to learn to swim and the cold water would trigger an asthma attack, you meticulously checked the pool's temperature to decide whether to leave the solar cover on or off so the water temperature would stay a comfortable, healthy eighty- to eighty-five degrees for me.
>
> You attended every baseball game and even gave up your chance for an interview with the governor when it meant you would miss my championship game.

You taught me how to drive and had the patience of Mother
Teresa after the driver's ed. teacher ridiculed me, called me an idiot,
and made me not want to ever get behind the wheel of a car.
You treated me like a man and listened to my every rambling, even
when I made little or no sense.

You protected me in a thousand ways. From the wasps nesting
on the porch, the bullies on our block, and even occasionally from
myself.

Donnie paused, and looked over the top of the letter at his father. He
was surprised to see Rocky's shoulders shaking as he and Tiny inched
toward the rear exit.

Everyone followed Donnie's gaze. After the door closed, he continued.

You always showed sincere interest in anything I was doing. And
when I made a mistake, and I made plenty, you always said, "It's
OK, pal." And when you said that, it was OK.
You showed me how to be a man, a good man, by your example.
You are genuine, honest, and true, Papa. And I am proud to be your
son. Thank you, Papa. I love you.

Freddie

Donnie gulped back his tears. Reverently, his shaky hand passed the letter back to Mr. Ricca.

Tom wondered whether his son's tears were for a lost friend, his
brother, or his own waning innocence? Perhaps his son had taken a giant
leap toward manhood today.

Now Mr. Ricca took Donnie's hand. He squeezed it as if he feared a
calamity might occur if he were to let go. Or maybe he was seeing his
own son instead of Donnie.

"I failed my son. I fed into his boyish dreams. He wanted to carry a
sword and shield and experience the glory of victory. But he didn't find it.
I should have told him that what he was seeking came at a high price."

He cleared his throat. "Our castle . . ." He thought better of using metaphors. "Our home is cold and empty. Our son's quest will not be put to a tune and be sung across America. All that is left is the sorrow of a mother and father who have lost the purpose for our lives." He broke down.

Tom and Donnie, like everyone in the place, wept along with Mr. Ricca.

"What your father is going to try and do for you should make you feel nothing but pride." Mr. Ricca eyed Tom and gave him a slim smile.

Tom returned the gesture with a brief head tilt that said thank you.

"It is a father's duty to protect his children. God . . . I wish I had known I could go in my son's stead. I would do just what your father is going to do." Mr. Ricca's voice gained strength as he spoke.

Mr. Ricca forced a smile out for Donnie. He gripped the young man behind his neck and pulled them head to head as if eager to be connected to warm flesh. He hugged him.

Then he spoke to Tom. "If I can help, all you have to do is call. Just hearing what you are doing has pulled me back. Today I was sitting in that corner"—Mr. Ricca pointed into the shadows—"going through the motions of living and not knowing why. And now I have found a reason. There is another way to fight this insane need for vengeance. I am going to help you, Tom."

As he let out a deep breath, Mr. Ricca looked as though his gaunt body had filled out the shrunken pieces.

He came back from the dead that afternoon. Donnie had never seen a resurrection, but he saw one that day.

The adults and the young people moved closer and surrounded Mr. Ricca. Some cried with him, sharing memories, while others discussed the reasons behind the war. By the time evening arrived, Mr. Ricca would leave the Wings on Fire Café revitalized.

"Son, it's time to go. Your mother will have dinner waiting." Tom slapped Donnie on the back. "You too, Frank."

As Donnie walked to the door, he said, "Poor Rocky. He screwed up in reverse. Again. What a chump."

"Donnie, don't talk about Rocky that way," said Tom.

"Dad, he has been on me since . . ."

"No! You don't understand. This morning his mom got notification that his father is missing in action, presumed dead. That's why he was drunk out of his mind. I know his father wasn't such a great example. He was a convicted felon and a drunk, but he was Rocky's dad. There are all kinds of families, and he was someone who will be missed and who was loved. You have to cut Rocky some slack, son."

Chapter 15

IT WAS TWO WEEKS AND ONE DAY LATER. At six a.m. it was cold, damp, and dismal, which was nothing new to Tom. That was the weather forecast inside his mind, even if he had a sunny smile showing.

He and his son were jogging, rolling along at a nice pace doing the airborne shuffle. Tom sang each stanza, and Donnie repeated after him. "C-130 going down the strip . . . C-130 going down the strip . . . Airborne Ranger gonna take a little trip . . . Airborne Ranger gonna take a little trip . . . stand up, hook up, shuffle to the door . . ."

Tom waited for Donnie to repeat the line of the cadence when Donnie burst out ahead. Tom turned on what he had left in him and ran hard, to finish in their driveway shoulder to shoulder with his son.

"Huh. Didn't think your old man had that in him, did you?"

"No crowing." Then Donnie grilled his dad, "What's your MOS?"

"My Military Occupation Specialty is . . . Ranger." Tom sang out the last part. "I'm a lethal weapon. So look out, boy." He danced around like Rocky Balboa, poking Donnie in the ribs. Tom chuckled. His son did not.

"Dad, stop it. This isn't funny. You're not a Ranger anymore. You have to fit in as a member of Twenty-Eighth Infantry Division. SBCT, Fifty-Sixth Brigade Independence."

The wall separating Tom and Donnie had crumbled that day at the Wings on Fire Café. Donnie was completely onboard, so much so that if Tom hadn't seen the gray hairs in his sideburns when he looked in the bathroom mirror, he wouldn't have known who was the father and who was the son. Well, he had wanted Donnie to commit to something and he had. It was Tom's training.

Every morning, while they were jogging and sweating, his son would lecture him. He listened because it was his son talking. Tom knew precisely what he was getting himself into.

Tom leaned over, resting his hands on his knees, trying to find more oxygen. "Yeah, I know, I know. I am part of Stryker Brigade Combat Team. Handling support missions. We are a lethal modular force." He straightened and slapped Donnie on the back. "I don't know what lethal and modular have to do with each other, but . . . are we through here?"

"No!" With his hands on his hips, Donnie walked around his father like a mean drill instructor. "My infantry rifle platoon has how many ICVs?"

"Four. You are a driver and Sergeant Steiner is your infantry combat vehicle commander." Tom could recite this forward and backward. "Three nine-man rifle squads and one seven-man weapons squad make up the platoon."

"Drop and give me forty."

"Shit." Tom was loving this time with his son, but a complaint was definitely called for. "We just jogged five miles." He decided the kid liked pushing him a little too much.

"No grumbling." Donnie checked his stopwatch. "You were three minutes and forty-five seconds off your mark for the run."

"I used to do five miles, averaging under six per mile." He thought, *God, could you just give me a little of my youth back?* Tom was back in the prayer business. The answer echoed through the pain in his muscles: *Not a chance.*

"*Used to* doesn't count." His son circled him, checking his form. "Get your butt down. Better. Back flat. Good."

Tom croaked out, "For my age, the regs say I only need to do twenty-five of these."

"Forget the requirements. Sergeant Steiner and the lieutenant want each of the men in the squad to max everything. The max in push-ups for my age is seventy-one. You're me."

"What's the minimum? Can I go for that?"

"You can. It's forty . . . if you're my age."

"You have a sadistic streak. I never knew that."

"Let's follow those push-ups with seventy sit-ups, soldier." Donnie squatted down, watching his dad, and grinned.

"Cruel." His words came out in ragged gasps that matched Tom's up-and-down motion. "Don't you think you are overdoing this a bit, son?" His pecs and biceps were screaming at him to surrender. "Fifty-nine, sixty, sixty-one." Tom collapsed onto the soggy, half-frozen ground. Tom's journey to fitness was a long road and Donnie was determined to shorten the trip.

"Sergeant Steiner is not going to take our exchange lying down. He's a real hard-ass. If you get inside the gates at Fort Dix for processing, he's going to try and break you."

"Still doubting the plan?"

"Keeping it real. I'd give this plan the same odds as winning the lottery, one in ten billion."

"So you are just along for the ride. Is that what you're saying, kid?"

"Dad, I know once you make up your mind to do something I can't make you change course. And I understand why you're doing this so . . . I'd rather be with you than against you."

"We're like Butch Cassidy and the Sundance Kid."

"No. We are more like *Toy Story*." Donnie laughed. "I'm Woody."

"That makes me Buzz Lightyear."

"No, Dad. You're Mr. Potato Head."

Tom and his son had started working out the day after their talk in Mona's front seat. But that letter from Mr. Ricca's son sealed their deal. They had been at it every day. The boy was determined to get his dad in shape. Sure, Donnie still had his doubts that this would work, but he didn't want his old man falling flat on his face, either.

From Tom's point of view, the road to fitness was nothing but uphill curves, and he couldn't ever quite get around that first turn. But with Donnie behind him, he kept pushing. Hell, if he was going to have a heart attack, Tom preferred to have it at home, anyway.

Frank joined them in the driveway.

"Now, there is the real Mr. Potato Head," chortled Tom.

Tom, Frank, and Donnie discussed everything. They met daily. In the morning, after Tom's physical training, Frank supplied coffee and CPR as needed.

This morning, Tom would have welcomed oxygen more than coffee.

"Take me to the house before my muscles freeze up and I'm stuck to the ground like dog crap," Tom begged Frank.

Tom slung one arm around Frank's shoulder and let his friend guide him toward the house to get ready for work.

"See you tonight, Donnie," said Frank for Tom.

Donnie gave his dad a big smile before he jumped into his car and headed to work.

"Did you see that?" asked Tom, beaming.

Frank chuckled. "Let's get you up the steps."

Once they were on the porch, Frank propped Tom against the front door and said, "Go inside. Take a shower. I'll grab my stuff and be back in fifteen."

Tom managed a single nod. Today he had sympathy for every jerk who couldn't chew gum and walk at the same time. He doubted if he could even do the chewing part. Everything hurt. He was having trouble sweating and stumbling at the same time.

At last, he made it into the house. Inside the door, he stopped and looked around. Leaning on the couch, he took a sip of the coffee Frank had donated and waited for the plumbing or the radiators to critique today's workout.

Nothing. "Well, all right." He toasted the silence with his mug. "Thank you very much."

Then a sustained, agonizing groan rumbled through the pipes.

This time he didn't yell. The house and Tom were in sync. "I know just how you feel." He patted one radiator as he took off his sneakers and went upstairs.

Since he had been working out, the shower had also been kinder to him. Like right now. He had a full four minutes of good hot water. Then it clanged out a warning before turning cold. Tom guessed the plumbing had quick military showers in mind.

"Thanks."

"Are you talking nice to the house?" asked Christine.

"Yeah, I'm making peace." Tom smiled and kissed her on the cheek as he stepped out of the tub. "I'll be home at the usual time and—"

"Frank and Donnie will be here, too." She turned away. "I like this routine. I don't want it to end . . ." The strength in her voice fell away.

"Honey, don't go there. Hey, think of me as this house, with all its quirks. And when the house makes noises, complain a little for me. If you look around, you'll see signs of me all over this place. I'm a slob."

She hugged him and handed him clean underwear. "You'll be late for work."

Tom knew she turned away so he wouldn't see her eyes filling up.

"And don't make peace with the house. It doesn't feel right." Christine gathered up Tom's sweats and damp towel.

EVENINGS WERE FOR PLANNING. Donnie's knowledge added a lot once again; Tom was amazed at his son's sharp mind. He often reminded himself that Donnie would be left behind to deal with his peers, the family, and all the shit people were certain to throw at him. But as Tom looked across the pool table at his son, he was sure the boy could handle it. Donnie had grown up fast in these last weeks. In Tom's imagination, bright medals of courage were scattered across his son's chest.

"So what do we do when you get to the medical part?" asked Frank. "This is the part I am most worried about."

"I'll handle it." Tom flexed his newly recovered muscles as though he was changing into the Hulk. "No problem."

"Right," said Frank. "Like how? What has your sugar been running?"

"Dr. Frank, two hours after supper, the reading was a hundred and twenty. I checked when I went upstairs to pee. I also had a nice crap, if you are interested."

The subject was serious. They all knew Tom's type 2 diabetes could sink the ship. Tom tried to reassure Donnie and Frank.

"Look, I have never felt so good. With all the exercising, I have lost five pounds of ugly fat." He slapped his gut. "I have been managing my diet, cutting back on starches and simple carbs. And I'm eating more whole grains. Does that pass your inspection, Dr. Frank?"

"Yes, that passes," said Frank, coming nose to nose with his friend. "But keep on it."

"Christ, Frank, you're getting to be a real nag."

"Yeah? Well, you haven't seen anything yet. So just keep watching your sugar!"

Tom knew Frank was hanging on to his guilt that he had gotten Tom into this tenuous position. He expected Frank to come across hot and red once in a while. Lately, his tirades were running faster and faster, chasing Tom's D-day, and Tom had to admit he was also getting a little jumpy.

"Guys," warned Donnie, who seemed to be the only adult in the basement at the moment, "what about that lawyer?"

"I talk with Jim Small regularly," said Frank. "He's researched the common law. He says it has a chance. The resistance to the way substitution was done back during the Civil War came from charges of class discrimination. Both the Confederate and Union draft laws allowed the wealthy to opt out. But since there is no coercion or money involved in this exchange . . ." Frank took a breath. "He's put together a good argument and is eager and ready. Jim was full of great comments. He suggested we talk to our local congressmen. Congressional support could help."

"I don't know how to talk to a politician." Tom thought a moment. "Ask Jim to write a letter and put in some good words, for me."

"Sure," said Frank. "He'll do it."

"He's a good Ranger. Biggest *small* guy I ever met. Get it?" Tom elbowed his son. Suddenly he could see Jim's huge black hand slapping an extra clip in his as they ran full out from the Republican Guard.

"We need him to be a great lawyer right now," said Donnie, keeping them all focused. "If nothing else, to keep us out of jail."

"Jim has a fantastic reputation," said Frank. "The criminals fear him in North Carolina."

"Can we count on him?" Donnie was all business.

"Of course. He's one of us." More seriously, Tom added, "He has two sons of his own now. So don't worry."

"Geez, Dad, what are we doing? This is stupid. All this foolish planning." Donnie threw down his pencil and did his nightly worry walk around the pool table. "For what? We'll never make this fly with the army."

"Son," Tom kept his voice even, "don't let me down now, we're almost there. Jim Small is key to the plan, and he knows how important this is to me."

"He has to be the one to 'hang in there.' You said he is in the reserve. Dad, do you have any idea how much pressure the army will put on him."

Donnie was the one who didn't understand, thought Tom.

He tried to explain. "He does what he says. Once a Ranger, always a Ranger. In or out of uniform, we can always count on each other." At another time Tom would have wanted Donnie to experience these unbreakable bonds. These friendships were the silver lining of military service.

"Jim called this afternoon and said he would meet us outside Fort Dix on Saturday," said Frank as he checked the calendar. "Wow, we leave . . . tomorrow."

The room fell quiet. Even the heating system went stealth. They all knew Tom's deployment date, but until this moment no one had actually said it. Now it was the Sherman tank in the room.

"Today is Thursday." Tom cleared his throat. "Tomorrow after work the three of us will drive over to Fort Dix." The reality was not to be avoided.

Tonight would be the long good-bye. Tom's heart started thumping in his chest as he thought of Christine. He and his daughter had already planned to have breakfast together in the morning for their farewell.

Knowing his wife, and Tom knew her well, she, like him, wouldn't want any fuss. "Keep it regular, everyday normal." Tom could almost hear her saying it. And he agreed. But damn, it had taken him all these years to feel right in this world, and now he had to leave Christine and return to another reality. This was going to be hard, probably the hardest thing he would ever do.

"Dad? Dad, are you listening?"

"Yeah. What is it, Donnie?"

"I talked to Mr. Ricca. He is coming up Saturday morning with a newspaper friend of his. They will meet us at the motel, too. We'll go in all together."

"That's nice. I can use the support. But I don't want to be in the *Inquirer* or anything like that." Tom wrote in the air. "'Crazy Old Guy Goes to War with the US Army!'"

"No, Tom," said Frank. "Mr. Ricca will only make noise if they try to deny your rights under the law."

"It's a good angle, Dad. The military doesn't like publicity."

When they finished, and since this time they were *really* finished, Donnie decided to spend the night in his old room. Side by side, father and son stood at the front door and watched as Frank shuffled home.

Tom said, "He seems to be moving a little slower nowadays, son."

"Yeah," said Donnie. "Don't worry. I'll keep an eye on him. I'll take care of them all, Dad."

Tom's arm came up around his son's shoulder and tightened.

Tom walked upstairs to join Christine, wondering when his son had become the family's guardian and he the dependent. All of his dreams were resting on that boy. He was filled with pride as he thought, *They are in good hands.*

Tom smiled. So far, so good.

Chapter 16

Donnie was driving. Frank was in the backseat, and Tom was riding shotgun. The lack of cheer made it feel like they were heading for the last roundup at the OK Corral, mused Tom. Of course, in a way, they were all going into battle. Challenging the whole damned US Army was not something to take lightly.

Tom laughed to himself, realizing this car was full of crazy people. Doing what they were doing was something that could be thought up only by the insane. And so, Tom calculated, that made him the head crazy. He listened to the music on the radio and tried to forget where he was headed.

As they traveled through Ephrata, they passed an Amish family in a horse-drawn buggy clip-clopping down the side of the highway. Nice tidy farmhouses offered warmth and shelter down straight dirt roads. Laundry flapped on the clotheslines. Fields spread out with their summer crops turned over. The earth was resting for the winter. Beautiful.

Scenes like that couldn't help but remind Tom that America was wonderful in its diversity.

So much emotion was coursing through him right now that it was hard to keep up with the slide show running in his mind. Last night had been tough. God . . . Tom's mind had him on speed dial. . . . *You sure gave me one hell of a partner. Did we both cry a lot? Of course.* But somehow, and Tom still couldn't figure out how it had happened, Christine had given him the strength he needed to leave her.

God, You knew all this, Tom reminded himself. *You made her. So thanks for being with us last night,* thought Tom. Then he added, even more softly, *Stay close.* A huge apple formed in his throat. He swallowed his sadness.

"Dad? What's the matter?" asked Donnie, glancing over at him. "You're turning all red."

"Nothing. A little warm maybe." Tom cracked his window.

The truth was Tom was blushing, remembering that God had been there for the sexy part of the evening, too.

"We are now officially in New Jersey," announced Frank, who continued to navigate from the backseat with an old-fashioned paper map stretched out across his lap. He didn't trust "Jill," their GPS narrator.

Tom had repeatedly told Frank and Donnie that they didn't need the map or the GPS. But they were determined to handle him.

Tom knew he could have found Fort Dix just by heading southeast. There were signs everywhere off Route 206. The military complex was formidable. McGuire Air Force Base and the navy's Lakehurst were close to Dix, as well as several other installations.

Four hours after leaving home, Frank's putrid green VW Rabbit pulled into Wrightstown. It was a military town from one end to the other. Tom had not seen so many uniforms walking the streets since he had been one of them.

They scouted out the main entrance to the base to get their bearings for the morning, then went on to their motel. It was late by the time they checked in at the Quality Inn and sat down to dinner at a local steak place.

The food was tasteless. The conversation was scant. All the smug self-assuredness the two men and the boy had possessed during their planning sessions had lost its pizzazz.

Tom noticed his son's eyes darting around. He reminded his dad about his Soldier Readiness Packet for the umpteenth time, "I had my SRP seven months ago. If they take you, they'll be looking to do yours again first thing."

"Stop worrying, son. And stop using the word *if* so much. I'm familiar with how things work. I have my old shot record with me if they want to see it. I don't have any medical or dental problems, so I should be good to go."

Frank gave him the look, code for *Sure you don't have any medical problems?*

"I brought my SRP," said Donnie without humor.

Tom's heart skipped a beat. His head involuntarily gave a shake from side to side. Sheer dread filled him when Donnie added, "Just in case."

"There's a lot of ways this could go." Frank reflected, "That includes a cell with iron bars."

Tom understood Frank was still worrying about his sugar and that he had decided to try to keep his diabetes a secret. Lying to the US government was a serious offense, but Tom had been adamant. He would not hand the army even one bullet to use against him. He'd pass his physical and that would be that. He knew there would be monkey wrenches thrown in, but, hell, he had been taught how to improvise. Tom tried to lighten the mood.

"Fortunately, I fit into your BDUs, Donnie. Now that's really something."

"Dad, they're called ACUs, active combat uniforms, nowadays. Don't date yourself. And you will be getting new camos with the rest of your equipment. They changed the pattern or something."

"Donnie, you don't have to go over this again and again. I got it. I've done it before." Tom's words rushed out, too loud.

After that they finished picking at their meals in silence.

It was close to eleven when they finally hit the sack. Frank peeled off for his room. Tom and his son headed to the double down the hall. Tom was glad Donnie was bunking with him. It was one of his fatherly intuition things. Donnie needed him tonight. And, if Tom was truthful, he needed his son.

At midnight, Tom was still staring at the ceiling and half listening to an old John Wayne western on the tube. He peeked over and saw Donnie doing the same.

"Kid, you better get some sleep."

"I was thinking. You've never worn IBA, individual body armor, before. I should have had you train carrying the extra weight. I screwed up there.

You'll be carrying about fifty pounds on you. That's equipment, plus water. Maybe more, depending on the weapon and rounds of ammo."

"Stop. They'll put me on a desk. And desk jockeys don't wear IBA."

"Everybody in Afghanistan does. What if they don't sit you in a chair?"

"Give yourself a break, son. You've done your part; now it's my turn." Tom turned back to the TV. A few minutes passed as he searched for the words he wanted. "You know, we are all acting like I'm going to be standing in front of a firing squad tomorrow. Christ, we have got to stop that! If I don't catch a desk job, what's the worst? I will be made a driver. And transport isn't a life-or-death job." Wrong words.

"When the government federalizes a National Guard unit, like it did right after 9/11, it's because they need manpower to participate in a war. So, be straight with me, Dad."

"I think I have a good shot at that desk."

"You don't know computers."

"I am an expert at organization and supply. And somewhere along the line they still have to hand someone a piece of paper." Donnie was shaking his head, so Tom continued. "Or they'll give me your job, driver. There are a million places to stick me—communications, motor pool, cleaning latrines. Even if my military occupational skill is 11B, they'll put this old man in some corner to stay out of trouble."

"Infantry," said Donnie softly. "Rifleman."

"Don't talk to your mother about any of this infantry stuff. You know as well as I do that every soldier starts out with that classification. Believe me, I see a pile of paper in my future."

"Driving is your backup plan. Did you read all the specs I gave you on the infantry carrier?"

"Yeah. I can see that ICV Stryker's controls with my eyes closed."

"I wish there had been some way for you to at least simulate using the M-17 periscopes. Damn!"

This was like listening to himself when he'd taught Donnie how to drive. Going over and over little details. Hey, come to think of it, that hadn't been all that long ago. "I'll be fine."

"Dad, the thing is huge!"

"Yeah, yeah. I know. It's twenty-three feet long. Hey, tell me more about this 'cage.'" Maybe if he kept the boy talking, he would finally exhaust himself and fall asleep.

"After some fatalities, they added these slats of armor on the sides. The slats are eighteen inches away from the body of the vehicle, so an RPG's impact is defused between the slat and the armor."

Tom heard his son's voice falter when he said "RPG's impact." It sent a chill racing through him, too. But he quickly said, "Go on, son."

"Our vehicles," Donnie tossed in his bed, "are all new. The way our new LT treats them, you'd think the army took the cost for them out of his pay. Of course, they are the first new armored vehicles the army has acquired in eighteen years."

Tom had been thinking about this Lieutenant Cogriff. From Donnie's description, no one liked the guy. From personal experience, Tom knew a good leader wasn't loved, but he was respected. This guy was neither.

"I want you to take my laptop with you," added Donnie. "Somebody will show you how to Skype me."

"That's going to be a hell of a lot more problematic than handling Steiner and your . . . my lieutenant."

They laughed, then went back to searching the ceiling. Silent good-byes hovered and swelled until they occupied every oxygen molecule in the room. Neither of them found any words they dared to speak that could express their deep feelings. They both sniffled.

"Get some sleep, son."

Donnie's shadow merely nodded.

Tom heard the sheets rustle.

Still, they both stared at the only light in the room and listened. John Wayne said, "Courage is being scared to death, but saddling up anyway."

Chapter 17

They hit Fort Dix's main gate right after the condemned man finished his hearty breakfast. Six somber men—Tom, Donnie, Frank, Mr. Ricca, his friend and fellow journalist Paul Jordan, and Jim Small—were crammed into Jim Small's SUV, which had one of those *Life Is Good* stick families plastered on the back window. The six of them looked like an assault team fated for nothing more dangerous than the aisles of a grocery store.

Tom stuck his head out the front passenger window and asked the MP for directions to Building A-117. Out of the blue, Tom remembered that in his earlier service days they had called the in-processing building "the meat factory."

Looking out through the van's tinted windows, Tom was struck by the high security 9/11 had generated. The MPs watched their van approach with the sharp eyes of shepherds guarding sheep.

Three MPs surrounded the van. They asked the curious group to vacate the vehicle. Donnie was dressed in ACUs. Tom carried his in his backpack. They were both ready for either outcome. Nobody raised an eyebrow. Two brawny MPs searched the vehicle while one watched over them. They used a mirror on a long rod to inspect the undercarriage. Then each of them was asked to produce identification.

Donnie showed them his orders. Mr. Ricca and his newspaper friend flashed their press credentials, while Tom and Frank pulled out their driver's licenses. Jim Small's active reserve ID, which listed his rank as a major, was the only piece of paper that elicited any reaction from the straight-faced MPs. When Jim's hard eyes locked onto the MPs, they immediately responded with a snappy salute.

Jim told the guards they were seeing Lane off, but he didn't specify which Lane.

In the end, one of the MPs handed Jim an authorization card. Tom let out his breath as they drove through the gate. They were in.

Reading the permit, Tom noticed it was valid only until four p.m. They were on the clock. With this warning to get out of Dodge before sundown clearly displayed in the front window, the van headed for Building A-117.

Finding their destination, the military entrance processing station, wasn't nearly as easy as the MP had made it sound. All the buildings looked alike. They wandered around for a bit. And with three former Rangers in the vehicle, they didn't even consider asking for help.

Finally, Donnie spotted some men he knew, and they headed in that direction. Outside a one-story brick building, on a worn patch of lawn that was mostly dirt, they found Donnie's entire guard unit.

The men and women paced, laughed, and mingled like gladiators waiting to be called into the arena. Several waved and acknowledged Donnie's arrival, but for the most part all the young people remained close to their families, ready to grab their last hugs and handshakes when given the signal. That is, all but one. That young man stood apart, by himself.

Tom observed with a chuckle that the lone blue-eyed, blond-haired soldier was about the same size as one of the leafless maple trees dotting the area.

"Hey, Donnie," called the jolly giant.

When the young man turned to face them, Tom was immediately struck by something in the kid's expression. Maybe innocence. He watched as the boy rubbed the top of his almost hairless head absent-mindedly and ambled closer.

"What happened to you?" asked Donnie, pointing to the boy's head.

"Getting a jump on the barber. Hoorah."

Donnie laughed and said, "Dad, everybody, this is Albert Hamkens."

"Nice to meet you, Albert," said Tom.

"Amazing," said Frank. "They're looking younger and younger."

Jim Small nodded agreement.

Albert stuck out his hand.

Tom took it. "How you doing, son?"

"You Mr. Lane?" Albert asked.

"Yep. But you can just call me Tom. Like one of the guys." After all, Tom hoped to be one of them soon, so he decided this was as good a time as any to put that objective in motion.

Tom winced as Albert pumped his arm.

"Sorry. I always overdo it. Guess I'm a little slow . . ."

"Albert, you're not slow," said Donnie.

Tom would bet the farm that this wasn't the first time his son had become Albert's defender.

"He keeps telling me that. But what I don't have up here," Albert knocked a knuckle hard on his own head, "I make up for here." The kid indicated his huge biceps, which stretched the thick fabric of his shirt as he flexed.

"I can see that." Tom was still working his hand, encouraging the blood to return to his fingers.

"You T-T-Tom?" Albert's eyes narrowed. He rubbed both sides of his chin. "I gotta call you T-Tom?" He pointed back and forth between father and son. "To confuse my dumb t-tongue." He thought another few seconds. And repeated the name as if it were a tongue twister he struggled to master. He stuttered trying to pronounce the *T*. Then he gave a big sigh. "Can I just call you D-Dad?" Albert's big, childlike face stared at Tom as he waited for an answer.

"Sure," Tom said. "I'm use to answering to that, too."

Tom's group, with Albert trailing along, migrated in with some of the other soldiers, parents, and friends. Donnie was just finishing introductions when Staff Sergeant Steiner made his entrance.

"You'll form a single line to file inside. No chatter. Have your paperwork ready. For now, leave your gear with your family members out here. You can say your good-byes after you get your billeting assignments.

Hustle up. Let's go!" The sergeant waved his arms like a traffic cop. "Stay on the sidewalk. Off the grass!"

A line quickly formed at the entrance to the building. Tom and his supporters hung back. "We'll go last," whispered Tom to his friends. He decided there wasn't any advantage to setting the place on fire in front of the rest of Donnie's friends just yet.

Albert seemed glued to Donnie's elbow.

"Ham!" Steiner screamed, as though the kid had done something wrong. "I'm talking to you, DA. Get your stupid self . . ." All the parents' heads turned toward the sergeant, so he brought it down a notch. "Fall in, boy."

Donnie answered the unasked question. "Dumb Ass, or DA, is the label the sergeant gave Albert."

"DA, get movin'," repeated Steiner.

Albert glanced at Donnie. "Aren't you c-coming?"

"Go. It's OK." Donnie slapped the big kid on the shoulder.

Tom's whole group slipped into line after Albert was inside.

When Tom started in through the door, Steiner stepped out in front of him to block his entrance. "Sorry." The palm of his hand rested lightly on Tom's chest. "Family waits out here."

"Sergeant Steiner, I am Thomas Lane. And I think you are about to experience something way beyond your pay grade."

"Sir, stand aside." Steiner glared at Donnie. "Lane, get your ass in here."

Donnie stepped right up to him.

"Sergeant Steiner, my father is going in my place."

This was Tom's job. He had never expected his son to do the challenging. But the boy stood firm, and his voice was strong, calm.

Tom had known his son had his personal doubts, but there wasn't a hint of it showing in his words or tone. The kid was honoring his father's wishes. Maybe Donnie had something to prove to himself. Damn, what a son God had given him.

"I told you, Sergeant, that this was above your pay grade. I am going in my son's stead, and I have the law on my side," said Tom. "Now, are you going to get someone, preferably above a butter bar, or are we going to choose up sides out here on the sidewalk?"

The sergeant eyed Jim Small and Frank, who had stepped up to stand shoulder to shoulder with Tom.

"I'm his lawyer," said Small. His shadow covered the slightly shorter but no less powerfully built Sergeant.

For a second, Tom thought the sergeant and Jim Small would have been an interesting matchup. They were both solid blocks of muscle. Of course, Small had the experience, but the sergeant had the swagger that screamed "street tough."

"And who are the rest of these men?" asked the sergeant.

Each person sounded off.

Frank beamed, his flabby body straightening as he chimed in, "Army Ranger retired."

"*Washington Post,*" said Paul Jordan.

"*The Daily,*" Mr. Ricca added. "Good morning." He took out a pad and pencil and asked, "Is that Steiner with one *n*?"

The sergeant did a lot of breathing and thinking. "You two," he pointed at Tom and Donnie, "come with me. Let's just have a little talk, in private."

Mr. Jordan stepped apart from the group. "Son, you wouldn't want us to make a scene here in front of all these kids' parents, would you?"

"It might end up splashed all over the front page of the *Washington Post,* or even better on YouTube." Paul Jordan was small in stature, but if you took in the whole picture—his expensive black suit, his white shirt and red silk tie, and the phone he held out indicating a video in progress—the man was transformed into a giant. "By the way, my paper has a circulation of more than five hundred thousand. I'm sure the army would love the publicity."

Tom watched the sergeant's reaction. Steiner's teeth locked, and his jaw muscles bulged abnormally. He tried to force a smile, perhaps for the camera. Tom noticed it didn't come out as the nice-guy look Steiner was trying for. Instead, the sergeant looked like he had just found a live snail swimming in his soup and wanted someone to pay for the insult.

"Sorry," Tom said. "We are a unit. We move together." He pointed to his team.

"Ya gotta love the power of the press," said Frank, keeping one eye on the sergeant.

Steiner made an about-face and disappeared inside. He returned, fuming even more than he had been when he'd left. Tom was surprised steam wasn't coming out of his ears. It was obvious the man was having trouble not boiling over.

"Follow me!" Steiner barked. "We are going to see the lieutenant."

Tom's personal army fell in behind Staff Sergeant Steiner.

"Keep up," Steiner commanded.

Suddenly Tom felt like a kid watching a parade. Everyone has this same reaction, mused Tom. You hear the beat of a drum and marching feet, and before you know it your own feet are following the throbbing pulse without you realizing it. That was just how Tom felt now as he followed Steiner. Yeah, the old ways were sneaking back. He made a conscious effort not to strut his stuff like Steiner.

Tom watched as the sergeant took eight deliberate steps down the cement away from Building A-117. When his combat boots met the main sidewalk, he made a sharp military right turn, took ten more steps, then did another of his precision directional changes onto the walkway in front of the adjacent administration building.

Deep inside Tom's head, another thought surfaced, because the army had taught him a lot more than just marching. He was hoping his other finely honed Ranger training was waiting its turn to materialize. He might need it sooner rather than later. He was sure this guy, Steiner, was just itching to push around a Ranger. The Sergeant's smirk when Small showed him his ID to "enlighten him," as Small put it, and when he pointed out that Tom was also a former Ranger, told Tom everything he needed to know. Well, so be it. Let the pissing contest begin, because no matter what he does to me, they cannot have my son.

"Geez, we could have taken a couple of steps, cut across, and been at the front door," whispered Frank in Tom's ear. "Is he protecting the dirt from being trampled? 'Cause I don't see no grass around here." Frank's broad hands panned the red clay patch where they had just been standing.

They all chuckled.

"He's marking his territory," Tom answered. "Making us fall in line, follow his lead."

Steiner whirled around to frown at Frank. His look, which Tom knew all sergeants had, shot out a ripple of attitude.

Tom chuckled.

Frank smiled.

They knew something Steiner didn't. If the sergeant thought he had a corner on attitude, well, he was about to meet his match, because those vibes had just reached Small.

"If you think you're going to piss on me, Sergeant, you are going to have to grow a few feet taller." Small wasn't about to take this punk's or anybody else's shit. "Remember, you are talking to your superior."

"Calm down," Tom cautioned everyone.

"Rangers lead the way" had been their motto; Tom had it burned into his memory, as did Frank and Jim. And today it was looking like he and his friends were having a little trouble standing at the end of the line.

But, he admitted to himself, he was loving this. "Most excitement I've had in years," Tom said to Jim and Frank.

"Hold a little of the attitude back," Tom suggested as Jim passed him. "I'm sure there will be more inflated egos for you to crush in here." Tom held the door open for his friends as they all mounted the three steps and filed inside.

From the outside, this brick administration building looked exactly like A-117. Once inside, they found themselves in an alcove with the toilets to their right and left. A couple more steps in and they were looking down two steps over the entire first floor. It was open above the partitioned office spaces and reminded Tom of a hospital nursery, where you could look in on all the brand-new, shiny babies. Yes, Tom thought. They were all "that" young. Abruptly he was older.

This building was obviously a sanctuary for paperwork, a place Tom's queens back at the shop would have envied, given their present, more antiquated, no-frills surroundings.

Individual prefabricated cubicles dotted every foot of the yellowed, scarred linoleum floor like pimples on a teenager's face. Of course, all these "kids" were wearing their ACUs. Hell, they were all teenagers, at least that's how they appeared to Tom. The hum of computers, people, and copiers gave the place an impersonal, processed feeling. The bland plastered walls seemed to be calling out, "Let's just dot all the i's and cross all the t's and move this chunk of humanity on to the next pile of paper."

Tom noticed the windows were old, tall single panes—heat-sucking windows like his own back home. Which explained why it wasn't all that much warmer inside than it was outside.

"These windows could use some of those insulated green curtain things Christine has on our windows," said Tom to his son.

Donnie, his head cocked to the side, frowned at his dad.

Tom shifted his feet. Funny how the mind works. What pops up. Tom was sure his train had a unique rail system. He had always known that. But it was amazing how thoughts of Christine came to him so quickly. For a moment, half of him wanted to head home. And what was even more curious, the other half of him walked a little taller, surrounded as he was by all these uniforms.

"Dad," said Donnie, "that is Lieutenant Cogriff. My platoon's commanding officer." He pointed out a cubicle.

The lieutenant's cubical was at the bottom of the steps. Tom noticed that the officer had been placed just close enough to the front door that he would feel its chill every time it was opened. Knowing how the army thinks, if that is even remotely possible, Tom deduced the lieutenant, or LT in the enlisted man's version, was the lowest of the low in the hierarchy of fresh new officers.

"Excuse me, Lieutenant," said Steiner.

The lieutenant's slight figure was slumped over a pile of papers, and a non-army-issue, faded red blanket was tucked in around his crossed legs. It seemed impossible that he hadn't noticed the group's presence, but his head continued to swing back and forth between his computer screen and a yellow legal pad as he scribbled on it.

Again the sergeant interrupted, "Sir."

"I have tallied up the equipment we have received against the requisition orders, and a few items are missing. The quartermaster says we received everything. I want my missing equipment found now." His pencil, a yellow number two, repeatedly hit the pad to emphasize his point.

Now the lieutenant's tiny beady eyes left his numbers as Staff Sergeant (SSG) Steiner whispered in his ear. He was obviously getting the short version of the problem.

Tom watched Cogriff's sparse eyebrows dance at an interesting tidbit. His thin lips, however, were fixed neatly in place; only the corners were ever so slightly allowed to turn upward. The image that leaped into Tom's mind was Robert De Niro's passive-aggressive, creepy smile in *Meet the Parents*.

Lieutenant Cogriff stood and scanned them. He was wearing what soldiers affectionately called "birth control glasses"—black and thick-rimmed, they definitely repelled the opposite sex. He reminded Tom of a nerdy accountant instead of a leader of men. His fine black hair, high and tight on the sides and back, was longer on the top. Wisps of it fell over Cogriff's forehead in a downward slanting line. He had what Tom's mother would have called a bad bowl cut.

Cogriff continued to talk to the sergeant within earshot of Tom and his group.

"And why can't you handle this parent, Sergeant?" His hands flew about as he talked. "Your time would be better spent outfitting our Strykers with secondary armament." The lieutenant's long-fingered, lily-white hands rested on his bony hips.

Tom watched the sergeant stiffen and instantly knew he did not like being linked with this pencil pusher.

"Sir, the fifty-caliber machine guns are being mounted as we speak."

"Very well. Go on . . . Go. Introduce me. Let's be done with this foolishness."

"This is the father of one of our soldiers who is being deployed, Thomas Lane. As I said, he has an issue with his son . . ."

With a dismissive flick of his hand, the lieutenant cut Steiner off before he could finish. "I am always glad to meet the parents of my men. I am Lieutenant Cogriff."

As if they had just magically appeared, he acknowledged Tom and then grudgingly the others with him. Tom took the lieutenant's outstretched hand, which felt soft within his. The lieutenant was as tall as Tom but much thinner. He reminded Tom of a new green tree with stringy branches.

"I am sure you have concerns, but don't worry . . ." he said, pumping Tom's hand as he guided him toward the door. "I'll take good care of your son. I take care of all my men. Now, if you will excuse me, the sergeant will show your son the ropes. We really don't have time for this little joke of yours."

Tom was being dismissed. They were standing at the door as Cogriff turned his back to them.

"Damn right I have concerns." Tom's voice came out full-bodied, like that Sumatra coffee he'd been drinking. "Like my son is not going. I'm going in his place."

The lieutenant froze. And Tom noticed that all of the people in the room stopped, looked, and listened.

"Come again?" asked the lieutenant, still not facing Tom but leaning over and in, as if he were giving Tom the benefit of his attention reluctantly.

Tom repeated himself. "I'm going instead of him."

"Why, that is ridiculous. Ludicrous." The veins on Cogriff's neck and face swelled, pumping a red hue into his boyish cheeks as he struggled to keep a weak smile on his face. "You people must be joking. What makes you think you can pull something like this on the United States Army?"

"This is your first command?" Small asked Cogriff.

The lieutenant stepped back as Jim Small's presence overwhelmed him.

Turning to Tom, Jim said, "Real green little fellow, isn't he?"

The group covered their snickers with their hands.

"I am Major Small." Then to the gawking audience, Jim shouted, "Is there anyone in here with a bird or railroad tracks on his shoulders?"

An inconspicuous door at the very back corner of the room opened. A tall, silver-haired man stepped out. He barely moved but stood ramrod straight, summoning Lieutenant Cogriff with a slight flick of his hand.

Cogriff scurried to the captain's side.

When the lieutenant returned to Tom and his friends, he said, "This way."

Once again they all fell in line, but this time following Cogriff, who had no beat to imitate.

"Well, now we are getting somewhere," said Mr. Ricca.

Paul Jordan, his friend from the *Washington Post*, said, "At last, someone interesting."

Tom pointed to the man waiting by the open door at the back of the room as they weaved through the partitioned maze. "Do you know him?"

"Oh yes," said Jordan. "He was slated for a high-level position at the Pentagon, but some trouble with his commanding general's two daughters put him back in the field."

Tom asked, "Is he that guy? The colonel caught naked with the sisters and a bottle of massage oil in the back of the general's limo on Pennsylvania Avenue?"

"The same," whispered Jordan. "Except I see he is a captain now."

Tom's newsman contingent now became more animated than they had been all morning.

"In the blink of an eye, his career was down the crapper." Paul Jordan beamed. "This is why I love my job."

The captain held the door open as the troublesome six and Lieutenant Cogriff crammed themselves into his tiny office. When Jordan passed by and looked the man in the eye, Tom swore the captain's face turned as colorless as snow.

Jordan whispered in Tom's ear, "Yep. He remembers me."

"I am Captain Wulf. Company commander." He shook each of their hands.

Tom felt a single prominent ring when they shook. He must have been a graduate of West Point. This conclusion was reinforced when the man conspicuously fiddled with his ring, a ploy to make sure everyone knew his pedigree.

Last, the captain shook Paul Jordan's hand, and said, "I am sure you still remember to spell Wulf with a *u*, not an *o*, Mr. Jordan."

Call him crazy, but Tom was kind of liking the captain. He had always admired straightforward types.

They all stood, since there were not enough chairs for them all to sit down. To Tom's surprise, the captain remained standing also. After the shuffling stopped, he asked Tom to explain.

Ingrained behavior seeped out. Tom stepped up as if called to report, then a slight smile escaped when he realized he had given away that he was ex-military.

"Sir, I don't mean to cause any problems, but I am here to take my son's place with his National Guard unit. I know you are not interested in the reasons, only the resolutions. But I think we can both be satisfied if you let me, us," Tom motioned toward his friends, "explain."

"First," Captain Wulf said, "I have one question."

Tom nodded his OK.

"Is this what you want, son?" The captain walked over to Donnie.

Damn good question. This guy hit on something the sergeant and the lieutenant had not taken into account. Obviously Wulf was interested in the men under his command. Perhaps he thought Tom was bullying his boy.

Tom surveyed his young son, who was standing tall and strong as he answered.

"Yes, sir. My father and I have discussed this, and I have agreed to this exchange." Donnie swallowed. "I believe in God and this country, sir, but my older brother was a casualty of this war and my family, my mother . . ." Donnie paused, then picked it up. "But, sir, I am still willing to go and support the men in my unit if my father is denied the privilege of serving in my place."

The room took on an uncomfortable silence. Tom's heart was pumping with pride-filled beats. A father doesn't get a lot of chances to be there at those brave points in his kid's life, but Tom felt he was getting his share of Donnie's greatest moments.

Looking at Tom, the captain said, "OK, then show me what you've got that would allow for this unusual exchange." Captain Wulf returned to his chair behind his desk.

Jim went into action. He introduced himself. Next the captain and Small reminisced. Mutual acquaintances and overseas duty stations were discussed. They had common friends. It was true: The army is a family. This review of one another's military history was common practice among career men. The two came away with the measure of each other and, most important, the measure of Thomas Lane Sr.

Jim had painted a clear picture of the situation, even throwing in a mention of his own children and his empathy for what Tom was doing.

Tom saw Lieutenant Cogriff fidgeting in the far corner, where Small had more or less forced him to stand when they squeezed into the room. The lieutenant was chewing on his bottom lip.

Tom was hoping Cogriff would remain there. He had the look of a backbiter.

"I see on your DD214 you are eligible for re-upping. You are highly qualified, Sergeant Major Lane, but you would lose all rank if the army lets you replace your son. Do you realize that?"

Tom nodded.

"Our maximum age is fifty-nine. At your present age of forty-nine, and subtracting your years of previous service, you could still complete your twenty years of creditable service for retirement by that age.

"This is a great letter of support from your congressman. JAG will want to read this."

Tom caught Jim's wink.

The captain paused, as if thinking, as he thumbed through all their documents. Suddenly it dawned on Tom why the captain was going through all these regulations. He was giving him ammo. Pointing out the positives. Like you couldn't re-up if you couldn't put in the required number of years before retirement. A lot of soldiers reenlisted for the retirement benefits. That was perfectly legal. Next, Tom was hoping he would tell them where the booby traps were planted.

"This common law you have shown me, which allows substitution, one man for another, is dubious. Christ, it's from the Revolutionary War, gentlemen."

Lieutenant Cogriff perked up with a legitimate smile.

Small started to speak, but Captain Wulf put up a hand. "Excuse me, Major. The people over at JAG, Judge Advocate General, headquarters will have to check this out." He waved the documents in front of them. "I don't have any say in that department. But," he leaned forward and interlocked his fingers, "if—and this is a big *if*—if this happens, Private Lane, you will still have to pass your APFT and medical examination." The captain's voice rose. "Do you understand?"

"Yes, sir." Tom stiffened. His body had come to attention and he hadn't even realized it. "I am prepared to meet the standards."

Captain Wulf was being crystal clear. Maneuvering around JAG and the medical and Army Physical Fitness Test would be Tom's biggest obstacles. Isn't knowing where the traps are waiting for you half the battle? Or was Tom's assessment optimistic? He glanced over at Lieutenant Cogriff. "Monkey wrench" was the first phrase that came into his mind.

The captain circled. "Before you are dismissed and make your way over to JAG, may I inquire why these gentlemen were included in your group, Private Lane?" The captain's head bobbed toward Mr. Ricca and Mr. Jordan.

Both Tom and his son started to speak, but Tom won out. "Just in case the army tries something tricky."

"Yes, I see. Everything that's newsworthy . . ." The captain directed his comment at Jordan: "And I suppose a protective father sells newspapers.

Be careful you don't taint your commendable reputation, Private Lane, or the army's. The United States Army is not forgiving."

Now the captain was speaking from personal experience. "Sir," said Tom, "I don't want publicity. That is not why I am here. Please believe me. I just want to keep my son safe."

"So does the army. That is something you and I can agree on. Until JAG says otherwise, Private Lane, I will assume this is a go. You will take your son's place in all ways. Do I make myself clear? He is nineteen, correct?"

Tom nodded. For a split second, Tom thought the worst was over. He soon discovered he was wrong.

"I will expect you to pass Physical Test at the standards for his age group. Do you understand?"

"Sir, he is more than twice his son's age," said Small. "This is highly unusual, not according to the regs, and unfair."

"Major Small, unfair is not in the army's dictionary. And none of what we are talking about here is regulation. I am asking for a demonstration of commitment."

Out of the corner of his eye, Tom saw Lieutenant Cogriff's lips curve up in a pleased expression.

Jim Small raised a hand to object further, but Tom stopped him. "I accept your terms. I understand, sir. "

And Tom really did. He had pushed for that same dedication from Donnie. Now it was his turn. Wulf was also telling him not to give them an excuse, not even the slightest, to use against him. But why was this guy, the captain, doing all this? It was clear the lieutenant didn't have a clue what was really being said in this room. The subtleties of this conversation were too involved for the new officer. But something was behind the captain's tactics.

"Good," said Captain Wulf. "Then Donald Lane may return home if JAG also passes on this. But he should be prepared to return if summoned."

Donnie nodded that he understood.

"Lieutenant Cogriff will take over from here, gentlemen. JAG is your next stop. I will call to apprise them of the situation. Someone will be expecting you. Good luck either way, Private Lane. I will be checking in with JAG on the legal ramifications of this dilemma. I will also be checking on your performance, if the exchange is allowed. Your lawyer will keep you updated. Dismissed!"

Tom's back straightened as he snapped to attention and threw up a salute.

The captain returned his salute with a smirk. Tom supposed it was because he wasn't officially in yet. The captain handed all the documents back to Jim Small. "I'll need copies of everything. And before Private Lane puts on the uniform, lifts a weapon, or sets foot in the barracks, I need to hear from JAG."

The group spent the next three hours at JAG headquarters. They told their story to one person and repeated it for several others. Each time, they moved up the chain of command structure. Finally, after Small threatened to spend the night and Ricca and Jordan started calling in the story to their newspapers, JAG declared a temporary truce. Tom would stay on a provisional basis.

They returned to where they had started and saw Lieutenant Cogriff and Staff Sergeant Steiner peeking out the window of Building A-117, waiting for Tom.

Jim Small asked Tom, "What do you want me to do?"

"Nothing. This is what we wanted. There is no reason to cause trouble. Challenging the whole damn US Army can wait for another time. Just keep the pressure on JAG and let me know the outcome."

Paul Jordan said, "That Captain Wulf was not the pompous man I knew. Do you mind if I do a little digging? Maybe we," he indicated Mr. Ricca, "could write up something, kind of a human interest story on you, Tom. It would give us a venue for follow-up if things get dicey."

"I think that's a good idea, Tom," said Jim. "He can do it without naming names."

Tom turned to Frank and Donnie. "What do you think? Maybe we should just wait for JAG's verdict?"

They both shrugged.

Tom watched Staff Sergeant Steiner and Lieutenant Cogriff step outside. They continued to talk as they looked and pointed at him. Tom now knew how a turkey felt the day before Thanksgiving.

"Here we go," Tom said. At last the lieutenant and the sergeant broke apart. Tom had no doubt they had been hatching a plan. The lieutenant went back into the administration building. Staff Sergeant Steiner peeled off, eyeing Tom.

"Private Lane, follow me. I'm personally going to help you get settled in."

Tom told everyone to go on home. "I'll be in touch," he said, wondering how the sergeant could make "settling in" sound so ominous. Then it struck him, of course: It's the US Army.

He glanced up at heaven, and as he followed behind the sergeant, he whispered to God, *This is some more of the fine print in your contract. Right?*

Chapter 18

"I, Thomas Lane, do solemnly swear that I will support and defend the Constitution of the United States against all enemies, foreign and domestic; that I will bear true faith and allegiance to the same; and that I will obey the orders of the President of the United States and the orders of the officers appointed over me, according to regulations and the Uniform Code of Military Justice. So help me God."

So this is it, thought Tom. He should have known Lieutenant Cogriff wouldn't let him rest his head on one of the army's pillows without taking the oath. Captain Wulf administered it in his office as soon as Cogriff made a fuss that Tom putting on the uniform wouldn't fly unless he had been duly sworn in first.

So here he was back in the army, semi-officially. It's a beginning. The captain said JAG would nullify the decision if his claim proved invalid. Tom cautioned himself to check that out with Jim Small.

The sheer delight in Cogriff's eyes when he took the oath said it all. Now Tom was his.

After the oath, Cogriff sent Tom off to the Central Issue Facility to load up. By the time he had collected all his equipment, Tom was wondering if they sold Bengay at the PX. He had forgotten he would be carrying a lot of extra weight, a full rucksack, IBA (Individual Body Armor), an ACH (Advanced Combat Helmet), and, of course, his assigned weapon, which he would pick up over at the arms room.

Now that he had his gear, Tom shed any and all remnants of his civvies. Socks, shoes, and underwear were discarded. He was khaki through and through. If he wanted to be part of his unit, there was no better way to do it than to dress, act, and talk like a grunt. In fact, it felt normal to be back in uniform the moment he slipped his feet into his desert boots.

One of the guys in his squad came into the barracks right after Tom had finished arranging himself and his gear army-correct.

"All dressed to play soldier?" The kid came ambling up to Tom with that "I'm king of this hill and you don't belong on my heap" attitude.

Tom nodded. As he met him halfway across the dayroom, Tom's own swagger returned without missing a beat. There was more of the Ranger on the way.

"So, you're Donnie's fucking old man."

"And I thought my gray hairs didn't show," Tom said. "But, kid, is that the best you could come up with?" It had taken Tom years to leave his colorful vocabulary behind when he rejoined the civilian race. A few hours back in the uniform and some interesting military expressions were already floating to the surface.

Tom gave God notice, thinking, *Could you play deaf for a minute? 'Cause I'm trying to fit in with these guys.*

He closed in on the kid. "So you're the no-pecker king around here. Jake, isn't it?"

Jake looked confused.

"Yeah, I know who you are. Try not to piss in your pants when you answer." Tom looked at his nails casually, as if grease or maybe blood was under them. He remembered that he had always won the "no flinching" contests.

The kid nodded. Jake's eyes flashed right and left. He jammed his hands in his pockets and worked his shoulders.

"Are we going to have a freaking problem here, Jake?" Tom took two slow and easy steps closer, and smiled. Out of the corner of his eye, he saw three more of Jake's friends trail in behind him and fan out.

One of them, Tom guessed by the boy's accent, was from either Newark or Jersey City. He said, "I never had Donnie pegged for such a pussy. Sending his dad."

Jake smiled.

Tom saw Jake's confidence increase when the numbers were in his favor. "Smart, Jake. 'Cause you will need help." Tom's smile broadened.

"We just want to show you around. Take care of you, old man," offered Jake.

Jake seemed to be the obvious leader of the group. So, Tom calculated, he'd have to either crush Jake or win him over. Then the rest would fall in line. Tom had never liked punks. But since Jake was somebody's kid, maybe he'd give this punk some latitude.

"Is it true you were"—Jake spat on the floor like he had tasted curdled milk—"a fucking hard-ass Ranger? Hard to believe, since your son is such a gutless wimp."

Tom's second thought was maybe not. He'd go with the crushing plan. "You want me to kick your sorry ass to prove it, kid?"

The pissing contest was short. Albert walked in. He came over and stood in front of Tom. "If anyone has a problem with D-Dad, they have a problem with me." The kid swelled up to his full, sizable mass.

"Albert, I can take care of myself," said Tom.

"Dad?" Jake laughed and repeated, "D-D-Dad it is. You finally found out who your daddy is, DA? Are they all as stupid as you down on the farm, boy?"

Tom's hackles rose. That sealed it. A little devastation was called for. Tom was sure that by morning "Dad" would be his unofficial name. Of course, there would be variations on that title with imaginative profanities attached.

Tom braced himself at Albert's back. He looked at Jake and offered, "Let's do this." He waved him forward. "I've got more important things to do. But this will only take a minute. So come on, you little snot-nosed shitbag." Tom's stance was wide, and he was light on his toes as he moved forward.

Jake's body stiffened as he brought up his hands to protect himself. His rigor was a sure sign of his inexperience. Jake lacked the fluency of a skilled fighter whose body was loose, ready to make a move. Jake only knew the theory.

Tom also understood that Jake couldn't back down after all his bluster. That was the first rule in any pissing contest.

As soon as Jake took half a step forward, Tom was on him. He ducked under Jake's wild swing, spun around him with his leg extended, and swept Jake's legs out from under him. The kid hit the floor hard. Then Tom came full circle to face the kid, who was lying on his back. Before Jake could even attempt to get back on his feet, Tom dropped a knee and the full weight of his body down onto Jake's chest. The ballpoint pen Tom had had in his hand when Jake entered was now neatly pushing in on the coronary artery at the boy's throat.

His face inches from Jake's, Tom said, "Boy, if this was a knife," he showed everyone the pen, "your blood would be on it. Death happens only once, son."

This was Tom's shock-and-awe campaign. And from the expressions on the faces of the other young men, including Albert, his goal had been accomplished. Now that he had met that mark, Tom reached down and jerked Jake onto his feet.

As Jake straightened his uniform, Steiner came in.

"What's going on here?"

Over the sergeant's shoulder, Tom spied Lieutenant Cogriff cross in front of the open door. Had he been outside the whole time listening? Had he sent Jake on this fool's errand?

No one answered the sergeant. Jake's pallor confirmed that something had happened, but Steiner didn't ask again. Instead he chased everyone out, sending Tom to the arms room to pick up his assigned weapon and the rest to the obstacle course. Tom felt like a kid who'd been given a time-out. Part of him wanted a little excitement. Then he decided it must have been the clothes looking for action.

As Tom walked by, he warned Jake in a soft, menacing tone. "Tell your friends— anyone who bad-mouths my son or Albert again will be sucking shit headfirst out of the latrine."

"DA, get over here!" Steiner screamed.

Over his shoulder Tom saw Steiner haranguing Albert and repeatedly hitting the kid on the back of the head as if to hammer in his message.

It was interesting how this didn't bother Tom all that much now. And he doubted if Albert felt Steiner was anything more than a bothersome fly buzzing around him. It was what Tom had been used to and what he would once again accept.

As a sergeant, Tom had used the same tactics. His own men had come to expect and even crave the verbal abuse he dished out. Taking it had made them feel strong, tough. And anything that sparked the belief that they were invincible just might give them an edge and help keep them alive. That refrain, "keep them alive," repeated itself in Tom's head. When it passed through a second time, it became "keep my son alive."

He would also have to remember that there was nothing personal about the United States Army. It was never you did something wrong, it was *soldier* or *private*. You were one of many, a small part of a much larger machine. And it was never I am pissed, it was your commanding officer, the army, or your fellow soldiers are pissed.

However, when Tom arrived to collect his weapon, he quickly discovered his case might be a little different and more personal.

Cogriff had already changed Tom's MOS from driver to gunner. Of course, he wasn't going to be carrying a nice light M4 carbine equipped with a M68 red-dot sight like everyone else. Oh no. Tom was going to be hauling around the M240B, a machine gun. It had a big-ass M145 optic, a PEQ4 laser aiming device for night, a fifty-round starter belt of 7.62, and a two-hundred-round belt of 7.62 in a drum. And let's not forget that he would have a nine-millimeter handgun with a seven- to thirteen-round magazine on his hip. So that little change added up to Tom carrying, along with his other gear, an extra 125 pounds plus. Cogriff had been a busy little . . . Tom almost thought "bee," but then changed it to "wasp." Yes, the paper pusher did have a stinger.

When a corporal handed Tom his weapon, he said, "Lieutenant Cogriff said you were a Ranger. Is that true, Dad?" The pudgy kid was energetically chewing bubble gum. He offered Tom a piece as he blew a bubble.

"No, thanks." Geez. That was fast. So his label was already traveling around post. "In another life, kid, I was a Ranger."

"The lieutenant also said to tell you you'll be qualifying with that," he popped a bubble as he pointed at the machine gun, "at the end of next week."

"Thanks." The battle between Cogriff and Tom had officially started. The lieutenant was pushing him toward failure. And Tom supposed the M240B he was hefting onto his shoulder was Cogriff's declaration of war.

"Hey, good luck. Once a Ranger, always a Ranger. Right? You guys are like those fucking musketeers. All for one." The gum chewer stuck out his hand to bump fists. "Good luck to ya." Then he stuck out his hand to shake.

Tom wondered, once again, what he was doing. The line was backing up behind him.

He quickly shook the kid's hand and felt a scrap of paper. When he was outside, he opened it. It said, "Hoorah. For Tommy." He smiled, thinking, *Yeah, for both my boys.*

Later Tom took off to find the barber. Albert offered to show him the way.

"Albert, I wouldn't volunteer a lot around here. But I appreciate this. Time to get the old head shaved." Tom rubbed his head.

"I don't have anything else t-to do. It's OK, Dad." He checked Tom's hair like he was looking for lice. "You got some white ones sticking out. My daddy didn't have a white hair in his head when he passed."

"What happened to your father, Albert?"

"A t-tractor accident. I was eleven. Mama says that's when I started having trouble talkin'. I was riding with Daddy when it happened."

"I'm sorry about your dad, Albert."

"It's OK. I don't stutter so much now; only when I'm nervous. My four older brothers and I tried to keep the farm going. It worked for a while. But we weren't any good at it. Mama sold it last year. So here I am."

As they walked, Albert told Tom he was from Indiana. "A corn-fed, pig-farming boy," is the way Albert described himself. He said he'd gotten so strong by lifting hogs up by their hind legs to be castrated.

"Then my daddy would slice their balls right off with one whack." Albert demonstrated. His hand chopped the air. "And then I'd paint this blue stuff on where he had lopped 'em off. That was all there was to it."

Tom and Albert had just reached the parade grounds as the story ended. Dusk was settling in when they heard the first trumpet notes of taps over the PA. The flag was being lowered. The quick flood of patriotism and memories threw Tom off balance for a second.

He had heard taps played many times. Mostly at the end of each day of his military life. But what hit him the hardest during the first notes were the men at whose funerals it had been played. Within the circle of the setting sun, Tommy's face materialized, glowing larger than the rest of the ghostly images.

Tom and Albert turned to face the American flag and saluted. Their eyes were riveted on the red, white, and blue. By the time the flag was properly folded and the last note of the trumpet was dying away, the sky had taken on a rosy glow.

Tom turned and looked at Albert.

The boy's tan cheeks glistened with tears. Albert wiped his nose with the back of his hand. "Shit. Sorry, D-Dad. You should have seen what a wimp I was at my daddy's funeral when they played it."

"It has the same effect on me. Don't worry about it, kid."

"Thanks, Dad."

For an instant, in these last rays of light, Albert looked like Tommy. His first child had not been as bulky as Albert, but they had the same fair hair. Tom blinked. He took this to mean God was telling him he was on the right track. Or was his family increasing? Did he have a third son now? He patted Albert on the back.

They walked on, and Albert said, "Hey, Dad, did you know the flag represents, 'a living country and is itself'"—he paused and scratched his chin before continuing to recite—"oh yeah, 'is itself c-considered a living thing'?" He smiled, pleased with his memory.

"Where did you learn that, son?"

"US Code, T-title 36. I memorized it for my dad. He said the

American flag is alive in each one of us whenever we pick up a gun to d-defend it. It's like protecting a person who c-can't do it for themselves. My daddy was army; that's why I joined this branch of the military."

"Albert, don't ever let someone convince you that you're not smart. That is the smartest thing I've heard all day. And your dad was right." Tom also wondered how many young men joined the service to follow in their parent's footsteps. Sadly, Tom thought, Tommy had. But not Donnie.

Tom's FIRST NIGHT BACK in the army was restless and sleepless. His bunk was right across from Albert's. They shared a college dorm-style room.

As Tom was dropping off to sleep, Albert told him that the men had started a pool, "Like the lottery." It had reached five hundred bucks within hours after Tom moved in. To win you had to be right in two categories: the number of days Tom would last and whether he would be walking out or going out feet first.

Tom wondered about those very same things.

Night was creeping toward morning. Lying in his bunk waiting for the sleep that didn't come, all Tom could think of was, *So here I am in hell. Hell is a happy place.* He repeated this to himself several times. He was happy because Donnie wasn't here. It was hell because he was sleeping in a lumpy, smelly narrow bed without Christine.

"In fact, it stinks," whispered Tom to himself.

Tom's olfactory discomfort increased. He got up and paced. Finally he sniffed at himself. His skin reeked. He took a shower. When he came back the odor was still there. The foul smell made him want to vomit. He followed the pungent odor and discovered that the disgusting stench was in his bed. At three a.m., Tom pulled the dirty underwear, socks, and soiled jock straps out from under his sheet and from inside his pillow. He took them outside and decorated the outside of the barracks door with them. It was part of the life, pulling pranks. But seeing who would pay in the morning would be even more fun.

It was his turn to mark his territory.

Chapter 19

BIG DAY. While the rest of the unit was out—in full battle-rattle sweatin', pukin', and eatin' dust, enjoying an extended PT because of the dirty laundry the sergeant had found—Tom was off to prove he was fit to also receive that same abuse. In other words, it was time for Tom's dreaded medical exam. He was seeing the docs. It was possible he might meet all of them, if JAG and Lieutenant Cogriff had anything to do with it.

The lieutenant made a brief appearance at the hospital. Tom saw him out of the corner of his eye as he waited outside the clinic. Now what was going on in the lieutenant's pencil-pushing, calculating brain? He didn't have long to wonder.

"Lane," said Cogriff.

"Yes, sir."

He checked side to side. "You have some influential friends here who have *suggested* I take good care of you. So I have a supply clerk job with your name on it when we arrive in Afghanistan. That is, if JAG approves, you get your SRP, and you cooperate."

Tom didn't respond. The guy wasn't a good actor.

"In front of these young boys I have to appear tough. You understand. We are mature men. But there is no reason we can't get along." He smiled. Then, louder, he said, "Carry on, soldier."

"Yes, sir."

Was it true? Did his note-passing mystery supporter or one of Jim Small's contacts put in a good word, pull some strings? A desk sounded good. But why was the lieutenant making nice with him? To throw Tom off guard? The better question: Who was this spanking new lieutenant trying to suck up to? Tom vowed caution.

What he did know from his experience was that a new lieutenant irritated everyone, especially if they put their noses into NCO business. Technically, Tom was Steiner's problem. And Cogriff's micromanaging was sure to be getting under Staff Sergeant Steiner's skin. That would make Cogriff not just Tom's enemy but the sergeant's, too. Things just got better and better.

As he returned to his chair to await instructions after putting on a hospital gown, Tom spied Cogriff chatting with one of the doctors. This was the second time Tom had caught him in the background of his new world. So he's trying to play all the angles. Keep the brass happy while the passive-aggressive little shit sticks it to me.

One of the JAG lawyers had met with Tom twice. He'd answered all of his questions during their first meeting. The second one, this morning, was more of a threat session than an exchange of legal information. The lawyer listed all the penalties and hardships and even the jail time Tom might avoid if he would just give up his foolish, impossible quest and go home. The "go home" part was appealing for about three seconds. Then the lawyer said, "And send your son back." *Clang*, a gong sounded in Tom's mind. After that, Tom told him not to bother him again, that his lawyer would handle everything. He scribbled Jim's cell number on a scrap of paper and handed it to the young lawyer to take back to his superior.

"Oh, what crap we weave," Tom whispered. He was immediately directed to the third floor for his first appointment. Bad sign. Everyone was ready for him, even the receptionist.

An hour into his exam and Tom was thanking God he had taken care of his ingrown toenail. He had never had such a comprehensive physical. They were searching his every nook and cranny for an excuse to throw him out. It was *painfully* obvious.

If Frank were here, Tom mused, he would be a nervous wreck.

Wearing a thin gown that tied in the back, Tom was glad all the exams were done in one building and he didn't have to chance his butt coming down with pneumonia as he moved from one facility to the next. The gown was also a sign to get ready to be prodded as far up the ass as was medically possible without general anesthesia. He steeled himself. They were going to come at him from both ends.

Shots, X-rays, dental exams—while he was still in his little hospital gown? Who could figure that one out?—eye exam, and blood work were all scrutinized. The last one was the part he disliked the most.

Tom had never minded the sight of blood, but needles were a whole other ball game. He had to do a lot of deep breathing with his head between his knees while they filled six tubes.

Every new medic in the place had a chance at him. His veins were as easy to see as a blue river in a landscape of snow. But several techs said he had tough skin and rolling veins, so again and again they would put that needle in and wiggle it around. And if one wasn't successful at it, there was always another eager new medic waiting in the wings. Tom was sure the army recruited its phlebotomy people from a long list of thirsty vampires.

Before leaving for the hospital that morning, Tom had done a finger stick to check his blood sugar. It was a little high, due to the stress, he supposed. But it was still within the proper limits. He was taking his meds like clockwork. And three days away from Christine's home cooking, he had lost another pound. So Tom was confident all these tests would come out well.

Still, Frank's warnings echoed. Frank had told him to resist telling them anything about his diabetes, and Tom had agreed. But if he got caught in a lie, all this would be down the tubes. He would be on his way to jail, and Donnie would be on his way to Afghanistan. And that was not acceptable.

So Tom figured he would invoke one of the army's own laws: If they didn't ask, he wouldn't tell. But he was just going to focus on the "don't tell" section.

Four and a half hours later, Tom was still shuffling from one drafty hallway to another. Hell, his little paper slippers were wearing thin. More of that time was spent waiting and walking than being tested. He had come to believe that in his present garb, the elevators were the worst. The cold air went right up and through the back of his hospital gown, even after they gave him a robe to cover his shiny white butt cheeks.

Humiliation after humiliation was being heaped on him, but Tom didn't care. Bring it on. He wondered if they thought having his ass hanging out would make him change his mind? If they did, they were underestimating him. And that was good.

After forty-five minutes of waiting in a drafty public hall on a cold plastic chair, Tom decided this was his chance to call the shop.

Cecilia answered and rushed to get Frank, as though Tom was calling from Mars or something. Tom heard both queens blubbering in the background.

Frank told him Jim had been in contact with JAG. "There's a conference call going on between them right now. So far, no news," said Frank. He also told Tom that Christine was having him over that night for dinner. And everything was "business as usual" at the machine shop.

"Frank, tell Christine I will call this weekend. The next three days will be pretty busy." Tom ended the phone call by saying, "Thanks, buddy, for taking care of things. You know, it's not too bad being back."

"Give 'em time," said Frank, the eternal optimist. "What are you doing right now?"

"The medical." Tom heard Frank snorting fast through his nose. When Frank got excited, the emphysema kick-started. "I'm cruising through this. Don't sweat it. Calm down."

"Oh yeah, sure. Watch it, or they'll have your ass behind bars for providing false information and I'll be sending your Christmas card to Fort Leavenworth."

"Thanks, Frank, for cheering me up. I'm glad I called."

As Tom hung up, he chuckled to himself. It was good to hear Frank's old, gravelly voice.

At last a corpsman came over and told Tom he could get dressed.

"Are you sure? I was beginning to think the nurses liked looking at these gorgeous hairy legs." Tom offered a peek.

The corpsman had zero sense of humor. "Be back here at fifteen hundred. You are going to see Colonel Chesney." That made the corps-man smile.

Tom was down to the final step of the process: the talk with the doctor who would review all his results. Dr. Chesney's office was one floor up. Tom had passed by it in his travels. But why did that kid give him the "you'll get yours" smirk?

It was two in the afternoon and Tom hadn't eaten anything since breakfast. He was feeling light-headed and needed to eat and take his meds. So he quickly dressed and grabbed some lunch in the hospital cafeteria, sneaked his meds, then came right back and waited for the doctor.

Right on the stroke of 1500 (that's three p.m. for civilians), Tom was called into the doctor's office. He put on his best manufactured smile. Tom rationalized that disarming his opponent was a tactic worth trying.

Dr. Ben Chesney, his full name written on a plaque on his desk that faced Tom, seemed a pleasant enough guy on first encounter. The colonel had a white coat over his greens. He offered Tom his hand.

Tom guessed he hadn't gotten the "get rid of Private Tom Lane" memo, because he was the first nice person he'd met all day. Tom and the doctor were about the same age. This would be a breeze.

"Take a seat, Private Lane."

The doc sat down next to Tom instead of retreating behind his desk.

Tom initiated the conversation. "Looks like you have been stationed at Dix for a while, Doc." Tom's index finger circled, indicating the pictures and diplomas covering the sunny yellow walls. "You even merit a window."

"Yes. I'm stationed stateside nowadays."

In addition to the family memorabilia on the walls were pictures of the doctor with troops.

"You were in the Persian Gulf," Tom commented. "And a few other interesting places, I see."

"I changed directions a few years back. Went to medical school in my younger days; army paid the bill. Now I'm putting those skills to use in a full-time practice."

Tom didn't say more. The doc was a member of Delta Force. Tom recognized the uniform in the pictures and the red patch with the black dagger on the sleeve. He had worked with a few of these secretive army bastards. They were referred to as bastards because they worked in small independent units and were mavericks.

This doctor had done counterterrorism, counterinsurgency, and national intervention operations. Covert missions like rescuing hostages and raids. In other words, the doc's MOS had been walking through fire. Suddenly that breeze Tom had thought he was going to ride on died down, and the corpsman's smirk flashed in his memory. They had Tom paired with the most hard-ass doc in the place.

It struck Tom that the photos of the doc and his buddies were hung as if in some special order. Categorized maybe. All of them had the exact same frames, were the same size, and hung on their own special section of the wall. They were lined up horizontally in rows of four, with two full rows and one picture starting a third row. Tombstones. It came to Tom in a rush. They were lined up like tombstones.

Dr. Chesney saw Tom checking the photos. He looked away, pulled a thick folder off his desk, and opened it.

"Let's see what we've got here, Private Lane. I'd like to review a few things. I know by now you have answered a hundred questions, but I promise there will just be a few more." He smiled. "I don't get many privates your age coming in that door. So I want to be absolutely sure you are fit for the rigors of duty."

"Shoot, Doc. I mean, yes, sir."

"We're a little less formal around here, so relax. Doc is fine."

Tom nodded. He sounds like a Delta—they never paid any attention to rank.

"Any history of heart problems, high blood pressure, diabetes, or thyroid problems?"

"Nope." Tom concentrated on the "don't tell" common law.

"Depression, alcoholism, we can skip the Pap smear section." Neither man chuckled. "How about cancer?"

"No to all of the above."

The doc checked boxes. "Good. Excellent. Just a few more."

"I'm healthy as a horse, Doc."

"It seems so. Any trouble pissing? Can you write your name in the snow? Prostate problems can sneak up on a man. Does your urine smell funny, sweet?"

"Nope. Can't say I have any of those problems. I'm not that ancient."

"How's your appetite? Any indigestion, foods you can't eat, high cholesterol, special diet, or reflux problems?"

"No. I answered all of these questions at least twice already, sir."

"Let me check your labs. OK. Are you on any medications?"

Tom hesitated, then shook his head to indicate a negative. Inside a voice counted lie number two.

"Now take off your shoes. I want to look at your feet."

"What?"

"Fallen arches. You know the army travels on its feet."

Big mistake, taking off my shoes. He should never have underestimated the doc. Tom never dreamed this guy would come at him from all sides. He was sneaky as hell.

"And how long have you been a diabetic?"

"What? I'm not a diabetic."

"I know that's what you said. And your previous medical history doesn't show it. Of course, you were in your twenties then. Now you've put on some extra weight and years. And your labs are borderline. I also see several areas of poor circulation on your feet. Which is why the spot where someone cut out an ingrown toenail has never healed properly."

Tom was dumbfounded. He could only stare.

"I gave you a chance to come clean, Private Lane. In fact, I gave you several chances. I asked you flat out if you were a diabetic, and you lied. I asked if you had anything in your urine, any dietary restrictions, and you said no. I asked if you took any medications, and you denied it. Shall we do a finger stick right here?"

"No. Listen, Doc—" Tom stopped short.

"Before you dig yourself in any deeper, you should know we do a broad spectrum analysis for drugs both in your blood and in your pee. And your blood work and urine panel confirms you are taking a hypoglycemic, I would guess one of the sulfonylureas. Now, stop jerking me around and tell me why I shouldn't have your lying ass riding my boot off this post. Why, and this part is strictly for my personal edification, does an old Ranger like you re-up?"

Tom was caught red-handed, or as his mother used to say, black-tongued.

He shifted into defensive mode. "I know you have been told to get rid of me. Who was it, Lieutenant Cogriff, someone over at JAG, Sergeant Steiner, or Captain Wulf?"

"No one dictates how I practice medicine, Private Lane. No one knows anything about your labs. Yet." He waved Tom's medical file at him and then threw it on his desk. "So tell me what is so god-awful important that it makes you want to go through all this shit to be back in the army. You've served honorably."

Tom's mind was whirling. What should he do? His eyes traced the flecks in the maroon and brown epoxy-coated floor.

"Tell me, damn it, or we are done here! And I don't want to hear any crap about getting even for 9/11. No hero shit. All the heroes I know are dead." The doc's eyes wandered briefly to the pictures.

The wall. His wall. It was a memorial. Just like the Vietnam wall down in DC. But this one was just for the doc, something he faced every day of his life. Tom recognized the pain in the doc's face. He had some of those same lines of grief etched on his own.

Tom's breath came out in a great whoosh. He didn't even know he had been holding it. He rubbed his hands hard and fast down his face and hid behind them while he thought. Could he trust this man? The faces on the wall said yes. But there was a lot riding on this moment, so Tom quickly asked God for a sign.

When Tom showed his face, he immediately heard an old familiar sound. He must have looked anxious, because the doc put a hand on Tom's shoulder to allay his fears.

"It's nothing to worry about. In this old building the radiators bang and clang like they're the percussion section in a marching band. It happens all the time."

This was Tom's favorite tune. "Doc, it's OK. Look, I'm here because . . ."

The doc straightened a misaligned family photo and nudged it away from the edge of the desk where it had been moved by the radiator's vibrations.

"I'm here because of my son. He joined the Guard at eighteen, a year after high school. He was just finishing his first semester of college when he was called up. And I want him to have a few more years of innocence. So I'm here to take his place. That's the simple version."

Dr. Chesney rocked back into his chair and then leaned forward again, resting his elbows on his knees. "Who cooked this bizarre plan up? It's amazing you got this far."

"Well, I've got the law on my side."

Tom told him the whole story about the Revolutionary War law Frank had found. And he told him he had a friend helping who was a lawyer.

"You're like that guy who said his son was in a runaway balloon. A publicity hound. Using your kid! Self-serving shit like this pisses me off! Service people deserve respect. They do an impossible job. I won't give you a medical release so you can parade around for the media and soil the uniform!"

"No! God, no. Please give me a chance to explain. Please, Doc." Tom motioned for him to sit. "Listen. I'm telling the truth. I'm not a wacko. I'm here for my son. Well, actually both my sons."

Agitated, the doc got back up and circled like a panther.

Tom was a little worried. The doc was a few years younger than he was and in excellent shape.

Dr. Chesney sat back down. He was thoughtful for a moment, then said, "Lane, Thomas Lane. I thought I had heard that name before."

"Yes, my oldest boy died three years ago in Afghanistan."

"Because of him I'll listen."

Something pulled Tom's eyes back to the family photo.

"Look, you have a family." Tom picked up the picture.

The doc and his wife had their arms around a girl about twelve and a boy about fifteen. They all had brown hair, and features from each parent were replicated in the children. It was an all-American portrait. Beside the photo, in an attached frame, was a poem. It had been written with a bright red coloring crayon.

Tom read the words that came after the poem, "I love you, Daddy." The signature was on the very edge of the paper: "Stan the dragon slayer." This was the only space where the young scribe could squeeze in his name.

Dr. Chesney jerked the frame out of Tom's grasp but did not return it to its former position. It rested on his knee. He glanced at it.

"Could you just take a minute to," Tom's thoughts stuttered, "to think about what I am saying as if it was your son, Stan? Because, Doc, it could be, in just three years." He pointed to the boy in the photo.

"He plays basketball," said the doc. "He's pretty good."

"My kid has a great hook shot." He clasped his hands and worked his fingers as if warming up to twiddle his thumbs. Tom's rough skin made a raspy sound.

"Stan's a sophomore in high school, right, Doc?"

"Freshman."

"OK. Stan and you will be having this conversation next year, when he is a sophomore. It goes like this. He comes to you to talk about college. You tell him you don't have the money for college, so you suggest the Guard to help pay for it. You cosign for him to join when he is seventeen. Before you know it, a few years have passed, Stan's in college, rolling along, getting great grades, has a serious girlfriend, and his unit is called up. And with the blink of an eye, your son's life changes direction. He is going to be one of the thousands being sent halfway around the world to a place where the people hate him, and he's going to be part of an escalation against terrorism. All because you wanted him to go to college but didn't have the money."

The doc was quiet, staring at that poem.

"He was proud of my service and looked up to his brother."

"Are you the father of *that* Thomas Lane?"

"Yeah." Tom felt uncomfortable and shifted in his chair. "Now it's his

brother, Donnie. Christ! I might have just as well bought him a plane
ticket to the Middle East right then and there." Tom's brain was firing
as fast as it could. He had to find the words to convince this man. "You
are responsible for your son. You're his father. It's our job as dads to keep
them safe, and that's why I am here. I have to undo, correct what I have
done to my son. Me dying isn't the most horrible thing I can imagine.
But my son . . . another son"—Tom swallowed—"he is nineteen years
old. It wasn't that long ago that he was going to the prom and worrying
that the corsage he picked out wouldn't match his date's dress. Christ, I
just taught him how to drive a stick shift."

"So you're not trying to make a joke of the army, get yourself on Twitter and YouTube?"

"No way. Do I look like a guy who wants this ugly face out there?
Doc, I don't even own a cell phone."

Dr. Chesney smirked, then turned silent again.

"I served in the military . . ."

"Yes, Private Lane, everybody knows you were a Ranger."

"That's not what I'm talking about. I just mean I am proud of my service. I believe in words like truth, honor, and justice for all. And I was willing to fight against those who opposed those principles. Do I think I am
a monster? No. Did I kill some people during the actions I was involved
in? Yes. Do I want my kid to be forced to make those choices and take on
those memories? You know what I'm talking about, Doc. We were never
young again after we experienced combat. And once you've seen war, you
never stop seeing it. Is that what you want for Stan?"

"I'm serving. My son won't have to. The war will be over by then."

"I've played that same tune, Doc. Don't count on it." Tom reached
into his breast pocket. "By the way, this is Donnie." He pulled out a
family picture and named each family member. "That's Tommy junior,
after me. But this time I don't want Donnie following after me. When
he first found out he was going to the Middle East, he stayed glued to
the TV. I put that fear in him. Checking the casualty counts every night.
Listening to stories of collateral damage, civilians, even children, crippled

and killed. I forced him to join the Guard. Now I'll do whatever it takes to keep him from that, to keep him safe. I have to. Less than that is surrender, my failure."

Both men grew quiet.

Tom murmured, "He thinks stuff over too much. And too much thinking can—" The doc interrupted, finishing his sentence.

"Can get you killed."

The doc still held the poem in his hand.

"Do you think I wanted to abandon my wife, daughter, and son, Doc? This family?" He held out the picture. "I know I can't choose a life for my son. Maybe he'll even join up at another time. But I can protect him a little longer. That's why I am here. That's all I'm doing."

"You're a white knight." Dr. Chesney stood and walked around before returning to lean against his desk. He cleared his throat. "Slaying dragons. That's what I use to tell Stan I was doing when I was deployed. He was three when I started reading him this Hilary Lind poem, 'The Dragon Slayer.'" He read the words his son had written:

> Within your soul a fire burns
> A love for king and kin
> Stout of heart and courage too
> Built to fight and win
>
> Shoulders broad and mighty hands
> To carry shield and sword
> Armed with virtue and with truth
> For service to your Lord
>
> Dragon slayer await the call
> To enter battles fray
> To face the dragons of your time
> To fight and win the day
>
> But for now enjoy the dream
> Of action, war and quest
> And lay your sleepy little head
> Upon my loving chest

Ben Chesney cleared his throat. "In this war . . . sometimes it's hard to recognize the dragons." The doc got up and reverently replaced the poem and family picture on the desk.

Tom said, "I never had a chance to say good-bye to Tommy. Maybe that was a blessing in disguise. I don't know. But what father is ever ready to say his last good-bye to his child without doing everything possible to save him? Because something told me, maybe it was God, that if I didn't stand in for my son it might just be . . ." Tom got choked up and couldn't continue.

"Your last good-bye," said the doc.

Tom waited. After a few seconds he added, "My boy and I are at your mercy. I'm committed to this course." He cleared his throat and waited. When he had better control of his emotions, he said, "That talking-to-God part . . . you're not sending me up to see the psych docs next, are you?"

"No. But if you had seen combat and hadn't talked to God, then maybe I'd send you."

The doctor paced faster, as if pushing a decision forward in his mind. Then he hurried over to his desk and sat down. Picking up Tom's medical records, he thumbed through until he came to the lab sheets. He scanned them again. Then he dashed to the door as though his feet were on fire.

"Nurse, bring me a urine cup. Oh, and a chem tube and syringe to test for drugs and blood glucose. Something is wrong here. These labs don't make sense; they need to be repeated."

"Doc, what are you doing? What good would repeating them do?" And more needles didn't appeal to Tom, either.

The nurse returned before Dr. Chesney could answer him.

She asked, "Do you want me to draw Dad's, sorry, the Private's blood, or call in a corpsmen?"

"No, I'll take care of this myself." The doc winked at her.

Tom assumed the wink meant that she, like everyone else in the damn hospital, was in on the "Dad" conspiracy and the doc was telling her he was doing his part.

"Do you have somewhere close by where I can fill that?" Tom pointed at the cup in the doc's hand.

After the door closed, Dr. Chesney gave Tom his "fox getting ready to steal the chickens" smile.

Tom's brow folded in on itself.

"A little privacy, if you don't mind." The doc went through a door into the adjacent bathroom.

Tom heard the doc's pee hitting the cup and then the toilet flushing and water running.

When the doc returned, he rested his arm on the desk as if he was going to challenge Tom to an arm-wrestling contest. But instead he applied a tourniquet to his own arm. Then, with a skill not displayed by those bloodsucking corpsmen Tom had been subjected to, the doc found a vein and filled a tube with his own blood.

Tom was speechless. Maybe he should go into politics? He guessed he had made a good argument. Tom was quick to confess, *I'm joking, God.*

"Doc, I didn't . . . this is too much. This is putting your career on the line. Not to mention your retirement benefits."

"You know, sometimes people talk about warriors like we are mindless machines, incapable of making independent decisions. But of course we are not. We feel it all. Maybe because of what we do, we may feel things more acutely than others. Every wound. Every loss. The ones we couldn't bring home. The ones we brought home broken . . . and who couldn't be put back together. And those are the feelings that keep us from becoming machines. We do an impossible job and make extraordinary decisions. *You* understand. When you came here you made such a choice: to go on a hopeless mission based on your feelings for your son. I'm doing the same."

He took some preprinted labels with Tom's name on them from a sheet inside the chart and plastered them on the urine cup and tube of blood. Dr. Chesney took the lab sheets with Tom's urine and blood drug analysis and glucose results out of the chart and fed them to the shredder. "I'll wipe them from the computer database later. Now get out of here. I'll take care of the rest."

"But . . ." Tom was overwhelmed and didn't know how to thank him.

"Oh wait. Roll up your sleeve. Don't start rolling it down until the nurse outside sees you doing it." The doc placed a fresh Band-Aid farther down on Tom's arm from where the other "vampires" had drawn blood. The ruse was complete.

"Also, stop by tomorrow and I'll give you a new sustained-release medication. I can get you down to one pill a day. You won't have the highs and lows you have been experiencing with the medication you're taking right now."

The doc shoved some samples into Tom's hand. Then he added, "I'll make sure you have what you need. I have friends, good friends, all over the world; they will help keep you supplied. But I need to check up on you for a few days with this new med. Lose some weight, watch your diet, and you might not need any medication."

"Doc, it's going to be hard finding reasons to come here too often. I mean, blisters won't cut it. And someone will get suspicious."

"Well, tomorrow I can handle. Come by early to pick up your medical release and I'll check you out. After that, come to my house on your off-duty hours." He shoved his address and phone number across the desk. "We live off the base. No one will know."

"Medical release? I got it. I . . ."

"Don't say anything, Private Lane. I might not be doing you a favor. You still have to pass your APFT."

"Doc, I—"

"Listen, Private Lane. The army has been my life. On the whole, it is not a bad life. But you can talk and talk to other people—family, friends, and nonmilitary folks—about what it is like, what we do and did during war, but they won't understand. They don't know that other world. Their world is looking for a bigger plasma screen and a great wine. We're cultures apart. Hell, most of them don't want to know what we do. But we know and we'll never forget. And sometimes in that other world we traveled by instinct. That's what I'm doing right now. I'm going on instinct. And my gut tells me this is the right thing to do."

The doc smiled and threw up his hands. "Who knows . . . maybe in some way what you are doing will benefit more people than just you and your son."

The colonel cocked his head to one side, before adding, "I have a feeling."

Chapter 20

"Seventy-one push-ups in under two minutes. Sit-ups: I want seventy-eight from each of you in less than two minutes. Two-mile run in thirteen minutes. Some of you haven't taken your PT test . . . yet." Cogriff posed like a puny imitation of General Patton.

Tom had never liked standing in formation in the half-light of early mornings. The dampness of the night still hung around, sending chills all over you. His battered carcass was quickly losing any body heat it had left from his warm bunk. His sweats did nothing to keep the cold at bay.

The entire platoon had been called out for PT at 0500.

Tom hadn't had an extra minute in the entire first week. He guessed that the news had traveled from the doc's blood, metaphorically speaking, to the lieutenant's ears. This was probably why Cogriff's big ears were almost as livid as his face in spite of the temperature. And the sermon the platoon was being forced to listen to was all because Tom had sinned. He had passed his medical.

Steiner was throwing everything at him. Tom had been doing extra duty every day. And, sadly for the army, he was still here. The start of his second week had prompted a special appearance from Lieutenant Cogriff.

If he had to listen to him too much longer, Tom thought, Lieutenant Cogriff might just drive him to drink, but never to quitting.

Tom knocked a wet clump of something half frozen off the toe of his sneakers. Frost crystals were forming on his exposed fingers and face. Didn't Cogriff know it was December? Tom guessed the lieutenant rarely experienced the weather without his nice warm, thick jacket.

Forty GI Janes and Joes, one hardly distinguishable from the other, had been standing here, fresh out of the steam heat of their barracks rooms, for forty-five minutes. Occasionally, each of them eyed Tom.

Tom was fully aware they were sending darts laced with promises of future retribution at him. He held back a yawn. If he didn't get his old body moving soon, he was afraid it might become a permanent fixture for birds to shit on.

The lieutenant continued flapping his lips. "I want a hundred and ten percent. We are the best. We will continue to be the best." He was back to messing in Staff Sergeant Steiner's territory.

"I will not allow one soldier," he stared at Tom, "to pull the rest of the platoon down. Most of you men have your SRPs. So I am sure you will want to encourage those who have not yet passed their tests."

Tom was the only one who had not passed PT. That was a no-brainer.

"Help them continue our high standards," said Lieutenant Cogriff.

Did the lieutenant really think anyone here wouldn't recognize a sack of bullshit when they heard it? Cogriff was standing up there with a bucket of red paint, handing out brushes. Tom figured he'd have bull's-eyes all over his body within an hour. You have to have been in the army to understand that what is said by someone like Cogriff usually means the opposite.

Tom noticed Staff Sergeant Steiner's knuckles were white and his face a contrasting purple. And Tom knew it wasn't because the sergeant was cold. For a half second he thought about shouting out, "There she blows," because truthfully Steiner looked like he might erupt. Was that fire coming out of Staff Sergeant Steiner's nose or just his breath in the cold air? *Inquiring people want to know,* Tom joked to himself. He kept his amusing thoughts private.

The lieutenant had interrupted PT. A big no-no. The platoon was Steiner's, and Steiner belonged to the lieutenant. That was the pecking order. Who was Cogriff to mess with years of military tradition? Tom was sure Cogriff showing up and showing off was something he had worked out on paper first. But, at least in Tom eyes, the eraser the lieutenant had glued to his butt wasn't changing a thing. Tom was staying, even if Cogriff set the whole platoon against him, as he was busy trying to do right now. Tom's name would not be deleted from the roster.

What some of these new grunts didn't know was that Cogriff was nothing. Tom had seen his kind before. It was what the sergeant wanted from the grunts that counted. They worked for him. Jake and a few of his buddies still hadn't grasped the facts of army life. Tom decided he might have to send them to night school.

The Sergeant had finally had enough. He tapped Lieutenant Cogriff on the shoulder and motioned for him to step to one side so the men couldn't hear their conversation.

They talked. Things became more animated. Tom noticed it wasn't going well. The lieutenant's finger jabbed back and forth between him and the sergeant.

The only person more angry than the lieutenant was Staff Sergeant Steiner. He was flexing his throbbing hands at the sides of his body. Tom could only suppose he was trying to keep himself from strangling the lieutenant. After all, it was something Tom was thinking of doing himself. If he had to choose a side, Tom would pick Steiner's. He was ready to jump in if the sergeant got carried away. Of course, his reaction might be a little slow, given the cold.

Captain Wulf interrupted the rising tempers. With a minimum number of words and one or two looks in Tom's direction, the storm passed.

Then the solution hit Tom. Shit! Their hostility would land on him. And sure enough, when the lieutenant walked off, Staff Sergeant Steiner barked, "Private Lane, set the pace! Push-ups!"

Tom snapped back, "Yes, Sergeant." Suddenly Tom was facedown in the half-frozen mud with the whole platoon following his lead.

"Lane, count 'em out!"

"Yes, Sergeant."

During the next five minutes, Tom felt he knew the pain of birthing a baby. Every muscle in his body contracted and ached. And if he had missed abusing even one muscle, *it* got his attention when they changed exercises.

Tom did forty-seven push-ups and fifty-eight sits-ups in the two minutes allotted for each standard. Not close enough to the max for a nineteen-year-old, and that was the goal Captain Wulf had demanded from Tom. Most of the other grunts in the platoon passed him after he ran out of breath, and they couldn't hear his count.

Several times when the sergeant turned his back, one of Jake's boys knocked Tom face-first into the frozen mud. And then Steiner would roar in Tom's ear and Tom would have to start the exercise all over again.

When the sergeant "invited" the platoon to take a nice, leisurely stroll with him, they all jumped to their feet.

"Yes, Sergeant!"

From somewhere deep inside, Tom had to admit the reply of the many voices sent a thrilling jolt through his blood. He fell in with the rest, smiling. That really irked Jake.

Staff Sergeant Steiner jogged alongside them as the platoon flag bearer started a cadence when they reached the end of the block.

"When I get to heaven, Saint Peter's gonna say, how did you earn your living, boy, how did you earn your pay? I replied as I grabbed my knife, I earned my living taking other people's lives, left . . . left . . . left right left on left right on left right left, left . . ."

Tom listened to the words and his chest swelled.

He jogged along easily. That cadence was something like the one he had chanted when he was a Ranger. *Danger Ranger*, he had yelled. Then he thought of that dragon slayer poem in the doc's office. And he checked out the young slayers all around him.

By the third hill, Tom was puffing. Of course, every time someone passed him, he got an elbow in the gut. Sometimes his fellow soldiers varied their payback and trampled on his feet or made an effort to trip him. He was forced to do the two steps forward, dodge to the right and one step back, fade left.

Tom noticed Albert was also lagging behind. The platoon was stretched out. They had just passed the six-mile marker. Tom's sneakers were soaked through and caked with icy mud. His legs felt like someone had tied cinderblocks to his ankles.

At the top of the hill, Tom could see the end of the run, where a warm breakfast was waiting, and suddenly his feet were a little lighter. It had taken only one week to fall back into the groove of looking forward to army food. That was both sick and understandable, Tom had decided. His diabetes needed regular feeding. And with all the exercise he had been doing, he'd eat anything. Of course, nothing could compare to Christine's cooking. Tom involuntarily drooled down his chin on his way up the hill.

Staff Sergeant Steiner joined the slackers, doing his "encouraging" in an ear-piercing bellow.

"Ham, get your lard ass moving!"

"Yes, Sergeant!" Albert replied.

"Move it, knucklehead. Show me what you got, DA!"

Albert tried sprinting the last hundred yards, but it didn't happen. There was no way the boy could make his bulk move any faster.

Tom was waiting for his turn. But the sergeant didn't harangue him. Nothing. Not a word. Steiner simply ignored him.

Tom was disappointed. He could use a push. Isn't that why people hire exercise coaches—to yell at them? It made no sense to Tom. Motivation, that's a big part of a sergeant's job. He wanted his share. Tom's pouting wasn't very armylike. Then he remembered how Donnie had jogged with him. And he missed his son.

Tom wondered if Steiner was smarter than he gave him credit for being? Then it came to him. Since Tom had once been a sergeant, he should have recognized the tactics. Steiner was using the old "please don't eat that last green bean. It's so good that I want it." You know, so kids will do the opposite. It worked. Tom quickened his pace.

He was the last to arrive back at the barracks. The platoon broke into separate squads and headed for shared rooms, quick showers, and food.

Tom noticed Jake, Cogriff's lackey, in a corner of the rec room, huddled up with his usual three guns for hire. He must be in a new phase of planning how to destroy me. Well, at least the kid is using his mind for something. Tom ambled off to the shower.

While they were washing, four at a time, Tom noticed blood pooling around the drain. He glanced around for the source. This is tricky when you are in the shower with a bunch of men.

It was Albert. The blood was pouring down his inner thighs.

Tom hung around until almost everyone had left for breakfast. Then he said, "For God's sake, Albert, what happened to you? You are bleeding, son."

"It's because I'm so fat, Dad. That's w-what the sergeant says."

"Son, believe me, there is not a speck of fat on you. You're just a big boy. Is it your thighs rubbing together?"

He nodded.

Had Albert's bottom lip just puckered? Tom did a double take.

Albert turned one raw, bloody inner thigh toward Tom. "But it doesn't hurt."

"What, are you nuts? Of course it hurts. What did you put on them?"

"Nothing. I can t-tough it out."

"Okay, this is what you do." Tom proceeded to instruct the kid on how to keep dry with powder. "Put Vaseline on your thighs and wear long cotton boxers that hug your legs so they don't rub. For now, until that heals, wrap them during the day, put some antibiotic cream on them"—Tom handed him his underwear—"and wear the long cotton boxers, too."

"Yes, Dad."

The boy just stood there looking at Tom. "Now, Albert. Go do it now." Finally Albert ran off to follow Tom's instructions. Albert was such a kid, a big kid.

Tom called out after him, "And put some of that on your heels and other parts of your feet so you don't get blisters. Carry an extra pair of dry socks with you all the time."

On his way to breakfast, Tom decided to check in with the doc. Unfortunately, Staff Sergeant Steiner waylaid him.

"Where are you going? The DFAC, the Dining Facility, is that way."

Tom's back stiffened. "I never picked up my actual medical release form, Sergeant." In the army it was common knowledge that it was wise to keep your paperwork in your own hands.

"At the two-mile marker, you were still off by four minutes. You aren't going to make the cut, broken-down old Ranger." Steiner turned his back to Tom and then changed his mind and turned back. "Why are you making trouble for me, old man? Do you like trouble? Is it your friend? Are you one of those shithead alcoholic, dope-using burnouts? Didn't have a life out of the corps, so you're coming back to find one? You don't belong no more, old man. Your kind get my men killed."

Tom remained stiff and silent. Steiner wasn't done.

Suddenly his jaw locked, and the skin on his face tightened, hugging his skull. "You qualify with your weapons in two days, and then it is your PT test. You've got nothing. You aren't fit for duty, old man. Give this up before you get one of my men hurt. Go home to your family."

He seemed disappointed by Tom's silence. Finally he said, "Go. Get out of my sight. And they want you over at JAG at fourteen hundred."

Tom saw the doc. And Dr. Chesney said he was doing well on the new meds. Another month of stable blood glucose and he might be off all medication. Tom picked up his medical release and headed for breakfast. But he wasn't fast enough. Albert met him at the door and said they had to get back to barracks. They were going to the obstacle course.

Great! Just great. He grabbed two granola bars and ate them as he headed back to his room to gear up. This would be his first exercise in full battle-rattle, outfitted as he would be when he went into combat, carrying every piece of his equipment—an extra 125 pounds. They had assigned Albert as his ammo bearer, so he took some of the weight off Tom. They were now officially a team.

Surprised but pleased he had survived the obstacle course, at 1400 Tom forced his stressed-out, messed-up body over to JAG headquarters. He sat on an extremely hard, straight-backed wooden chair. Irrationally, he fleetingly thought JAG had placed that cruel chair there just to torture him. But, fighting off paranoia, he came to the realization that his tender physical condition was the only culprit.

All the brass who were passing by stared at him. Now he knew how a man on death row feels.

Finally a full-bird colonel stuck his head out a door down the hall and summoned Tom. He walked what could be his last mile slowly and with caution. He had no other choice. Agony was his companion, especially when he stopped and then tried to start moving again. The bright spot of this physical torture he was experiencing would be minor compared to what might be said on the other side of that door, Tom decided. "It could get worse, soldier," he said to himself. He was thinking the army way now.

He stepped into a large conference room. Beige walls, rich woods, green carpet, leather-bound volumes, and artwork gave the room that official "legal" feel. Eight decorated colonels, all in their greens, fixed Tom in their sights. It seemed he commanded an audience everywhere he went. First at the hospital, and now here at JAG. Fame was not what he was seeking. Didn't anyone get it?

"Take a seat, Private Lane," said the Post Judge Advocate sitting at head of the table. She wore her greens fully decorated and had a straight, almost starched appearance, in keeping with that of most of the generals Tom had met. Her expression gave away none of her thoughts. Tom noticed when she turned to speak in whispers to the others at the table that her rich coffee-brown skin didn't dare to wrinkle or leave a single telling line on her handsome face. A lonely lieutenant sat in the general's shadow, poised to take notes.

Tom took the first empty spot nearest the door. He was glad to rest his feet, but again he was in one of those hard wooden chairs. When he looked down the long glass-topped table, he was relieved to see Jim Small's friendly face smiling back at him. Jim was the only person in the room who was happy to see Tom.

"Hey, how are you doing?" He got up and came over to slap Tom on the back. Then he took the seat next to him.

The pat on the back didn't have the comforting effect Jim had desired. Perhaps Tom's wince gave his delicate condition away.

Jim whispered, "You look like shit."

"Thanks." Tom asked, "What's going on?"

"Well, actually, a lot. But I'll let General Mitchell explain."

The general rose from her chair and all eyes followed her. There is always one guy who can make you or break you. And this was that guy. Or in this instance, that gal.

"We have examined your claim . . ."

Forty minutes later and after a lot of legal lingo, they stopped debating. They stared at Tom.

Isn't the last thing they get to always the meat of the matter? Both Tom and Jim leaned forward.

"We want this publicity to stop! That is part of the deal, Private Lane. Is that perfectly clear?"

General Mitchell's steely eyes felt like laser-guided missiles targeting him. Tom braced himself.

"You can have your chance, at least for the time being," the general continued. "We are not capitulating. This is a ridiculous prank. But until the secretary of defense and I reach a decision, you may continue. We will be meeting again in three days. At that time we will render our verdict."

Jim jumped up. "We will be challenging the verdict if it goes against my client. I will keep you all busy with appeals for the next five years."

General Mitchell's scowl set Tom's nerves on edge but didn't faze Jim.

"If you will let me finish . . ." She waited for Jim to sit back down. "If you fail to meet the standards at any time during your evaluation . . . you're out, Private Lane. Do you understand?"

"Yes, ma'am." Tom popped up. His back straightened.

"No publicity. It must stop now." The general's fist hit the table.

The sudden outburst made Tom jump. He felt the vibrations at his end of the table. He hazarded a look over at Jim and leaned in. "What publicity?"

"I'll tell you later." Jim stood. "I have no more power over the press than you all do. My client has not talked to the press, and I will continue to advise him not to give interviews. Of course, that is dependent on the outcome of the next hearing. I assume you will keep me informed? Furthermore, I don't want anyone from this office approaching my client unless I am present."

"Certainly." The general, composed after her brief explosion, shot to her feet and the meeting abruptly came to an end.

Tom was glad the conference room table had taken the brunt of her fury. Her eyes locked on to his as she walked by, and he felt some of the residual heat of her anger.

Suddenly Jim and Tom were alone out in the hall.

"You get run over by a tank?" Jim was a subtle man.

"Inside, I feel the way I look, only ten times worse," said Tom. "Now fill me in."

"The law is still on the books, so they can't deny you. It will probably be off the books as soon as the sun goes down. But we still need the sec def's stamp of approval."

"Great. Hey, wait. Do you mean *the* Secretary of Defense of the United States of America?"

"Yeah. We are playing with the big boys. So it all goes through him. We are dealing with the army, not the civilian community. Those two legal systems work very differently. But no sweat. I'll stick around for the next few days just to keep the pressure on and make sure that JAG doesn't pull some trick."

"So I'm home free?"

"From the looks of you, Tom, it's more like someone dragged you over home plate and then beat you with a bat. If you want to call that home free," Jim said, looking Tom up and down.

"Let's just say I'm adjusting to army life. When will I know for sure this is a go?"

"Yeah, well, it looks like three days. But that would be in military time, so it could be as much as a week. I'll keep on them. Until then, buy some Gorilla Glue and keep yourself together." Jim slapped Tom on the back.

He cringed. "Thanks for the vote of confidence."

"Sorry. I forgot you're hurting. I've gotta go. Call if you need me. And read this editorial." He shoved a newspaper into Tom's hand. "Those newspaper guys were right. Stuff like this might just push them over the top in your favor."

Tom took the section of the newspaper and read the headline aloud as he walked back to his barrack. It was a *Washington Post* editorial. The byline identified the writers as Mr. Ricca and Mr. Jordan.

"What a world! What a world!" You all remember that line in the Wizard of Oz, but do you remember what the Wicked Witch of the West said next? "Who would have thought a good little girl like you could destroy my beautiful wickedness?" As children, we all could imagine good overcoming evil. But do we believe it as adults?

Today we are confronted by terrorists who make their threats from faraway mountains. We live under a constant orange threat level, and we talk about a blood-and-sand-soaked war on the other side of the world. Thousands of our sons and daughters, our future, are fighting over dust and dirt that they will never call home. That world is no Oz, and that kid from Topeka facing a Taliban assault in Kabul certainly knows he's not in Kansas anymore.

But the deeper question is whether any of us will ever see Dorothy's Kansas again.

What kind of a world are we building for our children? Will it be a safer world or a more brutal world? Are we anything close to a compassionate society? Will we be proud of our legacy? Are we handing down a world where good overcomes evil, or are we simply accepting the lesser of two evils?

In a world increasingly influenced by fear, these are questions that need answers. Especially for the men and women in uniform who hunted down the Wicked Warlord of the East (Osama bin Laden), while at home we grow more suspicious of our neighbors and continue our futile search for a political wizard who can make it "right" again. Will we recognize "right" when we see it?

Some of us delight in the humiliation of our enemy. We justify illegal wiretaps and torture. We jail people without due process. Worse, these abuses, which would have been greeted before the World Trade Center tragedy with shock and outrage and as an affront to American values, are now not even debated on their ethical or moral grounds. Little by little, we are letting our fears trample the Constitution and the spirit of America. We are creating a world of terror inside our own borders.

The good news is that it seems we have time to reverse the trend, to take us back to a yellow brick road, to regain our Emerald City.

But where do we find these guardians of our nation's legacy? Fortunately, one of them has found us.

There is a single man who has cried out. "Enough! Stop! No more!" A man who has said that war will not scar his son's inheritance, his son's dreams, and his son's destiny. A man whose deed is not complicated but tremendously difficult. He has not broken any laws. He has chosen to go to war in his son's stead. A simple declaration that speaks volumes about American ideals without costing a dime or involving a run for political office. He is what this country was in the beginning and what we hope it will always be. He is a man who is willing to sacrifice for his convictions, his cause, and his son.

After all folks, isn't that what dads do?

THANK GOD MY NAME ISN'T MENTIONED was Tom's first reaction. Then the words of the editorial settled in. And he knew it was all true. He also knew it would be men like his son Donnie who would help form and guide the next generation. Tom was immediately comforted. Donnie could plan a future. Donnie would be part of a better future.

The idea of Donnie, the man, glowed bright in Tom's heart. Christine as a grandmother with Donnie's family, his little children over for holidays, running around the house, was a great picture. Tom held on to it.

But to make that future happen, Tom had to do more. He tucked the article in his pocket. Tom spent the rest of the day at the firing range shredding targets with the outline of a man on them.

Chapter 21

THE NEXT DAYS WERE MUCH MORE PHYSICAL than Tom remembered. He suspected the young "dog faces" learned to accept the punishment a little quicker than an old dog like himself.

Tom reproached himself, "Don't use the *o* word. Don't even think old." He was down to the qualifying phase of his training.

Weapons, the M16 series rifle, M4 carbine, M60, and his M240B machine gun, were a breeze for Tom. And that accomplishment gave his ego a much-needed boost. He was back—hoorah. Well, almost back; he still needed to pass that damned PT test.

It was the same with rocket launchers and mines. He could assemble and disassemble any weapon in his sleep, while in his head he was marching to Brooks & Dunn's "Boot Scootin' Boogie."

He was pushing to accomplish everything as fast as he could because the doc had hinted that command was going to put the squeeze on him. How and where they could pile more on, Tom couldn't imagine. His back was already bent at a ninety-degree angle from his present load. The doc didn't have details.

Logically, Tom thought the final decision coming down from JAG was his best hope, and it was the monkey he had been carrying on his back since day one. Three days came and went without a single word from JAG. Tom was as nervous as a rabbit living under a doghouse. Then Jim called. "Tomorrow," he simply said.

"Woo." He collapsed back onto his bed. Tom repeated aloud, "Tomorrow." JAG was ready to broadcast the direction of his life. He would be going to Pennsylvania or the Middle East. With either outcome a trip was involved. And most important, Donnie's future would be caught up and forever shaped by JAG's decision. It was a life-or-death decision.

With a gnawing sensation in the pit of his stomach, Tom continued moving forward as if nothing would change. He preferred that reality. He knew working out and wishing would not influence JAG. Prayer and hope were all that was left. They and his mental conversations with Tommy were what had gotten him through each day since he'd arrived. He felt close to his oldest son in these surroundings. Tom reminded himself to maintain a positive posture.

Right now it was back to business. Tom did not want to give the army the smallest excuse to deny him. He was pleased that his knowledge of land navigation, first aid, and protection against chemical and biological weapons had risen to the surface. There was new and better gear today, but the fundamentals remained unchanged. Target acquisition, communications, and visual-signaling techniques had been ingrained in Tom and had never left. Just like radio operation and map reading. Tom passed them all. He had his Expert Infantry Badge by the end of his second week.

Keep moving forward, that's the key, he told himself. Don't think; just do.

The skills of the rifleman were many. Tom had a lot to prove in a short span of time.

The military was so much more than just marching and shooting. It was eighty percent mind and twenty-five percent body. Youth gives you that additional five percent, Tom mused, wishing he had that extra energy. Preparing a soldier for every eventuality was something the military took seriously. Of course, the one contingency the army couldn't train you for was dying.

The words of Tom's very first drill instructor returned to him: "Did the United States Army teach you how to die, Private Lane?" The sergeant's spit had pelted Tom's face as he screamed at him while they were nose to nose. "Then don't!" Even now Tom could visualize that DI's eyes. He'd had a way of boring into you. As if planting that answer somewhere really deep could prevent death from ever visiting. And when he was younger, Tom had believed his DI had that power.

But now, at this time in his life, Tom had adopted a more universal, civilian version of the DI's code: Did fatherhood ever teach a man how to let his son down? Then don't! That thought fired Tom up.

With that in mind, Tom cautioned himself that he still had a journey to complete. He had to max PT, and right now he wasn't even close. On Wednesday he failed his mock PT test. But Rangers never say never; that's what the familiar voice inside his head reminded him. Tom laughed at himself. Sometimes he didn't think his body remembered as well as his mind that he had ever been a Ranger.

The twelve-mile tactical foot march was another hurdle. He had to do it within three hours. The closest Tom had come was three hours and twenty-seven minutes.

Give me a couple more weeks, Lord, and I'll be in great shape. Tom repeated that refrain to himself every few minutes while he dissolved in a puddle of his own sweat.

His feet and legs were giant blobs of raw meat. He bought more Vaseline at the commissary, plus extra-large Band-Aids.

The other day he'd overheard Albert telling some of the other guys to use the Vaseline. Tom found it both amusing and surprising that more of these tricks hadn't trickled down. Albert also prompted a few of the others of the importance of dry socks. The guys and gals in the unit were looking at Albert with new eyes. Their view of Tom was also changing.

Most reacted to Tom with either fear or awe. He supposed bringing down Jake a second time—after he and three other masked idiots jumped Tom outside the gate as he returned from the doc's house a couple of nights ago—had sent out the message not to mess with him. But the nods and quick "Hey, Dads" he was getting from more and more of his fellow grunts told Tom he was on the path toward acceptance. It was a slow but vital process if they were all to fight together as a cohesive unit.

Friction within a squad could lose battles and, worse, lives. That was the real reason Tom took exception to Cogriff as their leader and why

Tom was determined to fit in. It wasn't just Donnie's life or even Tom's that was on the line anymore. All these kids would have when the shit hit the fan was each other. They needed to know they could depend on one another. There would be no time for debate, no do-overs, no choosing sides. There would be just one side: us against them. And Cogriff would lead them.

Tom held the belief that a leader should epitomize strength, hope, and courage. He would be a man always moving forward in the right direction like a well-oiled, synchronized machine. Cogriff encouraged side taking. He interacted with the platoon only when he had a complaint. He didn't know what leading by example even meant. He never joined PT or brought encouragement to the rifle range. Tom chided himself that he was acting too much like a father, worrying about the kids in his platoon. But something inside told him Tommy approved.

Tom walked into the barracks and saw Albert enjoying Tom's rising "fame" vicariously. One of the GI Janes was asking Albert to ask Tom something. Her eyes traveled briefly toward Tom during the conversation. "Ask Dad" was becoming a common phrase.

The most popular "Ask Dad" was how Tom took apart his weapons and reassembled them at the speed of light. Tom had worked with Albert. He'd told Albert about his trick of listening to an upbeat song in his head; when he had the rhythm, it would keep him coordinated as he picked up the parts to his rifle and put it together. It had worked like a charm for Albert, who'd previously been all thumbs. Albert had beamed when he finished second in assembling his weapon. Tom was always first.

Now during drills most of Tom's unit would be head-bobbing to iPods or humming tunes, racing by all the other units and usually winning hands down. Of course, Cogriff took it not as an accomplishment, but as a personal slap in the face. The man could smile and scowl at the same time. Creepy. Steiner, Tom noticed, remained neutral, scary in his patient neutrality.

In Tom's daily talks with the family, he didn't mention Cogriff or his personal worries or activities. He didn't think himself noble or any bullshit like that. It was just that he wanted to get away from the military for a while, even if it was only temporary. The inside of his head needed a little R & R. Listening to the voices of the members of his family kept Tom pointed in the right direction.

But the relaxation didn't come easily. Tom feared failure. The PT test plagued him. Right now, when he wasn't sweating and his mind had a chance to kick in, tomorrow loomed much larger than PT. After tomorrow at JAG, the physical stuff might not be an issue at all.

He had this eerie feeling that the United States Army had something up its sleeve.

Chapter 22

Steiner pulled Tom out of morning formation. "Lane, the jury's in. Go! JAG wants you. Now!"

Tom felt shell-shocked. Should he make a run for the gate and freedom or face the consequences of all this . . . this sweat and pain, discourse, and derision he had forced on himself, his family, and the corps?

Again Steiner yelled, "Get your ass over there. They are waiting for you, Lane. You don't have time to change. Go, Private. Double time."

Tom responded like a programmed robot. But he didn't miss Jake's smirk or the delight on Cogriff's face as he jogged passed a window and the lieutenant stared after him. Did his two-faced lieutenant already know his fate? Tom didn't have time to decipher either side of the man.

Tom could only concentrate on moving one foot in front of the other as, keeping his eyes straight ahead, he jogged to JAG headquarters. He told himself with each beat of his feet that no matter what happened, he would never apologize or doubt his actions.

He ran up the steps of the newest and most stately building on the post. Its marble columns hovered above Tom like an evil omen. How could a small and insignificant human like himself go up against the mighty and commanding government? His grand quest . . . had it been folly? No. Because what those doubters didn't know was that he, Tom, was the government. The little guy wasn't powerless. And if they had forgotten, Tom was ready to remind them.

Tom's damp sneakers squeaked out his approach as he made his way down the hallowed halls. Ahead of him, he saw Jim waiting outside the same conference room where they'd had their first meeting.

"Let's go," said Jim, standing to tuck his blue tie inside his immaculately tailored black suit.

Tom pulled on his sweats. He checked the muddy trail of footprints leading to his present location. He froze in place. His confidence suddenly sprang a leak. "I look like crap," he said. Did he want to know the answer waiting behind that door? Did Jim already know the answer?

Jim put one hand on Tom's shoulder. "I don't know what they are going to say in there." His eyes flashed to the closed door. "We'll find out together. I have to let them know in no uncertain terms we are committed to pursuing this course. I'm sticking, buddy. We can handle this, whatever the outcome. We are ready."

Tom could only nod.

Jim stepped back and opened the door wide. They walked in shoulder to shoulder.

General Mitchell was not at the head of the conference room table as Tom had expected. In fact, only one person sat at the long table. But his formidable presence filled the room.

It was Secretary of Defense Jacobson. The top man. The man in charge of all of JAG, who answered only to the president.

He was a bony character. His keen eyes were set into an oblong, middle-aged face on which a sharp, concise mind had etched a fair number of scowl lines. His gray eyes, which reminded Tom of the pieces of steel he worked with at the machine shop, latched on to him and followed his every step without blinking. Now Tom knew why the international community had nicknamed him "the Hawk." He definitely felt like prey before this man.

Tom quickly came to attention.

"At ease, Private Lane." Jacobson's voice surprised Tom. It was deep and raspy, as if he was hoarse, getting over a bad cold.

He motioned for Jim and Tom to take a seat up close to him. Tom saw the scar at Jacobson's neck where he'd had a tracheotomy and remembered the man had been diagnosed with throat cancer. *He is battling a war of his own,* thought Tom.

After they were seated, Jacobson smiled.

Tom found this especially disturbing. He was about to give Tom some bitter medicine for sure. Tom prepared himself.

"Well, Private Lane, you have certainly caused a storm. I guess in a small way we should be grateful to you for pointing out this glitch in the system."

Tom and Jim smiled at each other and relaxed. Then General Mitchell walked in to join them. Everyone's face changed. The smiles had been premature and they stiffened. *Here it comes*, thought Tom.

Jacobson said, "Welcome, General."

"Thank you. Let's move on." She turned to Tom. "Most of the laws in our country came originally from England. Did you know that, Private Lane?"

Jim nodded. Tom answered, "No."

Jim spoke up. "When the first colonists arrived in America, they didn't have formal documentation of law. So the common practice became following the existing laws of their place of origin," he recited.

"That's a bit of an oversimplification," said General Mitchell. "Common law or case law developed from precedent. These are laws based on previous court or tribunal decisions rather than on legislative statutes. In a common-law legal system, the ruling principle was that it was unfair to treat similar facts differently on different occasions. Those decisions were binding for future decisions, especially if parties disagreed. In that case, the court looked at past precedents in relevant courts for the decision."

Jacobson sipped from a glass of water at his elbow. He folded his arms, letting General Mitchell continue to prepare the site for the smart bomb Tom was sure she was going to deliver.

The sound of ice cubes clinking around in the glass set off Tom's nerves.

The general continued. "If there was a dispute and a similar quarrel had been resolved in the past, the court was bound to follow the reasoning used in the prior decision."

"Stare decisis," cited Jim.

The general agreed, "Yes, correct."

Tom looked at Jim for a translation.

"It's what they call the principle," said Jim.

"Today most often lawyers hear the term *common law* used in reference only to marriage," said the general. "For legal purposes, someone is considered married and lawfully entitled to the benefits of their spouse after they have lived together for a sustained period of time. Say after seven years of cohabitation, they are legally married in the eyes of the justice system."

Tom brightened. He had heard about common-law marriage before. But he had never applied it to what he was trying to do or even considered that the two things were related.

Jim said, "General, there are other occasions when common law has been accepted. I would like to cite . . ."

The general held up her hand. "Let me finish. The common law 'In His Stead,' which you cited, was found to have been addressed and removed from the law books in many states. Paying for a substitute was prevalent in the north and south during the Civil War, but it is no longer legal."

Tom slumped back into his seat.

Again Jim spoke up. "I have done an extensive search on the law, General. And, remember, there has not been any money exchanged. Nor has there been any intimidation."

"Yes, I am sure you have, Major Small." The general watched Tom and Jim for a moment. She seemed to be deciding something. "Secretary Jacobson?"

"Major Small, your client's age was a factor." Jacobson's baritone articulation added weight to his words.

"Sir, the army has been consistently calling back its older reservist population," said Jim. "I understand they interact well with the Afghani people. The village elders relate to our older soldiers. I have numbers . . ."

"Enough. No statistics," said the secretary of defense. "Let's get on with this, as I see your lawyer has indeed done his homework. The laws of the Commonwealth of Pennsylvania— your congressman has emphasized this fact in his numerous letters—we have found to be an exception. Pennsylvania did not nullify or address the common law 'In His Stead' in their state constitutional laws. Therefore, Thomas Lane, you are now officially a private in the United States Army with all the rights and privileges of that attachment. You are hereby directed to serve in your son's place for the full duration of your son's enlistment. The United States Army shall recognize your service as fulfillment of Donald Lane's obligation."

Tom was stunned. His mouth remained open, his mind petrified by disbelief.

"Well, Private Lane, let me be the first to congratulate you." Secretary Jacobson stood to shake Tom's hand. "You are in the army."

Tom jumped up. He shook Jacobson's hand but didn't feel it in his own. He was completely numb.

Jim stood. He reached out and shook the secretary of defense's hand, saying, "Thank you, sir."

General Mitchell held an envelope out to Tom.

Tom was incapable of lifting his arm again, so Jim accepted it.

"May I remind you, there is no turning back, Private Lane. You are committed."

Tom mumbled, "Yes, ma'am."

"And, Major Small, if you decide to return to full-time service, let me know."

Jim smiled. "Thank you, ma'am."

Tom and Jim stood. Protocol dictates that the highest-ranking officer in a room leave any gathering first. Anything else would be an insult.

Tom staggered as if he was going to collapse. Jim held on to him.

Secretary of Defense Jacobson smiled. "Carry on, gentlemen. I am sure Private Lane has duties. Dismissed." Tom saluted. The general and the secretary of defense went out the door at the back of the room into another office.

Jim guided Tom out. The second they were outside the door, Tom collapsed like a deflated balloon.

Jim punched Tom on the bicep. "JAG gave you your clearance. Get happy, Private!" Jim was holding up the official-looking envelope Jacobson had given them. "May I read the official notice?" asked Jim.

Tom could only nod. He was still reeling from the affects of that smart bomb exploding inside his brain. But it wasn't only the shock waves he was feeling. Why did he still have a twitchy feeling?

THE NEXT MORNING, a Thursday, the army rolled up its sleeve and revealed the last ace they had been hiding from Tom.

While Tom was standing in formation, Staff Sergeant Steiner announced, "You are either fit for duty or left behind. It's time to step up or step out!"

"Holy shit!"

"What, Dad?" asked Albert.

The whole platoon had been called out. Albert and Tom were standing at ease at the back of their unit.

"This is an accountability formation," said Tom. Albert looked confused and Tom signaled, "Later."

Every major division in the army has what is called a "cycle" of deployment. There are three categories of DFR, or Deployment Readiness Force. The numbers denote the time frame for deployment. DRF-1 means the force is ready to deploy—bags are packed and ready to go, and they will be in the air within twenty-four hours. DRF-2 means the force is ready to deploy in forty-eight hours; with DRF-3, it's seventy-two hours.

Tom's heart stopped as he waited to hear which cycle his unit was on.

"Ready within twenty-four," barked Steiner.

Tom's mind whirled. We are DRF-1. I'm not ready. I needed my SRP to go. Or—the alternative elicited an extra thud from his heart—Donnie will be standing here.

This had been what the doc had warned him about. This was what they'd been planning.

They're speeding up the engine so I don't have time to catch the train by making the grade, said Tom to himself. This was Cogriff's coup de grâce.

"Jerk!" Tom said, aloud. Damn it! I am close, so close.

An inner, more logical voice calmed him. These were the times Tom gave God credit. This didn't mean they were leaving in twenty-four hours, just that they had to be ready to leave within that time period.

He could still do it. It could be up to two weeks before deployment. Or less. Not any more. This isn't over. He wasn't done yet. *Tricky dicks,* thought Tom.

The informational briefing continued. The sergeant then defined the code words as "Las Vegas," which would alert the unit that the order was real, not a drill.

Steiner emphasized, "When the alert comes, protocol dictates you will be locked down. After that warning, there will be no phone calls or communication with the outside. This is as real as it gets."

Tom had been through this before, and he understood the need to protect operational security. They didn't want any leaks. So Tom still had until the warning order was given.

The sergeant started to walk away, then turned back. "Consider this a Christmas present from the United States Army."

Tom smacked himself on the side of the head. Time to put it all on the line.

This was the good-bye stage of army life. Christine, the kids, and Frank were coming down this weekend. The doc had invited them all over to his house for Christmas dinner. Tom had been looking forward to some home cooking; he hadn't seen his family for almost three weeks.

Suddenly, he didn't care about food. Time was his enemy. Don't waste it, he reminded himself.

It was interesting that when it came down to this moment, what Tom wanted more than anything else was Christine. She was his first and last thought every day. It's odd that he had never realized before that she was his breath, his life-giving oxygen. She made his lungs rise and fall and his heart beat with joy.

Tom felt like a young child whining, "I want my Christine." He suddenly needed to hold her in his arms and be held by her.

He also would have to talk with Frank. Time to get *things* in order.

Tom did an about-face back to JAG headquarters.

Chapter 23

THE FAMILY ARRIVED AT THE MOTEL around ten a.m. on Saturday, which was Christmas morning. Uncle Frank was behind the wheel and Donnie in the shotgun seat. The womenfolk, Christine and Chrissy, were tucked into the backseat.

Tom had the day off and had been eagerly awaiting his family's arrival by the front door of the motel since eight. He didn't want to squander a second he could spend with them.

Christine had done all the shopping herself this year. And Tom had missed singing Christmas carols with her as they searched for gifts. Of course, they only sang in the car because Tom's atonal voice would have made even plastic elves hold their pointy ears. Once Tom had gotten a speeding ticket for singing. It was crazy, but true. Tom and Christine had been laughing and singing, having such a good time he'd forgotten everything, including the speed limit. Tom had always thought that had been the best ticket he ever got. It had been worth the pure joy they'd had together.

Tom reminded himself that these great memories were the kind he would take with him and could pull out when he needed comfort during their time apart.

Once they had unpacked the car, they all gathered in front of the Christmas tree in the lounge area, where the fireplace sent out a warm glow.

Chrissy got an iPod and Donnie, at his dad's suggestion, seat covers for Mona. Uncle Frank got a new Thermos. Christine had taken to packing his lunch every day and told him she would keep it filled. The kids and Frank were pleased with their gifts, adding the appropriate *oohs* and *aahs* afterward.

As usual, Tom and Christine "got" each other. Tom whispered in Christine's ear, "I have a little surprise for you later." His smile widened.

Christine blushed. "I've seen that surprise before, and it's not little."

They both laughed. And Tom thought, *All the more surprised will Christine be when I hand her my gift.*

Tom and his family, including Frank, arrived at the doc's house around five. The Chesneys lived in a nonmilitary neighborhood. Every street was filled with twinkling lights, glowing snowmen, and Santa with his reindeer. The nostalgic scene made the holiday come alive for Tom. He had always prided himself on being the first in the neighborhood to have his lights up.

Standing on the doc's front porch, Tom looked over at his son.

The boy must have read his dad's mind. "I put the lights up, and Santa's sitting in his usual place on the porch. Just like always," said Donnie.

"Just like always"—*what a nice way to put it*, thought Tom.

After they got in the front door and finished the introductions, Christine and the doc's wife, Joan, migrated into the kitchen. Tom was pleased they had taken an instant liking to each other. Donnie and Chrissy were dragged into Wii games and enjoying every minute they were spending with Ben's lively children, Stan and Mary. After Frank had a Bud in his hand, he fell into a soft chair with the excuse that he needed some stretched-out quiet time.

"The woman in the car talked all the way here," complained Frank with a sly smile as he jiggled one ear.

Tom figured he must have looked like hell, because right after that, Ben took him into his home office. "Let me check you out. What have you been doing? Volunteering to be a moving target?"

"Close. But I passed my twelve-mile march at five a.m. Two hours and fifty-seven minutes." It hurt to smile, but Tom tried anyway. "What do you think of that, Doc?"

"I think you are as insane now as you were the first time we met."

He made Tom shut up while he listened to his chest, did a finger stick, and checked his blood pressure.

"What's the verdict?"

"Tom, inside you are twenty, outside you are ninety, and your brain is functioning on a third-grade level. You're normal."

They both laughed.

The doc added, "I think you can go off medication." Tom started to clap, but Ben stopped him. "You need to keep doing your finger sticks, though."

"Whatever you say. By the way, I found out what they had up their sleeve."

Ben cocked his head to one side.

"My platoon is DRF-1. It's do or die tomorrow with the PT test. Cogriff's ultimatum came down today. Then he winks at me."

"That guy is strange. His father is some big-shot politician, so he's not without pull. Be careful and don't trust him."

"I'm taking my test in the morning. If I don't pass, I'm out."

"And Donnie's in. Why, that SOB," said Ben. "And he didn't even give you the weekend with your family?"

"Nope. Today is it. And tomorrow it's the firing squad at dawn."

Ben pulled out his best scotch and two glasses. It was something Tom had acquired a taste for during his visits. Ben poured them each two fingers. "That calls for reinforcements."

"Thanks," Tom said as he toasted his host. "Ben, I couldn't have done this without you." When the scotch came out, so did their first names.

"Yeah. I still don't think I am doing you a favor. But you sure have given a lot of people something to think about."

"I doubt that."

"Well, if nothing else, you have stirred the pot."

Tom looked at him curiously.

"There's been another article in the *Washington Post* about 'the dad.' And your story was picked up by newspapers nationwide. Your congressman is getting into the action, playing it coy, saying on-screen how he supports 'the dad' and siding with those who want peace. Don't look so worried. The congressman has not given them your name . . . yet. But all these stories are circulating on the Net. Various people are coming forward claiming to be 'the Dad.' Jerks!" Ben laughed. "You're becoming a legend."

"No. If anything, I'm a cartoon. And great, let those wackos have the fame and glory."

"Seriously, Tom, the country wants peace. There is a growing movement. One war after another, losing our best and tainting the next generation . . . well, people are looking for a better way."

"The people and my local congressman, who happens to be running for reelection, are with me. But how about the rest of the politicians? If they were truly representing the people, we would already have peace. At the least they would be promoting peace with the same enthusiasm as they do war. I don't hear or see any action toward peace." Tom sipped his scotch and ruminated. "I don't care about any of them. That boy out there is safe." He pointed with his glass at the closed door between the office and living room. "And he is all that counts."

"You're a marshmallow." Ben snickered. "You care about them all. I've seen you with Albert and the others."

There were both quiet.

"You've got a nice family, Tom."

"Thanks."

Tom and Ben had mulled over potential solutions for the problems of their world many times.

"The voluntary army sucks," said Tom.

"Tom, look who is joining. Kids, unemployed men and women with families who can't find anything out here. We promise them a bonus and money for education. To some of them, that money is more than they will see in their entire lives. It's a nice, fat, juicy worm."

"Surely there have to be other alternatives," countered Tom.

Their conversations often ended like this, with Ben suggesting a change of the system and Tom agreeing. But neither man could come up with a new democracy.

When Christine called, "Dinner's ready," Tom drained his glass. "We better get back to the ladies." As he opened the door, he asked Ben, "You're sure the newspapers still don't have my name?"

Ben shook his head. And then, just to annoy Tom, Ben added, "But it won't be long. The whole base calls you 'Dad.' And you know the army can't keep a secret. They have already caught the paparazzi snooping outside the gates."

The pleasant domestic scene at Ben's home ended around ten. Christine and Joan hugged at the door and promised to keep in touch.

The Lane family was subdued as they filed into the motel and whispered good-nights in the lobby. Tom had reserved three rooms. Chrissy had her own on one side of Tom and Christine. And Frank and Donnie shared the one on the other side. Doors joined the rooms so they could move back and forth between them.

Tom was aware that Chrissy was oblivious to what was going on here at the Quality Inn. And he wanted to keep it that way. She kissed her dad, gave him a hug, and had her ear reattached to her new iPod before she reached her room.

"Dad. I . . ." Donnie hugged his father.

"That desk job is shining brighter, son." He had not shared his new MOS as gunner with anyone. His family didn't need the extra burden.

Donnie's eyes filled and he hurried off with the excuse to catch the last of a football game.

Smart kids, good kids, thought Tom with pride. Instinctively they knew the husband and wife needed some time alone tonight.

Frank waved and disappeared.

Tom turned to Christine. "It's just the two of us. Are you ready for bed?" Tom's eyebrows danced. "Or maybe a nightcap?"

"I think the nightcap . . . first."

It was then that Tom noticed she still had her antennae and they were fully functional.

He suggested, "There's a little place next door. A local hangout. We can walk."

They sat at the bar, talking about the house, the kids, and work. They casually touched each other and held hands.

Finally Tom said, "This feels like a date." He felt himself blush. He hadn't done that in years.

Christine's blue eyes sparkled. "Of course it's a date, Tom. We've been on one for the last twenty-some years. Didn't you know?"

Tom saw the sexiest smile playing at the corners of his wife's moist lips. *God, that woman can set me on fire,* he thought. "Just remember that when the guys start buzzing around. We're not finished with our first date yet."

She put her small, delicate hand over his.

"Warm, soft," Tom said as he lifted her fingers to his lips. He turned her hand over and kissed her wrist. The feeling of her pulse against his lips sent him from smoldering to a five-alarm fire. He inched closer. They were at the dark end of the bar. His lips moved to her throat. Again his lips reacted to the quickening of her pulse against his mouth. That delicate little pulsating of a woman's heart that throbs with so much love. He was nothing without her.

She smiled and let her fingers play down the side of his rough face. Her hand cupped his chin, then slid down to rest lightly on his chest.

And could she tell, Tom wondered, that she was holding every bit of his heart in the palm of her hand? A touch from the right person can do that, take hold of your heart. Tom was experiencing that right now. The shiver she sent through him should have caused an earthquake. It had happened the first time Tom and Christine had touched. And here it was again. Now, just like the first time, he had never wanted anyone so much as he wanted her.

"Tom, are you deploying soon?"

How did she do that? It was like she opened up his skull and read what was stored in there. "It's possible. I don't know for sure."

She raised one eyebrow, which told Tom she knew he was lying. But this time, she didn't go for the confession. She let it go.

"I have to be back early in the morning to take my PT test. It's the last hurdle."

"Then I think I'll take you up on that other part of your invitation." Christine started to rise off the bar stool.

"Wait. I got you a present." Tom was pleased. For the first time in a long time he had truly surprised her.

"Tom . . ." she said, her face lighting up.

"It's nothing much." He pulled something sparkly out of his pocket and she leaned over so he could put it around her neck.

Christine gasped. Her hand came up to curl around Tom's gift.

It was a crystal heart-shaped pendant.

"I had the guy over at the PX write something."

Christine read what was engraved in the center. There were just two words: "Love Endures."

As soon as they were back in their room, Christine looked over at the desk and asked, "Is that your power of attorney and will?"

When did she see me lay them there? Then Tom remembered she had been through this before. Unwillingly the first time. Less willingly this time.

All servicemen did this prep before leaving for overseas duty. Christine had been expecting this. *As always, she is way ahead of me,* thought Tom.

He nodded and then his eyes misted over. Christine guided him to the bed and they folded into one another and did what they did best: they loved each other.

Tom had heard someone once say, "You are never so much in love as when you are saying good-bye." Perhaps it was true. But he had an advantage over others. He had an enduring love, a heart that never said good-bye.

A LITTLE BEFORE DAWN, Tom left his wife and crept into Chrissy's room. He watched her sleeping for a while. Without a cell phone or an iPod in her face, she looked very much like his baby girl again. He kissed her forehead and tucked her in. *She's so beautiful,* he thought. He took a moment to press her into his memory. He smoothed the blankets and pushed a lock of hair off his daughter's face. He watched the strands fall like threads of spun gold from his fingertips.

He spied Frank waiting for him in the hall as he slipped into Donnie's room. It was a mess. Donnie's clothes—nothing in black, Tom noticed—underwear, and leather boots were scattered about. *He's still wearing those boots*, thought Tom. Well, there was nothing wrong with taking little steps. He smiled. The most important changes were on the inside of his son. He loved the mess. This was his boy. His son. The struggle within Tom immediately subsided. Donnie smiled and rolled over as he dreamed. And Tom thought, *Another time, when you're a little older, you will be ready to take on a dragon. But this one, this dragon, is mine. Pleasant dreams, son.* The urgency to leave and the overwhelming desire to stay battled inside him. Tom tiptoed out.

He went back for one last look at his Christine. He wanted to lock into his senses every smell, texture, and feature of her. Stabs of pain, as if his very soul was being cut away, ran through Tom. He wanted to cry out, *God, take away this pain.* Instead, he inched the door closed and let the knife finish its grizzly chore of separating him from his family, his life.

Frank was waiting for Tom when he reached the lobby.

Tom pulled a thin white envelope out of the waistband of his sweats and held it out to Frank. "Stay with Donnie when he reads this. You know, if . . . I told Donnie . . . well, he'll try and take it all on himself. Help him."

The good-bye letter was a military tradition. One that brings God closer in the writing and forces the writer to face the fear beneath their bravado.

Frank took the sealed envelope. "You're in the first cycle?"

"Yeah. I'm taking PT for real this morning. I can't delay. They are trying to pull out of here as fast as they can and leave me behind. That would force Donnie into the next wave of replacements."

"Gotcha." Frank put the letter inside his jacket.

Tom noticed Frank was wearing his work clothes. They looked good and were a pleasant sanctuary for Tom's eyes, which had been filled with khaki. But that was the old life. Tom cautioned himself, *Don't even imagine yourself there. At this point it would be a torture too difficult to visit.*

Frank started to speak. "Listen . . ."

Tom's eyes fixed on Frank's name written inside the white oval on his jacket. "No. Don't. You and I did the right thing here. Don't ever doubt that. I am lucky to have a friend like you. You came through for me, Frank. I'm grateful. This is what I want."

They looked at each other. They wanted to say more but couldn't. It would have been too much. Tom couldn't handle it. Frank was his brother. He loved him that much. He was a brother born during a war in a faraway place. He'd arrived fully grown, wearing camos, holding a rifle, and standing next to Tom. And they had been standing by each other ever since. They hugged. And Tom left.

It was still dark when he stepped outside the motel. The lights at the front gate to Dix about a mile down the street were beacons in the darkness. Tom was glad it was close enough for him to walk. He needed time to reorient himself.

Leaving one world and entering another was never easy.

Chapter 24

As Tom made his way to the front gate, the rising sun glanced orange off the windows of many buildings. While the glass appeared to be in flames, night still lingered everywhere else. The shadows were long and tangled up with each other. Several times what he had thought were trees became people and what he had thought was one person became many. Fort Dix was stirring.

Voices, guards calling out as the sentries changed, and many booted feet beating as one swirled into the sounds of street traffic and fell into Tom's ears from every angle. It was impossible to distinguish the origins of this music that signaled the beginning of another day.

At the main entrance, Tom showed his ID and passed through. Off to one side a cluster of men argued with the MPs who had denied them entrance. Tom had walked passed WKYG and Channel 23 local news vans on his way to the gate. He supposed these were the bad press he had been warned to avoid. He smiled to himself. If they had known they had just brushed shoulders with "the Dad," he wondered, what would they do? He decided it was best he didn't find out.

Tom was scheduled to meet Staff Sergeant Steiner alone for his testing. Cogriff had chosen this quiet time and the isolated location. Since it was a holiday weekend, Tom expected very few people to be around. He would have preferred the dirt patch outside the barracks. Perhaps this was the lieutenant's idea of keeping him hidden, a low profile, although Tom suspected something more devious was about to take place. Still, he headed for the parade grounds. He had to go. He walked away from the large main hub of the post and down the less traveled path.

Reveille stopped him in his tracks. He came to attention and faced the direction where the American flag was being raised. He saluted. The army requires you stay at attention, saluting, until the reveille stops, even if you cannot see the flag. Respect was to be demonstrated. Tom liked that part of the army's teachings.

He waited in silence and thought about the blood and sacrifice buried inside the stars and stripes. Tom thought of Tommy, Donnie, Albert, and the young faces of the others in his platoon. They had no idea yet how very brave they all could be.

The reveille ended. The sky was almost fully lit. The ghostly moon was fading fast in the west. Tom pulled himself back to today's quest. He laughed at himself. *Quest?* A white knight, that's what the doc had called him. But if he failed today's test . . . he would lose more than his shining armor.

Returning to civilian life wouldn't suit Tom now. It was like the doc had said, "He had a feeling." Well, now Tom had that same very strong feeling. It had been germinating in him, slowly growing, but it was now in full bloom. This was where he was fated to be. What clinched the deal for Tom was that the "black," his PTSD, had not visited his dreams after his first week.

He breathed in and out, watching the steam escape through his mouth, and told himself to get on with it. Tom entered at the back of the parade grounds, under the grandstands. He followed the path of sunlight that cut through the middle of the tunnel. The dirt looked like a golden carpet. Maybe that was a good sign. He needed signs. He could use an edge.

Thoughts of luck were broken when Tom spied Lieutenant Cogriff waiting at the far end, near the tunnel's exit.

A low murmur grabbed Tom's attention, and he looked overhead as he passed beneath the spectator's stands. He dismissed it as an echo from something nearby. Staff Sergeant Steiner's half-lit form, hands on hips, was waiting on the sparkling wet grass.

As Tom exited the tunnel, he threw up a salute, paused, then skirted Lieutenant Cogriff. The lieutenant's eyes bore into Tom as if he had just stomped on his toes.

Full sunlight slapped Tom in the face. He crossed to Staff Sergeant Steiner, shielding his eyes.

When he reached the sergeant, a rumble from behind pulled Tom back around. Squinting, he checked out the stands. The sun, like a spotlight at the theater, was lighting up the bleachers. They were almost full. Had he missed something? Was there an event, perhaps a graduation ceremony today? But it was too early.

"You have a cheering section, Private Lane." The sergeant didn't sound happy or mad. As ever, he was just Staff Sergeant Steiner.

Half of Fort Dix had turned out for Tom? He was shocked. He checked out the faces and saw Albert's, in the first row, beaming back at him. He couldn't believe he had that many friends. Tom rolled his shoulders like a boxer warming up and waved.

They started calling out, "Dad, Dad. Go, Dad!" This was great. Lieutenant Cogriff's expression, however, told another story.

When the lieutenant stepped out in front of the crowd, the cheering abruptly stopped.

Tom suspected he was there to watch him suffer, be a witness to his failure, so that he could be rid of him once and for all. And then the lieutenant could say to whoever was pushing the buttons to help Tom, "It wasn't my fault. I did my best, but Lane failed."

Well, fat chance. Little did the lieutenant know his presence was encouraging Tom, not discouraging him.

"Private Lane."

Tom snapped around to the sergeant's voice. "Yes, Sergeant."

As required, the sergeant read aloud the standard from the Field Manual for a proper push-up. Then he called, "Demonstrate post." Jake, sporting a big smirk, ran out to demonstrate the exercise correctly. The sergeant also had him demonstrate the disqualifying behaviors as noted in the FM.

Jake, like the puppy he was, ran off the field straight to Lieutenant Cogriff.

"Max is seventy-one. That's what you need, Lane."

Like he needs to remind me of what I've been working toward for the last weeks, Tom thought.

On Steiner's command of "Get set," Tom got down on the wet grass and assumed the front-leaning rest position. His feet were twelve inches apart. He forced his body to form a straight line from his shoulders to his ankles. Every fiber in him resisted, but Tom ignored his body's complaints.

The sergeant took out his stopwatch. "On my command." He checked Tom's positioning, then yelled, "Go!"

Steiner hit the stopwatch, and Tom started pumping them out. He was careful to lower his entire body as a single unit and, when returning to the starting position, to fully extend his arms.

In no time Tom was sweating, and his pecs, shoulder, and tricep muscles were screaming, "Stop."

The sergeant counted them out. "Fifty-six, fifty-seven . . ."

Tom heard a low moan from the crowd when he repositioned his hands. But he was safe. The rules said they had to remain in contact with the ground all through the test. Tom made sure of that. But Tom was glad he had witnesses to back him up, in case Cogriff tried to pull something if, by some miracle, he passed.

Perspiration was blurring Tom's vision. The salt was stinging his eyes.

"Sixty-six, sixty-seven . . ." Steiner's voice penetrated Tom's pain.

He was concentrating so much on doing the exercise with speed and accuracy that until this moment Tom had no idea how many push-ups he had done. He was pumping like that little steam engine in the children's book. But how was he doing with the time?

The crowd joined in.

Tom felt their chanting and foot pounding come up to him from the cold earth under his hands. New energy recharged his muscles.

"Sixty-eight, sixty-nine, seventy . . ."

Tom glanced at the sergeant's hand rising to check the time. His finger was poised over the button of his stopwatch.

"Seventy-one," yelled the crowd.

"Time," yelled Staff Sergeant Steiner.

The crowd erupted.

Private Lane collapsed to the ground. Taking off his sweatshirt, Tom wiped the salt out of his eyes. Someone handed him a water bottle, and he drank. It was Albert.

Albert tried to massage Tom's shoulders as he praised his achievement, but it was too painful. Tom just wanted to be perfectly motionless for the period of rest they gave him between exercises.

The army had rules like at the Olympics. Tom had no less than ten and no more than twenty minutes between events.

Next would be sit-ups. He wasn't too worried about them. Tom's abs were in great shape. He had never gotten that mountainous beer belly some men develop. The push-ups and the run were his weaknesses. One down; two more tests to go.

Finally, Tom's ragged breathing slowed, and his heart stopped galloping.

"You've rested for seventeen minutes," warned Albert.

Hearing that the next event was about to begin, some of the soldiers in the stands yelled out, "Go, Dad. Get it on. Dad's one badass." Some of the other encouragements like, "Rad Dad," Tom didn't understand. He waved anyway and chalked it up to a generation gap.

Albert stood up to talk to the sergeant. This was major for Albert, who treated the sergeant like an unapproachable idol.

Then Tom stood and said, "I'm ready, Sergeant Steiner."

The Sergeant repeated the same routine of reading the standard and having good little Jake demonstrate. Again, Tom would have two minutes to perform as many sit-ups as he could. Seventy-eight was his goal.

Albert got down on one knee. "Let's go, Dad. I'll hold your feet."

The starting position was lying flat on his back with his knees bent at a ninety-degree angle. Tom's feet could be together or up to twelve inches apart. He chose apart.

Albert's meaty hands grabbed hold of Tom's ankles. "Ready," he said.

The heels must stay in contact with the ground during the entire test, and with Albert attached to his, Tom wasn't worried about breaking that rule.

Steiner said, "Get set."

Interlocking his fingers behind his head, Tom got into position. Taking a deep breath, he listened for the signal.

"Go," commanded Steiner.

Tom snapped up, being careful to raise his upper body forward beyond the vertical position. When he came down, the bottom of his shoulder blades had to touch the ground.

A cheer went up from the crowd. Suddenly Tom felt light. This was easy. He was counting in his head as well as listening to the sergeant.

"Twenty-five, twenty-six, twenty-six," the sergeant repeated.

A moan came from the cheering section.

"Keep going, Dad," said Albert. "Shoulders to the ground."

Tom cursed himself. He must have screwed up. If that were to happen, the scorer, Sergeant Steiner in this case, would repeat the number of the last correctly performed sit-up.

"Fifty-nine, sixty, sixty-one, sixty-two, sixty-three, sixty-three, sixty-three."

Boos and hisses came from the crowd.

Was Steiner trying to screw him? wondered Tom. What was going on here?

Albert cautioned, "Shoulders, Dad, shoulders."

Tom could feel the clock ticking down. He pushed himself, trying to pick up the pace.

"Seventy-five, seventy-six, seventy-seven, seventy-seven . . ."

The long moan from the crowd went right through him.

"Seventy-eight, time!" shouted Steiner.

Albert picked Tom up like a rag doll and swung him around. In his dizziness, Tom thought he saw a slight smile on the sergeant's face.

Albert put him down as everyone started piling onto the field. Albert yelled, "Give him room to breathe. Dad still has the two-mile run."

Tom started laughing hysterically and rolling around on the ground. They must have thought he was having a senior moment, because his supporters backed away. Had there ever in the history of the United States Army been such a to-do over the damn PT test? This was crazy. *Wonderfully insane*, thought Tom. And it hadn't gone without Tom noticing that this was pulling out the best from Albert. The boy was stuttering only infrequently.

Albert had said he was the youngest in his family and the smallest, which was hard for Tom to believe. He'd always been the follower, never the leader. But today Albert was showing his potential. He was speaking up and speaking out, and the others were listening to him. Of course, being six foot six and two hundred and forty pounds of pure muscle made the boy hard to ignore.

Again Tom took seventeen minutes of rest, then went over to the oval dirt track that circled the grassy field.

Staff Sergeant Steiner was waiting for him. He pointed to the middle of the track in front of the grandstands. That was where Tom would start and finish. The track was a quarter of a mile long. So to do the two miles, Tom had to go around eight times in thirteen minutes or less. The Sergeant would count his laps and call out the time as Tom passed by.

The sergeant read the Field Manual standard.

Tom set up on the line Steiner indicated and waited for the command.

"Go."

When he started out, his muscles felt short and tight. They were used to contracting, not stretching out.

The crowd hooted and hollered, doing their part.

After the first lap, Steiner shouted out, "Lap one, a minute eight."

A minute eight. Not good enough, and Tom knew it. He needed to average one minute five seconds to make it.

Then a rhythmic clapping joined him.

Tom picked up the pace for the next two laps.

Steiner shouted out, "Five minutes."

After the fourth lap, Tom was at six minutes and nine seconds. He was getting slower. *Where is that adrenaline that's supposed to kick in?* he wondered.

The clapping trickled away.

Tom heard his own heart thumping in his ears. Was he having a heart attack? He pushed on anyway.

"Lap five. Lap six," yelled Steiner, loud and clear.

Tom heard the crowd counting from a great distance away. He started the seventh lap as Steiner yelled out, "Time: ten minutes three seconds."

Shit, he wasn't going to make it.

A voice inside him shouted, "Get your ass in gear."

Wait a minute, that wasn't his voice. Tom took a quick look to his left and saw Albert, big, slow Albert, running up next to him.

The FM prohibits physically helping in any way. But it is legal to run with another soldier during the two-mile. As long as there is no physical contact with the soldier, pacing is permitted.

Albert was not only slow; Tom had heard him sing and knew he had a terrible voice. The kind that sends small children crying for their mothers. But that day, when Albert started singing "Boot Scootin' Boogie" to Tom, there was no sweeter sound.

When Tom crossed in front of the stands, Steiner shouted, "Eleven minutes seven seconds. Last lap!"

Oh God, give me strength, Tom prayed.

"Come on, Dad," yelled Albert.

When Tom rounded the first turn, he heard many more feet joining him.

It seemed everyone in the stands had come out to pace him.

"Stay back," warned Albert. "Don't touch him. Watch you don't disqualify him."

Then everyone was singing, "Cadillac black jack, baby meet me outback, we're gonna boogie . . ."

It was ugly. It was weird. It was great!

Then out of nowhere, Steiner was there beside Tom. He was watching to make sure Tom didn't receive any assistance.

Adrenaline shot through Tom. He flew out ahead of the crowd. Only Steiner was staying right with him.

When he crossed the finish line, Tom heard Steiner scream, "Twelve minutes eight tenths!"

He did it! Tom screamed, "Hoorah!" He danced around, his fists reaching for the sky. Then Tom was swallowed up by his platoon. Albert charged him as though he was sacking a quarterback. The boy threw Tom over his shoulder. Tom's ribs felt like they were going to break. Congrats included painful punches in the biceps and wrestling him to the ground with everyone piled on top. But Tom didn't feel a thing. His relief was all-consuming.

As they all started off for breakfast, Tom spied Captain Wulf emerging from the shadows. He gave Tom a head tilt and silent applause. At the top in the corner of the bleachers General Mitchell from JAG and Lieutenant Cogriff were having a clandestine discussion. Cogriff's head was hanging low.

Tom stopped at the water fountain for a drink and watched the general escape into the tunnel while Cogriff made a beeline for the sergeant. No doubt Cogriff was about to share the general's disappointment with Steiner. That's the way the army works. The pecking order is a stress reliever.

The reaming out of Staff Sergeant Steiner by the lieutenant was the loudest yet. Even from a distance, Tom could see saliva coming out in short, amplified bursts from between Cogriff's paper-thin white lips.

Steiner didn't seem to mind at all. He stood there, arms folded across his chest, and let the insults rain down on him. Obviously *Cogriff didn't know sergeants were waterproof,* thought Tom.

Later, when Tom had enough breath to talk, he called Christine. "Did you get home OK?"

"Sure. Frank ushers us around like we are a flock of golden geese. Did you pass?"

"Yes. Hon, you won't believe it. My whole platoon showed up to cheer me on." There was a long silence at the other end of the phone. Tom heard the radiators bang as the heat came on in the background.

Christine's voice was soft. "That's the house congratulating you.

I've been filling in for you. But it doesn't respond to me the way it does to you."

"That's because your pretty lips don't swear all that well."

They ended the playacting. Neither of them pretended well. They knew what each other's little inflections, pauses, or sighs meant.

"When do you leave, Tom?"

"I would guess this week. I'll try and send you a message, but it might not be possible once they lock us down."

"I feel locked away from you already." Christine's voice quivered. Then she yelled, "Oh my goodness!"

"What is it? Christine, are you OK?"

"Wait a minute. It's a news flash."

Tom heard the television blaring.

"Tom, you're on television. I'm looking at you right now."

Chapter 25

"CONFINED TO QUARTERS!" Cogriff had screamed through trembling lips. His eyes bulged.

On the day after Tom had miraculously passed the PT test, Cogriff had thrown a foot-stomping hissy fit.

In all Tom's years in the military, he had never seen anything like the display Cogriff had put on. He'd kicked the dirt and almost foamed at the mouth.

Tom had tried to explain that he could not control photographers with long-range lenses in trees, but Cogriff would not listen. Tom and his much younger platoon mates had been captured celebrating his victory on the parade ground the morning after Christmas.

That video, complete with sound bites of the GIs cheering, "Dad!" was what Christine had caught on the evening news—and what propelled command to come down hard on Cogriff. The old sayings "the buck stops here" and "shit runs downhill" had jumped into Tom's mind when he had been called out of formation to be assaulted by Cogriff's tirade.

Lieutenant Cogriff had said the video went platinum on the Internet.

Later Tom had found the pictures. He thought the best shot was of Albert hoisting him in the air, as though he had won a gold medal. Cogriff didn't like any of the pictures.

Now Tom understood why command had canceled all passes. He and his entire platoon had been confined to base. Tom had also been forbidden to go anywhere near the perimeter fence. The media was staking out Fort Dix en masse.

Tom had called Jim Small to try to stop his fame from snowballing but was told it was too late.

"You've gotten over 456,000 hits already," Jim had said. "And your congressman is taking advantage of the action and claiming you are his bosom buddy. The jerk has given interviews to every network."

But that wasn't the worst of it for Tom. His new celebrity status had set the guys in his unit against him. They could deploy at any moment, and now none of them could go home. This wounded Tom the most. That had been five days ago. But today it all became meaningless.

"How about a trip to Las Vegas, Dad!"

Tom stopped dead in his tracks. He lingered in the barracks common area staring at Albert. "What?" Tom asked.

Albert hit him on the back, and he stumbled forward two paces.

"It's official." Albert smiled like he had just won a trip to Disneyland.

Tom knew the routine. All communications, phone, e-mail, and Skype were now forbidden. Within twenty-four hours, Tom would be flying toward his ultimate destination, Afghanistan.

He couldn't contact anyone, but the army did have a heart, so the Family Readiness Group would notify Christine. Tom also knew he could count on Ben to let her know what was going on.

"The code has been given?" Tom's question was rhetorical. "Albert, when did you hear?"

"Sergeant Steiner gave the warning order about an hour ago. I covered for you. Lieutenant Cogriff wants the platoon all together for another one of his informational briefings right now."

For the first time since Tom had met Lieutenant Cogriff, he was interested in what the man had to say, as opposed to the intelligence info that command had sent down.

Tom dropped his rucksack on his bed, and he and Albert hustled over to the briefing.

Tom listened for the important details with all the powers of his former Ranger training. The lieutenant passed on a warning from command. GIs should be extra cautious approaching American soldiers in Afghanistan. The insurgents were ambushing troops wearing US uniforms.

Geez, this enemy—and make no doubt that was how Tom and all the other men thought of them; "insurgents" sounded too weak a term—knew how they fought. They are smart to be playing on our compassion, our mercy.

"Our one-year deployment will be spent conducting security operations near and around the Hindu Kush mountains," said the lieutenant as he put a check on his notepad.

He made it sound like they were going down the road and standing around the perimeter of a fruit stand. The rumor mill was circulating that Cogriff was already planning his political career. Clearly, the man only wants soldiering on his resume. He was banking on the fact that voters loved the warrior image. He would never get Tom's vote.

He had seen Cogriff's kind before. Tom referred to them as paper soldiers, political soldiers. If Tom could get a good look at Cogriff's pad, he was sure at the top of his to-do list was "congressman." The problem was that paper burns. Tom could only hope he didn't go down in flames with this complacent lieutenant. And he'd be damned if he would let Cogriff's folly harm one of these kids.

Tom's protective instincts kicked in. He wanted to keep each and every one of these sons and daughters safe.

Tom didn't feel less loyal to his own family. On the contrary, he felt enriched, as if his heart had increased in size. Hell, he was making room for all of them.

As Cogriff droned on, no mention was made that most units were assigned to forward operating bases. FOB outposts were small and close to the action. The whole reason for calling out the Guard was to maintain operational tempo so someone else could rotate home. Tom's Stryker platoon would be "outside the wire," meaning on the unprotected side of the walls fortifying his camp, conducting combat patrols shortly after their arrival. And yet Cogriff skipped that important information. Would Tom and his machine gun be with them? Or did his secret friend who had sent him encouragement and the words *for Tommy* still have a desk job for him?

Tom waited, hoping to learn something about the environment they would be entering. But nothing of substance was said. Did Cogriff know anything about Afghanistan? Sure, he had probably read the books. But had he talked to anyone who had been there?

"We're going to a hostile, landlocked country where the terrain and weather are as unforgiving as our enemy." Tom had told Albert prior to this briefing. "The temperature in December in the jagged landscape of the high Hindu Kush mountains could vary from snow and thirty-two degrees Fahrenheit during the day to twenty-four below at night, depending on the elevation."

That was damn cold. Tom had looked this stuff up and discussed it with one of the medics who had recently returned. And as far as Afghanistan goes, those mountains were the last place you wanted to be. Did Cogriff know any of this or care about it?

The lieutenant went on to describe their travel accommodations like a deranged travel agent who had booked a cruise in shark-infested waters.

"We will be flying on a commercial airbus for twenty hours with two stops for fuel. The second leg of our trip is to the transit center at Kyrgyzstan, which is a small country south of Turkey. There you will get to stretch out and sleep two nights in a bunk with fifty other guys snoring next to you. You might want to try some of the local cuisine. I'd recommend the rice and stew or murgh qorma."

He looked away from his notes and smiled like he had made a joke. But no one had gotten it.

"From there we take a C-130 to our final destination: Bagram Airfield in Afghanistan. You'll have two weeks to acclimate to the weather, people, and terrain. Then we will be sent out to our assigned destinations. We will be broken up into our individual squads and scattered around to fill in the holes as needed."

Tom pictured his hard-earned SRP file. The thin profile, his Soldier Readiness Packet, held nothing of the pain, sweat, and sacrifice it had cost him. Tomorrow it would be tucked under his arm as he passed from checkpoint to checkpoint, as they connected his face and tags with those records. It was a paper passkey to a world that traces its origins back over two millennia, whose culture maintains the same dress, religion, and customs as it did when the Silk Road brought trade from India into the region.

Tom didn't speak the language, understand their religion, or dress like the people who lived there. Their only common ground was guns and the fact that they both had many of them. He found nothing of comfort in that thought.

Tom assumed the Afghani people loved their children the same way Americans loved theirs. And that made him wonder, if we all have that capacity to love, then what does God think of us warring over his proper name?

Or are we simply oil profiteers?

Soldiers are a noble breed. Tom thought it would be a travesty of monumental proportions if their battles were fought for less than heroic principles. A line from an old movie jumped into his head: "Honor is a gift a man gives himself." Tom hoped to return home with his intact.

"Dismissed!" shouted Cogriff. "Lane, come over here."

"Yes, sir." Tom stood at attention.

"I think I have just the job for you when we get to Bagram Airfield in Afghanistan."

Tom waited. This couldn't be true.

"I have arranged for you to work at the machine shop. You should fit right in. And it will be a low-profile job. We must keep you hidden from this insane media madness." His hand flipped though the air. "I'm sure that will be reassuring for your family."

"Yes, sir."

"Dismissed."

Tom saluted and walked away, perplexed.

The unit's previous low grumblings gained momentum. Some soldiers headed over to Pizza Hut for a last taste of America. Others pulled out their cell phones to call home and share the news before realizing they couldn't do that anymore. The full weight of severed connections was being felt.

Tom was glad he couldn't call home because that had been his first impulse. He didn't trust Cogriff. He had told Christine they would put him in a noncombat position, but he never really believed his own lie. The mandatory blackout would give him time to see what developed.

There was one thing about this war that was unlike the others Tom had taken part in: communication possibilities. Now there were cell phones and Skype. Once they were settled in Afghanistan, Tom could contact home. It was both a comforting and bizarre idea. A little combat, then a peek at your daughter performing at her ballet recital. Was war becoming too convenient? He wasn't sure if he wanted his family to see the setting he was destined to inhabit.

As they walked back to barracks, Tom overheard a GI Jane talking about her seven-month-old daughter. She broke into tears. Her friends walked with their arms around her.

"Geez." That kid might not even remember her mom after a year's absence. Tom's pain was nothing next to hers. His heart went out to her. Good-byes were always difficult. He had said his own good-byes every day when he'd talked to Christine. If he had known those good-byes would have to last a year, he would have . . .

Tom stopped for a second and thought, what had he left unsaid? Then he decided he wouldn't have done anything differently. He had held nothing back. Christine carried all his emotions and love.

That night, everyone was wired, as though lightning bolts were running through them. If you get to this point and don't think you are a badass superman, then the sergeant hasn't done his job. He looked around the barracks. They were exercising. Sweaty guys were pumping out push-ups. Tom didn't join in; instead he checked his weapons over and over again.

He had been in this spot before and knew exactly how these kids were feeling. He was feeling the same way. Tom was truly one of them now—heart, soul, and entire body.

The expressions on their faces spoke of what was going on inside. They were thinking about their strength and how good they were with that rifle. Buddies were punching each other on the arms and wrestling on the rec room floor to prove their strength and valor. *They all needed this*, Tom reminded himself. They would do anything to drag out the power that comes with that rush of adrenaline.

Tom looked up at the ceiling and searched for God. He could almost picture him nodding saying, *Yeah, I'll be with you. I understand what is going on there tonight.*

It was vital that they swear oaths, cuss, and flex their muscles. Because tomorrow it would take everything they had to walk out that door and board that plane.

Tom packed and repacked his rucksack and cleaned his weapons. He thought of when he and Christine, hand in hand, had said farewell to Tommy. He tried to image what Donnie and Chrissy would be doing tonight. There were several women in his platoon, which was a new experience for Tom. It crossed his mind that he would have done this same thing if it had been his daughter instead of his son. Women, mothers, sisters, and wives were seeing action. Would Tom picture Chrissy's face if one of them was bleeding?

After the sergeant came in to "tuck them in" for the night, Tom noticed that things got quiet. Too quiet. Thinking quiet.

Faces, places, and previous life events flashed inside Tom's head as if to say *hang on to me, remember me.*

Tom lay in his own bed searching for . . . he didn't know what. Perhaps it was his own humanity. He wanted to make sure to take it with him.

From the restless sounds all around him, Tom knew everyone was doing their own searching.

In the next bunk, Albert was describing every barn, pig, and blade of hay back on his farm. He had been talking nonstop for more than forty minutes. The boy's droning about his escapades with his brothers—evidently, they had shot Albert out of a tree with a BB gun when he was eight years old—were amusing.

This was that point in time when you review your whole life. Hours later you realize the "what ifs" will tear you apart. So you stop thinking about the past and start praying you survive the future.

Tommy had gone through this sleepless night alone, thought Tom. He wished he had been there for him. The last minutes before his eyes finally closed, Tom whispered, *Thanks, God. Whatever is in the fine print of your contract, I'll sign on the dotted line. Donnie is safe.*

Chapter 26

"Let's move out," Steiner screamed. "Pick 'em up. Go! Go, go!"

It wasn't anything poignant for their final hours on American soil, just the sergeant doing his job. But to Tom, Steiner was a disc jockey broadcasting his life. At least, that is the way it felt as Tom's mission for his son ended and his next assignment, to go to Afghanistan and safely return home, began.

At an easy jog, Tom rumbled over to the airfield in the cold half-light of morning with the rest of his platoon. The pounding of their many boots marching in unison was setting the pace for Tom's life. His new life, which was about to begin.

For the next twelve months, Tom would be sleeping, eating, shitting, and fighting alongside these men and women from the First Battalion, Twenty-Eighth Infantry Division out of Harrisburg, Pennsylvania.

"Great morning, right, D-Dad?" Albert smiled.

"Yes, son." To Tom, Albert looked especially young today. The boy's stutter was back.

Outside the hanger, he fell into line with his treasured SRP tucked under his arm. The faces surrounding him were knotted up in private thoughts just like his own. Some of the kids—they would be fully mature within weeks, but right now they still seemed very young to Tom—plugged into their iPods. Their heads bobbed to music. A few played video games. Searching his mind, Tom thought of Christine and conjured up a vision of their lingering "first date" as they held hands and he kissed her wrists. Remembering things like this helped him to keep it together and prevented fragments of his soul from falling off and being left behind.

All of these warriors were in the same delicate emotional condition. Inside, they were struggling to sustain a measure of composure, of toughness to get through this processing, while an adrenaline rush fought in the opposite direction, making them ready to escape and wreak havoc.

Boots scraping across concrete echoed overhead inside the domed cavernous space.

"Stay in your line," screamed the sergeant.

Once again, Tom recognized the familiar taste of his own adrenaline. His heart rate could not be slowed. Fully dilated blood vessels made his thoughts sharp and crystal clear. He was breathing with the ease of wide-open air passages. In other words, Tom's instinct for survival had kick-started. He was ready to fight.

The same enthusiastic glow shined out of each one of these kid's faces. It was part of the rite of passage. All these soldiers were ripe to test their courage. They had been trained for this moment, and now it was here. They were burning, ready to get it on.

"Keep your gear with you." Steiner pointed outside, where the sun was trying to sneak through the cloud cover. "Out on the tarmac, get into formation until someone points you to your ride. No accidently getting on the plane to Cancun. That's for the guys who wear the stars."

"Beaches and girls in bikinis sounds good right about now," said Jake in a shaky voice. Everyone within hearing approved with low chuckles.

"Yeah," said Albert. "I've never been someplace like th-that."

"Relax, guys," suggested Tom. "Loosen up. We've got plenty of time for daydreaming. Remember, for the next twenty hours our only job will be standing or sitting."

Tom was back in that waiting room. Waiting was a soldier's worst job and one that fell into every gap of army life. You could work up a sweat in that imaginary confined space. Worse, it had the power to shatter your nerve.

The curtain on Tom's last tour of duty drew back. Bits and pieces of blurred faces, groans, and the aroma of fresh hot cordite took their bows as they emerged from his memory. Then they dissolved. But he knew they were not gone. They were in the wings, waiting.

After he finished processing, Tom fell into formation.

"Looks like we'll be one of the last units called to board the plane," Tom told Albert.

"Th-this will be my first t-time flying, D-Dad," said Albert. "And I'll be t-traveling in style. The army spares no expense. Look at that baby."

Tom watched Albert's eyes light up. The boy stared at the commercial airbus like it was a hot fudge sundae. "You'll be fine, Albert. Stick with me." When Albert heard those reassuring words, he moved closer to hang at Tom's elbow.

An hour later Tom trotted onto the plane with his unit. He flopped down in a seat.

For a long time after they had taken off, many of the soldiers still clung to their weapons. Tom guessed they needed that reassuring presence in their hands. Clearly the kids were scared. He relinquished his own weapon as soon as possible. He couldn't convince Jake and some of the others that they would not come under attack while flying. Tension dominated many of the passengers, and they kept a firm grip on their carbines for the next ten hours. At long last the sergeant ordered them to uncurl their fingers and give it a rest.

After the long, uncomfortable flight, Tom was happy to land in Kyrgyzstan. The Kyrgyz Republic is an independent state, located in Central Asia and bordered by Kazakhstan, Uzbekistan, China, and Tajikistan—a very dicey place to be, Tom decided, as he checked out the airbase security. He had never been any good with geography, but Albert had Googled where they were going earlier, so he had a vague idea about the soil he was about to put his feet on.

At the transit center, each unit was assigned to a zone inside a cavernous Quonset hut. They were given a chance for hot showers, hot meals, and beds. Tom tossed around which to do first as he searched for a bunk.

He weaved up and down aisles of double bunks, looking for a big sign indicating zone C. There were water stations everywhere. He drank his fill, knowing the arid climate was already trying to suck him dry.

After an extensive search he found the C zone and dropped his gear on the first empty bunk.

The sunlight showed through the prefab semicircular roof with such intensity, it was as if Chrissy had been there and bedazzled the place. With that thought, Tom's first smile in days dented his face.

Because he imagined the sweaty smell of a hundred GIs on the plane sticking to him like bubble gum to a shoe, he decided to do the shower thing before the sleep thing. Then he imagined Christine laughing at his fastidious behavior.

After the shower, Tom climbed onto the top bunk and let a long "Ahh" escape. He fell into a dead, dreamless sleep two seconds after his head hit the pillow. When he awoke six hours later to the same bright sunlight, he heard the snoring of a hundred other guys all around him. And the loudest was right below. He recognized the ragged z's as belonging to Albert, as though they were an old married couple.

Just as the latrine was calling his name and Tom was about to slide over the side, his hand came down onto something brown, cold, and sticky. Albert had brought him dinner. Thoughtful as the gesture was, Tom didn't eat it. He doubted anyone could or should.

This stuff didn't fit into any food category known to man. Smiling to himself, Tom decided it was a deep-fried refugee from a sci-fi feature.

He threw "it" in the garbage as Albert awoke.

"Dad, where are you going?"

"First to the latrine and then to dig out some MREs. Later, maybe you could show me how to do that Skype thing? I want to fill them in at home."

"Yeah, sure. It's easy." Albert rubbed his arms and legs to quicken his circulation. "The food is t-terrible around here. Hey, some of the guys are going to chow down on some of the local stuff the lieutenant suggested. Want to come?" Albert rubbed his sleepy eyes.

"Albert, don't eat anything uncooked. And tell the guys not to, either. They fertilize their crops with night soil, human excrement. That equals dysentery."

"Huh?"

"They put their own shit on the plants. And if you eat that stuff, you will have the shits for weeks."

"Thanks, Dad. I'll tell them."

Tom successfully accomplished his first Skyping adventure during the brief layover in the Kyrgyz Republic. Looking at each member of his smiling family on that small computer screen made them strangely less potent to Tom. Even though he knew it was a silly thing to think, it was as if they had been robbed of specific subtle qualities: Christine's skin looked less warm, Donnie's laugh sounded hollow. Tom had pressed them into his memory in one way, and now they had changed. Were they letting him go? Putting him behind them so they could get on with their lives? Isn't that what he wanted? He both understood and resented these thoughts.

Perhaps he was the one letting go? This distancing was precisely what he had promised himself he would not allow. Not this time. And yet could Tom be both a family man and a warrior? Was it physically possible to live these two separate and very different lives?

Chapter 27

IT WAS DAY FOUR OF THE TRIP. Packing the unit like sardines inside the C-130 seemed oddly appropriate for this the final leg of the journey. Discomfort would certainly be a constant companion going forward. Get used to it, Tom told himself.

Albert pouted, "I liked the other airplane better."

"Now we are flying army-style," quipped Tom.

The scene resembled one of his nightmares coming to life. Narrow, slinglike canvas seats hugged the profile of the plane's hull from front to tail, facing inward. Multiple rows with three seats across rambled down the backbone of the plane. It was a solid, shoulder-to-shoulder river of active combat uniforms. All remnants of the civilian sector had vanished.

From the stench in the plane and the traffic pattern up and down the aisle, Tom guessed many of the troops had not heeded his advice and had tasted the local delicacies.

Jake and Lieutenant Cogriff were doubled over for most of the flight. Taking a perverse pleasure in their discomfort, Tom and Albert struggled to control their laugher. Tom was thankful not to be stuck in the seats near the plane's bathroom in the rear. The stench was bad enough that it was crawling up to the front of the plane in powerful waves. Tom didn't want to imagine what the smell was like farther back.

The lieutenant was moving from seat to seat to get away from the foul odor.

Tom whispered to Albert, "You'd think by now the lieutenant would have figured out he is what stinks."

Albert belly-laughed.

Tom saw Sergeant Steiner also crack a smirk. The sergeant was growing on Tom. Or perhaps they had reached an understanding, one professional to another.

Tom's psyche was experiencing real highs and deep lows. He felt himself changing as he traveled farther from his family. Just before they left Kyrgyzstan, Tom had sent Donnie an e-mail. But with the time difference—the East Coast was nine hours behind—Tom didn't get a reply before they took off again. He was somewhat offended that his family wasn't hanging by the computer waiting for his pearls of wisdom. It may have been irrational, but nonetheless his feeling was real.

Tom had kept the tone of his e-mail light. He couldn't explain to them what he was feeling and thinking, because he didn't understand it himself. He had just talked about the flight and told them about Albert's farm. Albert had some pretty interesting stories; and since Tom and his family were city dwellers, he figured they would get a kick out of them.

Tom the Army Ranger had been a rough, foul-mouthed, scary guy. Figuratively speaking, Tom sensed that guy knocking at his door. He cautioned himself to hide Christine and the kids away in a small pocket somewhere in his heart. He needed them to be stored in a place that he could zip shut, where they couldn't see or hear that Ranger. The Tom who was a hard soldier would shock them. They didn't know that guy, and Tom wasn't ever going to introduce him to his family. Tom's greatest fear was that when this was all over "that man" would follow him back home, and he constantly prayed about it.

What was happening felt strangely two-faced, and in other ways it felt natural. For the first time in twenty years, he didn't want his family to be part of what he was doing. Although Tom knew this amputation had to be performed, he still suffered a sense of loss and betrayal. He had shared everything with Christine. That was their deal, the one they'd made as part of their new beginning after he quit the army. But that promise had to be put aside. Now he needed to carry a gun and his eyes needed to ferret out snipers. He had to self-protect.

"And my heart doesn't need body armor when I am with you, Christine."

Tom had spoken so softly he hadn't realized that his thoughts had been verbalized until Albert woke.

"What is it, Dad?"

"I think we're almost there." For now he would put his promise on pause. He was psyching himself up. Tom needed to focus. And thoughts of family were a diversion.

Staff Sergeant Steiner started preparing them a half hour before Tom heard the plane's wheels grind down. "Grab your weapons. Keep track of your stuff."

Albert gulped down the last of his gummi bear stash. Eyes jumped open. Weapons replaced iPods.

Jake yelled out, "Sergeant. Are we debarking tactical?"

"General, shithead," shouted back Steiner. "And your weapon better be pointing down at the ground. You shoot me and I'll be kicking your ass until you love the pain!"

And with that, the father, the husband, and the neighbor made his final exit. He was a soldier. Tom picked up his weapon and checked it over.

Albert and a couple of the others followed Tom's lead.

Tom's trained ears were the first to hear the sounds of war coming closer and closer. Jets streaked the sky. Black Hawk and Apache helicopters thumped in the air, intruding on his senses and drowning out the sound of the plane's engines. Tom braced himself.

Suddenly the plane was accelerating and climbing again to circle the field. The pilot came on the loudspeaker, saying, "Heavy fighting in the mountains to the east is delaying our landing. But don't worry; these Taliban strikes are over quickly. None of the insurgents have ever managed to get into the base."

The echo of mortar rounds, rocket fire, and grenades exploding ripped the squad's deployment out of the realm of narrative theory and into the bloody factual pool of reality. Game faces were fixed.

Chapter 28

THEIR GRAND INTRODUCTION TO BAGRAM AIRFIELD in Afghanistan ended up being anticlimactic. They landed without a hitch, which disappointed a few people. Jake, in particular, was talking the big game.

"My trigger finger is itchin' for action."

Tom wondered what the boy would do when things turned critical.

The next couple of weeks were nothing. The acclimation process was overrated. Maybe if the unit had come earlier, when the temperature hit the midhundreds, they would be complaining.

January at Bagram Airfield was actually kind of pleasant. Tom wouldn't mind a job here. But since he was spending a year in Afghanistan, he knew his turn to feel the heat—or the cold, depending on the duty—would most certainly come around.

Walking around the base, Tom could see they were in a valley. The mountains to the north had snow on the lofty peaks. At the highest elevations, the weather was extreme.

From watching the news broadcasts at home, Tom was familiar with the names of the cities he now heard mentioned daily. Places like Kabul, Kandahar, and Jalalabad. These places sounded exotic when there was an ocean between you and them. Now, when Tom heard them referenced, he immediately thought of dark-eyed danger lurking behind mud walls.

Charlie Marcus, one of the men in his unit, had been a high school English teacher before he was called up. He told Tom this area was the setting that had inspired Rudyard Kipling's *The Man Who Would Be King*. As he stumbled around holes caused by grenades and rockets, Tom wondered what Kipling would think of the place now.

"This is a gigantic installation," said Tom as he and Albert took a stroll around the base.

"Hey, there's a gym and an Internet lounge. All the comforts of home, right, Dad?"

"Yeah, just fabulous!"

The combined air force and army military presence was considerable. The base had an enormous facility for captured prisoners and detainees. Tom remembered Obama promising sixty million for the prison's expansion. Now he could see his tax dollars at work.

"I c-could get lost here, Dad."

"I agree."

Tom truly felt like a small fish in a very big pond. "This is good. I don't have to worry about reporters anymore."

"There are plenty of newspeople around, Dad. They'll find you if they want to."

"Albert, please, no giving them my location. Besides, their access is limited to specific areas here. I was getting a little stir-crazy back in the states."

The airbase was a busy American city within a foreign city. The local population in nearby Kabul was not allowed on base. But the landscape, arid air, and influx of Afghan military support were constant reminders to Tom that he was far from home.

With Albert's help, Tom had gotten the hang of Skyping. He talked to and saw Christine and the kids almost every evening (their evening was his morning). Having such instant access to home from Bagram Airfield was like being on a business trip, someone had quipped. So Tom tried that line on Christine. She didn't buy it.

"You never traveled for your job. And the jets, gunfire, and all the people in desert camouflage in the background blow that argument. Tom, they're carrying guns instead of briefcases. Nice try. But your business trip scenario is absurd."

Amazing. The woman's powers extended around the world. Maybe she had a personal satellite orbiting the earth. Impossible. But just thinking that brought Tom back to his old self for a time. And so, he learned, there were good and bad sides of Skyping.

After that, he was careful when he called. Most often, he did it after PT, when he could honestly tell Christine he was just exercising, eating, and sleeping. Tom didn't mention the attacks or the long wait for their turn outside the wire. All this make-believe—he couldn't come right out and use the word *lying*—was Tom's invisible C-wire (concertina barbed wire) to protect his family.

Albert, like every one of these kids, lived on YouTube, Facebook, or Twitter. Tom had regularly refused all of Albert's pleas to join the fun, just in case they were still showing his video.

During one of his talks with home, Chrissy had said his video was still getting hits. His daughter explained everyone at her school had seen it. She seemed to be enjoying her dad's fame. *But*, Tom thought, *what kid doesn't want to have a touch of stardom.*

But he still wouldn't watch anything on YouTube.

Lately, Tom had been noticing changes in bad-boy Jake. He supposed it was his fatherly instincts. Most of the unit was now accustomed to the alarm sounding for incoming fire, and only a few still ducked and covered. Jake was among those who continued to scrunch down, trying to be three feet instead of six feet tall.

Tom worried about that kid. Jake was getting scarily quiet. He decided to draw him out, in order to build his confidence. Tom and Albert started sitting with Jake at meals.

Jake accepted Tom's mentoring and started coming around. When he made fun of Tom's age, arranging for denture cream to be delivered to Tom at dinner, Tom was pleased.

This war was very different from Tom's last experience. Not only were there baskets full of "cherries," or inexperienced soldiers, arriving daily and being put into combat positions, there were also a lot more contractors. Tom had not remembered seeing this many in Iraq. Of course, he had left there early in the US occupancy. Here in Afghanistan, they were mostly former military personnel and experts in one field or another, like the guy Tom had met outside the latrine.

Mel—Tom only caught his first name—spoke with a southern twang, was probably in his late thirties, and was short and a little on the chubby side, with a mass of unruly curly brown hair. He did custom armor on the trucks and really knew his business. Tom asked him to look over their Stryker vehicles. They walked over to the motor pool.

When Tom spied their infantry carrier vehicles (ICV) at the front of the line being serviced, he took it as a sure sign they would be moving on very soon. He'd keep that morsel of info to himself. He decided to use this time to become more accustomed to the vehicles.

"The M1126 Stryker ICV is a beautiful machine," Tom said.

"Yeah. You'll be depending on it for protection during transport," Mel offered.

Mel said Tom's infantry squad could also count on direct fire support from the vehicle if they needed it. This was all new to the former recon Ranger.

"You'll be encountering more powerful IEDs, improvised explosive devices," said Mel, walking over to Tom. "The insurgents have been planting mines, fertilizer packed into empty plastic water bottles, in the twenty- to thirty-pound range."

"Yeah?" said Tom. "Back in Iraq, when we vacated an area we usually left behind our food, water, and our empties. So the locals could use the plastic bottles to carry water."

"Well, now some of them have found a new way to recycle," said the contractor. "They bury them in the sand with a pressure-plate trigger. They're moving up. More and more IEDs are in the five-hundred-pound and greater range." He smiled. "We're also seeing a few in the two-thousand-pound range. There's nothin' I can do for you if your ICV runs over that."

Was this good or bad information? thought Tom. "What are you doing now?"

"I'm doing an MRAP, a mine resistant ambush protection, on all these."

The contractor pointed to a long line of Stryker vehicles. It reminded Tom of the motor vehicle inspection station back home. At the end of the month the cars would be lined up around the block. Of course, none of them had armor plating.

"Repairs to the MRAP have been made on all these others," said the contractor. "The insurgents are keeping us real busy. Response to high operational tempo, you know?"

Tom did know. Boiled down, it meant seeing a lot of action. Just glimpsing the scarred vehicles made Tom think of Mosul in Iraq.

He had taken his squad in to rescue trapped soldiers after their vehicle had hit an IED. They took to the streets, searching for the SOB who remote-detonated the bomb. It was one of those adrenaline-charged housecleaning details—the kind that movies try to portray but can't, because sitting in the soft seats at the theater, listening to the action in surround sound, moviegoers can't hear or feel their own hearts pounding as though they are going to jump out of their chests.

He saw the block of dung-colored houses as clearly now as he had then. He and his squad were bursting into each house, not knowing whether insurgents or an Iraqi family sitting down to a meal were waiting for them. The vision sent the sweat pouring over him once again. Inside the first and second houses they had found nothing. From the window of the third the insurgents had opened fire.

Tom had given the command to return fire. Tom saw green. He was wearing his night-vision goggles. The insurgents broke and ran. Two young soldiers, one on Tom's right and the other on his left, fell. Both had sustained life-threatening wounds. They pulled the bleeding soldiers inside the house. Tom and the rest of his men fanned out to find and protect the trapped soldiers.

As the insurgents went out the back, one of them threw a grenade. A wounded and bleeding soldier named Pete—yeah, thought Tom, that had been his name, Peter—had knocked Tom down and thrown himself over him. Why? Why did Pete die for me?

He returned to the present and checked their vehicles for damage. All the operational knowledge and specs Donnie had forced on him during the planning stage of their In His Stead operation clicked into place.

The contractor's work area was a quiet place away from the hustle of Bagram. Mel had oldies playing on a battered radio. Tom took his time wandering from vehicle to vehicle.

All of a sudden, the top-of-the-hour news broke through Tom's respite.

Mel stopped what he was doing and screwed up his face. He moved closer to the radio.

He said, "They're talking about that 'Dad' guy again. Another father tried to take his son's place down in Mississippi. Man, those newspeople get hold of something and they're like gators. They latch on, lock down, and won't let it go." The contractor smiled and returned to his work. "You've heard about this guy, right?"

"Some," said Tom as he squatted down to check under a vehicle.

"I saw the dude on TV with his buddies." He paused. "You know, he looked a little like you."

Am I so obviously out of place? Tom asked himself. Was a private of his age that uncommon? "I'm not him," he said, a little too fast.

Mel smirked, as though he was onto the secret, but he didn't push. "Well, if I met that guy, I'd tell him I admire him. What he did for his son . . . I've got kids. They're too young for this madness. A father's love, right?"

"Yeah," said Tom. He was thinking of Donnie now and all the love that circulated between them. He patted the family photo he kept in his breast pocket. Distance was definitely not a barrier to love. "A father's love," repeated Tom.

Now, before the war took him over again, Tom let his family flow back into him.

"Hell, everyone is tired of this war," said the contractor. "They are having more and more incidents at the National Guard where parents are trying to do what that 'dad' did—serve for their kids. Geez, most of these kids can't find jobs, maybe have a kid on the way, and can't make any money back home, so they end up here. That's how I landed here, the bonus money. It's a crime. They should reinstitute the draft, even out the socioeconomics of those joining. Get my drift?"

Tom nodded. Yeah, he got his drift.

The contractor held out his hand as if to bump fists. "Peace, man."

Tom bumped fists. "Thanks for checking over our vehicles." He quickly turned away.

"Hey, don't worry about a thing . . . Tom . . . I'll take care of you." He winked and finished by saying, "Whatever you need. Remember."

As Tom walked back to his hut, thinking of Donnie's young face aglow with an unwritten, bright future, he whispered, "A father's love. So true. So simple. And pure. This war can't touch that now."

THE NEXT DAY TOM WAS CHECKED OUT by one of the docs on base, who told him he was on course and still didn't need to take medication. Ben continued to come through for him.

The doc must have made an impression. A day didn't pass when one of Ben's friends hadn't come up to Tom and asked what he needed. It was very reassuring.

Two Delta Force soldiers, freshly back from recon, stopped to meet Tom. They too were Ben's friends. They told Tom everything he needed to know, including what army-issued equipment worked and what didn't.

After their talk, Tom gave Christine a list of things to order and send out ASAP. "It's my belated Christmas list," he told her. When he had served previously, Tom's needs had all been met by the army. Now troops had to buy much of their own equipment, boots, CamelBak hydration system, and clothes, especially if they wanted gear that could be life saving. The army was slow on keeping up with their needs and the latest technology. Tom was hoping his order would arrive before they pulled out of Bagram for their forward operating base.

Signing off the computer, Tom approached Albert and asked, "Have you been glued to YouTube all day?"

"I watched a movie. But I'm signing on to YouTube now. Everyone is talking about a hilarious video that's circulating. It's this couple having a fight. Come on, Dad, watch it with me."

Tom turned away. "Albert, I don't want to see that junk." He noticed all around him soldiers in the Internet café, including Cogriff, were glued to their computer screens and eyeing him.

Albert pleaded, "Oh, come on, Dad. This is a good one. All the guys say so. Just this once."

Tom relented.

They started laughing their heads off as they watched a husband and wife quarreling like on the sitcom *Married with Children*.

"Now, this is funny, Albert," said Tom, getting into the spirit of things.

The couple's young daughter had taken the video and put it on the web. The numbers of viewers were jumping higher as Tom and Albert watched.

The father had a beer can in his hand and was throwing pillows off the couch at the TV. He'd throw three or four, then go over, pick them up, and do it again.

"Look. There he goes again, throwing those pillows." Albert laughed.

Tom stopped laughing when he saw it was an old picture of him in uniform that had been taken in the early 1990s that was on the tube. This man hated him. He was screaming at Tom's picture, "What the hell is this jerk trying to prove? What a dummy. We have to kill all those bastards! They should put people like this 'dad' in a mental institution!"

Albert looked over at Tom, "Sorry, Dad. I didn't know." He started to turn it off.

"Wait," said Tom.

The angry man's wife was rocking and knitting faster and faster while her husband was ranting. The video camera zoomed in on the wife. Finally she got up and threw the pillows at her husband, saying, "He's doing what you should have done, you lazy good for nothing! Our boy . . ."

Tom noticed that although the wife was just a little lady with black, gray-streaked hair, her burly husband shut right up. "I want my Luis to come home. Do you know how I feel every time that phone rings? I hurt, I tremble all inside."

The woman was holding her chest, and Tom was afraid she would have a heart attack. If she did, it would be because of him.

"That's what happens. My heart is all twisted inside me. And I wonder, is that call about Luis? Did he make it back from his patrol? He is all we have. What if I lose him?"

"He's a man now, Maria. Leave him be," yelled the husband.

She picked up the pillows and bombarded her husband again.

Crying, she said, "I want him home, safe, and in one piece. This is where he belongs. I don't know how much more I can take. My boy doesn't know these people. He doesn't hate them." When the mother dissolved into tears, her daughter stopped the video.

When Tom looked away from the computer screen, he noticed Cogriff watching him.

The lieutenant seemed to take pleasure in Tom's discomfort. He said to the men gathered in the dayroom, "Hey, aren't we lucky to have the famous 'dad' right here with us."

Jeers and applause accompanied Tom and Albert as they exited the room.

"I wish I had never seen that, Albert. I hope my family doesn't see that video." But from all the publicity it was getting on this side of the world, Tom doubted they would miss it. After that, Tom refused to set foot in the café and crawled into his shell.

Most of the enlisted soldiers thought it was cool to have a celebrity around, even if it was a relatively old man like Tom. They didn't like Cogriff much, so what he said didn't matter. But it did make an impression on Tom. His squad labeled him a prima donna and publicity hound. Some were mad at Tom. Jake switched sides again and spurred them on. About half had forgiven him. Tom decided he'd take what he could get.

He knew the army hated negative publicity. But this was beyond his power. A colonel from JAG had called him in to request Tom put something together in writing. It sounded to Tom like they wanted him to humble himself and apologize for his actions.

That was out of the question, he had told them. Tom didn't feel he had done anything that merited an apology. He was there for his son, plain and simple.

After that, he wouldn't have been surprised if the army stranded him for the duration of his deployment on top of the highest mountain peak.

Chapter 29

THE AFGHANI MOUNTAINS LOOMED HIGH AND OMINOUS over the valley cradling Bagram, and everyone in their shadow felt their presence.

Tom wanted the best gear if he was ordered to take on the Hindu Kush. His package from Taylor Tactical came just in time.

He and Albert were having a little post-New Year's pre-relocation celebration. Coke, gummi bears (Christine had put them in for Albert), and the best homemade molasses cookies in the world were a few of the highlights. They toasted and opened boxes.

Albert was very surprised. He loved the new lighter-weight vest for his body armor. And he was shocked that Tom had found hiking boots that had better support for mountainous terrain in his size, fourteen.

Minutes into their celebration, Tom and Albert got the message from Steiner to hustle over for a briefing. Tom's life was about to change direction. Time was moving faster, though at Tom's next stop he'd think time had come to a standstill.

Lieutenant Cogriff, Staff Sergeant Steiner, and a small platoon of forty men from Tom's original group were being sent to the northeast to the province of Nuristan, in the Waygal District.

One more mountain for Tom to climb. It had been only a short time since he had started on this journey, but Tom felt he had been struggling forever. Maybe because whenever he got to the top of one peak, all he saw was . . . another mountain. And at his present location, that thought could be taken literally. Tom thought of that line "The bear went over the mountain" and knew just how that bear had felt. All roads were leading uphill.

He honestly didn't know how many more mountains he had in him.

Divine guidance would be appreciated. Tom's eyes automatically rolled up, as if to say, "See me. Hear me."

Horror stories about the fighting at these small bases near the Afghanistan-Pakistan border had been circulating through Bagram. From these camps, small squads patrolled the trails through the Hindu Kush mountains. Tommy had survived his time on the mountain, Tom reminded himself, only to lose it in what should have been easy duty.

This assignment shouldn't have come as a surprise, after Tom's unpleasant encounter with JAG here at Bagram. He felt guilty that Albert and the others in his squad were being dragged up the mountain with him.

"Camp Dragon's Lair." Lieutenant Cogriff's voice deepened for dramatic effect.

The lieutenant needn't have bothered. The name said it all. Dragon's Lair—that was the forward operating base Tom was heading for.

He had a moment of déjà vu. Ben's poem, "The Dragon Slayer," echoed in his mind.

Tom tuned back in to Lieutenant Cogriff.

"It's no secret that NATO forces at these bases are attacked regularly. But the camp has never been overrun." Lieutenant Cogriff checked his notes.

Now, why wasn't that a comforting thought? And hadn't Tom heard that about Bagram the day he arrived? He identified an unsettling, prickly trend.

If Lieutenant Cogriff had thought this announcement would boost morale, there was a reason the lieutenant didn't have a marksmanship badge. He couldn't even find the target.

Tom leaned over to Albert and said, "Maybe Cogriff should look up the term 'pep talk.'"

The lieutenant saw Tom cover a smirk. His beady, predatory, birdlike eyes signaled that Tom remained at the top of his shitlist. He'd be paying for his insolence. The man was a certified schizoid.

But Tom had more important things on his mind right now. He hadn't heard anything more about the machine shop assignment. That had been a pipe dream and something he figured Ben had manipulated behind the scene. Steiner had suggested Tom might be headed for that duty and sent him over to talk to the sergeant in charge. But he hadn't heard anything more.

But if it happened, should he turn it down and stay with Albert and his unit? Tom felt a connection with Albert. What he would intend to do hinged on exactly how dangerous Camp Dragon's Lair was.

Cogriff obliged him. "Convoys are forbidden to travel the roads into the camp. They are too full of ruts for us to negotiate, increasing the possibility of us breaking down and becoming sitting ducks. And the areas that are passable are repeatedly seeded with IEDs."

"How do we g-get there, D-D-Dad?" asked Albert out of the side of his mouth. During new and tense situations, Albert's brain struggled as he formed his words.

"When you can't use the car, you call the local taxi service, Albert. It will be all right, son." Tom patted Albert's expansive shoulder.

Cogriff smiled. "A CH-47 Chinook will give us and our equipment a lift. These twin-engine helicopters do a lot of the heavy lifting around here, so two of our Stryker vehicles will be following us. With just forty of us going and some vehicles already at Camp Dragon's Lair, the rest of our ICVs will be going in another direction." The lieutenant scribbled on his clipboard, then asked, "Questions?"

After that uninspiring briefing from the lieutenant, Tom had a lot of questions, but he kept silent like everyone else.

"Lane. Over here."

"Yes, Lieutenant." Tom jogged over to stand ramrod still in front of Cogriff. Cogriff was wearing a smile that would creep out Dracula.

"I'm sorry I got your hopes up, but that machine shop job isn't going to happen."

Tom kept silent. The desk job option was in the rearview mirror. He had never expected Cogriff to let him out from under his thumb. But, for his family, he had kept the dream alive as long as he could. After he had given Christine his order for the hiking boots, she knew it would never materialize. But she never passed on her disappointment and fear. She just said, "If you wear out those boots, I'll order another pair."

Nonetheless, Tom's face burned with anger.

"Your buddies don't have your back anymore, Lane. You'll tough it out with the rest of us. There will be no more special privileges. No visits to the doctors for pep pills or whatever they have been supplying you. I couldn't catch you doping up, but from now on I'll be watching you. You stumble off course and I'll make sure you fall hard. I will take down you and all your friends." The lieutenant's jaw muscles bulged. "My friend at JAG has the paperwork in his hand. The moment you fall, your son steps up. I'll make that brat of yours my personal ass wiper! Do we understand each other, Private?" The man had worked himself up into a frenzy.

"Yes, sir."

"Dismissed."

As he and Albert walked back to their bunks to pack, Tom marveled at the depths of the lieutenant's hatred. The man's insane vendetta against him made him furious. Tom squeezed his balled-up fists so tightly blood seeped between his taut knuckles from where his nails pierced his palms.

Albert took hold of Tom and cautioned, "Don't do it, Dad. He's trying to provoke you."

The purple in Tom's face began to lighten. He hadn't asked for help. He hadn't set out to pit anyone against the lieutenant. He didn't know who was manipulating anything. Was it Ben or . . . Captain Wulf? Tom had thought Cogriff forced him to take the oath that first day, but now that he thought about it, that would be the captain's call. And Captain Wulf must have known about his medical clearance before Tom, or he would not have allowed Staff Sergeant Steiner to haul him out for PT.

And now I am all Cogriff's. He's been looking for a way to break me. Now he thinks he has found it. Only he miscalculated. He has only wounded me, and doesn't he know that is when your opponent is most dangerous. He should never have made this personal and threatened Donnie and these kids. Cogriff is in for a war he can't win.

"Hey, Dad, what did old p-pencil head say?" asked Albert.

"Nothing. Don't worry about it, son. Let's finish packing."

"D-Dad, what's it going to be like at the forward operating bases," Albert asked, interrupting Tom's thoughts.

Tom looked up from his rucksack. Jake and a few of the others moved in closer. "None of us have done this before," said Albert. "And the lieutenant gave us nothing."

Jake spoke up, "That's 'cause he doesn't know shit."

"All right, guys. The camp will be our hub." Tom painted a picture. "We will be spreading out from it and rotating in and out of small combat outposts in the mountains. Our Stryker vehicles will take us through the valley to a drop site. That's the usual deal. Then we will be hoofing it the rest of the way."

Some of Tom's worst experiences had been with force recon. The Taliban would be all over that mountain. He decided these kids didn't need to hear that, so he kept that bit of information to himself. Right now they had enough on their minds.

The lieutenant had also told them that at least one soldier in each of their reformed squads would be from the 101st Screaming Eagles. *No offense to the 101st*, thought Tom, but that didn't make him feel any better.

"The Taliban routes we will be watching will be on a rotating cycle. We'll be living on the mountains for long stretches. Supplies are usually dropped in after dark."

Tom had firsthand knowledge of the Taliban from his several tours in Iraq. He wasn't looking forward to renewing that acquaintance.

Everyone returned to packing without talking.

That night, Tom slept fitfully. His dreams came in short bursts: Chrissy falling off her bike and Tom missing catching her. Donnie three years old and trying to learn to throw a baseball, but Tom couldn't find the ball. Each dream was a snapshot of his failings.

The next morning Albert hovered close behind Tom as they lined up to board the Chinook. Tom noticed most of the others were sweating, and it couldn't be blamed on the weather, as it was bone-penetrating cold. Perspiration was running like a river down Albert's face. Tom slapped him on the back.

Staff Sergeant Steiner, followed by the lieutenant and then the grunts, trotted up the wide loading ramp at the back of the fuselage in full battle-rattle. It was almost sunrise. A faint, dusty, yellow hue flaked the horizon. It was late Saturday night back at home, Sunday morning here. In twelve hours Christine would be starting the ritual of her big Sunday dinner preparations. It would probably be chicken.

Maybe Tom would have the chicken and dumplings MRE tonight.

The crew of three—a pilot, copilot, and flight engineer—welcomed them with the standard commercial airline jabber. Each took a turn speaking a line. The flight engineer pointed out the exceptions to what his comrades had just said, "There are no tray tables, no meals will be served, and nothing will float. If you have to throw up, do it on the guy next to you, because I'm not your mother and I'm not cleaning up your crap." He ended by saying, "What a world, what a world."

Damn!

"You ain't in Kansas anymore. What nice, fresh-looking cherries," added the flight engineer.

Tom didn't feel like a cherry as he took his place on one of the canvas benches lining the sides of the Chinook. In fact, this was all very familiar. He checked his armpits. They were saturated with sweat.

Most of the soldiers around him were staring at the floor as if it might disappear. Jake's knuckles were fixed and white, one hand clamped around the frame of his seat, the other to his weapon.

But for some reason Tom's eyes flashed to the ceiling. Someone had pinned an American flag overhead. "Nice," Tom murmured. He elbowed Albert. "Look what's watching over us."

Everyone heard Tom and looked up. They smiled. The patriot button did it every time.

Even a brief relaxation of the tension was welcome.

Steiner talked to everyone, calming them. Beads of perspiration were coating Jake's upper lip.

Tom noticed the sergeant giving Jake a second look.

Once they lifted off, Tom watched Steiner excel at his job. He jabbered continuously. His burning discourse was accentuated by a random smack on the shoulder or a bang on a helmet. The sergeant's eyes bore into each man as if to say, "I mean you, you tough motherfucker!" and it made them believe him. Yeah, they were badasses ready for some hairy work.

Tom had once held the power to convince men that they were a killing force to be reckoned with, that they were invincible warriors. Not all his warriors had been indestructible.

Inside, each soldier was struggling to keep up with a sudden infusion of awesome strength. Tom had been here before and felt the potency of spirited words pumping him up. At the same time, he knew that better than half of these guys would be pissing in their pants when the first shot zinged over their heads. But right now, they needed this intense power that was churning inside them. Only combat could quench that thirst. They were ready to be what the US Army had trained them to be: killing machines.

As they looked out the window, the mountains came at them, hard and quiet. To Tom those peaks seemed to radiate more and more hate as the Chinook closed in. Black chunks of jagged rocks spelled out "Unwelcome." At the high elevations, snow covered the slopes. The same sharp terrain at a lower altitude was dotted with scrawny scrub vegetation. It was an impossible, foreboding landscape. Ancient paths had been worn into the solid rock and were visible from the sky. Tom guessed the slight color change marking the rock was where many feet had trod. The mountain seemed to be luring him in, saying, "Soon you and your enemies will be meeting on my trails."

They received their rounds of ammunition as the Chinook changed altitude on the descent into Camp Dragon's Lair.

Dragon slayer await the call
To enter battles fray
To face the dragons of your time
To fight and win the day

Chapter 30

IT WAS A STAR-SPANGLED-BANNER WELCOME. The insurgents brought the fight to the new arrivals. Tom had to wonder if this was a standard greeting.

The Americans answered from both the sky and the ground.

"Surprise, surprise," said Albert, suddenly sounding like that Gomer Pyle guy Jim Nabors had played.

Like a hen protecting her big, fat, and ugly chick, their escort, a Kiowa Warrior, buzzed around to position itself in front of their Chinook before opening fire on the mountainside. Her fifty-caliber fixed machine gun rapped out a tune. From inside the bird, Tom saw its music sending rocks and dirt clouds soaring.

Tom couldn't pinpoint the insurgents. The enemy blended in with the rock. And the mountain was still holding the shadows of night, like the camp below him.

A couple of the soldiers on the ground gave the pilot of the Chinook a thumbs-up, and Tom and his squad began their descent.

On board, the flight engineer went about his business as though it was just another day at the office. "Grab your gear and hold your ears. Don't leave nothin' behind." He smiled. "Club Med just can't wait to get you guys on the volleyball court." He tapped Albert on the shoulder. "Big guy like you will be real popular."

Albert paled, and Tom whispered, "Keep low, son."

The engineer's jest about Club Med wasn't far from the mark. Although Tom did spy something that could be a volleyball court in one corner of the camp, he knew the engineer meant that Albert made a big target.

"Saddle up!" Steiner screamed out. "Tactical deployment." The sergeant's command was followed by a chorus of sharp metallic snaps and clicks as ammo slid into chambers.

"If anyone shoots me, they will never find your body!" Steiner glanced over at Tom.

Tom briefly wondered why Steiner had repeated this warning. Could it be that someone had once shot him accidentally? It brought a smile to his face.

But Tom didn't have time to decipher it. He yanked the charging handle back on his machine gun, locked the bolt in the rear, and slid the charging handle back to the front. Tom placed the ammo on the feed tray with the first cartridge resting on the gap. With his left hand holding the belt parallel with the tray, he snapped the feed tray cover closed with a sense of purpose. His lips went dry. He gulped some water.

The locking and loading of weapons propelled this skirmish into the personal category. The insurgents were sending them a warm welcome. And Tom, like the rest of the men in the bird, was looking forward to saying "Howdy" right back at them.

The pilot set down on a small patch of dirt inside the camp's perimeter.

When Tom jumped onto solid ground and took up his position, he had only a vague idea of which way to go. The twin rotors of the big Chinook were kicking up a tornado. Small bits of dirt and rocks zinged off his helmet and body. Goggles kept his vision clear inside the dust cloud. Albert, his ammo bearer, was right on Tom's heels. He was counting on that.

When Tom turned back, their taxi had lifted off. Their job done, the Chinook and the escort were already disappearing behind the mountain peaks. Ten seconds on the ground, and Tom already hated those mountains. They cast a shadow over the entire camp.

"That's a show of force they won't forget," said the commanding officer of Dragon's Lair as he swaggered toward the new arrivals. The grisly captain had a MacArthur-like pipe in the corner of his mouth, clamped between his teeth. He wasn't very tall, and Tom had a hard time seeing him over the heads of the others. "At least until tomorrow." The captain's dark eyes looked around expectantly. "Where is Lieutenant Cogriff?"

The lieutenant stood and, after a shaky salute, handed Captain Chavez his orders.

The captain mostly ignored Cogriff after that, as he explained, "We engage these small groups of two to five insurgents a couple of times a week. They usually hit us in more than one position at the same time. See that mountain?"

Everyone looked up.

"They are always there, watching, waiting, looking down on us. Never forget that. We call it *La Parca*—that's Spanish for 'the Grim Reaper.' If you haven't figured it out yet, I don't like jokes about Hispanics."

With only a hint of an accent, Captain Chavez went on to say that their new home was overcrowded. "Increased operational tempo means that instead of four, it's eight men to a tent. Make it work. I don't mind a few touches of home here and there."

Tom noticed a colorful piñata hanging just inside the captain's quarters.

"Sir," asked Lieutenant Cogriff, "Where are the officers' quarters?"

"You'll share a tent with me." He turned back to the rest of the new arrivals, "Drop your gear. Look around. At thirteen hundred, you'll get a detailed briefing." He turned on Cogriff, "Lieutenant, first time outside the wire?"

Cogriff reluctantly nodded.

"Cogriff, follow me. Dismissed." The captain walked away casually, puffing on his pipe. Cogriff followed, walking as though he had a stick up his ass.

Tom and Albert found a tent with two free bunks and threw their gear on them. Tom warned Albert not to ask about the previous occupants.

The place was smaller than Tom had imagined. A couple of platoons equaling about a hundred men lived here. Seventy were US Army and the rest, thirty or so, were from the local police force. That number included the new arrivals. Tomorrow Tom and the forty guys he had flown in with would be broken apart to supplement the already-formed squads.

"Let's take a walk," Tom suggested to Albert. He added, "Bring your weapon. Always keep it with you . . . even when you are going to the latrine. And don't leave the tent without all your gear, full body armor. Do you understand?"

Albert nodded.

The Dragon's Lair was a rectangle 300 meters long and 100 meters wide. The setup was obvious. All eyes and firepower were focused on those damn mountains.

The camp had three mortars set up. One faced the east, one west, and one north. A mighty 155mm howitzer sat like a queen in the middle of the compound, surrounded by gabions filled with stone and earth. In some areas, the twelve-foot-high walls were the remnants of an older mud partition where a village had once been. The other parts of the compound looked like a deranged construction project. Sandbags piled twelve feet high, with odd pieces of lumber stuck in here and there, formed a couple of observation posts and some overhead protection from falling debris, rain, and snow. Gun ports dotted the walls.

Tom fingered one of the corrugated roofs. They deflected the heat in the hot months and protected them from snow in the winter. The tents, which were their living quarters, and three semipermanent structures made of plywood and a few four-by-fours constituted the hub of the camp. These "buildings" were the dining facilities that doubled as command center, the communications center, and storage.

Looking through one of the gun ports, Tom saw an observation post about fifty meters up the rise behind the camp. It was heavily fortified and stood like an out-of-place obelisk. It marked the forbidden territory between the village and base camp.

Tom stood on the top of a gabion and saw that Camp Dragon's Lair was well fortified and camouflaged. He also noticed that the scrub vegetation for as far as he could see had been shredded by gunfire.

On the east side of the encampment, a village of two or three hundred Afghans occupied a slightly raised mound. Afghani children played on the bullet-scarred rocks. The village was perched above a ravine where a river had once flowed. A small trickle of water still meandered down the valley. *Probably melted snow off* La Parca, thought Tom. He wondered if the camp shared their bottled water supply with the locals or if all those kids had to drink was that muddy sludge.

Tom and Albert walked the entire perimeter. A few scant rays of sunlight escaped over the mountain and fell inside their fortified walls. They didn't add any warmth or cheer.

The sound of the muezzin calling the villagers to prayer surprised Tom the first time he heard it. He reminded himself that it shouldn't have. This was what the Taliban had said this war was all about: religion. God. They had a grip on remote places like this, on a few mud huts filled with worshipers. He watched the people he was pledged to defend—heads covered, robes and rags fluttering in the breeze—on their way to the mosque.

The warrior in Tom wondered, *Had any of these villagers taken part in this morning's demonstration? Would they pray now and be forced by the Taliban to pick up their weapons later?* The Taliban's roots ran deep here. Tom could feel the emotion as he listened to the voices of those praying. Was their God the same one he was now asking to bring him through this?

At the captain's briefing, Tom found out that Staff Sergeant Steiner, the lieutenant, and he and Albert would be heading out before sunrise the next morning.

Captain Chavez explained they would be spending six nights on the Grim Reaper. "These frequent patrols are a necessary demonstration of the US Army's presence in the area. We keep the Taliban snipers on their toes and their supply routes closed." Chavez took a pull on his pipe before adding, "We are the plug holding back a greater flow of insurgents."

Tom was immediately reminded of his unpredictable plumbing back home. He'd never had control of it, either.

The first night was sleepless. It always was for Tom until he had labels for all the night sounds.

Albert's nervous voice came through the darkness. "D-Dad, why can't we leave when it's light and we can see those snipers?"

"The enemy does most of their troop movements under the cover of darkness. It's safer for us to do the same." Tom tried to quiet Albert's fears. "The guys in our new squad are good. They'll show us the ropes. Don't worry. Sleep."

Tom knew the drill. From their mountain perch they would radio back movements and confirm targets. Most of their sneak 'n' peek would be conducted in the darkness, looking through night-vision goggles. The squad would move at night and then settle in to watch specific areas and rest during the day. Mountain climbing in unfamiliar hostile territory with an inexperienced butter-bar lieutenant is what nightmares are made of—at least, what Tom's were made of.

Chapter 31

NINE GRAY GHOSTS FILED INTO THE INFANTRY CARRIER VEHICLE in somber silence. It was four in the morning. Snow peaked on the toe of Tom's boots. He kicked it off and stomped his feet, as though he was stepping into his home instead of an armored vehicle.

"Sunrise is at zero six hundred. Weatherman says it's going to be a lovely day in the neighborhood," sang their driver, Private First Class Dean.

"Well, that is not accurate," said Cogriff, eyeing the red-haired lad. "There is a chance of scattered snow at the lower elevations and a high of zero Celsius. Where we are going, at five-thousand-feet elevation, we'll see a whole lot more cold and snow."

"Just like the lieutenant said, another balmy day in paradise lost," inserted Steiner.

Cogriff and the driver were in the front seats, but Steiner was doing the talking.

"Sergeant, is this your first tour?" asked one of the veterans.

Corporal Kwan, Tom thought. He was still learning names.

"Third," Steiner answered.

Okay, now Tom was more at ease. Cogriff would be Steiner's problem. Then he wondered what happened to Steiner's last lieutenant.

Word had spread that this was the lieutenant's first combat post, and everybody was avoiding him like the plague. It wasn't his inexperience so much as his unwillingness to accept that he might have something to learn that didn't come from a book. He had spent most of yesterday practicing his Pashto instead of getting to know his men and the camp's fortifications. He practiced his language skills on his Afghani counterparts, and they had no idea what he was saying.

The vehicle rumbled down a semi-dry riverbed for more than an hour. It was the same muddy waterway that Tom had seen near the village. They traveled in silence.

The unspoken question floating among them was, *When will we hit an IED?* Putting their upgrades, the cage, and the mine resistant ambush protection to the test could certainly wait as far as Tom was concerned. He asked God to delay that trial.

Before they embarked, the captain had met them at their ICV. He'd said they swept this route regularly. Tom would have preferred a more precise assessment. But he did admit to himself that he trusted Chavez. He also understood that at some point he would be rotating through mine-sweeping duty. He needed to listen to the voices of the men who knew the territory. That was a daylight mission. Nothing sounded good here. But then that's why they say war is brutal.

Tom was once again glad Donnie wasn't in this place the rest of the world had both neglected and forgotten.

The ICV arrived at around five thirty at the back side of one of the smaller mountains in the six-hundred-mile Hindu Kush chain. It had taken them an hour and a half to travel nineteen miles.

Maybe that was good, considering there was nothing around there that Tom could call a real road.

Their vehicle had to stop several times to remove boulders from rockslides. Each time, they all got out to help, except for the lieutenant. It was an edgy endeavor. Their eyes kept darting up at the mountain and down the gorge, then back to what they were doing. The whole time Tom was wondering if the avalanche had been man-made or nature's doing. Either way the gorge was a trap waiting to snap.

Reaching their destination, the squad was quick to unload.

"A daylight return trip is sure to draw fire," said Dean out the cracked window. "Get my copilot in here." A blond soldier who had been helping them unload jumped into the passenger seat. The baby-faced Dean and his sidekick took off back to camp the moment everyone had exited from the vehicle.

Tom said, "See you in a few days."

As Dean waved, the wheels were already throwing up gravel. Then the ICV disappeared back into the gloom.

Tom's infantry rifle squad started their ascent on a wide, well-worn path. Corporal Kwan took the lead.

"This area faces northeast, so sun hits the mountain earlier than at the camp," said Kwan. "The more ground we put behind us while it is still dark, the safer we'll be. So look sharp and be quick."

Tom noticed they were traveling heavy. Two automatic riflemen hauled M249 SAWs (squad automatic weapons), seven thirty-round magazines, and two drums of linked 5.56mm bullets, each drum holding two hundred rounds. Two grenadiers carried M203 grenade launchers attached to their M4 carbines. They had ten to thirteen thirty-round magazines of the 5.56mm and fourteen forty-millimeter grenades.

The sergeant and Cogriff were armed with M4s and fourteen thirty-round magazines of 5.56mm. One of the other guys and Steiner were also team leaders, so they were lugging the additional weight of radios and signal equipment.

They hadn't been hiking for more than an hour when Tom noticed Cogriff sweating and sucking air.

Albert was equipped the same as the riflemen; as Tom's ammo bearer, he also had a tripod, plus 1,200 rounds, or six drums of 7.62. Tom didn't have an assistant gunner, so they were going light on ammo. Albert had picked up some extra rounds, but there was only so much the boy could carry.

While Tom was adding up all this firepower, he wondered what the reaction would be if a squad like this just happened to stroll around in Times Square. Would they be cheered as heroes? Or shot down by the police, mistaken for outlaws?

With a mental *yippee ki-yay*, Tom hoisted his M240 onto his shoulder. As the incline increased, it got heavier. His machine gun had all the bells and whistles: an M145 optic and a PEQ4 laser-aiming device for night. A fifty-round starter belt of 7.62 and a two-hundred-round belt in a drum rounded out Tom's load. For his nine-millimeter handgun, he had thirteen-round magazines.

They all wore full body armor front and back, and side plates. Tom's armor was under his load-bearing vest, which held extra magazines of ammo and a first aid pouch.

Understandably, it didn't take long before Tom was sweating. Not just a little sweat; he looked like he had just taken a shower fully dressed. This was all part of Cogriff's revenge. No doubt about it. Why else would he be carrying an extra 120 pounds, while everyone else was humping with only 80?

Tom's CamelBak contained about seven liters of water, and he would need every drop. He was thankful Captain Chavez had told them to use just their assault packs instead of the larger rucksacks.

The smaller assault pack had foot powder, dry socks, casualty feeder cards, enemy prisoner cards, flex cuffs, a poncho liner, stripped-down MREs (crackers and peanut butter), and extra batteries. "Essentials for every camper," Tom had joked at the time. No way was this anything like the supplies needed for the Boy Scout camping he and Donnie had done.

Could the army pile any more on? Tom took an extra-hearty pull on his water tube. Unless they had a way to change him into a four-legged mule, he doubted he could carry an ounce more.

They had been hiking for almost three hours when Staff Sergeant Steiner called a break. The altitude was beginning to get to everyone, especially the new guys. Tom was glad to see Cogriff was sweating profusely and breathing so hard he couldn't talk.

Tom guzzled down more water as their caretaker, Specialist Dombrowski, talked.

"By midday, we'll come up on one of our established outposts. It has good defenses and a small cave for shelter from the snow and freezing temperatures. Don't enter the cave until it has been checked for IEDs. We can cover the whole valley from there. They'll night-drop supplies, including fresh water, in to us. So keep hydrating."

When Cogriff signaled for them to start out again, he seized his chance to push the knife into Tom a little deeper. "Private Lane, take point."

Ridiculous. The guy with the machine gun doesn't take point. Tom checked the faces around him. There was no need for words; their expressions told him what they were thinking. The lieutenant was showing off his ignorance with red flares.

This was a joke. Tom didn't know the terrain. But he played along and hauled his weapon up onto his shoulder to follow orders. He figured the Screaming Eagle behind Albert would screech if he made a wrong turn. But he did worry about being a target. He couldn't rapidly defend himself with his weapons balanced on his shoulder.

They came across many intersecting paths. Some were vertical, indicated by ropes pinioned into the mountain. Others led into a multitude of crevices and caves. The mountain was like a monster with many scars. Tom noted some of that disfigurement was natural, but a fair amount of it was man-made.

Now Tom knew why Bin Laden had been impossible to find. There were hundreds of places for the Taliban to hide. They could be inches away, and he wouldn't know it until it was too late. "This colossal mountain has too many secrets," mumbled Tom.

The higher the squad climbed, the narrower the trail became. Large boulders and recent rockslides made forward progress slow to a cautious crawl. Tom picked his way around and up as the mountain threw him a curve. From just rock, the trail became wet rock, then ice-covered loose gravel. When he rounded the next bend, they were engulfed in a thick bank of clouds.

Kwan suggested, "Watch for snipers."

Everyone got smaller, and idle chatter stopped.

As Tom crept along, looking up and around instead of focusing on the footpath, his feet began to slip on the damp glacial boulders. Stumbling forward, he hit some loose pea gravel, dropped his weapon, and was surprised to find himself flying without a parachute.

Instinctively, Albert stretched out to catch Tom. He missed, and with a painful thump, Tom's body came up close and personal with an outcropping of rocks. He rolled off that ledge, slid down an embankment, and disappeared into the cloud bank.

Steiner and Cogriff were there in an instant. Albert had jumped down on the ledge and was lying on his stomach, crying out, "Dad! Dad!" No one answered.

They listened for only a few ticks on the clock before Cogriff ordered, "Move out. He's gone."

Albert continued to shout Tom's name as he began to sob. Cogriff held Albert in his stare and repeated his orders from between clenched teeth, "Move out!"

Poor Albert looked confused. "I th-thought there was a code not-t to leave anyone behind."

Tom would have been proud of the boy speaking up like that.

Then Steiner ordered, "DA, fall in at the rear with Lane's weapon. Kwan, take point."

Everyone started off again in abject silence. Albert took his position as he sobbed. Only the motion of his big shoulders conveyed the depth of his loss. Cogriff stuck around to put another nail in Tom's coffin as the rest of the squad passed by. "Not such hot shit now, are you, old Ranger?" he said, his constipated face leering at the spot in the clouds where Tom had disappeared.

Cocky son of a bitch, was what Tom wanted to say, as Cogriff's sarcasm penetrated his dazed mind. He was also tempted to yank Cogriff over with him, but he was still a little murky on exactly what had happened. The last thing Tom remembered was stumbling and sliding toward the great abyss. He had a flashback that Albert's big hand had pierced the fog.

In reality Tom had come to a stop about ten feet below the path on a narrow ledge at the edge of a precipice. Now he took a quick inventory and found he had not been seriously injured. Only the lump on his forehead was sore, and that hurt his pride more than anything else. He blew a thank-you kiss to the big boulder that his head had hit because it had also stopped him from going over. Tom waited to catch his breath before he pulled himself out and back onto the trail.

Tom caught up to Albert in no time, feeling a little exhilarated by his adventure. Cogriff looked disappointed and told everyone, "Keep moving." Tom saw a glimmer of a smile crease Steiner's face.

Albert's wet cheeks broke with elation. He was wordless and looked like he was going to cry again.

Tom said, "It was nothing. I came to a stop on a ledge just below the clouds."

"You've got blood on your face," said Albert, wiping his own face on his sleeve.

"It's just a scratch. Keep up, son." Tom knew the best way to get over fear was to keep going. "Let's catch up to the squad, Albert," Tom urged.

Around the next bend, the squad met their first resistance. A scattering of rifle fire changed chunks of rocks into lethal projectiles. The head of the column came to a halt.

Tom remembered this from being in Iraq. It was like being at the shooting gallery, only you were the yellow duck.

Kwan, at the head of the column, had the best view. He took cover behind a boulder and got low. Peeking out, he yelled, "Somebody get good eyes on this sucker!"

"Where is he? Where is he?" repeated Cogriff. His voice was an octave higher than usual.

Steiner's calm voice reached out to everyone, "Cover and maneuver. You know the drill."

"My shoes are slipping on the rocks. I can't move," screamed Cogriff.

Steiner grabbed the lieutenant by the collar, pushed him behind him, and shouted, "Go . . . go . . . go!"

Cogriff ordered, "You see something move, you shoot!" He pivoted around as he brought up his weapon. "Twelve clock." Cogriff's M4 split the air and sent rock clips pinging off Kwan.

"Watch it!" Kwan hit the deck.

"Dude, we gotta get closer," whispered Dombrowski to the lieutenant.

"Attack positions," ordered Cogriff.

The rest of the squad hugged the rocks and took cover wherever they could find it. Just in case of a situation like this, veteran soldiers were always looking for places to cover up as they walked. "Be prepared" was a great motto. Tom had been singing that to Albert for days. Now he was glad to see that Albert had taken his advice.

"It's too small an area," answered Tom.

Kwan inched forward to a broader area where there was plenty of protection. They were above the clouds, and the day was clear. He signaled the location of the sniper to Steiner. The Sergeant waited patiently, like a snake. When the sniper sent out a burst, the sergeant searched for him through his scope.

"Give me a target," whispered Steiner. The next time the sniper popped up, Steiner returned fire.

This was the game they played for at least thirty minutes, the sergeant, Kwan, and the sniper taking turns shooting and dodging bullets.

Doing nothing, Tom rested back against the rocks next to Dombrowski. The young specialist took off his helmet to mop his brow. Tom noticed a picture inside his helmet.

"Who is this?" asked Tom, removing the photo.

"My boy," said Dombrowski, adding, "I miss him."

"Cute kid. Your first?" asked Tom.

"Yeah. He was three months when I left. He probably won't know me when I get home."

"Believe me, a kid recognizes his father's love. You'll do fine." Tom thought of his family. Then took his own advice and got back into the action. "Let's roll with the beast," said Tom, providing cover as Dombrowski moved to a forward position.

Tom edged up close to Steiner. "I got a target." He pointed to a long fracture above and to the right of where the path curved. It lay parallel to the path, maybe two feet high at the most. The sniper was lying on his stomach. Tom figured that was the only way he could fit into that tight spot. They had expected to find the shooter in one of the many vertical crevices.

Steiner called Kwan to fall back.

"At least we're too close for rockets and mortars," said Kwan with a smile as he hunched down next to the sergeant. Tom admired the boy's attitude.

Tom listened in as Steiner told Kwan his plan. "When you move up, stay left near the edge of the path. The shooter will be forced to extend out to get eyes on you. Then go low and find cover. Give me a shot at that motherfucker."

Kwan nodded. He inched upright, his back scraping the rocks. When he was standing, he took off. He stayed left and, as he rounded the bend in the path, danced into a waiting crack just as Steiner let loose.

Steiner sent a prolonged burst blanketing the surrounding rocks to the right and above Kwan's position. Steiner riddled the target. After that no one returned fire. Tom's assessment of the insurgent location had been correct.

Tom heard a muffled groan. He passed that info along. Either Steiner had hit the sniper or splintering rocks had done the job.

The squad waited fifteen more minutes. Blood slowly oozed from the fissure. Tom figured that was their confirmation of a hit.

The lieutenant stood up and ordered the squad to continue on. The wounded or dead man was above them, and it would have been difficult to reach him. They left him where he lay.

With the sweat beginning to freeze on Tom's face, they reached the outpost. He was thankful to set up his weapon and put down his load. He and Albert checked out the cave after it was declared safe.

"Nothing that will blow us to kingdom come, but they left a couple of little bundles that could take you on a temporary trip to heaven." Kwan gave them a crooked smiled as he raised both hands palms out, "I'm only suggesting."

Tom walked over to where Kwan stood. "What are those?"

"Opium balls. Four of them. Each worth about sixty thousand in the United States. None of it has been processed yet." Kwan held out a black, oily-looking object about the size of a tennis ball, wrapped in a rag.

"Wow," said Albert. "And what's that stuff?" He pointed at several sacks that resembled bags of flour.

"ANAL, they call it. Ammonium nitrate, a component, along with aluminum, for making IEDs." Kwan gathered everything together in a sack and took it out to show the lieutenant.

Tom looked at Albert. "That's why we are here, son."

"We're the only show in town," added Albert. "If they don't have money, then they can't buy guns. Right?"

"Yeah, you got it, Albert. But it it's a little more complex than that. The counterinsurgency depends on denying the Taliban support from the locals so they can't operate. We are the wedge between civilians and the Taliban. Sometimes denying the locals their livelihood ticks them off, too." Tom and Albert staked out one corner and dropped their gear.

The hollowed-out cave in the rocks was just big enough for nine men. Tom felt warmer inside only because they were out of the wind; otherwise it was about as comfortable as a refrigerator, freezing cold inside and out. Rocks would be their beds.

Tom was thankful they had made it to the cave well before darkness. They had plenty of time to set up and settle in.

"Now that I remember," said Tom, breathing in deeply. "You can always smell it before you see it."

"You don't forget the stink of a slit trench," said Dombrowski, joking. "The shit ditch is at the back."

Later on, as Cogriff set up a perimeter and guard rotations, Tom was not surprised to hear the lieutenant reciting word by word from the manual. But Steiner made it work. Most of these guys knew the drill, and that reassured Tom.

Of course, Tom had been assigned the midnight rotation. But before standing his post he tried to catch a few z's, changed his socks, and ate something. He reminded Albert to do the same. "Use the foot powder."

The next lesson for Albert was a little more complicated. Tom took a moment to instruct Albert on the ins and outs of straddling a slit trench.

Later, when Tom tried to slip out for his midnight watch, Albert bolted upright. Despite the freezing temperature, the boy was soaked with sweat. He grabbed Tom's arm in a bone-crushing grasp and squeezed.

Was Albert still asleep? Tom wondered. He whispered to calm Albert as he removed his arm from the boy's grip. Tom spoke softly, as if he was talking to one of his children who was having a nightmare.

"It's OK. I'll be nearby. The first night in a cave can be intimidating."

"Dad, is it you?"

"Yes."

Albert apologized. "I'm sorry. I got scared . . ."

"Sleep now, son. Sleep the fear away," said Tom just as he had often said to Donnie. "And tomorrow you will be brave again."

Tom thought of how these young men mature in the blink of an eye. He mused, they grow up, then they grow hard. And then, if they are lucky, they grow old.

Chapter 32

I never knew coming down from a place so close to heaven could feel so good. That was Tom's last thought as he dozed in the ICV on the way back to camp. After sitting and sleeping on rocks, the solid seats inside the vehicle felt as cozy to Tom as his old recliner back home.

It was about ten degrees warmer in the valley, still winter, but oh so much more comfortable than *La Parca*.

Tom, like everyone else, had slept little during his time on the mountain. They'd moved each night to a new location, returning to the cave twice. They'd taken fire off and on. All in all, their mission had been accomplished. They had called in the location of two caravans. Now the drones would take them out or headquarters would send in a platoon to seize the drugs. The several bands of men they had encountered—Taliban fighters, Tom assumed—had been eliminated or driven back into their holes. No prisoners. Steiner made that clear from the get-go. Of course the enemy had remained faceless; all the skirmishes were at a distance.

It was easier climbing down. The new boots had paid off. Tom had his bearings and his load was lighter, minus some ammo.

Now Tom's lids were getting heavier with the lull of the rocking vehicle and the warmth thawing his frozen bones. He was having short spurts of dreams. In them, he was composing an e-mail to Christine. He would leave out the scary stuff. Every time they hit a crater left by an IED, he jerked awake. But in seconds he fell back to sleep.

He forced himself awake to listen to the driver when he heard the word *attack.*

The driver was filling them in on what had happened during their absence. "Last night, we got some pretty heavy action. The firefight lasted over five hours. The captain had to call Bagram for air support to end the skirmish. They sicced a drone on the bastards. Really brought down the hammer on them."

After that bit of information, Tom's brain wouldn't let his eyes shut. He was no longer exhausted. The adrenaline pump was operational.

About an hour into their homeward-bound journey, a couple of locals crossed their path. The two men were walking down the riverbed. It was everyone's highway. Cogriff ordered the ICV to pull over.

"Maybe we can make some friends and gather some intel."

"Honest to God, those were his exact words," repeated Tom to Albert, who awoke as Cogriff slammed the IVC door closed.

The lieutenant hopped out into the combat zone. The younger of the two Afghani men ran off. Big hint number one.

The remaining man appeared to Tom to have been beaten down or worn out from life. Tom watched him tremble in the presence of the lieutenant. His dark eyes held the wisdom of the ancients. He was dressed in traditional garb. But that red hair sticking out from under his *Kaffiyeh*, his head cover, was a big surprise for Tom. He had always imagined swarthy guys in these parts.

This man looked malnourished. His bony body lacked all vitality. He was nothing like the formidable enemy Tom had expected. The man walked with a limp or he would have run, too.

Through their interpreter, Tom heard his name. It was Lutfi. "It means 'friendly,'" said the interpreter. In an instant the interpreter and Lutfi got into an intense argument. It turned out that Lutfi was a village elder and the father of Camp Dragon's Lair's second interpreter, Ebadullah.

Corporal Kwan explained to Tom, "You met Lutfi's son, Ebadullah, the daughter in-law, and grandson, Guza, in camp. Ebadullah went against Lutfi's wishes when he volunteered to work with us. The old man says his son is dead to him now."

"That's too bad." He couldn't imagine ever denying his own children. "Guza's a cute kid. I've seen him around. So that's why they live inside our compound?"

"Not even close. Our first interpreter, Lutfi's oldest son, wife, and infant daughter were beheaded by the Taliban. After that the captain invited our interpreters and their family inside the wire."

"God! Unforgiving bastards," said Tom. "Kwan, this village elder, Lutfi, is he Taliban or a friend?"

"Who knows? He might be a believer or just plain scared." Kwan shrugged. "We have strict guidelines. No civilian casualties. Above all, hands off the village elders and holy men. If we bomb a house and a woman or child is killed, we pay a condolence call and give them twenty-five hundred dollars per fatality. Crazy war, right?"

"Yeah. Too bad the Taliban doesn't follow those rules." This is when Tom wished the bad guys were easier to peg. Maybe they could wear black hats, like in the old westerns. But here, friend and foe were all dressed the same. He admitted war occasionally forced roles to blur. He had most certainly worn hats of both colors.

His first life in the army had involved excursions into unfriendly territory and when he was loaned out to some agency—CIA most often, like he was a rental car—Tom had put on the black hat. But when the government waved the red, white, and blue and challenged Tom's core beliefs, he had responded to his country's call. Those ops still haunted him. Tom watched.

Lutfi trembled as Cogriff and the sergeant, through the interpreter, continued to question him. Hint number two.

Cogriff was offering MREs like they were chocolate bars, as if this was World War II.

Six soldiers fanned out with eyes on the mountains. The driver had his eyes glued to the periscope.

Steiner's ears were the first to pick up the sound of intermittent gunfire echoing down the gorge.

"Back! Back! Into the vehicle! Go!"

He forcibly hustled Cogriff into the safety of the Stryker.

"I've got movement on the mountain," yelled the driver. "He's above me."

Loose pebbles drifted down from above. Tom was nearest to the mountain. He was trying to get a bead on him for Albert, who was carrying his M4, while Tom had only his sidearm at the moment. Larger rocks began to cascade down the slope, throwing up dust and dirt and obscuring the view.

"Let's go," screamed Steiner, and everyone quickly retreated.

"Go! Go! Go!" Cogriff ordered, although the ICV was already on its way.

Tom watched Lutfi scurry away in the opposite direction. Was the man just frightened, or part of what was happening?

Ahead automatic gunfire increased.

With all the speed they could muster in the boulder-ravaged riverbed, the ICV headed toward the sound of a battle. Rocks dinged off the top and sides of the vehicle. At least Tom thought it was rocks. Inside it sounded like golf-ball-size hail was being shot at them from a cannon. It was deafening.

Their transport managed to make it another two hundred meters down the valley before Tom and the other occupants were rocketed out of their seats by a tremendous explosion.

Tom looked around and was glad to see they were all still intact. Metallic fragments and large boulders struck the top and sides of the convoy during the aftershock of the explosion. The sounds outside the ICV had been amplified by a factor of ten inside.

Everything happened in double time after that.

Tom seized the periscope. "Two Strykers in front of us. They must have been heading back to camp after an IED sweep along the riverbed."

He swallowed before continuing. "An IED ripped through the second vehicle. It's sitting in a mangled heap on its side fifteen yards in front of us. We'll have to go around."

Black greasy smoke billowed from the burned-out hull. As they passed the bombed ICV, Tom noticed the protective armor plate from under the vehicle had been driven through the roof. Everyone inside had died instantly.

He told Steiner, "It looks like it was targeted remotely."

"Yeah. Probably from the hills above us," he answered.

"They have the advantage of a sweeping view of the valley, while we have to dodge around to pick our targets," added Cogriff, finally showing he was learning something.

Tom yelled, "I've got two wounded men lying in the riverbed. They must have been topside on their vehicle when the IED exploded. They were thrown clear and smashed into the rocks."

Over the radio from the other ICV, Tom heard, "I've got a man wounded near you. He's on your left, firing his weapon from the cover of those large boulders."

"Stay put," screamed Steiner to the man in the rocks.

Specialist Dombrowski said, "Our other interpreter, Ebadullah, was in that vehicle. He and his family have been getting threats. Captain Chavez has been worried about retaliation. I've seen this before. This is a warning. If you help the Americans, you die."

Kwan maneuvered the ICV up closer to the wounded men as the rest of the squad prepared to open the back of the Stryker and recover them.

Cogriff said, "That explosion was a lot more than the five-hundred-pounders command said we could expect."

Steiner ignored him. This was no time for debate. It was time for action. He and four others took up positions outside the vehicle and began returning fire. "Lane, Ham, go get the wounded," ordered Steiner.

The other ICV had recovered and was targeting the hills using its remote weapons.

Tom and Albert dragged the two wounded men into the back of their transport.

Inside the ICV, Cogriff was desperate to contact base camp and have a couple of the Kiowas throw some rockets at the mountain.

Steiner screamed orders at Kwan to find targets using thermal imaging. Then he yanked the radio from Cogriff and called to Bagram. "We need a medevac now! One, maybe two, fallen heroes."

Tom scanned the rocks above, but there was no way to estimate the enemy's numbers. He and Albert set up the machine gun with their backs to the Stryker. Tom raked the mountain. His hands were saturated with the blood of the men he and Albert had carried. But his fingers never slipped from the trigger.

Both ICVs fired up their 105mm cannons. They boomed in the confines of the valley like a volcano eager to escape. The insurgents were outgunned. The assault from both vehicles was taking its toll.

At last, return fire from the mountain became sporadic, then it finally disappeared. Steiner didn't take any chances. He quickly evacuated the rest of the wounded, of whom there were now four, and scrambled to get out of there.

"Go, go, go!" Steiner screamed.

They would have to come back later to the twisted wreckage to collect what they could of the other fallen warriors. Pieces of that rifle squad would be hard to find.

It was a tight fit with three of the four wounded men inside. Strykers have a lot of electronics and are made for nine infantry at the most. There were twelve in Tom's vehicle now.

The pain and the blood were unavoidable. Cogriff went green and stiff-necked. He faced forward in the front passenger seat, his eyes glued to the electronics.

In the back, one of the wounded men was chatting as though he couldn't stop. He was in shock. Tom had seen it before. The other two men were in bad shape. They had been catapulted off the ICV and had hit the rocks hard; they were suffering from crushed ribs, skull wounds (they always bleed a lot), and multiple broken bones. Unfortunately, Tom had seen that before, too. He doubted if either of them would make it.

A familiar fleeting thought zipped through Tom's mind: It's not me. And he was glad.

Steiner spoke to the medevac. It was already on the way. When the ICV moved out of the narrow valley and hit a clearing, they would be waiting.

Tom leaned over the worst of the two men lying on the floor.

Men . . . that was an absurd assessment. The blond kid's chin with its light coating of fine whiskers trembled. He was the same kid who had been riding with Dean. Tom had said, "See you in a few" to him. Six days ago he had been smiling and young—and now this.

His gaze fixed on Tom. In the cramped interior, Tom could barely shift to wipe the blood out of his blue eyes with the dressing from his field kit. Tom smiled down at him.

"You're going to be alright, kid." What else could he say?

The boy smiled back as though he believed him. Hell, thought Tom, we all want to believe. Tom took the boy's hand and squeezed it. In that instant, Tom was transformed back into a father.

"What's your name, son?"

He bubbled out, "Sam." His chest was crushed.

After putting a pressure dressing on the mangled leg of the other soldier, the platoon medic inched over to Sam. "Give me room."

Everyone shifted.

"Sam, we've got a medic here who's going to fix you right up," said Tom.

Sam's grip on Tom tightened. His face twisted. Pain rolled over the boy.

Tom held on to Sam with both of his hands now, wishing he could transfer some of his strength.

The medic worked over the boy and then his eyes came up to Tom. He didn't say anything. His pause told all.

The medic pulled out a morphine syringe and injected the kid.

Tom knew the best the medic could do for Sam was to ease his passing.

Tom leaned in closer. "What did I tell you? You'll shake this off. I bet you are feeling better already."

Sam winced when he smiled. "You sound like . . . my dad. Shake . . . it off."

"If he were here, he'd be saying he's proud of you. You're a brave kid."

Sam coughed and fumbled at a pocket.

"Hey." Tom looked to the others in the vehicle. "Anybody. What's this kid looking for?"

Dombrowski answered. "When Sam gets scared, he listens to his iPod. He probably wants that."

Most of the guys looked away from Sam as if to deny this reality; if they denied it, it could never happen to them.

More than ten years of this shitty war, was what Tom was thinking. Kids dying and nothing changing. Anger boiled up into his mouth from his stomach. He felt like he was going to vomit but pushed it back down.

"I'll get it for you, son." Tom quickly found Sam's iPod and plugged him in. Thank God he had turned Chrissy's off often enough after she had fallen asleep that he knew how to work the damn thing. Little Chrissy, thought Tom. Having the image of her in his mind during these brutal conditions seemed oddly obscene to Tom.

"Here you go." After Tom plugged him in, he picked up Sam's hand again. It was colder than it had been.

The boy closed his eyes as though he were safe, somewhere else, in his music.

Maybe he thought he was back in high school at a dance with his girlfriend. It really didn't matter. He was in a happier place. That made the difference.

Sam's mouth fell slack.

"Sam, are you with me?" Tom asked. "Stay with me, son. This is nothing. You'll shake it off," he repeated.

Sam gave Tom's hand a feeble squeeze and said, "Right. This is nothing. Thanks, Dad. I love you."

When they cleared the mountain, Tom saw a couple of Apache helicopters hovering to make sure the landing zone was clear.

Tom and the others carried the wounded, including Sam, to the Black Hawk medevac. Tom noticed they already had body bags on board.

The lives of these men, some still in their teens, like Sam, were ending before they'd had a chance to begin. Tom's rage was hard to contain. If it were physically possible, he would stuff this war where it rightfully belonged: in a body bag.

Chapter 33

IT WAS MAY, AND THE WINTER OF TOM'S LIFE. Five months had crawled by—cold and hard, a single lonely day at a time, in the shadow of *La Parca*. Ten days of rain, sleet, and a lot of ice pulled thoughts of spring further out of reach. Snow at the higher elevations added an extra layer to his misery.

The days were small for Tom. He was at his lowest. How low could he go? He was learning there were infinite possibilities.

It was getting harder and harder for Tom to pull himself back from despair. Would this last forever? Was there a Guinness record for living on the edge of a knife?

Now when he looked at his shadow, Tom thought it was getting smaller. Had he left part of himself on the mountain? For sure his mind was fragmented, incomplete.

His mantra was "Live another day and the next one will come your way." Tom had heard that somewhere, but he couldn't remember where. It didn't matter, and it didn't make it less true. He struggled to shove some hope into each day.

Hope this patrol goes well. Hope Christine was sleeping better. She always had a problem if Tom wasn't next to her. He hoped Albert wouldn't take a hit. More and more he felt like a third son to Tom. Hell, he felt the same way about all these guys. Even Jake, who had grown miles since arriving here, although some of those miles were in the wrong direction—Jake was turning toward the darker end of the combat spectrum. He had an attitude of carelessness about his life and that of others.

When Tom looked at the dead insurgents in their forever sleep, their young faces were no different from Donnie's or Albert's. He wished he could save them all. Tom had thought that a million times over. Some of those older Afghani kids that he'd seen playing on the rocks the day he arrived at Camp Dragon's Lair were toting rifles now.

Tom had been doing regular rotations, just like all the horses on this merry-go-round. Five to ten nights on the Grim Reaper, day patrols, and then camp security. New people replaced those who were sick or wounded or had become heroes.

The captain ordered some new movies. Tom went through all the motions of enjoying *Avatar*. But it didn't feel right. Tom's normal happiness meter was all twisted up. The uglies in the movie were overtly cruel and loathsome. Here those distinctions were subtler.

Kwan had done some magic with the camp's Internet access. Now it worked ninety percent of the time. That was both good and bad. It was good because Tom was talking to Christine and the kids more regularly. They had enjoyed meeting Albert face-to-face. Tom was hoping these calls would relieve some of the anxiety he spotted in his family's forced smiles. But he could see in Christine's eyes it wasn't working. Each time they spoke, she clasped that crystal heart as if it were a talisman she had to hold tight or else risk losing her real heart, or maybe Tom's.

Tom had his own magic tricks. They were his ability to change his facial expressions in the blink of an eye. He didn't even need to practice or think about it anymore. Christine saying, "Hello" on the computer screen triggered Tom's plastic smile to slip into place. He had a treasure trove of these masks, each the appropriate camouflage for the expected emotion. He held himself in control. Don't let your pain affect the family, he told himself. Keep the crude animal you've been forced to change into on a leash. He felt like a fraud. The only time the old Thomas Lane showed his face was in the family picture Tom still carried in his chest pocket.

Tom's dubious fame was building a worldwide following. Donnie and Chrissy had so many e-mails coming in that they had to have them blocked, whatever that meant.

Incidents of fathers trying to serve in their children's stead were increasing. A few fights had broken out. Tom was not a man to incite people to go against the law. He resented his name being used for acts of violence. The peaceniks, religious leaders, and politicians were all choosing sides. They will latch on to anything to gain attention. Why don't these people get it? It was about love.

Chrissy and Donnie had some trouble with the media, too. They'd had to hide out at Frank's house a couple of times while Christine stood her ground and told reporters where they could put their cameras. There was nothing scarier than Tom's wife when she was guarding her chicks. That thought always made a big smile bloom on Tom's haggard face.

One of the helicopter pilots bringing in supplies had asked for his autograph. Tom refused. "I'm nobody," he had said. The copilot snapped a bunch of pictures with his phone. Tom supposed those would be circulating before the sun set.

The pilot had showed Tom a clip from the *Times*. It, too, was on the Internet, of course.

Tom read it. "The Secretary-General of the United Nations, who is from Egypt, made a surprise statement at the opening session of the United Nations. He challenged the group to strengthen their position on world security. Not from a position of military force, but from the resounding calls directly from the world's civilian populations."

The Dad story was resonating all around the world and stimulating an overwhelming hunger for peace. "'The world wants peace, a lasting peace, in the Middle East,' said the Secretary-General, adding, 'It should be pursued with all our vigor.'"

After Tom saw that news, he was optimistic. Maybe peace would come. But like anything political, it was tardy.

Tom was afraid it would be too late for him. Something had changed. He couldn't put his finger on it. Maybe he now needed the adrenaline rush that comes with *La Parca*. But on the other hand, he didn't feel anger or hate for the insurgents, the enemy.

"It's like I hate their weapons," Tom said to himself one day. He hated *them* threatening these kids. After one look at Guza, Tom and the boy were close, which reinforced his feelings. He didn't know how to describe it any better. At least God understood what was in his mind and heart, even when he didn't.

He did know he was glad to be here and have Donnie safely at home. And he didn't want to let any of these men at Camp Dragon's Lair down, not even Steiner.

One night when Tom pulled out a picture of Tommy that he carried, he shared it with Albert.

Albert had recognized Steiner in the background of the photo.

From that day on Tom had hounded Steiner to explain. Finally one dark and cold night on the mountain while they huddled in the cave, Steiner and Tom finally talked things out. Tommy had been Steiner's first lieutenant. Tommy had also been the guy who had accidently shot Steiner in the foot. He explained that Tommy was wrestling a weapon away from a stressed-out soldier, and boom. Steiner had been recuperating in the hospital when Tommy had died. And it seemed to Tom that Steiner was still carrying a lot of baggage, as if his presence could have changed the outcome for Tommy. He had been trying to keep Tom out of the action for Tommy's sake.

Steiner, Captain Wulf, and Ben had all been working together. It turned out Wulf had also known Tommy. "The machine shop was a sure thing until Cogriff made a stink. His father knows the commander at Bagram. Cogriff had him squash our plans," Steiner had explained.

Well, one enemy was now a friend, thought Tom, only the rest of Afghanistan and Cogriff to go. The lieutenant was definitely another story. He was still a dangerous hard-ass. But Tom was giving him some latitude. He had observed some changes. Maybe Cogriff was finally getting it.

Since their arrival, Tom had also noticed a change in their mission. Originally, it had been to build relationships with the locals. Because he was one of the older men in the camp, he and the captain had started to meet with Lutfi and the other village elders.

Tom had been the one to bring Lutfi what was left of his son's body. He had made sure Ebadullah was as clean as possible, in the Muslim way. He'd wrapped him in a plain, unsoiled cloth, according to their custom.

The captain and Tom had not attended the funeral, out of respect. But Tom and Albert had dug the grave and made sure it was aligned parallel to the Qibla, toward Mecca.

This small gesture of kindness had seemed to ingratiate Tom to Lutfi and the other tribal elders. But just when Tom was thinking their mission was on course, tensions returned. Taliban influences and threats from outside the village had to be the cause. So now the mission to win hearts had been replaced by just trying to keep a bullet from piercing his.

The other day Tom had decided that this must be what prison was like—just trying to hold all the pieces of yourself together until you've done your time.

Al-Qaeda, warlords, the Taliban, and deep tribal enmities made building anything lasting on a grand scale an impossible task. Tom thought the best approach had to be based on one-on-one relationships. But that too was difficult when you were being shot at. If the military presence was helping these people in any way, at this point Tom was not seeing it. So he was waiting—it always came down to the damn waiting—to know why he was here.

Good sign or bad, Tom talked to God sometimes five times a day. He told him all the things he couldn't talk over with Christine. His lost son, Tommy, frequently broke in on his thoughts at unexpected times. In the absolute dark of the nights spent on the Reaper he found himself watching the stars as if Tommy were there.

Back home, Tom never went to church. But in a strange way this place felt like the closest to God he had ever been. He smiled, thinking, as his eyes rolled up, *I'm at a pretty high elevation, so I should have good reception.*

As Tom's days at Dragon's Lair increased in number, so did the frequency of the Taliban's attacks. The Americans were getting hit on a more regular basis. Captain Chavez mixed up the times of the patrols so often that they had all stopped asking about the schedule outside the wire and instead just waited to be told what duty they had. The captain was doing everything he could to keep the insurgents from figuring out the rotation of duty. But the Grim Reaper had sharp eyes. As the captain said, someone was always watching.

Since the day that nineteen-year-old Sam, the blond kid, had died, Tom had become the unofficial dad in camp.

Tom had felt compelled to e-mail Sam's family after the army's death notification. Sam's dad and Tom had been in contact ever since. He presumed the connection with his son's friends gave Sam's father comfort. He told him how brave his son had been and that the last thing he had said was to tell his dad he loved him. It wasn't necessary to burst his bubble by saying Sam had thought Tom was his dad. That was just too complicated to get tangled up in. The boy's father was suffering, and Tom felt every emotion acutely. And yet Tom knew it could have been worse. It could have been another of his sons.

After the role of platoon dad was thrust upon him, the younger guys started coming to Tom with their problems. These were all men doing men's jobs here, and Tom was no Dr. Phil, but it became unavoidable. He did what he could. Dombrowski's problem was easy and fun. He was about to be a father. His wife was letting him pick their daughter's name. Every day he asked Tom what name he should choose. Tom advised him to pick one that meant something to him. He came up with Celina, which meant "moon" in Polish. First, he joked that his wife was as big as the moon. Then he said he loved the baby so much that his love would cover the moon. The moon in Afghanistan appeared to be twice the size of the moon back home.

The previous week, Tom had helped Kwan figure out a budget, which the corporal had then e-mailed back home to his wife. Tom guessed he must have done something right. Kwan's wife had been sending some of her mouth-watering spices for Tom to sprinkle on his T-rations. Those herbs could burn the army's overprocessed flavor out of anything.

The platoon had started out with plans to build a new school in the village, but that went by the wayside due to concerns for security. So Tom had Chrissy send him some writing supplies. The color crayons, pencils, Magic Markers, and paper were a huge hit. After Tom passed out all the goodies, the kids proved once again how much of a conundrum this place was. On one hand the mud huts and garb reminded Tom of ancient mystics, belly dancers, and fictional characters like Ali Baba and the Forty Thieves. On the other hand, most of the village elders and adult men, courtesy of the Taliban, were very familiar with what was being circulated on the Internet, YouTube, and Twitter. Hence, even the kids from the village had started calling him "Baba" (Arabic for "Dad"). Tom had hoped Baba was an endearment because of his gifts, not his dubious celebrity. But he didn't care. He also didn't care if they wrote Allah or God on their paper. At least, he figured, they were walking around with markers in their hands instead of guns.

Tom had been teaching the son of the deceased Ebadullah how to build things. Eight-year-old Guza had a real knack for engineering. His mother reminded Tom of Christine. She was a very determined woman. She wanted Guza to be educated. Her son was a cute kid, and he had bright orange hair like his grandfather.

This place hammered home the importance of parenting. The soldiers he fought alongside, as well as the children in the village, all looked to their elders in times of stress and insecurity. Even a substitute father, like Tom, would do. They hungered for guidance and the strength that only a parent could give. Tom realized that before he had come to war he had devalued his own role by putting work before family. He regretted that now. There was a lot of thinking time in this place.

Under the watchful eyes of the mountain and Captain Chavez, Tom and Albert had set up a rock filtration system for the village's water supply. Guza became their gofer, of course. They had run some pipes between the water to the filtration system and from there up to the village. Now their water came out clear and sweet. Most of the young women and a few of the elderly ones would show their appreciation by flashing him a smile when they thought the men weren't looking. The men, including the bony, red-headed man with the stringy beard, remained cautious and standoffish. Tom didn't blame them. If they were ordered to abandon Camp Dragon's Lair, the Taliban would move back in before the following nightfall. And they took revenge very seriously. Disappearances were common in the village.

Tom had also improved their camp's shower system. Small luxuries meant a lot. Now all the men could take a warm shower at least once a week. Tom liked doing things that weren't part of the war. It reminded him of his old self. It took his head to another place, even if it was temporary. None of them could forget for very long where they were. The Reaper wouldn't let them.

Yesterday, for the first time, he'd had to duck and cover while he was talking to Christine. Tom had wanted to explain but couldn't find the words. The war was just too much hell for her to ever comprehend. She'd let him off the hook as usual and changed the subject. But knowing his wife, she had an idea of what he was going through, and that was enough worry for her to carry.

"Hey, Dad, guess what today is," said Albert.

"I check the damn calendar every day. Just four months left, kid." About two months ago Albert had left his stammer up on the mountain.

Tom had passed the two-thirds mark. Inside, he celebrated with a little happy jig.

Albert did his own special version of dancing.

These young soldiers were something else, singing and dancing at every opportunity. Tom had joined in once and had thought he was singing the words to the rap song. But the music, like the lyrics, flew by too quickly and he had gotten it all wrong. The entire camp hadn't stopped laughing about it yet. He loved giving them something to smile about. They all had such strong spirits. As the days passed, Tom felt more and more right about being here with them.

The joy of their brief celebration evaporated as Tom climbed up to the north tower. Tonight he had guard duty. It was a little after 2200. After scanning his surroundings, he took a break from his night-vision goggles. The Tommy stars—he had come to name a particular group for his son—were spectacular. The cloudless sky was black velvet studded with diamonds. He imaged Tommy smiling among those stars. Here in the country where his son had died, he felt especially close to the boy. He often imagined it was just the two of them, on duty during the long nights. He could share his thoughts, his sorrow, and ask Tommy to forgive his failures. It was so dark that he couldn't deny the dominating presence of the stars. It was like when he was a kid—mesmerized by the stars. He would stare at them for long periods of time, until he was sure they were all moving. And for that instant he would believe in flying saucers and aliens. Impossible stuff. He let himself fall back into the memory of this pleasant fiction.

Tom jumped back into nonfiction when Guza climbed up the tower to give him his latest drawing. Tom did a quick critique and told him American cowboys didn't carry machine guns. Then he reminded Guza that he didn't belong in the tower at this late hour and that he should be in bed. He chased him to the ladder. Tom figured Guza understood about half of what he said.

Tom snapped his night-vision goggles back into place and scanned the north entrance to the camp and the outpost on the rise to his right. When he went back to star gazing, he was astonished to see a star wink at him. He quickly came to his senses and realized it was a muzzle flash. As Tom's tranquil fantasy smashed apart, dirt flew up in his face.

"I've got a visual. Movement to the north!" he screamed. The camp came alive. Multiple muzzle flashes were now as numerous as lightning bugs.

"Albert," Tom called down from his lofty tower, "get up here."

Tom immediately answered their attack with the chatter from his machine gun. He used his night-vision goggles to search out targets. The outpost was taking most of the fire and giving it back. Their perimeter fortifications, Claymores, and C-wire were unbreachable. Or so Tom thought.

An explosion, closer than Tom had ever before experienced, rocked the tower.

The next RPG hit the perimeter under the east tower. It came tumbling down. Jake rolled clear but came up hobbling. He jumped into one of the Strykers, started it up, and plugged the hole in the camp's fortifications where the tower had been. Jake used the remote night thermal-imaging camera in the ICV to pick out targets and blow the hell out of the mountain.

Captain Chavez ordered Steiner to take Tom's place and sent Tom to the north mortar. "Lane! Get that two-fifty-two in the game."

Tom had been filling in wherever needed since the captain had found out about his extensive experience. Right now the usual mortar crew was at the hospital in Bagram, one having been wounded and the other two suffering from dysentery.

Tom tried to get to the mortar, but another RPG exploded right in front of him. He had to dive into one of the nearby tents as debris rained down. When Tom looked up, there was Guza, pinned next to him. The boy hadn't made it back to his mother in the center of the camp.

"Stay!" Tom screamed. "Stay!" He hoped Guza understood his signal.

Kwan and Tom made it to the 81mm mortar at about the same time. Tom checked it over and there was no damage. They threw a missile in the tube and let her fly. From the wall they heard the captain on the radio, saying, "Up fifteen degrees!"

Tom adjusted the tube and in rapid succession sent four more rounds airborne. They kept hitting the insurgents for the next two hours.

Jake held his own from inside the Stryker. At one point, Steiner called out that the insurgents were within five hundred meters. Kwan and Tom adjusted to support the north wall and the outpost.

Tom thought the worst was over, but all of a sudden both he and Kwan were pinned down by grenades exploding all around them. They ducked behind the gabions guarding the mortars. When Tom glanced up again, he saw Guza wandering out from the tent. Blood streamed out of the boy's ears and nose, and he was covered in dirt. Guza was shell-shocked.

"Guza, down! Down!" The boy was completely out of it. Tom doubted he could even hear him over the cacophony of battle.

Random sniper fire zipped around them. Tom suspected it was coming from the houses at the edge of the village that were facing them. The outpost on the rise had turned our snipers loose to find the insurgents who were firing and hiding inside the homes of villagers. But they hadn't stopped them yet. And the danger for Guza was acute. He was wandering toward the battle, not away from it.

Tom jumped out of his shelter, screamed for Kwan to keep firing, and dashed for the boy. On the run he picked up a rucksack that had been hurled out of a tent by an RPG.

Tom must have been a juicy target, because the Taliban snipers increased fire. Dirt sprang up from the bullets hitting around his feet. He threw the ruck at Guza, as though it was the World Series and he needed a ninety-nine-mile-per-hour fastball for the last out and the win. The kid went down in a heap. Tom rolled over to him, and came up with the boy in his arms behind the sandbags at the perimeter. Cradling Guza, Tom catapulted himself behind the gabions with Kwan. He shoved the boy down behind him for protection.

Tom and Kwan continued to load and reload the mortar, as though they were robots on autopilot, until the captain called over the radio, "Cease fire!"

Tom looked at Kwan and said, "I thought we were going to have to fire up the 155mm there for a while."

Kwan just smiled. He was one of those silent types.

When Tom and Kwan stepped out from behind their shelter, Captain Chavez shoved the ruck Tom had thrown at Guza into Tom's chest. It was shredded.

"Don't ever do 'stupid' again," Chavez ordered. He gave Tom an extra push and glanced down at the small boy, who was still cowering where Tom had pushed him earlier.

The harangue from Chavez didn't sound sincere. But Tom couldn't really focus on him anyway. His damn shoulder, where he had landed during his acrobatic display, hurt like hell.

It was almost morning when Tom's head hit the pillow. Exhaustion didn't describe the depth of his weariness. His whole right side, from shoulder to hip, was bruised and already getting stiff. He had no idea whether after some sleep he would be better or worse. Tom tossed and turned, trying to get comfortable. Throbbing muscle pain wouldn't leave him in peace. He rolled on to his back as Steiner entered the tent.

"Lane. Catch."

Tom groaned and winced trying to snag the projectile with his left hand. He picked it up and saw it was a bottle of Motrin.

"Our medic checked out Guza. The kid's fine." Steiner smirked and said, "Hoorah."

Tom held up the bottle and said, "Thanks." But Steiner was already gone.

Tom remembered all the smirks and half smiles he had seen on Steiner's face, like when he passed his PT test, weapons certification, and his medical.

Unexpectedly, Steiner's "hoorah" sparked an old memory: Tom back at Fort Dix, picking up his weapon from a pudgy kid chewing bubble gum who had secretly pressed a piece of paper into Tom's hand. The paper had said, "Hoorah. For Tommy." Steiner had been sending him signals all along.

Chapter 34

It was December. Two weeks left. Fourteen days. Three hundred and thirty six hours and Tom would rotate home. He wouldn't be out of his commitment to Uncle Sam, but he'd be out of here. That comforting thought sustained him more than anything else.

And he had risen to the rank of E5. Cogriff had been livid when the captain jumped Tom up like that. But even after listening to Cogriff's whining for half an hour, Captain Chavez wouldn't have it any other way. He needed experienced men as squad leaders. The stresses of weather combined with the mountain climbing, and combat injuries were taking their toll on personnel.

Summer in Afghanistan had been brutal. Tom was glad to be through with that and feeling the pleasant chill of winter settling in. He'd take Jack Frost over losing five or ten pounds a day from sweating anytime.

This weather was perfect. It reminded Tom of that little nip in the air that accompanied Thanksgiving back home. When Albert woke him just before midnight, he had saliva trickling out of the corners of his mouth. He was confused, until he remembered that he had fallen asleep thinking about Christine's cooking.

As he pulled on his boots he lingered in his dream. He'd been sitting at the head of their dining room table. Christine was opposite him, looking as yummy as peaches and cream, with that damn sexy apron tied around her tiny waist. Frank was on one side of him and Donnie was on the other. Chrissy was sitting close to her mom. And Tommy was back home, sitting in his customary place right next to his brother. Even after he was fully conscious, Tom's dream didn't lose any of its flavorful appeal.

"Oh, Lord, I can almost smell it. It's Friday back home. That's chicken parm night. It won't be long now. Let the old meal routine commence," Tom said to Albert as he licked his lips and rubbed his hands together vigorously. "You'll have to sample my wife's biscuits, Albert."

Tom took the family picture out of his pocket and looked at them. He often stared at it for long periods of time.

"Sowing your winter crops again?" asked Albert with a chuckle.

"Yep. Planting the family and the old me back inside." It was Tom's way of starting to come down off his personal *La Parca*.

He had been letting Christine creep into his mind more often recently. Although she had never really left, he'd had to put her away for a while on a back shelf in his mind. Now he was preparing for their reunion. He'd been an old, flabby guy when she'd last seen him. Tom hiked up his pants, thinking, but I'm coming back a lean lover, baby.

From day one in Afghanistan, Tom had learned that physical fitness would be a vital factor in making it out of this place alive. They all did daily calisthenics. Then *La Parca* followed up with its own personalized aerobic torture. It was necessary. If he weren't fit, the mountain would eat Tom up and spit him out.

So Steiner had been right to push him like he had back at Fort Dix. Tom understood that now. None of his previous experiences in the army had ever prepared him to fight in terrain this treacherous and unforgiving.

When my physical fitness test comes around again, Tom thought, *I'll breeze through it.* Christine is going to go crazy over this body I'm bringing home.

Tonight Tom's squad had guard duty from 2400 to 0700. Cogriff did the scheduling, so most often Tom got the midnight shift.

Unexpectedly Captain Chavez appeared at Tom's elbow on the wall at the northeast corner lookout. He cautioned, "Keep an extra sharp lookout."

"Things have been quiet for the last week."

"Too quiet, Tom. And tonight I had a dream that a scorpion was crawling up my leg. It woke me from a sound sleep."

Tom nodded. The captain's experience and instincts made his assessments accurate 99.9 percent of the time, so everyone paid attention when he asked for vigilance.

Tom had to admit everyone in the camp felt something was off balance. It was the kind of calm where the murmurs of small groups of villagers make the hair on the backs of the soldiers' necks stand at attention.

At 0500, Tom heard the gurgle and splash of water running down the hill from the village. At first he thought it was nothing. But then he remembered that this wasn't when they were scheduled to flush their water delivery system.

Tom wondered if the Taliban insurgents were trying to cover up their movements. He scooted over to the next gun port at the east wall. He saw shadows, like leaves being blown by a fall night's wind. People were scurrying in and out of the houses in the dim remains of moonlight.

Tom called over to the outpost.

"Same thing. We're watching. There are a lot of them."

Nowadays the whole camp slept fully dressed except for their boots. That had started a couple of days ago when Chavez had ordered everyone to stay ready. Tom had been prepared since he put one foot down into this dirt.

Creeping along, he woke up Chavez.

The captain was up and out in a flash. He went to the tower and searched the surrounding flat ground. Nothing.

He came back and crunched down shoulder to shoulder with Tom at the east wall. "Nothing. I didn't see anything."

Tom started to relax, until the captain added, "And I don't hear anything. Lane . . . where are the crying babies, night birds, and those mangy dogs growling over the garbage? There's nothing."

Tom's eye went to his gun's scope. "No nightjars over the garbage heap." Normally he heard the birds cackling all night, fighting over scraps of food.

Tom's knees turned weak, like they had that time he'd gone on the Tower of Terror in Disneyland with Tommy and Donnie and experienced a thirteen-story free fall. But this feeling didn't leave, like when the ride stopped.

"Lane, quietly wake everyone up. Get them to their posts. Take your squad to the north wall. Tell Steiner to take his squad to the west. You two will take on the mountain. Cogriff will be in command of the south."

Even in the dark, Tom could tell the captain was smiling.

"He can't get into trouble there. I'm going out to the east outpost nearest the village to get a closer look."

Tom's body stiffened. Everything felt different. The air he was breathing was thick; his heart and all his bones sensed danger. It wasn't adrenaline; every single cell in his body was just scared. Was that candle he had been burning from both ends getting low? Did he have any more tricks up his sleeve to cheat death?

Tom crept from tent to tent, man by man. Without a word, one by one, the soldiers gathered their weapons to join their cheerless squads for battle. Tom's instincts told him they were about to be tested . . . as they had never been tested before.

In position, they waited. Forty minutes passed. Then another thirty. It would take another two hours for the sun to completely clear the mountain. They waited as if they were statues.

A half hour before dawn, Tom heard the call to worship echoing through the village.

"Allahu Akbar, Allahu Akbar, Allahu Akbar, Allahu Akbar."

He knew the routine. The muezzin chanted, "Allah is most great" five times each day at the beginning of prayers. Tom fleetingly thought everything was normal. Then he realized the voices of the responding worshipers were all wrong. Too strong. Too young. Too many.

The captain came over the radio from the outpost. "All the women, children, and old men must have left during the night. I don't see a one."

The outpost was about fifty yards away and uphill from the camp. Tom saw the silhouette of Chavez scanning the village through his scope.

"Eyes sharp down there, Dragon's Lair. I'm advising command at Bagram that something big is about to go down."

Tom was still hoping the captain was wrong, but if the insurgents tried to get inside the camp's fortifications, they had picked on the wrong camp. Dragon's Lair's defenses were solid, just like the men. Captain Chavez was a strong, intelligent leader and had made the best possible utilization of both men and materials.

Too late, Tom would realize his optimism was misplaced.

The insurgents launched their brazen attack just as the sun's first rays came over the lowest ridge to temporarily blind the men at the east wall of Camp Dragon's Lair.

From the northeast outpost, Tom saw Captain Chavez put his hand up to guard his eyes from the bright blast of sunlight. A sniper and the brilliant rays hit him at the same time. The captain's blood-soaked left arm jumped in a violent awkward motion as his scope flew out of his hands. He never faltered. He commanded, "The village. Return fire!"

Tom's eyes darted back to the north, toward the Grim Reaper. He blinked to help his eyes adjust to the lingering darkness, then switched to his night vision and saw his nightmares come to life.

A sea of cloaked figures, still obscured by the shadow of the higher mountain, crawled over the open space between the mountain and the camp. The floor of the valley undulated with sinister intent. Wave after wave of men came down off the mountain and advanced. They covered the floor of the valley. And they had but one objective—to crash down over Dragon's Lair and annihilate everyone.

This was Tom's wake-up call on Christmas morning.

And then, as they say in the movies, "all hell broke loose." The militants' assault came from multiple directions.

An RPG ideally located in the village near the outpost did its worst. Its blasts took out the small forward outpost during the first fifteen minutes of the battle for Dragon's Lair. Tom swiveled around and opened up with his machine gun to cover the captain and his men as they retreated the fifty yards back inside the camp's perimeter.

Tom raked that house repeatedly until the walls fell in on whoever was inside. He peppered every house on the rise that faced them. Then he had Albert launch grenades into the houses. All the time Tom was thinking, who picked this unholy ground for this isolated camp?

One of the men fleeing from the outpost was carrying his machine gun with him. He had taken hits to both legs. The captain, although also wounded, dragged him along with the help of a third soldier. The wounded man never dropped his weapon.

Tom noted that there were already two wounded soldiers in the first minutes of the battle.

When the captain and the men were clear, Tom had Kwan launch a couple of mortars into the abandoned outpost. Albert kept the machine gun in the action. Tom wanted to make sure the militants weren't going to use American ammo or the outpost site to get above them.

Suicide squads in groups of three or four men rushed down from the mountain behind a stream of automatic weapon fire and a rain of RPGs. For a while, the bullets were coming so thick that the camp's occupants couldn't lift their heads above the wall. On the east side of the camp an identical team of insurgents came at Dragon's Lair from the village. Tom saw their plan. They were trying to set off the Claymores by throwing themselves over the C-wire to make a corridor inside the camp's defenses for the rest.

The Claymores had wisely been set up on the most likely paths into the camp. But they could be detonated only by handheld clackers. Tom commanded them from his tower and had the safety switches on so the insurgents' rush to become martyrs would accomplish nothing. Tom and Albert cut them down before they got within five hundred meters of the camp walls.

A reckless waste, thought Tom as he tracked the battled on two fronts: north and east.

Before one of the wounded insurgents died, he triggered the bomb on his vest, at least a two-thousand pounder, and its shockwave threw a couple of soldiers at the top of the wall over.

Snipers had everyone pinned down. The traces of sunlight escaping the Reaper now made using night-vision goggles impossible. At the same time, that murky wave of insurgents crawling on their bellies was getting closer and closer. They were still hidden in the shadow of *La Parca*, and Tom couldn't see them clearly until they separated from the darkness.

This was a well-thought-out, coordinated attack.

The captain said the insurgents were simultaneously hitting another small camp to the south, and that Bagram too was under attack. In other words, the camp's usual air support was unavailable. Even the unmanned aerial vehicle was doing reconnaissance somewhere else. Captain Chavez sent a message on the radio to his subordinates: "We are on our own."

Tom watched as Jake scurried outside the wire to help the wounded who had fallen off the wall. The boy was fast; he'd been a sprinter in high school. At moments like this, Tom was glad he and Jake had made peace. He watched with fear and pride as Jake came hustling back to the barricade, one man under each arm.

The heads of snipers popped up from the rise near the village. It looked like they had Jake in their sights.

Tom yelled to Albert, "Snipers! Take down those bastards!" The boy was good, Tom thought with satisfaction.

Albert had his eye glued to his scope. As fast as he took one sniper out of action, another popped up in his place. Tom did his best to provide cover for Jake with his machine gun.

Jake called up, "Clear."

Albert yelled, "Jake, there's one more, farther out on your right."

Jake was taking fire but was determined not to leave anyone behind. He started out again.

Tom checked the open ground around him. Then he saw it. "Jake, no!" Tom screamed, with all the power of his lungs. "Back! Back!"

Jake didn't hesitate to obey. Tom saw Jake's right hand fly in the air as he turned and started weaving his way back. He still wasn't home free when the insurgent in US Army camo raised up to take his shot. Albert put the militant down before the martyr could pull the trigger.

When Tom checked, Jake was already back at his post. The medic had bandaged his hand and he stayed in the action.

Albert looked at Tom.

"He was wearing the wrong boots," Tom said. "Remember our briefing back at Dix?"

They didn't have time for chatter; they needed to focus on the job. "Get some more ammo up here, Albert."

They were two hours into it with the insurgences nearing the camp's perimeter laced with C-wire, when the camp's howitzer 155mm fell silent.

Tom missed its reassuring, booming voice. He called over to Kwan. "What's going on over there?"

Like many of their weapons, it needed to cool down. Dragon's Lair was holding its own, but just barely. They were paying dearly. They had three KIAs and seven wounded.

Tom heard the captain calling Bagram for a medevac. "Be advised, we are in a bad situation."

A long twenty-five minutes passed before the familiar throbbing of the Black Hawk swooped over Tom's head. It was hard to see anything with the debris and dirt filling the air. The Black Hawk appeared to have a single Kiowa flying as sidekick.

Then Tom heard the radio crack. It was the chopper pilot. "Be advised . . . we got hit . . . north side of aircraft . . . belly. We'll have to go back. Landing zone too hot." As they banked away from the camp, the Kiowa fired its two Hellfire missiles into the mountain.

The side of the mountain roared and chucks of the black rocks crumbled, but the insurgents kept coming. Most of them were off the mountain by now and steadily advancing.

The Taliban forces were as well armed as the camp. They had rocket-propelled grenades, machine guns, and mortars. Tom estimated there were at least four hundred militants coming at them. Four to one was not good odds. The barrel of his 240 was starting to glow hot.

The insurgents had been planning this attack for a long time. It was like the captain had said: "*La Parca* is always watching." They knew exactly where to target to do the most damage to the camp's defenses. They took out the observation post and tried to demoralize the troops by taking out their leadership. But they had screwed up. The captain was still in full command.

Tom had been worried about the consequences if they lost the captain. A commanding officer must hold his men's confidence and hopes. He is the guy who forces them to keep moving, guides all their choices, and makes all the tough decisions. In other words, Chavez kept everyone advancing in the same direction. What would they do if he could no longer command? Cogriff filling those shoes wasn't something Tom wanted to consider.

The insurgents' gun crews were accurate, and during the third hour, they tried again and again to take out all the mortars. But luckily, the captain had relocated one of them just yesterday. The other two fell to the insurgents' RPGs, along with one of the camp's stockpiles of ammunition. Dragon's Lair still had one functioning mortar but was running low on ammo for it.

Tom had never been in a firefight that lasted this long. He was fatigued. He imagined the other men all felt the same way. But no one ever let up. One of the wounded men, whose toes had been blown off by a grenade, put a rucksack filled with water bottles on his back and was making his rounds on his hands and knees.

Now the Taliban was going after the Strykers with their RPGs. Cogriff and one other soldier inside a vehicle were getting hammered, but their weapons were never silent. Just in time, the lieutenant had gotten it.

Suddenly Tom's tower took a hit from an RPG. He and Albert jumped clear as the structure collapsed around them. Tom came up hobbling, his old injured shoulder screaming with pain.

He and Albert picked up the machine gun and ammo and ran for cover. Tom heard the thud of a sniper's bullet more than he felt it as it nicked his ear. Blood trickled down the left side of Tom's face, but they quickly set up the machine gun on the sandbags and went back to work.

"Not long 'til full sun," said Tom.

"Yeah, then we can see who's killin' us. Great."

"Albert, come on"—Tom pivoted his weapon to the right as he

fired—"each dawn brings new promise. That's what a sunrise is all about." His words were smudged with the grunts and groans of repositioning to a low crouch. "They'll send reinforcements . . ." Tom stopped in midsentence.

Over the radio, he heard the captain say, "We're running low on ammo over here. I've got fifteen wounded and unable to fight."

They were in a serious way. Worse than Tom had imagined.

"Albert, I'm going to make an ammo run." Tom was proud of the boy. Albert never said a word. He took the machine gun and did the job, opened fire on the insurgents.

As Tom passed a hole in the east wall, he saw that the militants were inside the wire and within seventy-five meters of their position.

Tom commandeered Jake, and together they grabbed some boxes of ammo and sprinted across the compound to the east wall.

Grenades and bullets kicked up the dirt around their feet and buzzed around them like angry bees.

Tom slid up next to the captain.

"We're in bad shape," said Chavez. "I've got to get these wounded and dead out of here. We need water, ammo, and reinforcements. Anyone who can still pick up a gun and fire, send them back on the line."

The fastidious Lieutenant Cogriff showed up looking like he had been rolling in the sand. "I have one undamaged ICV left."

Tom looked at Chavez. "Do you want me to set off the Claymores?"

"Yes! Give me the damn clackers," said Chavez.

"Those Claymores are our ace in the hole if a breach of our defenses is threatened," countered Cogriff.

"What the hell do you think this is?" screamed Chavez.

The east wall had been hit the hardest. There were more wounded men than not. Blood didn't just speckle the ground and sandbags; it had soaked in and started to pool.

Tom and Jake ducked down as the Claymores exploded all around the perimeter. Then they used the lull in the action to start dragging and carrying. Making run after run. Taking a body one way and returning with ammo. Their hands were never empty. Back and forth, Tom picked his way across the compound. He didn't pay attention to whether the men he was dragging were dead or alive. He practically threw them at the medic.

The medic was set up inside the dining hall. It was overflowing with ravaged humanity. They were out of pain meds. Treatment was a bandage to stop the bleeding or a long rest in a nearby tent that had become the mortuary. Those were the only two options. Tom announced that the captain needed help. All the wounded who could still pick up a weapon chose to return to their friends, even if it meant they were still bleeding or dragging an arm or a leg.

The Afghan militia, many of whom had become close with the soldiers of Dragon's Lair who had trained them, stayed to fight and die with them.

The pause in the action after the Claymores went off was brief. Going into the fifth hour, the militants were gaining ground. Jake took his last hit while making another valiant ammo run.

Tom saw him lying out there in the center of the compound like a target and felt he couldn't leave him like that. He had no breath in him, but he ran out and scooped Jake up. The boy was already gone by the time Tom got him to the medic. When Tom went in to lay twenty-year-old Jake down in the mortuary, he saw Chavez. He had taken a fatal shot to the head.

Lieutenant Cogriff was now in charge. Tom didn't know if the lieutenant even knew.

The insurgents' mortars had so badly damaged the Strykers that their sole use was as a shelter from enemy fire. Just about everyone in camp was wounded or injured, some more seriously than others. Too many. But still the camp's weapons were never silent and remained active.

Tom's ears were tuned in to the cacophony of battle. Any change in the deathly music—the pop, pop of the carbines, the rat-tat-tat of the machine guns, the boom followed by the explosion of the shell spit out by the 155mm—and he was on it. When the 155mm artillery ran out of ammo, Steiner and Tom were on their radios. "It's not possible we ran out of shells," said Tom.

Steiner countered, "I've got Kwan searching for more. We had an overabundance of projectiles when the battle started. But this attack is stretching us thin everywhere."

The barrels on many of the soldiers' weapons, especially the M4 carbines, were so overheated they were jamming.

Cogriff grabbed the radio to advise Bagram. "They've got us pinned down. We're clean out of ammo for M777 howitzer 155mm and low on everything else, including water and medical supplies. Our casualties are high. The insurgents are within fifty meters of our walls."

Tom was pleased and surprised to hear some steel in the lieutenant's voice.

Tom calculated the distance. Fifty meters. That was within hand-grenade range.

Just as he had the thought, first one grenade, then another, landed in the center of the compound.

For a second no one reacted. Earlier, rocks had been thrown in over the walls and most of the soldiers thought they had been hand grenades. Tom understood that the militants were using all their tricks to flush them out of their fortifications into the sights of their snipers. So it was hard for him to tell whether they were grenades or rocks.

This was real. The earth convulsed. Tom was airborne. Dirt and dust clouded Tom's vision when he hit solid ground.

Albert was hit. Tom jumped on the boy to cover him as more grenades rained down around them. He dragged Albert behind the closest barricade. The boy had some shrapnel in his thigh.

"It's nothing, Dad. I'll shake it off."

"Yeah." Tom had too often used that phrase with sad results. "Go! Get the medic to stop the bleeding."

Steiner crouched down next to Tom. "Listen!" he yelled. "Listen!"

"I hear it."

Their faces brightened.

Steiner slapped Tom on the back as Cogriff scurried in next to them.

"Steiner. Release smoke!" Then Cogriff radioed the A34 fighter pilot. "Be advised, we need you to come in hot. They're on us."

Steiner squeezed the lieutenant's hand over the radio and added, "We need your cannon fire within ten meters. Break."

The pilot's calm voice faltered, "Come back."

"Ten meters," repeated Cogriff, nodding at Steiner.

"You kidding me? Be advised that is high risk," said the pilot. "I repeat high risk. Over."

Tom looked at Cogriff as the lieutenant said, "No shit!"

Tom and Steiner smirked. This was the first time they had heard Cogriff say anything with more force than "gosh," "darn," or "damn."

Steiner grabbed the radio out of Cogriff's hand. "You need to get these guys off us. Now! Ten meters. Over."

"Roger that," said the pilot. "Ten meters. I'm inbound with missiles."

It was the seventh hour into the battle when the day exploded. To Tom Dragon's Lair had been transported to the surface of the sun. The earth surrounding the camp was on fire. The village went up in a blaze. Flames and debris rained down over Tom and everyone in the camp. Chunks of the east wall were blown away. Some of the Afghan friendlies lived on that side of the camp.

"Guza!" Tom screamed.

He took off through the flames in the direction of where he'd last seen Guza and his mother. Injured insurgents were running wild and blind for the protection of the inside of the camp. Tom came eye to eye with a militant who couldn't have been more than sixteen. He was a pathetic warrior, all skin and bones rattling around in rags.

Tom passed him by. He heard the Black Hawk coming in behind him. Its rotors cleared a path through the flames and dust. Tom found Guza and his mother. She was hurt, bleeding profusely from her wounds. He picked her up and, with Guza trailing behind, carried her back to the medevac.

Cogriff was at the corner of Tom's vision, laying down covering fire. The flames were spreading through the plywood sections of the camp.

The crew chief told Tom, "Another helio is on the way. She'll have to take the next bus."

"No. Wait," Tom begged. "Take her and the boy."

"I'm full up."

Albert hobbled closer. Standing behind Tom, he raised his gun and mouthed, "Take them."

Tom thought his stern expression changed the medic's mind.

"OK, OK. Get her in here," said the flight medic over the crew chief's objections. "I gotta get these wounded back to base. This is their golden time."

That was an expression the flight medics used when referring to the period of time they had for saving a critically wounded person.

As soon as Tom laid Guza's mother down, the medevac lifted off. As they rose off the ground in a storm of bullets and dust, Tom heard the flight medic's benediction—"Jesus Christ, save us. They're all alphas"—directed at the pilot. The medics usually radio ahead the condition of their passengers. Alpha was the designation for the most seriously wounded.

Dragon's Lair and its remaining soldiers were still taking sporadic gunfire from the dazed and confused insurgents. Tom and Albert forced Guza to duck down behind a barrier with them.

Guza broke free, chasing after his mother. They were peppered with small arms fire. Tom shoved the boy to the ground. He'd have to get Guza on the next helio.

Suddenly, Tom felt a numbness spreading through his right leg. Covering the boy with his body he waited for the next medevac to touch down.

The bird landed.

Things were getting fuzzy for Tom. It was hard for him to get to his feet.

As if from far away, Tom heard Albert yell, "Dad! Get back behind the barricade. Fall back! They're everywhere! Cogriff says we are abandoning camp, they're inside the wire!"

Tom's mind snapped to attention and he got low.

The remaining soldiers watched and laid down cover fire as, one after another, the remaining wounded were loaded on the transports. The fighter pilot was doing his part to keep the massing insurgents off the camp as they struggled to evacuate.

Over the radio Tom heard the fighter pilot telling Bagram, "Dragon's Lair's is an anthill swarming with insurgents."

Two more Black Hawks had arrived. Their 50mm machine guns were a welcome sound to Tom. They were going to make it! He, Albert, and Guza would be OK. Somehow, he managed to stand upright and shoved Guza into a helio. He went back to help Albert.

"See, what did I tell yah?" Tom pointed at the glowing orb of the sun, now full overhead.

Steiner called out, "The militants are rallying for another assault. Get ready!"

The pilot of the Black Hawk came on the radio, "OK. Last load. Time to get out of Dodge!"

Tom and Albert stood up as if they were one person. They were leaning heavily on each other, holding their side arms in their free hands.

And then out of the corner of his eye, Tom spied that ragged kid he had seen earlier. The boy pulled a handgun from his pants. Tom's first thought was the gun was bigger than the boy. He got off four rounds before his weapon stopped working. Albert took two.

"Dad," Albert screamed, reaching out for Tom as he faltered. "Dad!"

Tom held Albert to him and kept going, half dragging the much larger man. It took all of Tom's strength to prop Albert up against the helio. But he didn't have enough left in him to lift him up and in alone. The crew chief and flight medic had their hands busy; one of the wounded was bleeding out. The inside of the medevac was so full of bleeding flesh, Tom couldn't tell were one person ended and another began.

A wounded Steiner, firing from inside the copter, put down his weapon to help Tom. He clawed at Albert with his good arm, pulling him the rest of the way inside the bird next to him.

When Tom looked back to see if everyone was on board, Cogriff went down. *He must have caught a ricocheting bullet,* thought Tom.

Insurgents were pouring in through the breach in the east wall. They came screaming and howling at the helio.

Tom turned to go back for Cogriff.

Steiner screamed, "No, Tom. Don't. He'd leave you."

Tom half turned and just smiled. "I'm not him. I figured it out! That's why I'm here. To bring you all back."

"Dad! Baba! No, Dad!" echoed the mingled voices of Albert and Guza. Blood was dripping from the interior of the helio, staining the earth. Dragon's Lair still wanted more of them.

Tom had managed to lift Cogriff in a fireman's carry over his injured shoulder. But by the time he got near the Black Hawk, he was having trouble moving his legs. Tom stopped. He flopped down onto his knees, still holding the unconscious Cogriff against him.

Steiner jumped down and limped over. He pulled Cogriff out of Tom's arms and hurried back, as best he could, to put him in the chopper.

Then Tom stood up.

"Baba," said Guza, holding out his hand for Tom and crying.

Steiner had to restrain the boy to keep him in the chopper. "Tom, come on!" screamed Steiner.

"They're too close." The pilot called, "I'm getting out of here!"

"We aren't leaving without Dad," threatened Albert. His big hand crunched down on the pilot's arm.

Tom got to his feet and stumbled a couple of steps forward before staggering back toward the insurgents. He weaved around like a drunken man. He stopped at the young insurgent who had shot him and Albert. His side arm came up to boy's head. They looked into each other's eyes. Tom let his arm fall and his weapon slide out of his hand.

In broken English, the boy asked, "You . . . the 'dad'?"

Dazed, Tom didn't answer the boy.

The crippled old man with the stringy red beard, Lutfi, screamed,

"*Tegga!*" All the weapon fire ceased. Then the Afghan stepped forward. "You are the one? Baba? The 'dad'?"

Tom stared into space at something no one else could see. Was it the stars? He smiled. Then blinked. The fingers of one hand reached up to the heavens as if to take hold. When he spoke, it was a soft whisper. "It's so bright." He smiled and reached out. "T-o-m-m-y." His hand flew to his chest, where the family picture rested.

Tom Lane smiled at Lutfi and fell forward into the arms of his enemy.

Steiner limped over to the Afghan chief with his revolver drawn. "I'm not leaving without him!" Bleeding from multiple wounds, dragging his leg, and his weapon pointed at the insurgents, Steiner tried to pick Tom up but faltered.

The ragged boy wandered closer.

With great effort Steiner aimed at the Afghani chief.

The chief came eye to eye with Steiner. "We will help you carry him."

All his reserves spent, Steiner's weapon fell into its holster. Together the Afghan chief, the ragged boy who had shot him, and Steiner bent down and lifted Tom. Gently they put him down inside the chopper.

The elder Afghan chief turned to Steiner. "We have heard about this 'dad' who suffers for his son. My father was a martyr when the Soviets came, as were his four brothers. My sons are all gone, their blood poured onto this ground. Guza is my grandson. His blood could have joined theirs. This 'dad' has saved the only remaining member of my family. You see how he loves this 'dad.'"

Steiner turned and saw Guza clinging to Tom.

"Perhaps . . . this man has shown us another path," continued the chief. "A path with a future. One that does not require the blood of our children."

The battle at Dragon's Lair had lasted for nine hours. It had taken the highest toll of American lives in any single battle thus far in Afghanistan. The final count was seventeen American heroes and thirty-seven wounded. The number of dead and wounded insurgents was uncountable. It was estimated that more than half lost their lives.

But for now enjoy the dream
Of action, war and quest
And lay your sleepy little head
Upon my loving chest

Chapter 35

Frank's hands were trembling as he knocked on Christine's hotel room door. It had been a year since the famous battle of Camp Dragon's Lair. Donnie, strong and confident, stood by Frank's side. The young man buttoned up his suit jacket. He put a supportive hand on Frank's shaky shoulder.

Frank turned and looked at Donnie, and for a moment, he saw the father instead of the son.

"Come in. We are almost ready," said Christine as she opened the door to her and Chrissy's hotel room. "Your sister is still primping." Then she saw Donnie. "You are very handsome, son."

Christine walked to the floor-to-ceiling windows that made up one wall of their suite. "Frank, come over here. Look at this view." When Frank was closer, she linked her arm through his. "Did I thank you for coming with us?"

"Yes. Too many times," Frank stared out the window. Neither of them was really seeing the view. Their eyes were on the stars. They were hoping Tom was looking back at them.

"You know, Tom wouldn't have gone for all this fuss."

"But I think he'd have liked to see inside the White House." Christine patted Frank's reddening face. For all of them, emotions overflowed at unexpected times.

Frank shrugged. "Sometimes I'm doing something, like getting a greasy burger at the roach coach, and I'd swear he's standing next to me."

"Me too," Christine said, patting Frank's hand. "When the house groans, I hear him grumping back."

Tears threatened, and instinctively Donnie walked closer and put an arm around his mother. "Okay, gang. Let's get this show on the road. Chrissy, get out here. The limo is waiting."

The cameras flashed, and the crowd was overwhelming when the Lane family stepped out of the St. Regis, one of Washington's finest hotels.

Christine was elegant in her simple black dress. Chrissy was dressed in yellow, like the sun, which her father had once said she epitomized for him.

Donnie and Frank, like knights-errant guarding their women, maneuvered Christine and Chrissy swiftly through the crowd and into the White House. They were escorted to chairs in front of a podium that carried the seal of the President of the United States.

As the event unfolded, Christine's knees began to shake. While on the outside her emotions appeared to be under control, inside they were ripe and blossoming. She whispered to Donnie, "I don't think I can get up and read in front of all these people."

Her son squeezed her hand. "If you can't, I will stand in your stead."

The ceremony in the East Room of the White House began before more could be said.

The President walked to the podium. "We are here to honor one man." He paused. He looked around the room. "Wow! Think about that for just a moment.

"Can one man make a difference? It is the wish of every president who has gone before me and who will come after me that his or her presidency will have a positive impact on Americans. But can we do it? Can one man or one woman make a difference? I ask myself that question every day.

"Then I remember: Mahatma Gandhi was one man. Albert Einstein was one man. Martin Luther King was one man. These men have proven that not only can one man make a difference, but even more important they also remind us that one man can trigger great good. These few men had mighty ideals. And their actions are still being felt in our world today.

"And, like them, let us all pray the results of Thomas Lane's actions will be everlasting. Out of the billions of people on our planet he has achieved something the rest of us could not do. He is a man above the rest. He reached such distinction that his ideas, his presence, and his actions shouted so loud that we could not ignore him. That is something. I never imagined when I took the oath of office that my presidency would have the privilege of being part of the fantastic changes that are laid before the world community because of just one man. For he has proven without a shadow of a doubt that the axiom is true, one man can make a difference, a positive difference."

Everyone applauded.

Pride shone on the faces of the Lane family.

"And now for our awards ceremony," said the President.

"Did I hear a plural there?" whispered Donnie. It was a rhetorical question.

"The man we are honoring never held a lofty position except with his family. Thomas Lane demonstrated both kindness and peace through his actions as a soldier. He was a man truly for the people and of the people. And most impressive is that he touched millions with his honest, self-sacrificing expression of love for his son, all our sons."

Christine dabbed at the few tears swimming over her cheeks.

"And this will be a surprise for the Lane family . . ."

One looked to the other, puzzled.

"Tonight we are making history," continued the President. "Only one other man, General James H. Doolittle, has had this honor bestowed on him. That is, until tonight. I am happy—no, delighted and thankful—to bestow posthumously upon Thomas Lane both the Medal of Honor and the Presidential Medal of Freedom, this nation's two highest honors." The President applauded. "Mrs. Lane, will you come forward?"

Christine smiled and half stood up, saying, "Could my son do the honors?"

The President nodded, "Of course."

Donnie rose and walked to the podium with his shoulders squared. There was a slight gasp as everyone noticed the striking resemblance between the father on the poster and the son who stood next to it. Donnie cleared his throat.

"My family and I are honored by the distinction bestowed upon my father. This is not my award, and not my family's. It is my father's. Therefore, I think I should let my father speak for himself. This letter"—Donnie held up several lined sheets of yellow paper—"was written before his deployment. He was a man of simple pleasures and often boiled things down to the bone. He made most of his decisions with his heart, as you will hear in his letter. And although this letter was meant for the Lane family, I think it has something in it for all of us." He cleared his throat. "My father wrote:

> Dear Christine, Donnie, Chrissy, and Frank,
>   When I decided to write this letter and leave it with Frank, I was uncertain as to the words to put down that might bring you all comfort. And, of course, I wanted an opportunity to once again have the last word.

A few people in the crowd chuckled before Donnie continued.

> Dads like to have the last word, even if we have to whisper the astute lessons life has taught us. Because one of those lessons, if it is heard, sometimes just might plant the seed of an idea that will bloom into greatness within our children.
>   I know you already understand, but I just need to say it again. I love you all more than my own life. Donnie, I want you to understand that giving you life a second time was not a difficult choice. It was an honor.
>   Chrissy, I see the divine in your every smile.
>   Christine, there is no way to measure the phenomenal love you have given me. I feel your spirit wherever I am. It is as if "we" magically became one mind, one heart, one love. You did that. You are the best part of me. Know I am always with you.

Christine's hand went to the simple crystal pendant at her throat. Chrissy, Frank, and Christine linked their arms together.

Donnie smiled down at his family from the podium. There was so much love there. He briefly wondered if this was what his father had seen when he looked at his family nightly around the dinner table. And he instantly understood how one could sacrifice his own life for another person when it all came from love. He would do it in a heartbeat for any one of those three people. He smiled.

And as his smile stretched into a grin, he realized he still had a lot to learn from his dad, because he had quantified, and therefore limited, his love. That was something his dad had obviously never done. "Let me continue."

> A day does not pass when I don't visit a memory of things we all did together: family dinners, Donnie and I fishing side by side, Chrissy and I feeding the ducks on the pond, or Christine and I on our enduring first date. Remember these moments, and I'll be there with you.
>
> Donnie, during the planning of my adventure I had numerous opportunities to witness the amazing man you will become. I don't know what profession or skills you will someday employ to make your living. One part of me would like to see you bend your mind and not your back. And as the pay differential between executives and skilled workers expands every year, so does out ability to appreciate and grasp the link that should exist between these groups. But whatever your collar, white or blue, remember that a man's job is his most distinctive characteristic. It is these choices and what we make of them that determines how a boy becomes a man. Your job might not be glamorous, but if you take pride in your labor it will do you credit. Lead by example. Treat your peers as you would your family, with respect and honesty.
>
> Manhood doesn't automatically come with the accumulation of years. True manhood only comes to those with the capacity to take the needs, hopes, and even the fears of others and make them your own. Strong principles, honor, integrity, and respect are as

important as broad shoulders. Hold on to your values. They will clear away the insignificant from your eyes so that you will see what is truly valuable in your life.

With an unusual clarity, as I wrote this I discovered that every person who has been a partner in my life altered me in some great or small way. And each has added a little seasoning to your old dad. The resulting "concoction" that became me was only possible because of the others who passed through my life. I know you all will develop many friendships. I am encouraging you not to let one person slip by without making contact. Cherish these people. They will give you more than you give them.

By the way, one last lesson: Giving friendship when it is not wanted, loving when you get none in return, and caring when everything inside you says that the person is not worth it are marks of a man's greatness and give him credit.

At the beginning of my mission, I had a nagging feeling there was something going on beyond just you and me, son. As I prepare to deploy, that feeling grows stronger. And not just because I have a lot to make up for. I deeply believe that Afghanistan is the place I should be. I prayed to God for this gift, to go in my son's place, and He granted it. I have always known that He only makes package deals and that there is always a catch. I thought the complication that came with my deal was leaving my family. But I had it all wrong. It was an opportunity, not an ordeal, that God was giving me. I will do my best for those I meet along my journey. And at the end, I am hoping God considers our contract worthwhile.

Donnie, keep Mona tuned and under seventy. Thank you so much for being the son that you are. I know much of this letter was meant for Donnie, but he carries the greatest burden if this letter is delivered.

These are my final thoughts. I wanted them to be all about life and love. Because you see, although I went to war, I found more friendship and love on the battlefield, than enemies and hate.

I love you all,

Dad

P.S. By the way, if Frank is still hanging around outside, see if your Mom has something cooking, and invite him in.

A few more chuckles erupted when big old teddy-bear Frank half stood, acknowledging that he was the hungry neighbor.

"There are a few more pages to my mom and sister, but we would like to keep those private." Donnie glanced at his mother.

"You have heard my father's thoughts, and now I would like to share a few of my own. For most of my life my father seemed a vaguely distant man, someone who dressed in his work clothes even on his day off. A man who habitually worked late. We had a routine in our house, and I am sure it is the same in many other homes. When my dad walked in our front door, he was the center of my mother's attention; dinner was waiting, and we children hustled to our chairs around him at the table. After dinner my dad resided in the recliner in front of the TV, to fall asleep watching *Jeopardy*. That was the signal for the house and its occupants to fall into quiet conversation to accommodate this routine. Apart from our fishing trips and games of pool, which decreased in frequency as I got older—I grew to believe my blue-collar father and I had little in common—we spent very little time together."

Donnie smiled. "And I have to admit that not too long ago, I thought manhood meant being able to legally drink and get a driver's license, moving out of your parents' home, financial independence, and breaking away from that ritual I just described. You see, my father never gave me the 'how to be a man' lecture." Donnie took a deep breath and blew it out. "Instead he tried to show me. But until he forced this switch on me, I had not truly seen what he was teaching me. We all use elusive words like love, devotion, sacrifice, and friendship every day. But do we *see* them in action? Can we feel them inside us? I now understand the kind of man my father was, and I can say he showed me what he felt and he felt it all.

"That nightly ritual I described was a sign to his family of his dependability. He was telling us that although we all might move in different directions, he would always be waiting for us when we returned. He might be asleep in his recliner, but he would be there for us.

"This," Donnie raised his father's letter in the air for all to see, "is our first father-son, deep philosophical conversation. And it's a keeper. He has given my mind and my heart a code for living my life. He once told me that 'he couldn't live with himself if he did nothing.' I know part of him was thinking about my older brother, who had been killed in Afghanistan. And his reasons aren't important. Actions are what counts. He made it clear he would do everything in his power to make sure I had a future. I didn't fully understand why at the time.

"That is, until sitting side by side in the front seat of Mona—by the way, Mona is a 1969 Chevelle Malibu—my father and I discussed the need for a 'just cause,' for an individual to take extraordinary measures."

Donnie looked up as if seeing and hearing his father once again. "You see, I was his 'just cause.' He believed so very deeply in me that he was willing to give all he had for that belief. After that talk I saw through different eyes . . . I saw through his."

Donnie straightened his back and squared his shoulders. "I'd like to accept these medals, on behalf of my father and my family." Christine, Chrissy, and Frank stood up.

"On behalf of the Afghan mother and son my father saved." Guza and his mother stood up.

"On behalf of all the soldiers, both American and Afghan, who my father served with at Fort Dix and in his last hours." Albert, Steiner, Ben, Cogriff, and a skinny Afghan boy stood up.

"And on behalf of what the world and my family hope will be the beginning of a lasting peace in the Middle East." At the side of the room, a dozen Middle Eastern heads of state and tribal leaders stood. And among them was the Afghan chief with the bright red beard.

Acknowledgments

The author would like to thank Alice Peck, an impeccable editor, Shaun Butcher U.S. Army, who helped with the details, Dorie McClelland for the professional interior layout, and George Foster for designing a book cover that emulates my emotion for the story. And as always thank you to my husband Frank who encourages me through the tough times and makes all things possible with his enduring love.